W9-AJX-536

MASSACRE CANYON

Center Point
Large Print

Also available from Center Point Large Print:

By William W. Johnstone with J. A. Johnstone:
  Sidewinders Series:
    Deadwood Gulch
    The Butcher of Bear Creek
  The Family Jensen Series:
    Helltown Massacre
    The Violent Land
    Hard Ride to Hell

By J. A. Johnstone:
  The Loner Series:
    The Big Gundown
    Rattlesnake Valley
    Seven Days to Die
    The Bounty Killers
    Trail of Blood
    Killer Poker
    The Blood of Renegades

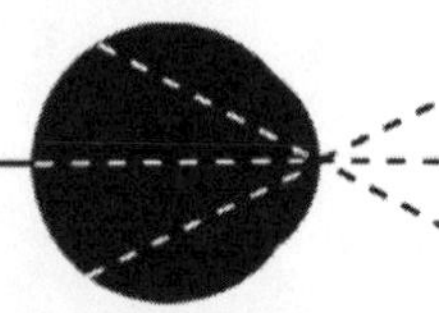

This Large Print Book carries the Seal of Approval of N.A.V.H.

THE FAMILY JENSEN

MASSACRE CANYON

William W. Johnstone
with J. A. Johnstone

CENTER POINT LARGE PRINT
THORNDIKE, MAINE

This Center Point Large Print edition
is published in the year 2014 by arrangement with
Kensington Publishing Corp.

PUBLISHER'S NOTE
Following the death of William W. Johnstone, the Johnstone family is working with a carefully selected writer to organize and complete Mr. Johnstone's outlines and many unfinished manuscripts to create additional novels in all of his series like The Last Gunfighter, Mountain Man, and Eagles, among others. This novel was inspired by Mr. Johnstone's superb storytelling.

The text of this Large Print edition is unabridged.
In other aspects, this book may vary from the original edition.
Printed in the United States of America on permanent paper.
Set in 16-point Times New Roman type.

ISBN: 978-1-62899-112-3

Library of Congress Cataloging-in-Publication Data

Johnstone, William W.
[Family Jensen.]
Massacre canyon : the Family Jensen / William W. Johnstone, with J.A. Johnstone. — Center Point Large Print Edition.
pages cm.
Summary: "Bounty hunter Luke Jensen catches one of Kroll brothers away from his gang. When the gang ambush and take him prisoner, Luke's brother Smoke is drawn into the fight. With Smoke Jensen comes fire—adopted son Matt and lifelong friend Preacher, who storm into battle to save Luke from the Krolls"—Provided by publisher.
ISBN 978-1-62899-112-3 (library binding : alk. paper)
1. Jensen, Smoke (Fictitious character)—Fiction.
2. Large type books. I. Johnstone, J. A. II. Title.
PS3560.O415F46 2014
813′.6—dc23

2014008481

MASSACRE CANYON

Book One

Chapter 1

Luke Jensen pressed his back to the wall of the corridor beside the hotel room door and raised the long-barreled Remington revolver in his right hand until it was beside his head. He waited patiently, a tall, rangy, muscular man with a rough-hewn face and a neatly trimmed mustache that matched the dark, slightly curly hair under the thumbed-back black hat.

Any minute now, the springs on the bed inside that room would start to squeal, and Luke would know that it was time to kick the door open and throw down on Mordecai Kroll. It was a shame to interrupt a man's sporting fun with a particularly good-looking redheaded dove, but Luke would make an exception for Mordecai Kroll.

He would take any advantage he could get over a cold-blooded, rattlesnake-mean killer like Kroll.

There were bad men . . . and then there were men like Rudolph and Mordecai Kroll. If there was a state or territory west of the Mississippi where they weren't wanted by the law, Luke wasn't aware of it. He had seen reward dodgers issued on them from Texas to Montana, from Missouri to California.

Their list of crimes was as long as the list of places offering bounties on them. Murder, rape, robbery, arson, kidnapping, extortion, assault, horse theft, cattle rustling . . . Come up with a violent crime and chances were the Kroll brothers had committed it at one time or another.

At some point they had probably pried the gold fillings out of a dead man's teeth.

As a result, if Luke could bring in Mordecai Kroll, dead or alive, he stood to earn the biggest payday of his career as a bounty hunter. The rewards for Mordecai added up to more than ten thousand dollars. The only way Luke could ever top that would be to corral Mordecai's older brother, Rudolph, who had even bigger bounties on his head.

Of course, if he could get both of them, Luke thought, he would collect enough to give up his dangerous profession. He could afford to buy himself a cattle ranch somewhere, like the Sugarloaf spread owned by his brother Smoke.

But he couldn't buy the goodwill and the friendship that Smoke had earned, nor did Luke know of any store where he could waltz in and buy himself a smart, beautiful wife like Sally Jensen.

No, he was just a bounty hunter, and while he might aspire to more, it was doubtful that he would ever achieve it, especially considering the fact that he wasn't as young as he used to be.

Since that was the case, he would concentrate

on doing his job he told himself, instead of standing in the dim, dusty second-floor hallway of a rundown hotel in a little town in Arizona and daydreaming about what might have been. He stood a little straighter as he heard the bedsprings squeak on the other side of the door.

"Get on with it, Mordecai," Luke muttered to himself. "She's a whore. She's not expecting flowers and poetry."

He'd been coming out of an eatery a short time earlier when he spotted Mordecai Kroll emerging from a saloon across the street arm in arm with a rather buxom redhead. The young woman had a shawl around her shoulders against the evening chill, but it didn't do much to conceal the ample bosom that threatened to escape from the low-cut neckline of her dress. She still had her looks, which meant she hadn't been working as a soiled dove for very long.

Mordecai appeared to be half-drunk. He stumbled a little as the two of them moved along the boardwalk, but the redhead didn't let him fall. Both of them seemed to find his rotgut-induced clumsiness hilarious.

Luke had moved quickly into the shadows of the alley next to the café and studied the two people on the other side of the street, just to make sure he really saw what he thought he was seeing. He'd heard rumors that the Kroll gang had been spotted in this corner of northeastern Arizona, not far from the border with New Mexico Territory, and he had drifted in this direction to have a look around.

It was hard to believe he'd be lucky enough to run smack-dab into Mordecai Kroll like this. Even more astounding was the fact that big brother, Rudolph, and the rest of the gang didn't appear to be anywhere around.

Mordecai must have slipped off without telling the others, Luke thought as he studied the outlaw. He had seen countless posters with a variety of drawings of Mordecai Kroll on them, and the man with the redheaded whore matched up with those likenesses. He had the same angular features, the same bushy eyebrows, the same shock of fair hair, the same lanky build.

That was Mordecai Kroll, all right, Luke had decided. No doubt about it.

He followed them to the Sullivan House, which was a pretty fancy name for a second-rate hotel. Through the front window, which fortunately wasn't as grimy as it might have been, he had seen the clerk behind the desk take a key from the pegboard on the wall and hand it to Mordecai. Luke's keen eyes had no problem reading the number 14 printed on the slip of paper tacked to the wall under the peg where the clerk had gotten the key.

From there it was simple to slip in the rear entrance and go up the back stairs. He found Room 14 about halfway along the corridor with a threadbare carpet runner, faded wallpaper, and a lamp burning dimly on a table at the far end. The hallway was deserted except for Luke.

While he stood there waiting, he heard laughter and voices from inside the room. A man and a woman, and both sounded like they'd been drinking. That confirmed he had the right room. He slipped one of the Remingtons he wore in cross-draw rigs from its holster and waited.

The doorknob of another room clicked as it was turned. The door opened and a man stepped out into the hall. It happened too quickly for Luke to hide, and there was no place to conceal himself in this corridor anyway.

The man stopped short and his eyes got big with fear. He was tall and skinny, with a prominent Adam's apple. He wore a tweed suit and a derby. The clothes had seen better days. Luke pegged the man for a drummer of some sort.

Carefully, Luke lifted his left hand and pressed the index finger to his lips in a signal for silence. The man took in the bounty hunter's rugged face, the dusty black shirt and trousers, the pair of revolvers. He swallowed hard, which caused his Adam's apple to bob up and down. Then he backed into his room and gingerly closed the door behind him.

Smart man, Luke thought. Whatever was about to happen, that hombre didn't want any part of it.

Luke hoped no bullets punched through the thin

walls between rooms. He would do his best not to fire a shot, but that really might be too much to hope for.

The bed noises from inside the room got louder. Luke got ready to make his move. He planned to kick the door open and rush in. If Mordecai was on top, it ought to be a simple matter to wallop him over the head with the Remington and knock him out. If he wasn't on top, that would complicate things. He might be able to reach for a gun before Luke could stop him.

Luke was counting on the booze to slow down Mordecai's reactions long enough for him to get the redhead out of the way. Then he and Mordecai would just have to take their chances against each other.

A thought flashed through his mind as he stepped away from the wall, drew his other Remington, and turned toward the door. With a quarry like Mordecai Kroll, some bounty hunters would start shooting as soon as they kicked in the door. If some of the bullets wound up in the whore, that was just too bad. They could always claim that Mordecai shot her, and chances were that nobody would question the claim.

Luke had never been that sort of man. He hadn't lived a blameless life, not by a long shot, but he liked to think there was a core of decency in him, instilled there by the sheer fact that he was a Jensen, even though for a long time he hadn't used the name and had called himself Luke Smith instead.

He had thought that he had good reasons for doing that. It had taken meeting his long-lost brother Smoke to show him that he was wrong. Now he was proudly once again a Jensen and would remain so.

He lifted his right foot and drove the heel of his boot against the door right beside the knob, as hard as he could. The jamb splintered under the impact and the door sprang open.

Luke leaped through the doorway with both revolvers thrust out in front of him. Either Mordecai or the redhead had lit the lamp on the small dressing table, so a yellow glow filled the room and revealed that the bed was . . .

Empty.

But the redhead stood beside it, still fully dressed, bent over with both hands resting on the mattress. She appeared to be frozen in that position with a look of terror on her face, and in that frozen instant of time, Luke realized why.

She had bounced the bed up and down and made it sound like both occupants of the room were romping on it, but that wasn't the case. In fact, Mordecai Kroll was all the way on the other side of the room, holding a shotgun that he pointed at Luke.

Flame erupted from both barrels as Mordecai triggered them.

Chapter 2

Luke's quick reflexes were all that saved him. He dived forward as the terrible boom of the shotgun's discharge filled the room. He hit the floor hard on his belly. The double load of buckshot passed over his head. A couple of pellets stung his legs as the loads spread, but that was all.

He angled the Remingtons upward and fired both revolvers. Mordecai had already darted to the side and barely avoided the .44 slugs, which ripped into the wall.

At least the bullets were traveling at such an angle that they probably went well over the head of anybody in the next room, Luke thought as he cocked the guns to try again.

If Mordecai had fired just one of the shotgun's barrels, he could have finished Luke off with the second one. The weapon was empty, though, so he was forced to swing it as a club. The twin barrels hit Luke's left-hand revolver and knocked it over into the other Remington as the guns discharged again. Still unscathed, Mordecai slashed at Luke's head with the stock.

Luke rolled out of the way of the blow and twisted on the floor so he could hook a booted foot between Mordecai's calves. He jerked hard with it and swept the outlaw's feet out from under him. With a startled yell, Mordecai went over backwards.

Luke started to scramble up, but Mordecai recovered quickly enough to kick him in the chest. That knocked Luke back against the bed. He was off-balance and sprawled against the side of the mattress.

Mordecai had been able to hang on to the shotgun. Even though he was fighting for his life, a cackle of vicious glee exploded from him as he rammed the shotgun's barrels into Luke's belly. Luke doubled over in pain and fell forward on his knees.

Since he was already bent over and low to the floor, he drove forward and butted Mordecai in the belly. The breath *whoofed* out of Mordecai's lungs as he fell on his butt. Luke surged ahead and planted a knee in the outlaw's groin. Mordecai groaned, and Luke smelled rotgut whiskey and spicy food.

He had the advantage now. He smashed his right-hand gun against Mordecai's jaw. The impact slewed Mordecai's head around. While Mordecai was stunned, Luke cracked the barrel of his left-hand gun across Mordecai's right wrist. That finally made Mordecai drop the empty shotgun.

Luke kneed him again and took some vicious

satisfaction of his own from the agonized, high-pitched scream that Mordecai let out. No man could take punishment like that and keep fighting for very long. Mordecai Kroll was no exception. He curled up in a quivering, whimpering ball of pain.

Luke shoved himself up and staggered to his feet. His chest rose and fell hard from the effort and the sheer desperation of the fight. He eared back the hammers of both Remingtons and pointed the guns at Mordecai, even though the outlaw seemed helpless at the moment. Without taking his eyes off his prisoner, he asked the redhead, "Are you all right, gal?"

No answer.

Fearing the worst, Luke backed a couple of steps toward the door and glanced to his right so he could see on the other side of the bed. The young woman lay there, and she wasn't pretty anymore after what the buckshot had done to her face. A pool of blood spread slowly around her head.

Luke cursed bitterly. He didn't blame himself for the redhead's death; Mordecai Kroll was the one who had pulled the triggers on that shotgun. But Luke regretted what had happened, just as he always regretted what happened when somebody innocent got in the way of a cold-blooded killer.

He stepped closer to the mewling outlaw,

leaned down, and struck again with the right-hand Remington. The blow knocked Mordecai out cold and shut him up.

The sound of rapid footsteps in the corridor made Luke swing toward the door. His guns came in line with the opening just as a man appeared in the doorway. His eyes widened at the sight of the Remingtons pointed at him, and he took a quick step back.

"Whoa, hold on there, mister!" he said. "Don't shoot!"

Luke spotted the badge pinned to the pudgy hombre's vest and lowered the Remingtons. The lawman had a six-gun on his hip and carried a Winchester, but he made no effort to point the rifle at Luke.

"Take it easy, Marshal," Luke told the newcomer. "The shooting is all over."

To prove it, he holstered the left-hand gun and started reloading the two chambers he had fired from the other Remington. He had to break the revolver open and expose the cylinder to do that.

The lawman stepped into the room and asked, "Anybody hurt in—" Then he stopped short and gulped as he spotted the redhead's legs sticking out on the far side of the bed. He leaned over to look, jerked upright, and a sick, greenish expression came over his face.

"I didn't do that," Luke said. "You can see for yourself that the poor woman was killed with a shotgun. That bastard on the floor is the one who did it."

He snapped the Remington closed again and nodded toward the senseless Mordecai Kroll.

"Who . . . who's that?"

Luke started reloading the other gun. A man in his line of work often needed all the firepower he could get. He said, "That's Mordecai Kroll."

"The outlaw?" The local star packer sounded like he couldn't believe it. "Mordecai Kroll was in my town? Really?"

"You can see him with your own eyes. Surely you have wanted posters on him in your office. You can compare the likenesses on them to Kroll in the flesh if you want, after you've gotten him safely behind bars."

"I'll do that. If that's Mordecai Kroll, I reckon that makes you . . . what? Some sort of bounty hunter?"

"That's right," Luke agreed dryly. "Some sort of bounty hunter. My name is Luke Jensen."

He could tell that the marshal had never heard of him, which was all right. Luke had never sought notoriety. That was one reason he had kept his true identity a secret for many years. He didn't want to bring shame to his family over the failures and tragedies of the past.

He had put all that behind him now. Anyway, there was no way he could ever be as famous as his brother Smoke, who quite possibly was the fastest, deadliest gunfighter the West had ever known. Despite all that, Smoke had built a reputation as a solid citizen, so Luke supposed there was hope that a bloody-handed bounty hunter might become respectable someday . . . but for now he was content to lie low and do his job.

The marshal suddenly looked even more worried. He said, "If that's Mordecai, where are Rudolph and the rest of that wild bunch of theirs?"

"I have no idea," Luke replied honestly. "I just spotted Mordecai on the street a little while ago. He had that young woman with him and appeared to be drunk, so I decided to follow him and see if I might have a chance to take him into custody."

"You don't really talk like most bounty hunters I've run into," the lawman said with a slight frown.

"I read a lot," Luke said simply.

That was true. He always had several books stuck in his saddlebags, and he picked up more whenever and wherever he had a chance. In the lonely existence he had led, sometimes it seemed like books were his only friends. They were certainly the only ones who were always there for him.

The marshal's thoughts must have gone back to what he had been talking about before. He said, "You must not've been able to get the drop on him like you hoped."

"He must have spotted me following him," Luke said, and once again that note of bitterness was in his voice. "He forced the girl to make the bedsprings bounce and squeal like they were busy. Then when I kicked the door in, he was ready and cut loose at me with that greener. I barely got out of the way."

"Yeah, but Sheila didn't," the marshal said with a gloomy expression on his face. He shook his head.

"That was her name? Sheila?"

"Yeah. Not a bad sort, for a whore. She seemed to genuinely like folks. I reckon she probably would've stopped feelin' like that if she'd stayed in the business long enough. Maybe it's a blessin' that she didn't have the chance."

Luke couldn't bring himself to feel that way. Any life cut short before its time was a bad thing. But he wasn't going to argue philosophy with the local badge-toter in an Arizona cowtown.

"We'd better get Kroll locked up while we've got the chance," he said.

"Yeah, we don't want the others to show up while we're takin' him down the street." The marshal sounded like it would have been all right with him if Luke hadn't captured the infamous outlaw. Now he had to worry about the rest of the Kroll gang riding into town to bust Mordecai out of jail. With a sigh, he added, "I'll have to get the undertaker up here to take care of Sheila, too. Not to mention the damage to the hotel from the blood and the buckshot and the bullets and such."

Luke would have been willing to bet that this wasn't the first time blood had been spilled in the Sullivan House, nor were those bullet holes the first ones that had been put in the walls. He would pay the proprietor for the damages, though. With the rewards he would collect for capturing Mordecai, he could easily afford the expense.

He rolled Mordecai onto his belly and took a strip of rawhide from his pocket. Some bounty hunters carried handcuffs, and Luke had a pair of the metal bracelets in his saddlebags, but the rawhide served well for tying a prisoner's wrists together, too, with the advantage of being compact and lightweight. It wouldn't clink against something at a bad time and give away his presence when stealth was important, either.

Mordecai started to come around as Luke jerked his arms behind his back and lashed his wrists together with the rawhide. He pulled the knot good and tight and wasn't any too gentle about it. Then he took hold of Mordecai's arms and hauled the outlaw to his feet.

Mordecai yelped in pain and cursed.

"Careful," he said.

"Like you were careful when you practically blew poor Sheila's head off?"

"Was that her name? Hell, if she don't have sense to duck, it ain't my fault, is it?"

Luke drew his right-hand Remington, pressed the muzzle to Mordecai's head just behind the right ear, and pulled back the hammer.

"If my thumb happens to slip, it's not my fault, is it?" he grated. "Anyway, all the reward dodgers on you say dead or alive, so it doesn't really matter, does it?"

Mordecai stood stiff as a board now. He must have realized that his callous remark had pushed Luke a little too far.

The local lawman broke the tense spell by clearing his throat and saying, "Uh, Mr. Jensen . . . we said we were gonna lock him up. . . ."

"And so we are," Luke agreed as he got control over his anger. He lowered the Remington's hammer and slid the revolver back into leather. "But if you're smart, Kroll, you'll keep your mouth shut for a while. Just remember . . . dead or alive."

Chapter 3

Marshal Jerome Dunlap sighed in obvious relief when the cell door clanged shut behind Mordecai Kroll. He had told Luke his name while they were marching the prisoner up the street and into the squat stone building that housed the local marshal's office and jail.

Luke said, “Turn around and back up to the bars, Kroll, and I’ll untie your wrists.”

Kroll did as Luke told him. When his arms were free again, Mordecai brought them around in front of him and massaged his wrists as he glared at Luke.

“You’re gonna be mighty sorry you ever crossed trails with me, Jensen,” he said. “That was your name, wasn’t it?”

“That’s right,” Luke said.

With a sneer, Mordecai told Dunlap, “You better make a note of that, Marshal, so you can tell the undertaker what name to put on this dumb bastard’s grave marker.” Mordecai paused, and then went on. “No, wait, that’s right, you’ll be dead, too, so you won’t be able to tell the undertaker a damned thing.”

He laughed raucously. Luke ignored him and turned back to the marshal’s office.

Dunlap followed him out of the cell block and dropped the big ring of keys on the desk with a jangling thump.

“I’ll have to send to St. Johns for the sheriff,” he said. “That’s the county seat of Apache County. We can’t hope to hold Kroll here in this cracker box of a jail.”

Luke thought the marshal was underestimating the building’s strength, but Dunlap had no deputies and it was certain that just the two of them wouldn’t be able to withstand an attack in force by the entire Kroll gang. The sooner they could get Kroll to the county seat and surround him with armed, experienced deputies, the better.

"Have you got a telegraph office here?" he asked.

Dunlap shook his head.

"No, I'll have to send a rider to St. Johns. Fella who owns the livery stable has a boy who carries messages for me sometimes. Got a fast horse, too."

"How long will that take?"

"Start him first thing in the morning, the sheriff ought to be back here with a jail wagon and some men by nightfall."

Luke nodded and said, "So we've got to wait less than twenty-four hours."

"Twenty-four hours can be a mighty long time when you've got trouble rainin' down on you," Dunlap pointed out.

He was right about that, Luke thought. But all they could do was hope for the best.

"You mind stayin' here while I go roust out the undertaker and tell Benji Porter I need him to ride to the county seat in the mornin'?"

"Go ahead, Marshal," Luke said. "I'll keep an eye on Kroll."

Dunlap nodded. He looked like he would be glad to get out of the office. Luke wondered briefly if the marshal would come back tonight or manage to be occupied elsewhere. He didn't think

Dunlap would abandon his duty like that, but you never could be sure about people.

Once Luke was alone in the office, he looked at the few wanted posters that were pinned to the wall. He figured that Dunlap had to have more reward dodgers than that, unless the marshal had been using them for kindling, so he took a look in the scarred old desk. In the second drawer he found a big stack of the posters.

He didn't have to flip through them for very long before he came across one with a drawing of Rudolph Kroll on it. The man staring out balefully from the penciled likeness was considerably older than Mordecai, but Luke could see a slight resemblance in their craggy faces. Rudolph was dark where his younger brother was fair. His nose was bigger, and underneath it was a thick, dark mustache that drooped over the corners of his mouth. If anything, Rudolph Kroll looked even meaner and more filled with hate than Mordecai, although such a thing didn't seem possible at first glance.

Luke found posters on some of the other members of the Kroll gang in the stack: Fred Martin, Calvin Dodge, Pete Markwell, a handful more. All of them ruthless, hard-bitten, dangerous men, even if their reputations weren't quite as bad as that of the Kroll brothers'. Luke had no doubt that any one of them would have killed him in an instant if given the chance.

He didn't intend to provide them with that opportunity.

"Hey!" Mordecai called from the cell block. "Hey, Marshal, you still out there?"

Luke put the wanted posters back in the desk drawer and closed it. He stood up and went over to the cell block door to ask through the barred window in it, "What do you want, Kroll?"

"That you, Jensen? Where's the marshal?"

"Busy. If you don't want anything, shut up."

"I didn't say that. I could use some coffee. My head really hurts where some big dumb son of a bitch walloped it with a pistol."

He chuckled at his own cleverness, or what he regarded as cleverness, anyway.

Luke had already noticed the coffeepot staying warm on a pot-bellied iron stove in a corner of the office. Several tin cups sat on a small shelf to the side. He supposed it wouldn't do any harm, and since there was a good chance he would have to stay awake all night to guard the prisoner, he decided he ought to have a cup for himself.

"All right, but don't try anything," he told Mordecai. "I'd just as soon put a bullet in you as look at you."

He poured thick, black coffee into one of the cups and took it over to the desk where he picked up the key ring. He had seen which key Dunlap used to lock the cell block, so it was simple to unlock it. He drew one of his guns as he used the other hand to carry the coffee into the cell block.

Mordecai was in the first cell on the left. Luke told him, "Back off all the way over there under the window. Take a step in this direction before I tell you to and I'll blow your kneecap to hell. You'll have a bad limp when you walk to the gallows."

"You're mighty confident," Mordecai said as he backed over to the far wall. "I'm gonna enjoy watchin' you die."

Luke just grunted. He bent, reached through the bars, and placed the cup of coffee on the cell's stone floor. Then he backed up well out of reach and said, "All right, you can go ahead and get it now."

Mordecai did so. He took a sip and made a face, then said, "Has the marshal been boilin' this stuff for a week? It tastes like it."

"I wouldn't know," Luke said. "I can take it back—"

"No, no, that's fine."

Mordecai sat down on the bunk, took another sip, and sighed.

Luke had encountered scores of outlaws during his career as a bounty hunter, and few if any of them had ever given much thought to the havoc they wreaked in innocent lives. Despite knowing that, he asked, "Doesn't it bother you that you killed that girl?"

"It wasn't my intention that she come to any harm. I just planned on killin' you."

"Because you saw me following you?"

"Yeah. See, you thought I was drunk . . . and I was. But I got highly developed instincts, like a wolf, say. I can sense danger. And when I saw that some fella was skulkin' along on the other side of the street, it got me curious. Figured you might be after the bounty on my head. So I decided to set a little trap for you." Mordecai took another drink of the coffee and then added, "I can sober up in a hurry when I need to."

"What if I hadn't been after you?"

The lanky outlaw shrugged.

"If the gal had bounced that bed up and down for a few minutes without nothin' else happenin', I would've said that my suspicions was wrong, and then we would've put the bed to better use. But I wasn't wrong, and you come bustin' in, and . . . well, you know what happened after that."

"Yeah," Luke said. "I do. Finish your coffee."

Mordecai grinned and said, "Now, don't rush a man. I'm a prisoner now. You got to treat me decent." He sipped the coffee again. "You want to kill me, don't you?"

"More than you could ever know."

He didn't say anything else, even though Mordecai took a couple more gibes at him. When the outlaw finished the coffee, Luke had him set the cup through the bars and back off again.

Mordecai cooperated. He might be a loco animal in a lot of ways, but he had enough sense to know that if he gave Luke the slightest excuse, the bounty hunter would ventilate him.

Luke picked up the cup and went back into the office. He locked the cell block door and sat down at the desk again with a cup of the strong black brew for himself. A few minutes later, Marshal Dunlap came in.

"Got those chores taken care of," the lawman reported, almost as if he were the deputy and Luke was the one in charge. "The undertaker's collected Sheila's body, and Benji Porter will be settin' out to fetch the sheriff at first light. All we got to do is sit tight and wait for somebody to show up and take Kroll off our hands."

"And hope it's not his brother and the rest of the gang who show up," Luke said.

"Mister, I'm not hopin'," Dunlap said fervently. "I'm prayin'."

Chapter 4

Despite the marshal's worries, the night passed quietly with no sign of trouble. He and Luke took turns sleeping and napping on the old sofa on one side of the office, but nothing disturbed them.

Early the next morning Dunlap went over to the café and brought back breakfast for both of them and for the prisoner.

"I went down to the stable, too," he said as he and Luke were eating. "Abner Porter told me his boy left for St. Johns before dawn. He's mighty excited to be helpin' out in something like this, Abner said."

Luke frowned over his flapjacks, eggs, and bacon.

"He's not so excited that he'll go spreading it all over town about Kroll being locked up here, is he?"

"Well, you know, I didn't think to say anything to him about that. I might should'a told him not to say anything except to the sheriff."

Luke bit back the sharp comment that tried to spring to his lips. Marshal Dunlap was just a small-town peace officer who probably never had to deal with anything much worse than a drunken cowboy or miner.

Luke stood up and went into the cell block. Mordecai sat on the bunk eating his breakfast. Luke looked at him through the bars and asked, "What were you doing here in town by yourself? Where's your brother and the rest of the gang?"

"You think I'm gonna tell a no-good bounty hunter where to find Rudolph and the rest of the boys?" Mordecai laughed. "You're plumb dumber than I thought, Jensen."

"Yeah, I suppose you come and go as you please, don't you? You want to come into town for a drink, maybe a poker game, and a little slap-and-tickle with a dove, you don't have to ask your brother's permission."

Mordecai snorted and said, "Damn right I don't. Rudolph knows better than to try to put a halter on me."

"So he doesn't know where you are."

"Hell, no! I don't have to tell him every time I—" Mordecai stopped short and frowned. "Blast it, Jensen, you're tryin' to trick me!"

Luke left the cell block without saying anything else. Even though Mordecai was probably a habitual liar like most outlaws, Luke thought his tweaking of the man's pride had prompted him to tell the truth without thinking. Mordecai had slipped away from the gang on his own. He had probably done similar things before. With any luck, it might be several days before Rudolph Kroll got worried enough to go looking for his little brother.

By that time, Luke would have turned Mordecai over to the sheriff of Apache County and the outlaw wouldn't be his responsibility anymore.

During the day Luke saw a number of townspeople lingering on the opposite boardwalk. They stared across the street at the jail and talked animatedly among themselves. He knew that word had gotten around town about the notorious

Mordecai Kroll being locked up in there. It would have been difficult if not impossible to keep that quiet, he supposed, especially considering what had happened to the unfortunate, redheaded Sheila.

Since Mordecai's capture was already a subject of much gossip in town, there was no point in saying anything to Dunlap about keeping such things quiet. Luke just kept his eyes open and waited for the sheriff to arrive.

As Dunlap had predicted, that happened late in the afternoon, after a long, thankfully boring day. The sheriff's arrival brought even more excitement to the town, since he rode in at the head of a posse of a dozen deputies surrounding a sturdy jail wagon pulled by a team of six black horses.

Dunlap unlocked the marshal's office door, and he and Luke stepped out to greet the newcomers. The sheriff, a tall, stern-looking man with iron-gray hair, swung down from his saddle and gave Dunlap a curt nod.

"Marshal," he said. "I hear you've got a prisoner for me."

"You make it sound mighty simple, sheriff," Dunlap replied with a relieved smile. "This ain't just any prisoner. It's Mordecai Kroll."

"So I'm told." The sheriff turned to look at Luke and extended his hand. "Sheriff Wesley Rakestraw."

"Luke Jensen," Luke introduced himself as he shook hands with the lawman.

"I hear you're a bounty hunter."

"That's right," Luke said warily. Most lawmen didn't care much for bounty hunters. He supposed they thought men like Luke were encroaching on their job of bringing lawbreakers to justice.

Rakestraw didn't appear to be that sort, however. His expression was bland and noncommittal. Maybe he was more interested in the fact that a mighty bad hombre was locked up where he couldn't hurt anybody else, rather than in who had brought him in.

"No sign of Rudolph Kroll or the rest of that bunch the Kroll brothers run with?"

Dunlap fielded that question. He said, "Nope, it's been peaceful since last night, sheriff. Kroll's locked up inside, and nobody's tried to get him out."

"Good," Rakestraw said with a nod. "Tomorrow morning we'll take him back to the county seat. It's going to take some time and burning up the telegraph wires to sort out exactly who has first claim on him." The sheriff smiled faintly. "There are plenty of people lining up for a crack at hanging Mordecai Kroll."

Luke said, "It's what, twenty miles to the county seat?"

"Twenty-two," Rakestraw said.

"You brought enough men with you to get the prisoner there safely?"

"I think you'll find that my deputies are the best in the territory, Jensen." A smug look came over Rakestraw's face. "We can handle anything that comes up."

Luke wasn't so sure of that. According to everything he'd heard, the Kroll gang numbered about a dozen men, the same size as the group of deputies Sheriff Rakestraw had brought with him.

But Rudolph Kroll might be able to call on a dozen or more other hardcases to ride with him if he set out to rescue his brother from the law. That might be too much for Rakestraw's posse to handle.

What they really needed, Luke decided, was a whole cavalry patrol. He wasn't sure the army would go along with that, however, even for an outlaw as notorious as Mordecai Kroll. Besides, there was no telegraph office here, so contacting the military authorities wouldn't be easy.

Their best bet would be to hustle Mordecai to St. Johns as quickly as possible, before Rudolph Kroll found out what was going on.

"I think we should move the prisoner tonight," he told the sheriff.

Rakestraw raised an eyebrow and repeated, "We?"

"I'm coming with you," Luke said.

"I don't figure that's necessary. I can put in the

reward claims for you, if that's what you're worried about."

"No offense, sheriff, but I'd rather handle that myself."

Rakestraw's weathered face tightened. Despite what Luke had said, he *was* offended. Luke didn't mean to question the sheriff's honesty, but he was accustomed to handling his own business.

"Suit yourself," Rakestraw said, "but we're not starting back to the county seat until tomorrow morning. You're welcome to ride along with us then if you want to."

Luke nodded. He supposed that would have to do. If nothing else, the jail here would be much better guarded than it had been the night before.

Rakestraw turned to his deputies and ordered, "Dismount and get set up, men. Tom, take the wagon down to the livery stable and see to the team."

The deputies responded crisply. Several of them, each packing two revolvers and carrying a Winchester, went into the jail to watch over the prisoner. The others began positioning themselves around town where they commanded a field of fire all around the jail. If anybody tried to get in there who wasn't supposed to, somebody would be in position to pick him off.

There didn't seem to be anything left for Luke to do here, so he nodded to Dunlap and walked away. He had put up his horse in the livery stable the previous evening, before he stepped in the café to get some supper, and he hadn't had a chance to check on the ugly, hammerheaded dun since then. That was where he headed now.

When he reached the stable he found a middle-aged man and a teenage boy unhitching the team of blacks from the jail wagon. He said to the youngster, "You'd be Benji, wouldn't you? You followed the sheriff and his men back here after fetching them."

"That's right, mister," the boy said. "And you're that bounty hunter. I heard all about you."

"Did you happen to say anything to folks in St. Johns about Mordecai Kroll being in jail here? Other than Sheriff Rakestraw, I mean?"

The liveryman said, "Now hold on a minute. Don't make out like my boy did anything wrong, Mr. Jensen. The marshal didn't tell Benji not to say anything. You can't expect a boy to keep quiet about something this excitin'."

Luke shook his head and smiled.

"I didn't mean to imply that you'd done anything wrong, Benji," he said. "I'm just curious how many people know about Kroll being captured."

"Well, I reckon I did tell a few people about it . . . and you know how things get around. . . ."

Luke nodded and kept the smile on his face, although not without effort.

"That's fine, Benji. I appreciate you being

honest with me." He took a silver dollar from his pocket and tossed it to the boy, who caught it deftly. "That's for the fast ride you made today. That was good work."

The youngster beamed and said, "Thanks, Mr. Jensen!"

Benji's father seemed mollified now. He said, "That dun of yours is a good horse, Mr. Jensen. Not much to look at, but I can tell he's got sand. You gonna be leavin' him here another night?"

"Yes, it appears that I will be," Luke said, not bothering to add that he would have preferred to leave for the county seat immediately with the prisoner and the sheriff's posse. From what he had seen, the road between the two towns was good enough to follow in the dark.

The decision was out of his hands, though. He lingered at the stable for a few more minutes and reached into the stall to scratch the dun's head, then left. He hadn't gotten a hotel room before he ate supper the night before, and after that he hadn't had a chance to do so, spending the night in the marshal's office instead. So finding a place to sleep tonight was the next order of business, he supposed.

He was on his way along the boardwalk in search of a better hotel than the Sullivan House when a voice called from behind him, "Mr. Jensen! Mr. Jensen, if I could speak to you for a moment, please!"

Luke stopped and turned. He was curious because the voice that had hailed him belonged to a woman.

But he wasn't expecting her to be a woman beautiful enough to take a man's breath away.

Chapter 5

She was almost as tall as he was, so she didn't have to tip her head back much for her eyes to meet his. Those eyes were a rich, deep brown, he noted, almost as dark as the thick, dark brown hair pulled into a bun at the back of her neck.

The woman wore a gray hat with a little brown-and-white feather attached to it. Her traveling outfit was the same shade of gray and had a thin layer of dust on it, so Luke knew she had been on the trail. That traveling outfit was snug enough to reveal an intriguingly curved shape.

Her skin had a golden tint to it, and her exotic good looks made her even more striking. Luke wouldn't have been surprised to see a woman like her in the finest restaurant or hotel in San Francisco, but here in this little Arizona Territory settlement, she definitely looked out of place.

At the same time, she had such poise as she smiled faintly at him that he realized she could make any place belong to her, instead of the other way around.

"Do we know each other, ma'am?" he asked, even though he was sure he had never laid eyes on this woman until this minute. He would remember if he had.

"No, we've never met," she said. "And it's miss, not ma'am. Miss Darcy Garnett."

Luke touched a finger to the brim of his hat and said, "Pleased to meet you, Miss Garnett. I'm Luke Jensen. But then, you seem to know that already."

"Of course. You're Luke Jensen, the famous bounty hunter. The man who captured the notorious Mordecai Kroll. Everyone in St. Johns is talking about you today."

Luke managed not to grimace. In his business, having a reputation sometimes came in handy, but most of the time it didn't.

"You came here from St. Johns?" he asked.

"That's right," Darcy Garnett replied.

"Followed the sheriff and his posse all that way?"

"I certainly did."

"Why?"

"To talk to you, of course," she responded without hesitation.

"Then I'm afraid you've wasted your time," he told her. "I'm about the most uninteresting hombre you'll ever run across."

"I don't believe that," she said. "And I'm sure my readers will agree with me."

Again Luke had to control the impulse to make a face. As they talked, he had started to have a sneaking suspicion that Darcy Garnett might be a journalist. He had run into inquisitive newspaper reporters before and sometimes could recognize them before they started asking their questions. Usually he told them he wasn't interested in talking and stalked off, not caring whether or not he was rude.

That would be harder to do with a lady.

"You work for the newspaper in St. Johns, do you?"

For the first time Luke saw a faint crack in the cool, reserved façade Darcy Garnett put up. She said, "Actually, no. The publisher there doesn't believe in female reporters. I told him that back in Pittsburgh, a woman who signs herself Nellie Bly is writing regularly for one of the papers there, but that didn't change his opinion. I'm hoping to sell a piece about the infamous Kroll brothers to *Harper's Weekly*, and your stirring capture of Mordecai Kroll is just what the story needs to cap it off."

"So you want me to tell you all about it."

"If I could get a firsthand account from the man who brought Mordecai Kroll to justice, no editor would turn down the story. Especially if you could tell me about the tragic death of the unfortunate young woman who was killed, too."

Luke felt a flash of anger go through him. He hadn't known Sheila, but she was dead and this woman regarded her death as nothing more than something that would help her sell a story to *Harper's Weekly*.

"I don't think I have anything to say, Miss Garnett," he told her with a shake of his head. The words came out a little harsher than he intended them to, but he didn't really care.

"Please, Mr. Jensen," she persisted. "The people deserve to know—"

"Most people know more than they really want to about the bad things in the world. And those bad things sure include men like Mordecai Kroll."

"Then you won't give me an interview?"

"That's what I just said, isn't it?"

Anger sparked in her eyes. Her mouth tightened into a line and she said coolly, "All right. If that's the way you feel about it, I won't argue with you. Anyway, Sheriff Rakestraw has already promised me his full cooperation."

For some reason, that rubbed Luke the wrong way. He hadn't particularly liked the sheriff. Rakestraw seemed a mite too full of himself, and his confidence when he talked about how he and his men could handle the Kroll gang if need be had bordered on arrogance. Reckless arrogance, in fact.

Even though he didn't really know the sheriff, Luke figured it would be just like Rakestraw to give Darcy an interview that made it sound like *he* was the one responsible for capturing Mordecai Kroll. Luke didn't much care what people thought about him; if a high public opinion was important to him, he never would have become a bounty hunter.

But he didn't want anybody making any claims that might damage his chances of collecting those bounties. Say Darcy Garnett did sell a story about the affair to *Harper's Weekly* or some other magazine or newspaper, and it made Sheriff Rakestraw out to be the hero. The men in charge of the banks and railroads and stagecoach lines that had put out those rewards for Mordecai might use that as an excuse to drag their feet about paying him.

Luke wasn't going to put up with that, not if all it took to prevent it was talking to an attractive young woman for a while.

"Hold on a minute," he said. "I guess it wouldn't hurt to answer a few questions for you."

She smiled, and this time he thought he saw a flash of triumph in those brown eyes. She had tricked him into going along with what she wanted by bringing up Rakestraw, he realized. Somehow she had guessed that he wouldn't want the sheriff trying to hog all the credit. And he had to admit that she'd been right.

"Excellent," she said. "Were you on your way to the hotel to get a room?"

"I was," Luke said.

"So was I. Why don't we have supper tonight in their dining room? That'll give us a chance to talk."

He nodded and said, "All right." He supposed he ought to clean up a little first, even though he was really too old to worry about trying to impress a woman like Darcy Garnett.

"We'll meet in the lobby at . . . six-thirty?" she asked.

"I'll be there," Luke said.

He had misjudged her. She was really a charming, intelligent young woman with a passionate interest in justice. That was the only reason she wanted to see Mordecai Kroll and the rest of the gang get what was coming to them. It didn't have anything to do with helping her career as a reporter.

Or maybe that was what she wanted him to think, Luke warned himself as she smiled across the table at him.

Regardless of her motives, he found himself enjoying the time they spent together. He liked having dinner with a beautiful woman as much as the next man, even when he knew it wouldn't go beyond that.

And Darcy was beautiful, no doubt about that. She had changed into a dark green gown that came up fairly high but left the elegant curve of her throat uncovered. She wore a choker with a tiny gem set in it that went well with her flawless skin. Her hair had been let down, brushed until it shone, and then put back up again in an appealing arrangement of curls.

She far outclassed him, he thought, but at least he had washed up and shaved, changed into a clean black shirt, and even put on a string tie made of braided rawhide with decorative silver tips. That was about as fancy as he could get when he was out on the trail like this, hunting for badmen.

The Talmadge Hotel—a definite step up from the Sullivan House—had bottles of wine available with dinner, and Luke had ordered one. He wasn't really a fancier of fine wines, but one every now and then was nice. He'd had a couple of glasses as they ate, and that gave him a warm glow, even though he was far from being drunk.

"You really don't speak like I'd expect a bounty hunter to speak," Darcy said. "You seem like an educated, cultured man."

"Don't give me too much credit," Luke told her. "My education has come largely from books. As for culture . . . I get to Denver or San Francisco from time to time. I like to take in a play when I'm there."

"What about the opera?"

To Luke, the opera was just a bunch of

caterwauling, but he had been acquainted with some young ladies who seemed to enjoy it, so he'd learned to tolerate it.

"That depends on the company," he answered Darcy's question diplomatically.

"The opera company, you mean."

Luke took another sip of wine and shrugged. Let her draw her own conclusions.

"I'd like to visit San Francisco with you sometime," she said. "I think it would prove interesting."

Luke thought so, too. He was starting to wonder if maybe he wasn't too old for her after all.

"We still have to talk about Mordecai Kroll, though," she went on.

"That's not nearly as pleasant a topic."

"No, but it's what my readers will want to know about."

After he had enjoyed her company all through dinner, he knew he couldn't back out of the interview now. He downed the rest of the wine that was in his glass and told her about the trap Mordecai had set for him. He didn't try to make himself look better as he explained what had happened. She stopped him a few times to ask a question, and he answered them as honestly as he could.

"That's terrible," Darcy said when he was finished. "That poor young woman."

"I reckon I'm partially to blame for what

happened to her," Luke said. "I walked right into that trap Kroll set for me. Kicked my way into it, rather."

"But he's the one who tried to murder you. As far as I'm concerned, her death was his fault, and that's the way I'm going to write the story."

"Well, I appreciate that," Luke said. He poured more wine for them, then mused, "Any man who makes his living with a gun has to deal with things like this sooner or later, I suppose. I know Smoke carries around a lot of old ghosts with him—"

He stopped short as he realized he had said more than he intended to say. He hoped Darcy hadn't noticed, or if she had, that she wouldn't recognize the name.

That hope was dashed right away. Darcy leaned forward with an excited look on her face and said, "Smoke? You have to tell me, Luke. Are you related to the famous gunfighter Smoke Jensen?"

Chapter 6

Luke hadn't meant to reveal that. Even though he was using the Jensen name again, after many years of calling himself Luke Smith, he didn't particularly want to publicize the fact that he and

Smoke were brothers. Not for his sake, but for Smoke's.

Although, Smoke probably would be the last person to be bothered by being related to a bounty hunter. He had been an outlaw himself at one point in his life, long before he settled down to become a respectable rancher.

While Darcy Garnett smiled expectantly across the table at him, Luke mentally cursed himself for his slip of the tongue. He would have liked to blame the wine he'd drunk for that moment of carelessness, but he knew that wasn't the case. Darcy had a way of relaxing a man just by her sheer presence and making him more inclined to talk.

It wouldn't do any good to deny the relationship now. Most people on the frontier had heard of Smoke Jensen, even if Luke Jensen was unknown to them. Darcy probably wouldn't believe him if he tried to say that he and Smoke were friends and that was all.

He nodded slowly and said, "Smoke is my brother."

"I didn't know he had any brothers other than Matt," Darcy said.

Luke could have pointed out that Matt Jensen was an adopted brother, not a blood relation, but that might have sounded petty. He hadn't met Matt yet, but Smoke had told him all about the young man. Smoke had taken Matt under his wing when Matt was an orphaned boy, and he and the old mountain man Preacher had raised him into a fine frontiersman who was making a name for himself as a scout, gunfighter, and all-around adventurer. One of these days they would all get together, Smoke had said, but so far that hadn't happened yet.

"Smoke and I didn't see each other for a long time," Luke said carefully. "I wasn't able to go home right after the war, so I sort of got separated from my family for a while."

"Something happened during the war to keep you from going home?" Darcy asked.

Something had happened, all right. . . . Betrayal, murder, a fortune in stolen Confederate gold . . . For a moment Luke's thoughts went back to those dark days at the very end of the war, but he dragged them into the present again and told Darcy, "You go through all that killing and it changes a man. I figured I'd drift around for a while, and before I knew it that turned into fifteen years."

"Amazing," she murmured. "I think you have quite a story, Luke Jensen. I could talk to you for hours. And you said you weren't interesting!"

He shook his head and said, "I don't think that would be a very good idea."

"Are you sure?" Her lips curved in a subtle smile that promised a great deal. "I think we'd both enjoy getting to know each other better."

Luke pushed his chair back.

"I'll be riding to St. Johns early in the morning with Sheriff Rakestraw and the posse," he said. "Reckon I'd better get some rest."

Darcy looked disappointed. She said, "It's really not that late—"

"I didn't get much sleep last night," Luke broke in, "what with standing guard in the marshal's office and all. I enjoyed our dinner, Miss Garnett."

"You should call me Darcy."

He ignored that and went on. "But I'll be saying good night now."

"You're sure."

"Positive," Luke said, even though there was a part of him that really wanted to keep talking to her and eventually accept the invitation she seemed to be offering him. He hadn't been with a woman in quite a while.

But Darcy Garnett wasn't some trail town whore. That was the sort Luke usually looked to for female companionship. She was a lady, and he wasn't going to take advantage of her journalistic ambitions.

She sighed and said, "Well, then, thank you for dinner, and for telling me about your capture of Mordecai Kroll and answering my questions. I'm sure it'll make a stirring story."

Luke got to his feet and nodded to her.

"Good night, then."

"Good night, Luke."

The way his name sounded coming from her lips almost made him reconsider, but then he turned and left the dining room. He had told her the truth when he said he was tired. And Sheriff Rakestraw wanted to start for the county seat at first light.

Luke was going to be mighty glad when Mordecai Kroll was locked up in the jail at St. Johns.

Despite the weariness that gripped him, Luke's slumber was restless and haunted by violent dreams ranging from the war on up to the desperate fight in the hotel room with Mordecai. He was more than happy to get up early the next morning. Doing something was always better than remembering and brooding.

It nagged at him that he had told Darcy Garnett about being Smoke's brother. He wondered if she would be willing to leave that out of the story she sent to *Harper's Weekly*. She probably wouldn't want to, but he figured it wouldn't do any harm to ask. As he went downstairs to the lobby with his saddlebags slung over his shoulder and his Winchester in his left hand, he decided that he would write her a note and leave it with the clerk for her. He was sure he would be on the trail to St. Johns with Rakestraw and the posse before Darcy got up.

The lobby was empty. Luke went to the writing

desk tucked into one corner and quickly wrote a note for Darcy in his neat script. He thanked her for her company at dinner and asked her to consider not saying anything about Smoke in her story, since it was supposed to be about the Kroll brothers and Mordecai's capture, and Smoke hadn't played any part in that.

The request might not do any good, but at least he had tried, he thought as he slipped the note into an envelope and sealed it.

The clerk still wasn't at the desk when Luke went over to it. He hit the bell that sat on the counter, and the clear note from it made the door behind the desk open a moment later. The clerk came out, yawning and running his fingers through his rumpled hair.

"What can I do for you, Mr. Jensen?" he asked.

Luke held up the envelope and said, "I'd like for you to give this to Miss Garnett when she comes down."

"I can't do that, sir," the clerk said.

Luke reached in his pocket for a coin, but the clerk stopped him by raising a hand.

"No, sir, Mr. Jensen, I mean I really can't do that," he said. "Miss Garnett isn't here anymore. She checked out and left town a half hour ago."

That news took Luke by surprise and made him frown. He asked, "Was she headed back to St. Johns?"

"I'm afraid she didn't say, sir."

Luke looked at the envelope in his hand. The message it contained didn't mean a blasted thing anymore. He crumpled it into a ball, tossed it to the startled clerk, and said, "Then throw that away for me, would you?"

He left a couple of gold pieces on the counter to cover his bill, turned, and walked out of the hotel.

The sun wouldn't be up for another hour, but the jail wagon was already in front of the livery stable as Abner Porter and his son Benji hitched up the team. Sheriff Wesley Rakestraw stood by and watched with a rifle tucked under his left arm. He gave Luke a curt nod of greeting.

"Quiet night?" Luke asked.

"Very," Rakestraw replied. "I have a hunch Rudolph Kroll doesn't know yet that his little brother has been taken into custody."

"Or maybe he's waiting to ambush you on the road between here and St. Johns," Luke suggested.

"If he tries, he'll get an unpleasant surprise. Every one of my deputies is a marksman."

That was all well and good, Luke thought, but if the posse was outnumbered by two to one or more, it might not be enough to make a difference.

"The café is already open," Rakestraw went on. "There'll be time to get some breakfast before we start."

"I'll just see to saddling my horse first," Luke said.

When the dun was ready to ride, Luke walked

over to the café. The sheriff and several of his deputies were already in there. He sat apart from them and washed down a hearty breakfast with several cups of coffee. He felt considerably better when he walked down to the jail.

The wagon that would take Mordecai to the county seat was parked in front of the building. Two of the deputies stood on the boardwalk holding Winchesters. They gave Luke hard stares as he went inside.

Marshal Jerome Dunlap sat behind the desk with a worried look on his face. He said, "I'm glad to see you, Jensen. I'm ready to have that varmint out of my jail, so things can go back to normal around here. I don't reckon I slept more than an hour last night."

Rakestraw came in a minute later, followed by four deputies. All five men wore grim expressions.

"Has the prisoner had his breakfast?" Rakestraw asked.

"He sure has, sheriff," Dunlap replied.

"He's ready to go, then."

"More than ready. At least I'm ready for him to go," Dunlap said again. He took the ring of keys from a nail on the wall and went to the cell block door.

Luke was aware that he was barely breathing. A feeling of tension gripped him like a physical fist. His instincts told him that something was bound to happen. Hell had a habit of breaking loose in situations like this.

Instead, Rakestraw and his deputies brought Mordecai out of the jail and locked him in the back of the sturdy wagon without incident. Mordecai had an arrogant grin on his face as he climbed into the wagon, as if he expected his brother to show up and rescue him at the last minute, but as the door swung closed Luke caught a glimpse of the fear that abruptly appeared in Mordecai's eyes. The big padlock snapped closed. The deputies, mounted now, surrounded the wagon and Rakestraw called out a command. The vehicle lurched into motion. Luke rode behind the group of lawmen.

Mordecai Kroll was on his way to jail . . . and ultimately to the gallows, if there was any justice in the world.

Chapter 7

Two months later

Rugged peaks loomed over the big old adobe house on all sides. The wide canyon in which it sat was accessible from the south through a mountain pass. From the north, a creek flowed into the canyon, but it was bordered by high, sheer cliffs that not even a mountain goat could have climbed, and it ran deep and swift through dangerous rapids where jagged rocks stuck up like a giant's fangs. A man would risk his life trying to navigate those rapids, and a few guards with rifles could make the canyon's southern entrance impassable.

For those reasons, this isolated canyon in the Superstition Mountains made a perfect hideout for the Kroll gang.

The little creek also provided enough water before it disappeared underground to support some vegetation, making the canyon one of the few spots of green in this brown, black, and tan wasteland. Cottonwoods and hardy grass grew along the stream. Farther from the water, manzanita, barrel cactus, and the majestic, somewhat eerie saguaros covered the landscape.

The big house had two stories, with terraced steps leading up to its entrance and a balcony along the second floor at the front. From there Rudolph Kroll could see much of the compound that was also surrounded by a high adobe wall with wrought-iron gates set into the main entrance. The barns and corrals, the long, low bunkhouse, the blacksmith shop, smokehouse, and granary all testified that once this had been a hacienda instead of an outlaw stronghold.

Kroll wasn't sure what had happened to the

early Spanish settler who had established this ranch. More than likely he and his family had died screaming at the hands of the Apaches.

All Kroll knew for sure was that when he and his men retreated to this canyon after pulling one of their jobs, they were safe. The law wasn't likely to find them here, and even if that happened, they could hold off a small army.

Yes, it was safe here, Kroll thought as he stood at the wall around the balcony and looked out over the hideout with the reddish light from the setting sun washing over his face . . . if you had enough sense to stay in the canyon and not sneak out to get drunk and dally with whores.

If you weren't as stupid as his little brother, Mordecai!

A massive, bearded man wearing a long vest decorated with Indian beadwork in intricate patterns came onto the balcony behind Kroll and said, "Supper's ready, boss. You want the woman to bring it out here?"

Kroll considered the question for a moment and then shook his head.

"No, Galt, I'll come inside in a few minutes," he said.

Galt grunted and nodded. He retreated through the French doors into the house.

Kroll had spent a considerable amount of money repairing and refurnishing the buildings of the abandoned rancho when he decided to make this the gang's headquarters. He didn't mind admitting that he enjoyed luxury. Growing up on a hardscrabble farm in Kansas before the Civil War, there hadn't been any of it. There hadn't been much of anything except squalor, backbreaking work, and near-starvation. Mordecai was younger. He didn't really remember much about those days or understand what that life had been like.

And that ignorance was one of the things that made him stupid.

Kroll turned away from the spectacular view and went into the house. This was his bedroom, but a table was set up so that he could take his meals here, too.

An attractive, middle-aged Mexican woman named Valencia brought his meal in on a tray and placed it on the table. She shared Kroll's bed from time to time. There were other women here to serve the gang's needs, too, some of them very young and beautiful. Mordecai hadn't needed to leave the canyon just because the itch was on him. He could have satisfied it without setting foot out of the stronghold.

No, as soon as Kroll had received word of Mordecai's capture from one of the spies he had spread out across the southwest, he knew what had happened. Mordecai had slipped out of the canyon out of sheer defiance. He didn't like his older brother riding herd on him all the time.

They had clashed repeatedly over that issue, as well as over the way Rudolph ran the gang. Like most young men, Mordecai thought he knew everything.

Now he was locked up, sentenced to death.

"Is there anything else, Señor Rudolph?" Valencia asked. She was slender, with a beautiful face and hair as dark as a raven's wing except where it was touched with silver threads that just gave her more character.

"No," Kroll said, then changed his mind and went on. "Yes. Light a fire before you leave."

"*Sí, señor.*"

There was a big fireplace on the other side of the room. Most nights here in the higher eastern slopes of the Superstitions, the temperature was chilly enough that the warmth from a fire felt good. That would probably be true tonight, too, but Kroll had something else in mind.

He sat down to eat. The meal was simple fare—corn bread, beans, ham—but it was what he liked. Valencia had left a glass of tequila on the table, too, along with the bottle. That warmed Kroll as well.

Tonight, however, the food seemed tasteless in his mouth. After toying with it for a few minutes, he pushed it away.

Valencia had kindled the fire in the fireplace. She stood in front of it now, silhouetted by the growing flames behind her. When she saw that

Kroll wasn't eating, she asked, "Is something wrong, señor?"

He shook his head.

"Just not hungry tonight, I suppose," he said.

"Would you like for me to take it away?"

"Yes, *por favor*. But leave the tequila. And send Galt back up here."

She nodded, gathered up the food, and left. When she was gone, Kroll reached over and picked up a magazine that was lying on the table.

It was a recent edition of *Harper's Weekly*, brought to the hideout in a load of supplies from Phoenix. The woodcut illustration on the cover depicted a scene of violent gunplay between two men. Under the picture were the words "Daring Capture of Desperado Mordecai Kroll."

Rudolph had read the story inside the magazine at least a dozen times since Galt had given it to him. It was written in florid, breathless prose by someone named D. J. Garnett and told how Mordecai had been captured in a small town in Apache County by someone named Luke Jensen. Although Garnett didn't spell it out, it was obvious to Rudolph that this man Jensen was the lowest form of life: a bounty hunter.

The story ended with Mordecai being taken to St. Johns to be held there until jurisdiction was decided. Rudolph had kept up with the rest of the story through newspaper accounts and reports from his spies. He knew that even though warrants for Mordecai's arrest had been issued in more than a dozen states and territories, Arizona authorities had refused to give him up. He was wanted in this territory on numerous counts of murder, rape, and robbery. Eventually, he had been taken to Phoenix to stand trial on those charges.

Rudolph had considered trying to rescue his brother from the law while Mordecai was being transported from St. Johns to Phoenix, but in the end he had decided the risk was too great. Fearing just such an attempt, the territorial governor had asked for help from the army, so Mordecai was guarded during the trip by soldiers as well as deputies. The word was out, too, that the soldiers had unofficial orders to shoot Mordecai down if it looked like he was going to escape.

Once the trial began, it hadn't taken long for Mordecai to be found guilty on all counts and sentenced to hang. He would have been dead already if some of the states where he was wanted hadn't continued their efforts to have him brought there for another trial. All this legal wrangling had delayed things, and while that was going on, Mordecai had sat in Yuma Prison under sentence of death, waiting to be hanged.

Just because Rudolph had been forced to bide his time didn't mean that he had given up on getting Mordecai out of there. But the simple fact of the matter was that this wasn't a job for a bunch of outlaws. It required more finesse than that.

Kroll stood up, slapped the rolled magazine against his thigh, and walked over to the fireplace carrying a freshly topped-off glass of tequila. He stood there sipping the liquor and watching the flames until the big outlaw Galt, who served as his majordomo here at the hideout, came into the room behind him.

"You wanted me, boss?" Galt rumbled.

"That's right."

Kroll opened the copy of *Harper's Weekly* to the story about Mordecai's capture. Some of the paragraphs concerning Luke Jensen mentioned that Jensen's brother was Smoke Jensen, the famous gunfighter who now owned the Sugarloaf ranch near the town of Big Rock, Colorado. The author touched on Smoke Jensen's own notorious history and played up the fact that he was one of the most dangerous gunmen who had ever slapped leather. Perhaps even the most dangerous of them all. . . .

Rudolph Kroll's mouth tightened into a grim line as he read that passage again. An idea had begun to form in his head. He needed Luke Jensen, not so that he could take vengeance on the bounty hunter, but for another purpose entirely. Everything might depend on it.

Anger surged up inside Kroll. He threw the glass in his left hand into the fire. The glass shattered, and the tequila that was still in it ignited and went up with a *whoosh!*

In the next heartbeat, Kroll flung the magazine into the fireplace, too. The flames, burning even hotter because they were fueled by the liquor, consumed the pages in a matter of moments. As the cover illustrating Mordecai's downfall curled and blackened into ash, Kroll watched it and said to Galt without turning around, "I don't care what it takes. Bring me Luke Jensen."

Chapter 8

Skunk Creek, Wyoming

The town lived up to its name, Luke thought as he walked the dun along the settlement's muddy main street. A cold rain sluiced down and dripped from the low-pulled brim of his hat. But even in the rain, which usually washed the air clean, the place smelled bad. Something about the seeps along the edge of the creek that ran behind the buildings, he supposed. Didn't really smell like polecat, but it was bad enough on its own.

He wore a slicker, but of course the stubborn rain had found ways to worm trails under the oilcloth and soak his regular clothes. That meant

Luke felt cold and clammy and wanted nothing more than to find a nice hot fire to sit beside, so he could dry out some and warm his bones.

Instead, there was a good chance that in the next twenty minutes he would either have to kill somebody . . . or be killed himself.

It was only the middle of the afternoon, but the thick gray overcast made the sky look like dusk. Because of that, the lamps were already lit in most of the buildings along either side of the street in the block where Skunk Creek's business establishments were located. The windows showed up as yellow rectangles in the gloom.

One of those businesses was the Panther Saloon. A while back, somebody passing through Skunk Creek had recognized the bartender there as Andy Eggleston, who was wanted for fatally gunning down a deputy marshal during the getaway from a botched bank robbery in Rawlins, Wyoming Territory, a year earlier. Eggleston must have believed that Skunk Creek was far enough away from Rawlins to be safe, but he was wrong about that.

The man who had recognized him had told somebody else, who had mentioned it to somebody else, and eventually the news had drifted to Luke in Cheyenne. He recalled having a poster on Eggleston in his saddlebags, and when he dug it out, he saw that the bank had put an eight hundred dollar reward on the would-be robber's head. The town council had added a couple of hundred to it in order to make the total an even one thousand dollars. That wasn't bad.

Of course, he wouldn't need a bounty like that if all the rewards due him for the capture of Mordecai Kroll would come through. As usual, though, the banks and railroads and state and territorial governments were taking their own sweet time about paying him. If a fella owed money to any of those places, they wanted it right then and there, and you were in trouble if you didn't pay up.

But when the dinero was supposed to go the other way, it was a different story. Then it was, *Risk your life killing or jailing this no-account bastard for us, and we'll get around to paying you for it when we're damned good and ready.*

Those thoughts were running through Luke's mind when he spotted the Panther Saloon up ahead on the left. The letters on the sign nailed to the front of the awning over the boardwalk had faded, and the dim light of the rainy day made them even harder to read. Once Luke made them out, though, he angled the dun in that direction.

"Soon as I'm finished in there, we'll find you a nice, dry stable, old-timer," he said.

The dun flicked an ear.

The saloon had bigger front windows than most of the buildings, but they were so dirty that not much light filtered through them. At this time of year the double doors at the entrance were closed, instead of being open with just the swinging bat wings in them. A couple of benches where idlers could sit and spit and whittle when the weather was nice flanked the doorway.

Three miserable-looking saddle mounts with their heads drooping were tied up at one of the hitch rails. Out of habit, Luke checked the brands as he reined the dun to a stop. All three horses were from the Block K. He had never heard of that spread, but he assumed it was a ranch somewhere not too far from Skunk Creek. Three of the hands, unable to do any real work because of the weather, had ridden into the settlement to pass the afternoon, he supposed.

He dismounted and grimaced as his boots sank into the mud. They came loose with sucking sounds when he stepped up onto the boardwalk after looping the dun's reins around the hitch rail. In an effort to get some of the mud off, he stomped several times as he headed for the doors, but the sticky stuff clung stubbornly.

He was sure this wouldn't be the first time somebody had tracked mud into the Panther Saloon.

Before he went in, he leaned his head forward to let more collected rain water drain off his hat. He unbuttoned his slicker and flapped it to shake off some of the moisture, and not coincidentally, to give him easier access to his Remingtons. With that done, he grasped the knob of the left-hand door, turned it, and went inside.

The air outside was chilly and dank, but inside the saloon the atmosphere was hot and oppressive. He'd be lucky if he didn't catch his death of the grippe, thought Luke . . . if he didn't get holes blown in him during the next few minutes.

The heat came from a pair of big potbellied stoves in opposite rear corners of the low-ceilinged room. The bar was to the right, with a tarnished brass rail running along its base and several spittoons sitting in front of it. Half a dozen mismatched tables were scattered haphazardly to the left. In the back was a small open space for dancing and an old piano that probably hadn't been tuned since Stephen Foster was a boy. Nobody was around to play the piano, and there wasn't a woman in the place as far as Luke could see, so the dance floor was going unused, too.

Only one of the tables was occupied. The three cowboys who went with the trio of Block K horses outside sat there with a bottle of whiskey on the table between them. They were doing some serious drinking, apparently, and concentrating on the job at hand, so they barely glanced at Luke as he came in and closed the door behind him.

The man behind the bar was tall, with thinning blond hair and a beard. He wore a soiled apron over a flannel shirt with the sleeves rolled up to reveal the sleeves of a set of red long-handled underwear. He had an empty glass in his right hand and used a rag in his left hand in an attempt to polish it. The glass had too many greasy fingerprints on it for the rag to do much good.

The beard was new, but other than that, the bartender looked just like the picture on the wanted poster Luke had folded up and put in his shirt pocket. The paper might be a little damp now, but it would still be legible.

The bartender nodded and said, "Nasty day out there, ain't it, friend?"

"It is indeed," Luke said. "Longfellow claimed that the best thing a man can do when it's raining is to let it rain."

The bartender frowned slightly.

"Can't say as I know the gent you're talkin' about, but he's right. Can't do a blamed thing about the rain except try to stay out of it."

"Which is exactly what I'm doing," Luke said. "Can I get a beer?"

"Sure." The man filled a glass mug that was also heavily coated with fingerprints and slid it across the hardwood. "Four bits."

Luke dropped coins on the bar and picked up the mug. The beer was as bitter and tasteless as he expected it to be, but at least it cleared his throat a little.

"Don't think I've seen you in Skunk Creek before," the bartender said as he went back to his futile glass polishing.

"I just rode in," Luke said.

The man laughed.

"I hope you're just passin' through. There's not much here worth stayin' for."

"You own this saloon?"

"Naw," the bartender replied with a shake of his head. "Just work for the old man who does. He's got the rheumatism, so he don't get around very well anymore, especially when the weather's damp like this. But I don't have anything else to do, so I don't mind runnin' the place pretty much full time."

He held the glass up to the light, studied it for a second, sighed in defeat, and set it aside. Then he stuck out his hand.

"Harvey Lawdermilk's my name."

"Now that's funny," Luke said as he took the man's hand. "Ever since I came in the door, I've been thinking that you look familiar to me, but that's not the name I put with your face."

Alarm lit up in the man's eyes as Luke suddenly tightened his grip.

"I would've sworn you were Andy Eggleston," Luke went on.

The bartender tried to pull away, but Luke jerked him forward over the bar and at the same time reached across his body with his left hand and palmed out the Remington in the right-side cross-draw holster. He brought the gun crashing down on Eggleston's head.

Eggleston collapsed across the bar. His arm hit the mostly full mug of beer and sent it sliding off to crash on the floor in front of the bar. Luke leaned back and hauled harder. Eggleston wound up sprawled senseless on top of the bar.

Luke heard chair legs scraping on the rough floor and glanced over his shoulder to see the three cowboys starting to their feet with startled expressions on their beard-stubbled faces. He swung the Remington in his left hand in their general direction and said sharply, "Sit back down, boys. There's nothing going on here that you need to be involved with."

"But you walloped Harvey!" one of the men exclaimed.

"Are you holdin' up the place?" another asked.

"Now, if I were an outlaw I think I could find a more lucrative place than this to rob," Luke said. He took the folded reward dodger from his pocket, shook it a couple of times to straighten it out, and held it next to the face of the unconscious "Harvey Lawdermilk" to be sure he was the same man.

"Son of a bitch!" the third cowboy said. "That's Harvey on that ree-ward poster."

"That means he must be an outlaw," one of the other men said.

"That's right," Luke told them. With that explained, he holstered the revolver and reached for one of the rawhide strips he carried so he could tie Andy Eggleston's wrists behind his back before the fugitive came to.

One of the cowboys said slowly, "That means . . . you must be a bounty hunter, mister."

"Right the first—" Luke began.

The sound of guns being cocked interrupted him.

He glanced over his shoulder, saw all three cowboys pointing revolvers at him, and dived for cover just as flame spurted from gun muzzles and shots began to crash like thunder.

Chapter 9

Bullets smashed into the bar and sent splinters flying where Luke had been standing a hairsbreadth of time earlier. He sprawled full length on the sawdust-littered floor, which stunk of spilled beer and rotgut and vomit. A quick roll carried him against the legs of the nearest table as more slugs chewed into the floorboards next to him.

He grabbed the table legs and heaved. The table overturned and provided a little cover for him as he yanked one of the Remingtons from its holster. He had no idea why the three cowboys from the Block K were trying to kill him, nor did he care.

As more bullets thudded into the overturned table, he thrust the Remington around the side of it and triggered two shots. He couldn't tell if he hit any of the cowboys, but the flying lead was enough to make them scatter.

One man headed for the nearest potbellied stove which would have made good cover if he had reached it. He was a little too slow. Luke snapped a shot at him and drilled him through the thigh.

The wound made the cowboy lose his balance and pitch forward as his leg folded up under him. His arms went out instinctively and wrapped around the stove, embracing it as a man would a lover. His face rammed against it, and he screamed as the heat cooked and blistered the skin of his face and hands.

The other two men had turned over a table of their own and crouched behind it as they hammered shots at Luke. The table he was using for cover had taken a lot of damage. As it began to splinter and come apart, several slugs punched all the way through the wood and whistled perilously close to Luke's head.

He holstered his gun, grabbed a couple of the table legs, and surged to his feet. Holding the table in front of him like a battering ram and yelling at the top of his lungs, he charged across the room toward the men trying to kill him. The unexpected attack startled them enough that they stopped shooting for a second.

That gave Luke enough time to crash his table into the other one and knock it back against the two men, who sprawled on the floor from the impact as wood snapped and cracked. They wound up lying on their backs with the wreckage of two tables on top of them, along with Luke's weight.

He rolled off and drew both guns as he came away to his feet. A quick step and a swift kick knocked the gun out of one man's hand. Luke pointed a Remington at the other man's face and eared back the hammer.

"Throw it away!" he rasped. "Now!"

The man did so, sliding the gun a good ten feet across the dirty floor. Luke was breathing hard, and he was mad. The cowboy must have realized he was only a slight pressure on the trigger away from getting his brains blown out.

Luke backed off. His left-hand gun covered the two men lying in the debris of the broken tables; the right-hand gun pointed toward the cowboy lying beside the stove, moaning in agony from his burns.

"Crawl out of that mess," Luke told the two men he had just disarmed. "Stay away from your guns. Make a move I don't like and I'll kill you."

"Sure you will," one of the men said as his face twisted with hate. "That's just what a damn, no-good bounty hunter would do!"

"I'm going to ignore that for the moment, as long as one of you tells me what the *hell* is going on here!"

"Ain't you figured it out by now?" asked the man

who had spoken up. He and his companion stood together, their arms half-raised. "We're wanted."

Luke narrowed his eyes and stared at them. He didn't recall ever seeing either man before, or their likeness on a wanted poster, either.

"So that's why you tried to kill me? You thought I was after you?"

"You come in here, pistol-whip Harvey, haul out a wanted poster of him and admit that you're after blood money. . . . What in blazes were we supposed to think?"

"Oh, I don't know," Luke said. "Maybe that I was after *Harvey,* you idiots!"

The second man looked over at the one who'd been doing the talking and said, "He's got a point, Rance. If we'd just kept our mouths shut, this gent likely would've taken Harvey out of here and left us alone." His eyes widened as something else occurred to him. "Then we could've helped ourselves to all the booze in the place!"

"Shut up!" Rance said. "How was I to know? I mean, those stolen Block K broncs are right outside. He had to've seen 'em."

"You shouldn't be talkin' about stolen broncs. Didn't you hear the fella say he didn't know nothin' about that?"

"He already knows we're outlaws, you fool! We tried to blow holes in his hide!"

"Because you said we oughta!"

Listening to those two wrangle was actually a

little entertaining, Luke thought, but he wasn't really in the mood for it. The fact that the third man was lying on the floor a few yards away with his face half burned off sort of put a damper on the humor. The burned man had fallen silent now, which told Luke he had probably passed out from the pain.

"Go pick up your friend and tend to him," Luke said. "And while you're at it, tie up Eggleston."

"Who?"

"The bartender. The one who's been calling himself Harvey Lawdermilk. His real name's Andy Eggleston. He tried to rob the bank over in Rawlins and killed a man getting away."

"Harvey done that? Dang, he seemed like such a nice friendly fella."

Luke waggled the right-hand Remington.

"Go on and do what I told you."

"You're takin' us all in?" Rance asked.

"That's the general idea. I'll get your names once you're tied up."

"You really don't know who we are? You wasn't after us?"

"Sorry to disappoint you, boys," Luke said, "but you brought this on yourselves."

Both men wore expressions of total disgust as they went to help their friend.

Skunk Creek was too small to have a jail or even a local lawman. The blacksmith had a sturdy smokehouse, though, and he was willing to rent it to Luke so that it could serve as a temporary lockup. The price was a little exorbitant, but Luke figured he had no choice but to pay it.

The settlement didn't have a doctor, either. Luke got some lard from the café and rubbed it on the burned man's injuries. That was all he could do for the unlucky varmint.

He didn't feel too sorry for any of the cowboys. It had been their choice to start shooting at him.

By the time all that was taken care of, night had fallen, and it was a dark night indeed because of the overcast. The rain had tapered off, but it was still a steady drizzle as Luke went back to the café to get something to eat.

The woman who ran the place had graying red hair and was built like a tree stump. She wasn't very friendly, but she was a decent cook, Luke discovered when he sat down to a meal of steak, fried potatoes, and greens. The peach cobbler with which he followed it was even better.

"Is there a hotel or a boardinghouse in this town where a man can get a room for the night?" he asked the proprietor.

"In Skunk Creek?" The woman laughed. "Nobody stays overnight in Skunk Creek unless they have to, mister. Hell, none of the people who live here would stay if they had anywhere else to go. What you can do, though, is ask the Swede down at the livery stable if he'll let you sleep in his hayloft. If he ain't been drinkin' enough to feel argumentative, he'll usually let travelers do that."

Luke nodded and said, "I'm obliged to you."

"I'd let you spend the night at my place," the woman said, "but you're not really my type. No offense, but I like men who are a little younger and better-looking."

Luke chuckled and said, "None taken. Although with cooking like this I'd think you'd have more suitors than you could handle."

"Ain't no such thing, mister. Ain't no such thing."

Still smiling, Luke headed for the livery stable a few minutes later, leading the dun. The poor horse had been standing in the rain for a couple of hours. He needed a nice warm stall, a good brushing, and some oats or grain. A dry hayloft didn't sound bad to Luke, either.

The mud still sucked at his boots with every step. As he approached the livery barn he saw that its big double doors were closed, but a line of light came through the little gap between them and told him that a lantern was lit inside.

The doors weren't latched or barred. He grasped the one on the left and pulled it open enough to take the dun inside. Light spilled around them as they entered.

A stocky, broad-faced man with a shock of blond hair stood inside, fiddling with some harness. He nodded to Luke and asked, “What can I do for you, mister?”

The Scandinavian accent wasn’t strong, but it was enough to confirm that this was the Swede, Luke thought. He said, “I need accommodations for my horse and for myself as well. The woman at the café said you might be willing to let me pitch my bedroll in the loft.”

“Oh, yah, sure. There are some bugs and rats up there, but not too many, mind.” The man didn’t look up from whatever he was doing with the harness. Luke tried idly to figure it out but couldn’t really tell. “There’s an empty stall right yonder. You can put your horse in it. I’ll get to him in a few minutes.”

“All right.”

The hair on the back of Luke’s neck prickled a little as he led the dun into the stall that the Swede had indicated. He had gotten a sudden hunch that something wasn’t right here, but he couldn’t tell what it was. The Swede certainly seemed harmless enough, despite his preoccupation with that bit of harness.

Luke unsaddled the dun, dried him with a rag he found hanging in the stall, and carried his bedroll and Winchester back into the aisle between the rows of stalls.

“You’re that bounty hunter fella, aren’t you?” the Swede asked, still without looking at him. “The one who shot up the Panther Saloon.”

"The gunplay wasn't my idea," Luke said. He was getting a little irritated now by the liveryman's attitude. "I had captured the man I was after without firing a shot. It was those other three hombres who decided to turn it into a gunfight."

"That'd make you Luke Jensen."

"Yes, what—"

Luke stopped short as he realized that he hadn't told anyone in Skunk Creek his name. That meant someone else had given it to the Swede. Someone who had to be looking for him.

He dropped the bedroll and brought the rifle up as he heard a rush of footsteps behind him. The Swede dropped the harness he had been pretending to fiddle with and dived for the open door of his office. Clearly, he wanted to get out of the line of fire.

Luke whirled as several figures lunged from the thick shadows deeper in the barn and charged at him. He got a shot off with the Winchester, but couldn't tell if he hit any of his attackers. Before he had a chance to work the rifle's lever, a couple of men crashed into him with diving tackles and knocked him off his feet.

He landed with bone-jarring force on the hard-packed dirt of the aisle. The impact jolted the Winchester out of his hands. He reached for one of the Remingtons, but a booted foot slammed into his ribs and rolled him onto his side, trapping that hand. More kicks rocked him and sent pain exploding through his body. A boot heel caught him in the temple and made the world blur and spin crazily.

"Remember, don't kill him!" a man's voice ordered. "We need him alive!"

"But we can bust him up some, right?" another man asked.

"Oh, yeah. Bust him up. Make him pay for what he did."

Luke hadn't even caught a glimpse of any of their faces. He didn't know who they were or why they were doing this.

But given his line of work, he had made plenty of enemies over the years. Obviously, one of them wanted some special vengeance on him; otherwise, the attackers wouldn't be under orders to keep him alive. If it had been a simple matter of revenge, they would have gone ahead and killed him.

That was the last coherent thought he had. Everything after that was a blinding tide of pain that carried him away to oblivion.

Chapter 10

When Luke came to, he felt the surface he was lying on rocking back and forth and bouncing as well. Everything around him was utterly dark, so he couldn't tell where he was. The blackness was so absolute that he had to blink his eyes to be sure he actually had them open.

A pounding ache filled his head. That came as no surprise to him. He had been knocked senseless enough times in his life to recognize the feeling as the aftermath of another brutal assault.

It was a good thing he had a thick skull, he thought.

When he tried to remember what had happened to him, at first he couldn't. Then the details began to seep back into his brain, fuzzy and disjointed at first, but eventually they formed a picture which made a sort of sense, although it left many questions unanswered. He tried it out by thinking through it.

A group of men—half a dozen, he estimated, although there could have been more—had ridden into Skunk Creek looking for him. They must have been on his trail for a while and had finally caught up to him in the squalid little settlement.

Rather than searching for him building by building, they had figured he would show up at the livery stable sooner or later and had gone there. They had taken over the place and waited in the shadows. The Swede must have had several guns pointed at him the whole time he was talking to Luke.

The men had told the Swede Luke's name and ordered the man to make sure of his identity when he came in. That explained the Swede's odd behavior. He had been in fear for his life and had been trying to follow the orders the mysterious visitors had given him. As soon as those strangers were certain that Luke was the man they were after, they had jumped him, had kicked and stomped and hit him until he was out cold.

That brought him right up to the moment, Luke thought. The questions that remained were:

Who were these men?

Who had sent them after him, and why?

And what was he going to do about it?

He could answer the last of those questions. For the moment he would do nothing. He was tied hand and foot, with his arms pulled back and his wrists lashed together behind him. He checked, and another rope ran from his bound wrists down to his equally fettered ankles, pulling him into an odd, uncomfortable shape that left him totally helpless.

Sooner or later, though, his captors would have to cut him loose, and when they did . . .

His mouth stretched in a wry grin at the thought. When they did, more than likely he would still be helpless, because he was bound so tightly that he couldn't feel his hands or feet. He wouldn't be able to stand up or grip a gun.

He had to wait and be patient. If they ever gave him a chance, he needed to be able to grab it.

In the meantime, the best thing to do might be to investigate his surroundings. The unsteady motion made him a little sick, but he tried to ignore it. It would help if he kept himself occupied. He couldn't move much, but he managed to squirm to one side until he came up against a wall.

He rolled so that he could explore the wall's surface with his hands. It felt like the same sort of thick, slightly rough planks that were underneath him. He twisted, pushed with his feet, and worked himself up into a sitting position with his back leaning against the wall and his legs drawn up to the side.

Luke had been on a few boats in his time. The rocking motion reminded him of being at sea. It wasn't bad enough for that, he decided. He became aware of a steady, rhythmic thudding, and that told him what he wanted to know.

The sound came from the hooves of a horse or mule team striking a road. He was in an enclosed wagon with the bed suspended on leather thoroughbraces that were old and not very strong anymore, hence the swaying and bouncing.

Luke scooted himself along the wall to his left until he reached a corner. The sound of the horses' hooves wasn't as loud here, so he assumed he was farther away from the team, which would make this a rear corner.

Inch by inch, he slid over to the other rear corner. His best estimate was that the wagon was eight feet wide.

He continued his awkward explorations and determined that the closed wagon bed was roughly eight feet by ten feet. He got his feet under him, braced his back against the wall as best he could with his hands tied behind him, and tried to stand up. That took him a while, as well. He hadn't straightened to his full height when the top of his head bumped the ceiling.

The dimensions of his temporary prison were familiar. Even though he hadn't found them, he would have bet that steel rings were set into the floor so that chains could be attached to them.

He was in a jail wagon, the same sort of vehicle into which he had prodded countless prisoners at gunpoint over the long years he'd been a bounty hunter.

That realization made him lean his head against the wall and laugh. It seemed as if the universe was having its own private little joke at his expense.

After thinking about it for a while, he decided that it was night outside. Even a tightly constructed prison wagon had tiny gaps between the boards in places, and daylight would come through them.

That theory was confirmed after an interminable time when a very faint gray glow appeared here and there. Dawn was approaching.

Luke had already figured out that the rain had stopped because he couldn't hear it anymore. He wondered what direction his captors had gone from Skunk Creek.

He also wondered if somebody in the settlement would let his prisoners out of the smokehouse when the Swede told everybody about what had happened. *If* the men who had captured Luke had left the Swede alive.

Luke hoped they had. He didn't really care what happened to Andy Eggleston or the three outlaws who had stolen horses from the Block K. If the blacksmith had any sense, he would turn Eggleston over to the law himself and collect the reward. The three horse thieves might wind up being hanged as, well, horse thieves.

Once they tried to kill him, they deserved whatever they got, as far as Luke was concerned, although they had seemed more stupid than vicious.

The light coming through the cracks got brighter. Luke saw that he'd been right about the steel rings bolted to the floor. He was surprised that his captors hadn't fastened his bonds to one of them. Maybe they had figured he was trussed up good enough like he was that he couldn't get away.

So far they would have been right.

The light got brighter, and eventually the wagon lurched to a halt. Luke lifted his head and yelled, "Damned well about time! Get me out of here!"

He didn't see any point in pretending not to be awake. They were going to be checking on him anyway, he was sure of that.

He heard a clunk that he recognized as the sound of a padlock being unlocked, then the lock rattled in a hasp. The door swung back, and after being locked up in absolute darkness and then thick gloom for so long, the light that came into the wagon was blindingly bright to Luke's eyes. He tried not to flinch from it but couldn't help himself.

"Haw! Squeamish as a rabbit!"

The loud, harsh voice made Luke angry, but there was nothing he could do about the scorn . . . other than mark it up in his mind as one more score to settle later.

He couldn't see the man who had spoken except as a dark, hulking shape against the light. The man went on. "A couple of you boys get in there and drag him out. I want to get a look at this hombre who's so important to the boss."

More shapes loomed. Luke felt the wagon shift under him as men climbed into it. Strong, rough hands took hold of him and dragged him toward the opening. When they reached it, they dumped him on the ground outside.

His eyes had started to adjust by now. He could make out more details about the men who stood around him, grinning. The leader seemed to be an ugly man in a long sheepskin coat. Tufts of rust-colored hair stuck out from under the battered old hat with a tightly curled brim that was tugged down on his head. With his stringy neck and beak of a nose, the man reminded Luke of a buzzard.

"You know who I am, bounty hunter?" the man said.

"Can't say as I—" Luke began, then stopped as a name popped into his memory. "Hell! You're Dakota Charlie Payne."

"That's right," the man said proudly. "Dakota Charlie his own self. Meanest man north of the Missouri River. That's what the newspapers done called me. You can look it up."

"Hear lately you've been riding with—"

Once again Luke stopped short as a memory came back to him. Payne just grinned wider and said, "Ay-yuh, that's right, Jensen. I ride with the Kroll brothers. All these fellers do. Rudolph Kroll, he's the one sent us to fetch you. I reckon he ain't happy with what you done, catchin' his little brother and bein' responsible for him gettin' sentenced to hang and all."

"Mordecai Kroll had it coming to him. He deserved whatever he got."

"He ain't got nothin' yet," Payne said. "They're still waitin' to drop him through the trapdoor."

Luke hadn't known that. He hadn't kept up closely with the story, so he had assumed that Mordecai had gone to the gallows before now.

The fact that the younger Kroll brother was still alive might put a different face on this whole affair.

Payne turned to the men with him and said, "Somebody get a fire goin' and boil some coffee. We'll stay here and let the hosses rest for a spell 'fore we get back on the trail."

"Where are you taking me?" Luke asked.

"I thought I done told you that. To see Rudolph. Don't know what he's got in mind to do to you, but I'll bet a heap it won't be pleasant." Payne waved a hand. "Throw him back in the wagon."

"Wait just a damned minute!" Luke objected. "Can't you even cut a man loose long enough to tend to his needs?"

"Go ahead and piss yourself," Payne said with a vicious grin. "Reckon you'll be doin' that by the time Rudolph gets through with you, anyway!"

Chapter 11

Luke had been through some hellish experiences in his life, including being shot and left for dead, but the next ten days were as bad as anything he had ever experienced. From dawn to dusk, and often after dark as well if the trail was marked well enough, Dakota Charlie Payne kept the wagon and its outriders moving. From the few brief glimpses Luke got of the outside world, he thought they were heading in a generally southerly direction. Maybe a little southwest.

He didn't see much of the world, though. For the most part his entire universe was the inside of the jail wagon. His muscles grew so cramped and weak from being tied up that he wasn't sure he would ever be able to walk normally again. Payne and his other captors gave him barely enough food and water to subsist on, which contributed to his weakened condition. His beard and hair grew, and he supposed he was starting to look like a man who had been trapped on a deserted island.

"Robinson Crusoe Jensen," he muttered one day as he remembered the character from a novel he'd read.

The heat during the day began to grow worse,

which was another indication that they were heading south. It had been chilly in Wyoming, but nothing like it would be later in the autumn and winter. The season was still early enough in autumn that the days in certain parts of the southwest could be quite warm, even hot.

He had caught up to Mordecai Kroll in Arizona, Luke recalled. There was a good chance the gang's hideout wasn't too far from where Luke had captured Mordecai. So the heat made sense if Payne was really taking him to Rudolph Kroll.

The brutal outlaw had no reason to lie about that, as far as Luke could figure.

Luke could tell by the slant of the wagon when they were traveling through mountainous areas. They had been climbing for a full day, moving slower because of the angle, when the trail leveled out for a short distance, then began to descend slightly.

They had just gone through a pass, Luke thought. He had no idea where and it might not matter, but he had been thinking about anything and everything, trying to keep his mind strong even as his body grew weaker. During the endless hours he had quoted poetry to himself, recounted the plots of numerous novels, even quoted Scripture. Anything to keep his brain from sinking into a mental morass.

The quality of the light told him it was the middle of the day, but a short time later the wagon stopped. That wasn't too unusual—Payne had called midday halts before—but Luke sensed that something was different about this one.

One of the men unlocked the wagon. As usual, several of them stood guard, holding rifles or pistols, while two men dragged Luke out of the wagon and dumped him on the ground.

This time, however, Dakota Charlie Payne approached Luke with an enormous Bowie knife in his hand.

"I could carve you from gullet to gizzard with this, Jensen," Payne said as he flourished the knife. "It'd be just what a lowdown bounty hunter deserves, too. But you know I ain't gonna do it."

He hooked a boot toe under Luke's shoulder and rolled him onto his belly. A second later Luke felt the tug as Payne used the Bowie to cut the rope holding his wrists and ankles together.

That allowed his legs to straighten out. Cramped muscles screamed a protest at that. Luke tightened his jaw. He wasn't going to let them hear a sound out of him, not even a whimper.

A moment later, he could tell that Payne was cutting the ropes on his ankles, too. They came free.

"Get him on his feet," Payne ordered.

Luke's feet were so numb they might as well not have existed. He could only hope that they weren't permanently damaged. Four men took hold of him, two on each arm, and lifted him.

They set him upright. His legs folded up like strings. He would have collapsed if the outlaws hadn't been holding him.

"Walk him around some," Payne snapped. "We got to get him movin' again."

The men dragged Luke back and forth as they tried to force his muscles to work. His legs flopped limply at first, but then he felt sensations creeping into them again. Even his feet began to prickle with an intense feeling of pins and needles. He gritted his teeth again in order to remain stubbornly silent.

While they were tormenting him like this, he looked around. They were on a lane lined with junipers, but through the gaps between the trees he saw rugged peaks rising all around. This was a high canyon in some mountain range that was unknown to him, although some of the landscape did look vaguely familiar as if he had seen it years earlier.

In the distance, a creek with cottonwoods growing along it twisted its way through the canyon. Luke's gaze followed the stream to where it flowed past a number of buildings. He saw barns, corrals, what looked like a bunkhouse. This was a ranch, he thought, or at least it had been at one time.

He began taking a few stumbling steps. He still would have fallen if not for the men holding him up, but he could tell that his iron constitution was asserting itself. Given time, rest, and exercise, he wouldn't be a cripple after all, and that knowledge came as a huge relief to him.

Of course, he reminded himself, if Rudolph Kroll killed him five minutes from now, it wouldn't really matter, would it?

He had already figured out that this was the Kroll gang's hideout. Had to be. Why else would Payne and the others have brought him here? Why else would they be forcing him to walk? They were about to turn him over to Rudolph Kroll.

"All right," Payne said after a few minutes. "Move the wagon."

One of the men climbed to the driver's seat and lifted the reins. The team of horses hauled the wagon out of the way, and for the first time Luke got a good look at the main house. It sat behind a flagstone patio at the top of about twenty terracelike steps. At each end of each of those steps sat a potted cactus.

The house itself was big and sprawling, with a red tile roof in the Spanish style and a walled balcony on the second floor. The windows were decorated with wrought iron. It might have been the home of a Spanish don outside Seville, Luke thought.

The man waiting at the top of the steps was a far cry from a nobleman, though. He was an outlaw, plain and simple, an evil man with a hawklike face and a dark mustache. Luke recognized him from plenty of wanted posters.

Rudolph Kroll.

Standing behind Kroll and to one side was a massive bear of a man wearing a long, beaded vest and a flat-crowned brown hat. Probably Kroll's segundo, Luke thought.

Kroll had his arms crossed over his chest as he looked down the steps and regarded Luke with an expression of pure hatred. Clearly, he was waiting for something.

"All right, Jensen," Payne said as he prodded Luke in the back with a rifle barrel. "Up you go."

Luke didn't know if he could make it up the steps, but pride stiffened his back and his legs. He lifted his right foot and felt the muscles trembling, but they obeyed his commands well enough for him to set the foot on the first step. Now to see if the leg would support his weight when he started up.

It did. The steps were wide enough that he had to plant both feet on each one, shuffle forward, lift his right foot and then his left foot to the next one, and repeat the process. It was slow going, but he kept his head up and met Rudolph Kroll's cold stare with an equally chilly, defiant one of his own.

Kroll might be about to kill him, but whatever his fate might be, Luke was going to meet it on his own two feet, and he was thankful for that.

It seemed to take an hour for him to climb the steps, although he knew it wasn't really that long. Finally, he lifted a foot to the patio and forced his body up for the last time. He stood there facing Kroll, who stood ten feet away.

"Luke Jensen," Kroll said, his voice deep and powerful but with an undertone of harshness that made it sound almost like the growl of an animal. "I've been looking forward to this meeting."

"That makes one of us," Luke rasped. He hadn't used his voice much during the journey here. It sounded like the squalling of a rusty gate to his ears.

"Do you know why I've had you brought to Massacre Canyon?"

"That's what you call this place?"

"The hacienda probably had some other name. Don't ask me what it was. But the area is known among the Apaches as Massacre Canyon, which probably refers to something that happened here, I don't know." Kroll gave a curt shake of his head. "None of that's important. I had you brought here because of two brothers."

"You and Mordecai," Luke said. "Tell me, have they stretched his neck at the end of a hang rope yet?"

Luke didn't want to be tortured any more than he already had been. He would rather goad Kroll into pulling a gun and shooting him, if it came down to a choice like that. A quick, clean death, even if it was at the hands of an ugly bastard.

But surprisingly, Rudolph Kroll smiled. He said, "You're only half right, Jensen. This is about Mordecai, all right. And no, they haven't hanged him. I've paid off enough lawyers and politicians to keep him alive for a while. It's really about two other brothers, though: you and your brother Smoke."

Luke's breath froze in his throat. His heart seemed to stop in his chest. Was Kroll going to go after Smoke to complete his vengeance?

He might wind up with more trouble on his hands than he expected if he did that.

"You see, I know all about the famous Smoke Jensen," Kroll went on, obviously very pleased with himself now. "His exploits are legendary. If everything that's been written about him is true, there's never been anyone else like him in the history of the frontier."

"All those yarns just scratch the surface," Luke muttered.

"I'm glad to hear that," Kroll said. "It makes me even more convinced that I made the right decision. You see, I figure if there's anyone who can get my brother, Mordecai, out of the hands of the law and bring him back here safely to me, it's the famous Smoke Jensen. And that's exactly what he's going to do."

Kroll's face twisted into a hate-filled snarl.

"Or else I'll send his own brother back to him

carved into bloody little pieces. Isn't that right, Galt?"

The bearlike man in the beaded vest fingered the handle of a machete tucked behind the red sash around his waist and smiled in anticipation.

Book Two

Chapter 12

The smell of wood smoke drifted through the night air to the men who sat their saddles in the thick shadows under a grove of trees. Somewhere not far away, a campfire burned.

"Varmints have got confident they lost us," one of the riders said quietly, his voice barely above a whisper. "They figure they don't have to cover their trail no more."

"They're wrong about that," another man said with the eagerness of youth. "They're gonna find out just how wrong. Isn't that right, Smoke?"

"I intend to get back those horses they stole, Cal," Smoke Jensen said. "Whether or not we do that peacefullike . . . well, that's up to them."

The first man who had spoken said, "It won't be peaceful. They're horse thieves. They know we'll just string 'em up if they surrender, so they'll fight."

That brought a chuckle from Smoke.

"Don't be so bloodthirsty, Pearlie," he told his foreman. "Don't you know the days of hang-rope law are over? Just read the editorials in the newspapers."

Pearlie snorted.

"I got a better use from them dang editorials and the papers they're printed in. It has to do with a little buildin' with a quarter-moon cut in the door."

Smoke smiled in the darkness. Pearlie wasn't long on patience.

But he was probably right about what was going to happen, Smoke reflected. The eight men who had hit the Sugarloaf's horse herd a few nights earlier and run off more than forty fine saddle mounts weren't very likely to give up peacefully. Their natural response to a challenge would be to slap leather.

Pearlie knew that because he was kin to their breed. In the past, he had been an outlaw and a hired gun, although he had never stooped so low as to steal horses. Meeting Smoke Jensen had changed his life, but the lessons learned in those old, wild days were still with him.

Smoke had heard the owl hoot on dark, lonely trails himself, back when he was younger. In the days following the death of his first wife, Nicole, he had been outlawed for a time. Wanted posters with his name and likeness on them had circulated among the frontier law offices, and rewards had also been posted on "Buck West," the name Smoke had used for a while.

All the charges against him were bogus, but he'd had to live as if they weren't in order to survive. He had lived among men who had no regard for the law, and he knew how they thought.

In a firm voice, Smoke said, "We're going to give them a chance to surrender. If they will, we'll take them back to Big Rock, turn them over to Monte Carson, and let the law take its course."

Monte Carson was the sheriff in Big Rock and one of Smoke's best friends.

Smoke paused, then before his foreman could object he continued. "But Pearlie's right. In all likelihood they'll put up a fight. If any of you boys aren't ready for that, you can wait here and nobody will think any the worse of you."

That wasn't strictly true, of course. Anybody who backed out would be an object of scorn among the other hands who rode for the Sugarloaf.

None of the other seven men spoke up. After a moment, young Calvin Woods said, "Shoot, Smoke, you know better than that. Let's go get the sons of—"

"Hold on there, son," Pearlie cut in. "You know Miss Sally don't like you cussin'."

"Dang it, I'm not a little kid, Pearlie! I'm about to ride in there and trade shots with a bunch of no-good horse rustlers, aren't I?"

Smoke knew his friends would squabble for as long as he would let them, so he said quietly, "Come on. Let's go take a look at the layout."

The nine riders moved slowly up the draw they had been following. The smell of smoke from a campfire grew stronger. They were too close to the horse thieves' camp for talking and it was too dark to see more than a few feet, so Smoke signaled to Pearlie to stop and dismount. Pearlie passed that signal on to Cal, who passed it on to the next man and so on, until the party from the Sugarloaf had come to a halt and the men had swung down from their saddles.

With a faint whisper of steel on leather, the men withdrew their rifles from saddle sheaths.

They left the horses there and continued on foot. Smoke led the way, slipping along the draw with a stealth that would have done an Indian proud. The men who came behind him were almost as quiet. He spotted an orange glow up ahead and knew they had almost reached their destination.

The horse thieves had pushed their four-legged loot hard during the past few days. Smoke and the men with him had been on the trail first thing the next morning after the raid and probably could have caught up sooner, but Smoke had wanted to lull the thieves into thinking they had escaped pursuit. That would make it easier to take them by surprise and maybe avoid a fight.

He wasn't worried about his own hide if it came down to gunplay. He had already dodged so many bullets in his life that he figured he was living on borrowed time. Nor did the thought of taking the law into his own hands and dealing out hot lead justice to the horse thieves bother him.

But even though they were always ready to back his play, whatever it was, Smoke wanted to lessen the risk to Pearlie and Cal and his other men. Cal had suffered a couple of serious bullet wounds in the past, and since Smoke's wife, Sally, regarded the young man almost as an adopted little brother, he didn't want Cal to get shot up again.

When it came down to the nub, though, Smoke would do what he had to do. He wasn't going to let those thieves get away with his horses.

The draw opened up into a flat about fifty yards wide. On the far side was a ridge with trees growing on top of it that stretched for several hundred yards in each direction. A little creek tumbled down the ridge in a waterfall and formed a pool at the bottom. Smoke could see all that in the glow from the campfire.

Off to the right, the thieves had built a corral out of poles and brush that backed up to the ridge. The stolen horses were in there, docile at the moment because the wind carried the scent of the other horses away from them. Smoke hadn't planned it that way, but he was canny enough to take advantage of it.

A couple of men stood near the corral, holding rifles and puffing on cigarettes. Two more sat beside the fire passing a flask back and forth. The other four thieves were stretched out in their bedrolls, asleep. At least two of them were snoring.

Smoke and his men were beyond the reach of the light from the campfire. He motioned for them to spread out and encircle the camp. They ought to be able to pin the horse thieves against the bluff and with any luck force them to surrender.

"Pearlie, stay with me," he whispered to his foreman. "We'll brace them head-on."

"Now you're talkin'," the former gunhawk breathed.

Smoke's keen eyes followed the other men as they worked their way to right and left, keeping to the shadows as much as possible. After a minute, he lost sight of all of them, but he knew where they were and how long it would take them to get into position.

When he judged that he had allowed enough time, he nodded to Pearlie, who whispered, "You sure you don't want to just cut loose on them varmints, Smoke?"

"I don't bushwhack anybody, even horse thieves," Smoke replied. "Come on."

He stepped out of the darkness at the head of the draw and walked toward the fire. When he was just outside the circle of light, he stopped and called, "Hello, the camp!"

The two guards near the corral stiffened and lifted their rifles. The two who had been drinking by the fire bolted to their feet and reached for their guns. The four who'd been asleep started thrashing around in their bedrolls.

"Stand where you are and keep your hands away from your guns!" Smoke shouted. "You're covered!"

From the darkness sounded the metallic ratcheting of Winchester levers being worked. The familiar, menacing sound made the horse thieves freeze.

"What the hell is this?" one of the men beside the fire called angrily. "Who are you, mister, and what gives you the right to throw down on us?"

Smoke moved forward into the light. He was a man of medium height with sandy hair under his brown Stetson, and the most impressive thing about him physically was the unusual width of his shoulders, which were powerfully muscled, as well as his arms.

Yet some indefinable something about him said that here was a man to stand aside from. It might have been the utter calm and confidence with which he carried himself. That confidence never spilled over into arrogance, though. Smoke had learned humility early on in his life, and he had never lost that quality.

Plenty of men could claim to be fast on the draw, but none were faster than Smoke Jensen. Not Frank Morgan, Ben Thompson, Matt Bodine, Luke Short, or any of the other legendary gunmen known from one end of the frontier to the other. Not even Smoke's adopted brother Matt, who had already developed quite a reputation as a shootist after only a few years, could match his speed and deadly accuracy with the twin Colts he wore.

So when he answered the outlaw's question by saying, "My name is Smoke Jensen," everybody in the camp instantly knew the name. He added, "I'm the man who owns those horses you stole, so that's what gives me the right. I'm calling on you right now to throw down your guns and surrender."

The man at the fire sneered. He had a pointed, foxlike face, and long dirty hair tumbled from under the battered hat he wore with its front brim turned up. He said, "Yeah, well, I'm callin' on you, Jensen. I'm callin' on you to eat lead and die!"

No sooner had that shout rung out from the horse thief than guns began to roar along the top of the bluff. Muzzle flame bloomed in the darkness like crimson flowers and slugs whipped past the heads of Smoke and Pearlie, prompting the foreman to yell, "Damn it! It's a trap!"

Chapter 13

Eight men had stolen the horses from the Sugarloaf and drove them this far. Smoke was certain of that from the tracks he and his men had followed.

But nothing prevented those horse thieves from joining up with another bunch of outlaws. Obviously, that was what had happened. And they had set a trap of their own, leaving the original eight by the campfire while settling down atop the bluff to ambush any pursuers that caught up.

Too fast for the eye to follow, Smoke's hands swooped to the butts of his guns and brought the Colts out of their holsters. The barrels came level and smoke and fire began to belch from their muzzles. The hail of lead that erupted from his guns scythed through the men around the campfire. They jerked and jittered as .45 slugs ripped bloody holes in them.

Despite giving up his gunfighting ways, Pearlie was still faster on the draw than most men, too. His revolver blasted and brought down one of the guards near the corral. The other man fired his rifle, but he hurried his shot and the bullet went over the heads of Smoke and Pearlie.

The sudden racket, along with the smells of powder smoke and blood that abruptly filled the air, spooked the stolen horses. They began to lunge back and forth in the makeshift corral as they tried to find a way out. The barriers erected by the rustlers wouldn't hold up under such punishment for long.

Smoke and Pearlie backed away as they continued trading shots with the men who had been left in the camp. Cal and the other Sugarloaf hands, who were spread out to the sides, concentrated their fire on the riflemen up on the bluff. The battle might as well have been a terrible storm, with gun thunder substituting for the regular kind and muzzle flashes clawing through the darkness like bolts of lightning.

The men who had been sleeping near the fire had managed to throw off their blankets and leap to their feet, only to run into bullets from Smoke and Pearlie's guns that knocked them down again. In a matter of chaos-filled seconds, all eight of the horse thieves were on the ground.

One man reared up again. Blood from a wound streaked his face, but he had guns in both hands and roared curses as he triggered the weapons at Smoke and Pearlie.

Smoke snapped a shot at the man with his left-hand Colt. The outlaw's head jerked back as the .45 round bored into his brain. He swayed on his knees for a second, then pitched forward onto his face.

Rifle bullets from the top of the bluff kicked up dirt around Smoke's boots as some of the riflemen up there tracked him in their sights. Cal and the other men were making things hot for those bushwhackers, but they hadn't given up the fight.

At that moment the brush barrier collapsed and the horses stampeded out of the wrecked corral. Smoke and Pearlie had to leap backwards to avoid being trampled as the panic-stricken animals pounded between them and the fire.

The surging mass of horseflesh provided cover for them, however, and so did the roiling cloud of dust kicked up by the hooves of the stampeding horses. The dust filled the air all around the camp and made it impossible to see. Smoke and Pearlie took advantage of that to fall back into the mouth of the draw. Smoke bellowed, “Sugarloaf, come on!”

Cal and the other cowboys began converging on the draw, firing their rifles on the run as they fell back. Smoke kept calling out so they could home in on his voice through the choking, blinding cloud of dust. Bullets still whined here and there, but they were like phantoms because no one could tell exactly where they were.

Smoke counted the men as they ran into the draw. When he reached the right number, he ordered, “Back to our saddle mounts, boys. We’ll have to round up those horses.”

“What about the horse thieves?” Pearlie asked. “We gonna round them up, too?”

“I haven’t forgotten about them,” Smoke replied with a grim note in his voice. “Anybody hurt?”

A couple of the men had been grazed by flying lead, but the injuries weren’t serious. The wounds could be tied up with bandannas, and the men would be fine until they got back to the ranch.

Cal said, "Smoke, I think I heard hoofbeats up on that ridge a minute ago, and I know there weren't as many men shootin' at us there at the end as there were at first. Some of them lit a shuck. Wouldn't surprise me if all of them have by now."

"It wouldn't surprise me, either," Smoke agreed. "Once they saw their trap didn't work and the horses broke out of the corral and stampeded, they decided to cut their losses and run."

When they reached the spot where they had left their mounts, Smoke said, "Pearlie, you and Cal come with me. The rest of you fellas follow the horses, gather them up, and start 'em back to the Sugarloaf. There are a half dozen of you. You ought to be able to handle them."

"Where are you going, Mr. Jensen?" one of the cowboys asked.

"To see if we can find those fellas who bushwhacked us." Smoke's voice was hard as flint as he added, "I don't like being bushwhacked."

Somebody was going to find that out before too much longer, to their everlasting regret.

Smoke and his two companions climbed their horses out of the draw and headed one way in the night while the rest of the group from the Sugarloaf set off in the other direction to look for the stolen horses.

The horses might have run a mile or so when

they stampeded, but probably not much farther than that, if any. They might have scattered some, though, which would make them more of a challenge to round up. It could easily be morning before the Sugarloaf hands had them all gathered and on the way back to the ranch.

While the shooting was going on, Smoke had tried to count the number of muzzle flashes he had seen on top of the ridge. Of course, he had been a mite busy at the time, gunning down the horse thieves by the campfire and the corral, but he was fairly certain he had seen rifle fire coming from six different locations up there. If all the ambushers had survived, that meant he and Pearlie and Cal would be facing two-to-one odds if they caught up to the men.

Smoke had faced worse odds in his time. Much worse.

They circled wide of the horse thieves' camp. Some of the outlaws might have still been alive, although Smoke doubted it. He was in no mood to check on them, however. They could fend for themselves. The important thing as far as Smoke was concerned was that they were all too shot up to represent a threat anymore.

The moon and stars provided enough light for the three men to see where they were going. Smoke found a place where their horses could climb to the top of the ridge. With rifles held ready, they rode slowly along it until they reached a spot overlooking the rustlers' camp. Sure enough, all eight bodies were sprawled around the fire, which was burning down now with no one left alive to tend it.

"This is where those varmints were lurkin', all right," Pearlie said. "Reckon we can pick up their trail?"

"We're going to try," Smoke said.

He dismounted, struck a match, and used its light to look around. A few yards away, he found some empty shell casings. The brass gleamed dully in the matchlight.

A few yards back from that point Smoke spotted hoofprints. He hunkered on his heels, snapped a fresh lucifer to life with his thumbnail, and closely studied the tracks.

Every set of hoofprints was different, although sometimes the things that set them apart might be so small that most people would never see them. Smoke had been taught how to track by one of the canniest scouts who had ever lived, the old mountain man known as Preacher, so to his eyes a set of hoofprints might as well have been a sign chalked onto a blackboard. He could read them that easily.

Pearlie and Cal knew what Smoke was doing as he ranged along the bluff and continued his search by matchlight. When he returned to the horses, he swung up into his saddle and gave a decisive nod.

"Looks to me like they came in from the east and headed back the same way," he said.

"What's in that direction?" Cal asked.

"There's a settlement about fifteen miles yonder," Pearlie said. "You been there, Cal. Place called Fletcher's Gap."

"Oh, yeah," Cal said. Moonlight gleamed on white teeth as he grinned. "Not much to it, just a wide place in the trail, but the fella who runs the one store has a pretty daughter, right?"

Pearlie snorted.

"Trust you to remember that, boy," he said.

Smoke turned his horse's head to the east and said, "That'll be our first stop. Maybe somebody there will know something about the men we're looking for."

"And if they don't?" Pearlie asked.

"We'll keep looking."

Chapter 14

The sun wasn't up yet as Smoke, Pearlie, and Cal approached Fletcher's Gap several hours later, but the eastern sky was rosy with impending dawn.

They had come down out of the mountains a short time earlier, through a pass that Smoke knew gave the little settlement its name. Fletcher's Gap. The town, although calling it by that designation was generous, was about a mile out on the flats, where the grassy plains began that stretched all the way to the Kansas border and beyond.

Smoke had spotted the settlement as they rode down the sloping trail and had counted six buildings. He thought back to previous visits and remembered a trading post, a livery stable and a blacksmith shop run by the same man, and a saloon. The other two buildings were houses. Another memory came back to him. The trading post and saloon were owned by a pair of brothers, each man operating one of the businesses.

Nothing much here to attract a bunch of horse thieves, or men in the market to buy some stolen horses. Smoke figured the hombres he and his friends were tracking fell into one of those categories. But they might have stopped to pick up some supplies.

There was also a chance some of them had been wounded during the ruckus several hours earlier and could have stopped here in search of medical help.

They weren't likely to find much along those lines in a place as small as Fletcher's Gap.

Now that the light was better and growing brighter by the minute, Smoke cast back and forth looking for tracks, just to make sure they were going in the right direction. It took him about a quarter of an hour to locate a number of hoof-prints left by horses heading east. He dismounted, studied the tracks for only a moment, and then nodded to Pearlie and Cal.

"This is them, all right," he said. "They probably took off from the ambush one by one, but they've rendezvoused and are traveling together again. And they're headed for the settlement, all right."

He mounted up and they trotted toward Fletcher's Gap. Out here on the wide-open plains there wasn't much cover, so anybody who was up and about in the settlement and looked to the west would see them coming.

That worried Smoke a little. The three of them might be riding into another ambush. But they would deal with that when the time came, if they had to.

Smoke didn't see any activity around the buildings, nor were there any wagons parked in front of them or horses tied up at the hitch racks. Pearlie and Cal noticed the same. Cal said, "Looks like a ghost town."

"Yeah," Pearlie said, "but I don't recollect hearin' anything about the place bein' abandoned."

"Could be everybody's still asleep," Smoke said. "It's still early."

"Maybe. I don't have a good feelin' about this, though."

Smoke couldn't argue with his foreman. He

didn't have a good feeling about the situation, either.

When they were within a hundred yards of the nearest building, which was the blacksmith shop, Smoke said quietly, "We're going to split up. Cal, you head left. Pearlie, go right. I'm going straight up the middle. When you go, take off in a hurry."

"You reckon on drawin' their fire, if they're waitin' for us," Pearlie said.

"That's right. Ready . . . *now!*"

He dug his heels into his horse's flanks and sent the animal leaping forward. At the same time he leaned forward in the saddle, pulled his Winchester from its sheath, and worked the repeater's lever to throw a cartridge into its chamber.

The flat crack of a shot sounded in the early morning air.

Smoke spotted the puff of powder smoke from a corner of the blacksmith shop. He returned the fire, cranking off two quick rounds. Shooting from the back of a galloping horse, he didn't expect to hit anything unless it was by sheer, blind luck, but he knew he could come close enough to make the bushwhacker duck for cover.

More shots rang out. Smoke glanced to the right and left and saw Pearlie and Cal riding hell-bent-for-leather. They were throwing lead toward the settlement, too. Smoke hoped any innocent folks kept their heads down.

The horses belonging to the men they were

pursuing had to be hidden inside the livery barn. As Smoke charged into the settlement, he saw a man lean out from the opening into the hayloft and fire a rifle at him. Guiding the horse with his knees, he snapped the Winchester to his shoulder and pressed the trigger. The rifle went off with a wicked crack, and at this range it was a different story. The man in the hayloft doubled over and dropped his rifle as the slug punched into his belly. He toppled out of the opening.

Smoke had already flashed past by the time the bushwhacker hit the ground in the limp sprawl of death.

He couldn't see Cal and Pearlie anymore. His friends were around behind the other buildings. Smoke knew he could trust them to take care of themselves, and besides, he had his own problems to handle. More shots blasted from the front porch of the trading post. Smoke's gaze swung in that direction and spotted a man crouched behind a rain barrel, firing a six-shooter at him.

Smoke's Winchester spouted flame again. The high-powered rounds tore through the upper part of the rain barrel and into the man behind it. If the barrel had been full of water it might have slowed down the slugs enough to stop them, but a recent dry spell had left the level low. Smoke had figured that would be the case when he aimed his shots.

The force of the bullets threw the man back

against the trading post's front window. The glass shattered and sprayed glittering shards into the air. The bushwhacker landed with his legs still hanging over the window sill and didn't move again.

That was two of them down, Smoke thought, and from the sounds of gunfire echoing from other parts of the settlement he figured Pearlie and Cal were doing some damage as well. He would have liked to take one of the enemy alive in order to question him and find out more about who was responsible for the theft of the horses, but that might not turn out to be possible.

Somebody had shot at him from the rear of the blacksmith shop, Smoke recalled. That couldn't have been the man he shot out of the hayloft. That hombre hadn't had time to get up there. As that thought went through Smoke's brain, he wheeled his horse back toward the smithy.

The shop door stood open. Smoke dropped from his saddle and ran toward it at an angle, stopping before he got there to press himself against the building's front wall.

"If you're in there, mister, throw your gun out and come out behind it with your hands in the air," Smoke called. "Nobody's going to shoot you if you give yourself up."

Silence came from the shop.

Smoke reached out with the barrel of his Winchester, hooked the partially open door with it, and threw the door all the way back. That didn't draw any fire.

But a second later he heard a sudden curse, followed immediately by a shot and a howl of pain. Somebody was hurt in there, possibly an innocent citizen of Fletcher's Gap.

Either that or it was a trick.

Smoke couldn't afford to take that chance. He went through the door low and fast.

Another shot blasted, the muzzle flash bright and garish in the gloom of the shop's interior. Smoke spotted the big forge. A man crouched on the far side of it and aimed a revolver at him for a second try.

Before the man could pull the trigger again, a shape loomed up behind him. A big, balding man with blood on his shirt and his right arm hanging limp swung a hammer in his left hand. The hammer smashed into the gunman's left shoulder and drove him to the ground, shrieking in agony. Smoke figured that terrible blow had shattered every bone in the man's shoulder.

He took a quick step and used the Winchester's barrel to knock the gun out of the man's other hand. The bushwhacker collapsed, no doubt passing out from the pain of his injury.

"Hold your fire, mister," rumbled the big man who had struck him down. "I reckon if this fella's out to kill you, we must be on the same side."

"I'd say the same thing about that bullet hole

in your arm," Smoke replied. "Are you all right?"

The big man glanced down at his injury. He shrugged his other shoulder and said, "I will be. This don't amount to much."

Outside, Pearlie yelled, "Smoke! Smoke, where are you?"

"In here, Pearlie," Smoke called. He looked at the big man again and went on. "You're the blacksmith and liveryman here, aren't you?"

"That's right. Jasper Hargrove. And you're Mr. Jensen, from the Sugarloaf. We've met a time or two." Hargrove grinned. "When I heard a couple of these damned fools talking about buying some horses stolen from your ranch, I knew you'd be along directly to hand 'em their needin's."

Smoke smiled. Pearlie came into the barn and reported, "Me an' Cal cleaned out the rest of these rats, Smoke. Hope you didn't figure on any of 'em livin' through the altercation."

"This one did," Smoke said with a nod toward the man Hargrove had struck down. "We'll have a talk with him when he wakes up."

Pearlie squinted at the unconscious man and said, "I'll fetch a bucket of water. See if we can't hurry that along a mite."

As Smoke suspected, a couple of the men they had followed to Fletcher's Gap had been wounded in the earlier fight, and the group had stopped here to patch up their injured and wait to see if anybody was coming after them. While they were doing that, they had herded all of the settlement's inhabitants into the saloon and had been keeping them there at gunpoint, with the exception of Jasper Hargrove, who was the unofficial "mayor" of Fletcher's Gap. He had hidden in the livery stable, in a storm cellar hollowed out under the tack room. When the shooting started, he had crept out and slipped into the blacksmith shop to try to get the drop on the man posted there.

That hadn't worked out, at least not at first, as Hargrove collected a bullet through the arm for his trouble. But he had gotten a second crack at the gunman and put the opportunity to good use.

While the storekeeper's daughter—who was as pretty as Cal had said but obviously smitten with the burly blacksmith—was bandaging Hargrove's arm, Smoke questioned the gunman with the broken shoulder. The man spent most of his time groaning in pain but finally admitted that he and his companions had met the horse thieves to take the stolen animals off their hands.

"Everybody knows the Sugarloaf raises some fine horses," the man said through teeth gritted against the pain. "And Josiah, he said that all those stories about you were just so much hot air, Jensen. He said we didn't have to worry about you comin' after us." The man moaned again. "That damned fool!"

"Who's Josiah?" Smoke asked.

"Big hombre, wears a buffalo coat and a hat with a feather on it, like a Injun."

That matched the description of the man he had knocked through the trading post window with a couple of bullets, Smoke recalled. Josiah wouldn't be making any more unwise plans.

That seemed to be the end of it. Hargrove promised they would tend to the injured man as best they could and send a rider to the next town over, where both a doctor and a deputy sheriff could be found. Smoke was more than happy to leave the citizens of Fletcher's Gap with that responsibility.

He was tired and just wanted to go home.

It was late in the afternoon before he and Pearlie and Cal rode up to the big ranch house that was home to Smoke and his beautiful, dark-haired wife, Sally. A number of the cowboys had gathered around to greet the three men, anxious to hear about whether or not they had caught up to the bushwhackers, and one of the men must have told Sally that Smoke was back because she was waiting on the porch for him.

She wasn't alone, however. Smoke had already spotted a familiar horse tied to the hitching post in front of the house. Monte Carson stood next to Sally. The big lawman had a solemn look on his face, and that was enough to make Smoke's instincts start warning him that more trouble loomed.

The other hands clustered around Pearlie and Cal to get the story from them. Smoke stepped up on the porch, took Sally into his arms, and kissed her. The passion between them had never dimmed and never would. As she leaned back a little in his arms, she asked, "Are you all right, Smoke?"

"Right as rain," he told her.

"Then so am I." She moved aside but kept an arm around his waist. "Monte rode out earlier. He has a message for you."

"What is it, Monte?" Smoke asked, his voice calm and level despite the alarm bells going off in his brain.

"Well, now . . . I don't rightly know," Carson replied. He took an envelope from his shirt pocket and held it out.

"You delivering the mail now in addition to being sheriff?" Smoke asked dryly.

"This didn't come by regular mail. A man came to my office, said he knew that you and I are friends, and asked if I'd see to it you got it. Something was off about him, Smoke. I never saw him before, but I could tell he was a wrong one."

"What did he look like?"

"Big. Big as a grizzly bear, and about as hairy as one, too. But he talked like an educated man."

Smoke shook his head and said, "He doesn't sound familiar."

"That's right. He said you wouldn't know him,

but that you'd want to read the letter he had for you. I told him I'd see that you got it. I figured you'd want to get to the bottom of whatever it is, and that's the fastest way."

Smoke finally took the envelope and looked at the wax seal.

"You didn't open it."

Carson smiled faintly and said, "Don't think I wasn't tempted. But we've been friends a long time, Smoke. I respect your privacy."

"I'm not sure I do," Sally said. "Open it and find out what this is all about, Smoke."

With a chuckle he didn't particularly feel, Smoke broke the seal and slid a folded piece of paper out of the envelope. He opened it and read the words printed on it in a neat, precise hand.

Then his face turned as gray and hard as stone. Sally gasped, and Monte Carson, even though he and Smoke had been friends for a long time as he had just said, took a step back.

He couldn't help it. Smoke looked like he wanted to kill somebody.

And when Smoke Jensen felt like that, anywhere around him was a dangerous place to be.

Chapter 15

Smoke thanked Monte Carson for bringing the message out to the ranch and asked him to stay for supper, but he didn't offer to share the contents of the envelope. He could tell that offended his old friend a little, but it couldn't be helped.

"Guess I'd better head on back to town," Carson said, "but I'm obliged for the offer of supper. Another time."

Smoke nodded.

"All right, Monte. Thanks again."

Carson untied his horse, swung up into the saddle, and rode away. When he was out of earshot, a frowning Sally asked, "What was that all about, Smoke? You don't normally act so mysterious. You hurt Monte's feelings by not telling him what that says."

She nodded toward the message that Smoke still clutched in his hand. He had to fight back the impulse to crumple it in anger.

"Let's go inside," he said. "I'll tell you all about it."

Once they were sitting down in the parlor, Smoke held up the paper and said, "This is a letter from a man named Rudolph Kroll."

Sally shook her head and said, "I don't think I know him. I don't believe I've ever even heard of him."

"No real reason you would have, but the name's familiar to me. The man's an outlaw. He and his brother have a gang that's run rampant all over the frontier."

"Wait a minute," Sally said. "I think I've heard the name after all. Something about a trial . . ."

Smoke nodded.

"Mordecai Kroll, that's Rudolph's younger brother, was captured over in Arizona a while back, put on trial for his various crimes, and sentenced to hang. He's still there, waiting while several other states and territories are in court trying to get him extradited so they can try him, too."

Sally put a hand to her mouth and her eyes widened.

"I remember now," she said. "There was an article in *Harper's Weekly* about him. And it said he was captured by . . . Oh, my God, Smoke, it was Luke who captured him!"

A while back, Smoke had discovered that his older brother, Luke, long thought to have been killed in the waning days of the Civil War, actually was still alive and had been making his living as a bounty hunter for the past fifteen years under the name Luke Smith. Gravely wounded, Luke had wound up at the Sugarloaf to be reunited with his younger brother and nursed back to health by Sally. He had helped Smoke handle some trouble, and Smoke had made it clear to him that he was welcome to stay, that he would always have a home here if he wanted it. But Luke had chosen to resume his drifting ways, although he had dropped the Smith name and called himself Luke Jensen again.

Smoke nodded in response to Sally's exclamation and said, "That's right. And now Rudolph Kroll, Mordecai's brother, has captured Luke. He's threatening to kill him unless . . ."

"Unless what, Smoke?"

A faint, bleak smile touched Smoke's lips as he said, "Unless I break Mordecai out of Yuma Prison and return him safely to Kroll's hideout."

Sally stared at him in silence for a long moment, then shook her head.

"You can't do that," she said. "That would make you an outlaw, too."

"I know. That's why I didn't tell Monte what was going on. It's better for him if he can honestly say that he had no idea about any of this."

Sally frowned and said, "You can't be thinking about going along with what Kroll wants."

"Luke is my brother. For fifteen years I thought I'd lost him." Smoke's voice hardened. "I'm not going to lose him again to some outlaw."

"So you'll become a fugitive yourself? That's insane, Smoke. And it doesn't even take into account the fact that you probably can't break this Mordecai Kroll out of Yuma. It's supposed to be impossible to escape from that prison, isn't it?"

"Men have done it," Smoke mused. "It's just that there's not much place for them to run when they do. That southwestern corner of Arizona is pretty much a hellhole. The authorities have Apache trackers, too, and they send them out after escaped prisoners. It usually doesn't take long to run them to ground."

"So, you see," Sally said, "you can't do it." A speculative look came over her beautiful face. "You'd have better luck trying to find out where Rudolph Kroll is holding Luke and rescuing him."

Smoke smiled again. For all her beauty and tenderness, Sally had a fierce streak in her as well. She had taken up arms against their enemies more than once in the past, and given a good account of herself, too. Even though her first impulse was to worry about the dangers involved, deep down she didn't want to let Rudolph Kroll get away with kidnapping Luke and threatening his life, either.

"The Kroll gang has pulled jobs all over the West," Smoke said. "There's no telling where their hideout might be. I could search for years and maybe never find it. The law could settle things and hang Mordecai Kroll any day now, and if he dies, Luke dies. So there's no time to waste."

"If you don't know where the hideout is, how are you supposed to take Mordecai there if you get him out of prison?"

"I figure Rudolph Kroll plans to have someone meet us and take us there, or else he'll get word to me some other way of where we're supposed to go. He wouldn't be going to this much trouble if he didn't have things worked out."

"This is just . . . revenge," Sally said angrily. "He's tormenting you as Luke's brother because of what he thinks Luke did to his brother."

"I reckon you're right about that. That's the way a vicious outlaw like Kroll would look at it."

Sally leaned back in the rocking chair where she sat, spread her hands, and said, "So what are you going to do? You can't help Mordecai Kroll escape without risking your life, and even if you succeed, it'll ruin our lives."

"I don't know," Smoke said. "I'm starting to have a glimmering of a plan."

"And there's something else," Sally went on. "Say that you do it. You break Mordecai out of prison and take him to the gang's hideout. You know good and well that when you get there, Rudolph Kroll plans to kill both you and Luke. He can't afford to let you go when you know the location of the hideout."

"I thought of that right away," Smoke admitted. He held up the note from Kroll. "I can tell from this message, though, that there's something old Rudolph doesn't know."

"What's that?"

"I've got a secret weapon on my side," Smoke said with a smile. "Two of 'em, as a matter of fact."

Matt Jensen's eyes narrowed as he looked along the stage road to the narrow gap up ahead where the trail ran between two rugged bluffs topped with boulders.

"Is that the place, Salty?" he asked the grizzled old jehu on the high seat beside him.

"Durned tootin' it is," Salty Stevens replied as he flapped the reins against the back of the six-horse hitch to keep them going. The road ran up a slope to the gap, and the stagecoach always slowed down on this stretch.

Matt had a shotgun propped up beside him with his left hand holding it as the weapon's butt rested on the seat. His Winchester was right behind him, riding in the fringed sheath he had removed from his saddle and lashed to the railing that ran around the top of the coach. The six-gun on Matt's right hip and the Bowie knife sheathed on his left hip completed his armament.

If he needed more than that to handle any trouble he and Salty ran into, chances were not even a Gatling gun would be enough.

This leg of the stagecoach run in southern

New Mexico Territory had been plagued with holdups recently, enough so that most potential passengers thought better of it and found some other way to get where they were going. Wells Fargo's business was down as well, to the point that the express company had joined forces with the stagecoach line to offer a substantial reward for the robbers.

Matt, who spent most of his time on the drift, had happened to be in Silver City when the reward notice was posted next to the door of the Wells Fargo office. Being low on both funds and supplies at the moment, this seemed like a fortuitous circumstance to him.

He opened the door and went in.

Only one person was in the office, standing behind a paper-littered desk wearing a harried expression. She was a young woman, and the expression didn't make her any less lovely as far as Matt was concerned. In fact, he thought the strand of rich brown hair that had worked its way loose from the arrangement of curls on top of her head and fallen over her left eye just made her prettier. She blew the strand of hair away from her face and said, "Yes? What can I do for you?"

"I'm looking for the Wells Fargo agent," Matt said.

"You're looking at her," the young woman snapped. "For the time being, at least."

"Oh." Matt grinned. He was big, brawny, fair-haired, and the ladies seemed to find him reasonably easy on the eyes. It might be a challenge to charm this one, though, considering the impatient mood she seemed to be in.

Good thing he liked a challenge, thought Matt.

"I saw the notice posted outside about the reward," he went on as he jerked a thumb over his shoulder. "Are you still looking for somebody to sign on as a shotgun guard?"

The woman looked a little more interested now. She ran her gaze over the big young man standing in front of her clad in jeans, a faded blue bib-front shirt, and a tipped-back black Stetson. She said, "That's right. You want the job?"

"I could use the reward," Matt admitted honestly.

"What about some bullet holes in your hide? Could you use those, too? Because there's a chance that's what you'll get."

"Life's full of chances," Matt said as his shoulders rose and fell. "Good and bad. Can't have one without the other."

"Ah. A frontier philosopher. What's your name? Socrates?"

"Matt Jensen."

The name didn't seem to mean anything to her. That came as no surprise to Matt. Mostly it seemed that everybody west of the Mississippi, as well as many of those east of the big river, had heard of his adopted brother, Smoke. Matt was starting to make a name for himself as well, at least in certain circles, but he was far from achieving the same level of notoriety as his older brother.

"You've seen the notice. You know there's been trouble on this run."

Matt nodded and said, "Yep. You wouldn't be offering a reward if there wasn't some risk. But I've handled trouble before."

"You don't have to take the job to go after the reward, you know. You could try to track down the gang on your own."

"Yeah, but that seems like an awful lot of trouble," Matt said. "If I'm on the stagecoach, they've got to come to me."

For the first time, a slight smile appeared on the young woman's face.

"That's true," she said. "You'll have to pass muster with the driver. He works for the stage line, not for Wells Fargo. But if he agrees, the job is yours. My name is Janice Mullins, by the way."

"It's a pleasure to meet you, Miss Mullins. It's not often you find a lady running a Wells Fargo office. Especially not a lady as—"

She held up a hand to stop him before he could finish the compliment.

"It's *Mrs.* Mullins," she said, "and I'm only running the office because my husband broke his leg and is recuperating. So I'm afraid the reward for those outlaws is the only one you're going to get here, Mr. Jensen."

"Oh." Matt grinned again to hide his disappointment. "That's all right. I'm not fond of outlaws. Not one little bit."

"Then welcome aboard," Janice Mullins said. "We can use your help. Salty should be down at the stage line office, or in the barn behind it."

"Salty?"

"The regular driver on this run," Janice explained. "I'm a little surprised he hasn't been scared off, too."

"It takes a lot to scare off Salty Stevens."

Matt had understood that comment as soon as he met Salty. The old-timer "still had the bark on," as the saying went. His bristly white beard and weathered face testified that he had plenty of experience. His eyes were deep-set and surrounded by permanent lines from squinting in the sun. He wasn't big, but he was wiry and tough as whang leather. Matt liked him immediately, and the feeling seemed to be mutual.

Because of that, Matt found himself now on this stage to Lordsburg, swaying slightly on the seat next to Salty as the coach approached the gap. There were no passengers, but a Wells Fargo express pouch was locked in the box under the seat, and Janice Mullins had stressed the importance of it reaching its destination.

"How many times have you been hit on this run?" Matt asked Salty.

"Me personally, twice," the old-timer replied.

"Other drivers, four more times, all in the past couple of months. Those gents quit, but not me. I'll be danged if a bunch o' no-good owlhoots are gonna make me holler calf rope."

Matt chuckled at Salty's cantankerous reply, and then asked, "Has anybody been killed so far in these holdups?"

"No, but it ain't been from lack o' tryin'. Them desperadoes have burned powder at us ever' time."

"What about this gap up ahead? Have they ever stopped the coach there?"

"Nope. But I figure it's just a matter of time. Perfect spot for a holdup, ain't it?"

"Perfect," Matt agreed. And he had a crawling feeling on the back of his neck that he recognized as his instincts trying to warn him.

Something was going to happen here, or he was going to be very surprised.

It would happen soon, too, because as the road leveled out again and entered the gap, Salty took his whip from its holder, popped it over the heads of the team, and yelled, "Hi-yaaahhh! Move along there, you gol-dang hunks o' crow bait!"

The horses surged forward against their harness and the coach picked up speed. The other end of the gap was about fifty yards away.

The coach never reached it. Salty had to haul back hard on the reins and shout, "Whoaaa!" as a huge boulder landed in the road with a resounding crash.

Chapter 16

The coach was going fast enough that it and the team almost plowed into the boulder anyway, even though Salty threw his weight against the reins and kicked hard against the brake lever. The vehicle rocked and swayed on its leather thoroughbraces and finally skidded to a halt a few yards short of the boulder, which had landed right in the middle of the road. If it had been to one side or the other, Salty might have been able to steer past it.

The shooting from the sides of the gap started before the stagecoach even came to a stop. Matt saw powder smoke spurting from several different places along both rims. He brought the shotgun to his shoulder and loosed one barrel at the rim on the right side of the gap, then swung the weapon smoothly to the left and triggered the other barrel. With all the rocks up there it was likely the robbers had good cover, but with buckshot spraying around, it was possible some of the pellets might find their mark.

Matt dropped the empty shotgun on the floorboards of the driver's box and twisted to pull the Winchester from its sheath. In a continuation of the same move he vaulted off the box and dropped lithely to the ground.

At the same time, Salty leaped down on the coach's other side. As soon as he caught his balance, he drew the Colt on his hip and started blazing away at the hidden robbers.

The problem was that they were caught in a cross fire, Matt thought as slugs continued to whine over his head. There was really no place they could hunt cover except underneath the stagecoach. That might be enough to stop most of the lead from finding them, but they would be pinned down if they did that, unable to stick a head out without the risk of having it shot off.

On the other hand, out in the open like this they were in an even worse position. The road agents were bound to get the range pretty soon, and then he and Salty would be in real trouble.

They met at the rear of the coach, crouched there, and returned the gunfire from the rims. Over the roar of shots, Salty yelled, "Dang it, we're in a bad spot here, Matt! Looks like we're gonna get kilt for sure!"

Something nagged at the back of Matt's brain, some sense that more was really going on here than he realized. With that prodding at him, he said, "These outlaws haven't gunned down anybody who surrendered, have they?"

"Not yet!"

"Maybe we'd better throw down our guns."

"Dadblast it! Surrenderin' eats at my craw—"

"Better than getting a bullet through it," Matt pointed out.

Salty raked his fingers through his beard, yanked off his battered old hat with its turned-up brim, and threw it to the ground in exasperation.

"All right!" the old-timer said. "Our bosses are gonna be mighty disappointed in us, though."

Matt listened to the sound of slugs hitting the coach and said, "Maybe. Maybe not."

"What?"

"I'll explain later. For now . . ."

Matt straightened, tossed the Winchester out into the open, and stepped away from the coach with his arms raised and his hands high in the air. Immediately, the shooting from the rims stopped.

Salty threw his revolver down and raised his hands, too, as he moved a few steps from the vehicle. Carefully, Matt lowered his left hand, reached across his body, and slid his Colt from its holster. He tossed it to the ground next to the Winchester.

His skin crawled a little as he stood there in the open. He had based his actions on something too nebulous to even be called a hunch. If he was wrong, he and Salty could expect to feel bullets smashing into their bodies at any second.

Instead, the gap became eerily quiet as the echoes left over from the gun thunder rolled away.

Less than a minute later, the sound of hoofbeats broke the silence. They came from behind the stagecoach. Matt and Salty turned to look as several riders entered the gap through the same end the coach had used a few minutes earlier.

Matt counted four men trotting toward them, all holding revolvers. The robbers wore long brown dusters and brown hats with the brims pulled down. Bandannas covered the lower halves of their faces, so nothing was visible except their eyes. The guns in their hands were steady as they covered Matt and Salty.

Movement glimpsed in the corner of his eye caught Matt's attention. He turned his head and lifted his gaze to the rim on the right. Several more duster-clad outlaws had stepped out of concealment to point rifles down at the stage-coach. Matt's gaze swung to the left. More of the men stood on that side of the gap.

He and Salty were well and truly trapped.

The riders reined in. Without speaking, one of them motioned with his gun toward the driver's box.

"Dadgum it, I know what you want," Salty grumbled.

He started to lower his hands, and the outlaw jerked his gun in a signal that the jehu should keep them raised.

"Jehosaphat! How do you expect me to get into the box without puttin' my hands down?"

The man who seemed to be the leader of the outlaws pondered that for a second, then nodded and gestured again with the gun.

Two of the riders followed Salty to the front of the coach while the other two stayed where they were with their guns pointed at Matt. Salty had the key to the box's padlock on a ring on his belt. He unlocked it and reached inside. The riders tensed, as if worrying that the old man might have a gun hidden in there.

The only thing Salty took out of the box was the express pouch. He stepped back and said, "That's all that was in there. Have a look for yourself if you don't believe me, dang your hides."

Satisfied that the box was empty, the leader reached inside his duster and slid the revolver into a cross-draw holster. He snapped his fingers and made a motion for Salty to toss him the pouch. Salty did so, and the man caught it with ease.

The riders started to back their horses away. Salty said, "Blast it, are you gonna ride off and leave that big ol' rock in the middle of the trail? I can't get the coach past it! I'll have to back outta here, turn around, and go back to Silver City!"

The leader shrugged. Judging by the look in his eyes, he found Salty's dilemma amusing.

The four men turned and galloped out of the gap. Matt cast a glance toward the guns he and Salty had thrown down. He was a little surprised the outlaws hadn't taken them, but he wasn't going to turn down even the smallest stroke of good luck.

He couldn't take a step toward the weapons, though, because the men on the rims still had rifles trained on him and Salty. Clearly, they weren't going to budge until the four who had ridden into the gap had made their getaway.

From where he stood beside the box, Salty said, "Dang varmints are downright creepy, the way they don't talk."

"Is that the way it was the other times they held you up?" Matt asked.

"Yep. Threw lead until we didn't have any choice but to surrender, then closed in around us and made me open the box. Never said a dang word, even when they were lootin' valuables from the passengers. Always just motioned and pointed."

"How come nobody ever told me about this?"

"Wasn't any reason to, as far as I can see," Salty said with a frown. "And Miz Mullins, shoot, as far as I know she may not even know about it."

The information might be important, though, Matt thought. For one thing, it fit in with the vague theory that had begun to form in his brain.

The outlaws on the rims began to withdraw. One by one, they disappeared as they moved back out of sight, and each time that happened, Matt heard rapid hoofbeats a moment later. They were mounting up and galloping away to rendezvous with the four who had taken the express pouch from the coach.

Finally, the last man vanished. Salty lowered his arms and said, "Danged well about time! These meat hooks o' mine were about to fall off."

Matt went quickly to the guns and picked up his Colt and Winchester. He holstered the revolver and started to hurry past the stagecoach, but he paused for a moment to study the dozens of bullet holes in the vehicle.

"Yeah, they really shot up the old girl," Salty said. "We're lucky we ain't ventilated, too. But she'll still drive all right once I get her turned around and started back to Silver City."

"You'll have to make that trip by yourself, Salty," Matt said. "And I'm sorry, but you'll have to do it with one less horse because I'm taking one of the team."

"What!" Salty was aghast. "You can't do that. It'll take me until the middle o' the night to get back if I have to do it with three horses."

"Can't be helped. I'm going after those outlaws."

"By yourself?" Salty frowned. "There was a good dozen of 'em. Besides, you signed on to be the shotgun guard."

"I signed on with Wells Fargo," Matt pointed out. "Anyway, there's nothing left to guard. They already got the express pouch."

"Yeah, but . . . if you catch up to 'em, you'll get yourself killed!"

"I'm after that reward, remember? In order to collect, I have to corral that gang."

"You . . . you can't do it on your own, dadblast it!" Salty sputtered. "I'll come with you. We'll take two of the horses."

"What about the stagecoach?"

"When it don't show up in Lordsburg, the station manager there will have the sheriff send some deputies out to look for it. They'll find it here. It sure ain't goin' nowhere."

Matt considered the idea. He was used to operating on his own most of the time, but Salty was an old, cool-nerved campaigner who kept his head under fire. With the odds what they were, it could very well come in handy to have him along.

"All right, but you'd better leave a note with the coach so whoever comes looking for it will know that we're not dead. Tell them that we've taken up the trail of the outlaws, and maybe those deputies will come after us."

Salty nodded solemnly and said, "That's a mighty fine idea, Matt. One thing, though . . . you'll have to write the note. I can pop a whip and cuss out a dang stagecoach team and shoot the whiskers off a gnat at fifty yards . . . but I'm a mite shy on book learnin'!"

Chapter 17

Salty advised him which two members of the stagecoach team would serve best as mounts, and they unhitched the horses.

"How are you at riding bareback?" Matt asked.

"Shoot, I never knew what a saddle was until I was twelve years old!" Salty replied with a contemptuous snort. "There's a couple of old blankets in the rear boot that we sometimes wrap around any cargo back there that might be fragile. We can use them as saddle blankets like the Injuns do and cut up some o' this here harness to make bridles out of. It'll be like some fancy lady takin' a ride in the park on a Sunday afternoon!"

Matt smiled. He didn't think it would be exactly the same, but having the blankets and bridles were certainly a lot better than nothing.

Within a few minutes they were ready to go. Salty drove the coach over as close to the side of the gap as he could so the horses they were leaving behind would have some shade.

"Wish we could leave 'em some grain and water, but there ain't none," he said. "Well, the poor brutes shouldn't have to be out here for too long, prob'ly not even overnight. We're facin' a future that's a whole heap more uncertain, if you ask me."

"We'll find out," Matt said.

He carried a stub of pencil and some paper with him, folded up in his pocket, and he had already used some of it for the note they'd be leaving behind for the deputies. He closed one of the coach doors on it so that part of it was sticking out and would be noticeable flapping in the breeze. The deputies ought to see it right away, but even if they didn't, somebody was bound to find it sooner or later.

With those things taken care of, Matt and Salty climbed up onto the horses and rode back out of the gap the way they had come . . . and the way the four outlaws had departed.

Picking up the trail wasn't difficult. It didn't appear that the holdup men had even tried to hide their tracks. They must have believed that they were safe as they rode off into the rugged badlands of southern New Mexico to rejoin their comrades, since a stagecoach couldn't follow where they were going. Maybe it had never occurred to them that somebody could unhitch a horse from the stagecoach team and pursue them that way.

Once Matt and Salty were away from the road, the terrain was pretty bad. Stretches of hardpan alternated with bands of volcanic rock that could cut a horse's hooves to ribbons if the rider wasn't careful. Salty warned them away from depressions filled with sand that would "suck down a man or a horse," according to him. Deep ravines slashed across the earth as well, forcing travelers to detour around them, and sometimes they had to circle towering pinnacles of rock as well.

Matt had been through this region before. It was still just as ugly and intimidating now.

The tracks weren't too hard to follow, though. They were easy enough to see where the ground was sandy, and in the rocky stretches Matt was able to spot the tiny marks left behind by horseshoes. A few times it seemed that he and Salty had lost the trail, but after a little searching they always picked it up again.

Matt also saw where the other outlaws joined the ones he and Salty were trailing. He kept count and decided that there were an even dozen in the gang, as he had estimated during the holdup.

The tracks led north toward a range of small mountains. Matt asked, "Do you know what those are called?"

"Them's the Armadillo Hills, on account of they're shaped sort of like armadillos. See what I mean?"

"I don't know," Matt said dubiously. "They don't look much like armadillos to me."

Salty snorted and said, "Do the Grand Tetons really look that much like a gal's bosoms?"

"They never have to me," Matt replied with a smile.

"Well, there you go. A fella sees what he wants to see sometimes, and the fella who named them hills thought he saw armadillos."

"Fair enough," Matt said. "Does anybody live up there? Any mines or ranches or anything like that?"

"Not that I've ever heard tell. They're about as empty and useless as any place on earth, I reckon."

"Sounds like a perfect place for a gang of outlaws to hole up, doesn't it?"

"It does, at that," Salty agreed.

The trail pointed unmistakably toward the Armadillos. Due to the ruggedness of the terrain, it took the rest of the day to cover the relatively short distance to the mountains. Night was falling as Matt and Salty reached the slopes.

"We gonna make camp?" Salty asked. "We ain't got no supplies, not even any jerky."

"We'll stop and let the horses rest for a while, but then I think we'll do some exploring."

"In the dark?"

"It's pretty clear those road agents didn't think anybody would follow them. Maybe they're still being careless."

"Oh," Salty said. "You think maybe we'll spot their campfire."

"I think there's a chance of it," Matt said. "Not

only that, but these horses have to be pretty thirsty by now. If the outlaws have a camp up here, it'll be in some place where there's water. If the horses smell it, they'll take us right to it."

Salty regarded him with narrowed eyes and said, "You've done some manhuntin' before, haven't you, son?"

"A little," Matt admitted. "And I had a couple of really good teachers when it came to taking care of myself."

"Who might that have been?"

"I'll tell you all about it later," Matt said, "providing we come out of this alive."

After the horses had had a chance to blow, the two men mounted up again and rode slowly into the hills. Or mountains, Matt thought. Whatever name they went by, they didn't amount to much.

An hour or so went by. By now full night had fallen and millions of stars had put in an appearance in the black sky, casting their silvery light over the stark landscape. The moon hadn't risen yet.

Suddenly, the horse Matt was riding lifted its head. A second later, so did Salty's mount.

"I ain't seen no signs of a campfire," Salty said quietly, "but these two nags sure act like they scented water."

"I agree," Matt said. "Let's give them their heads and see where they take us."

The horses climbed steadily toward the top of a

ridge. As they neared the crest, Matt abruptly smelled something, too: the aroma of stew simmering in a pot.

He hauled back on the makeshift reins. Salty did likewise, and Matt whispered, "They're close. I can smell their cooking."

"So can I," the old-timer said, "and it's remindin' me it's been a heck of a long time since I et somethin'!"

"Maybe we can do something about that before too much longer."

"What? Waltz into that owlhoot camp and ask if we can stay to supper?"

"We'll see," Matt said. "For now I think we'd better leave these horses here."

They slid down from the horses' backs and looked around for something to hitch the reins to. Failing to find anything in these barren hills, they settled for letting the reins dangle to the ground and placing rocks on them. That wouldn't hold the horses if they got really spooked, but it was the best they could do.

On foot, they climbed to the top of the ridge, knelt there, and took off their hats to risk a look. Matt didn't think the starshine was bright enough to skylight them, but there was no point in taking unnecessary chances.

The ridge fell away on the other side into a broad depression. A dark streak marked the stunted vegetation along a small stream. Matt had been sure the outlaws had to have a source of water, and this proved he was right. The little creek probably rose from a spring, twisted through the badlands for a mile or so, and then plunged back underground.

Half a dozen adobe huts lined one bank of the stream, the sort of crude *jacals* that peasant farmers built in this part of the world. At some point in the past, a small group must have tried to make a go of farming here in these hills, only to give it up. Even with water, the soil was so poor that it wouldn't produce much.

The *jacals* made good quarters for a gang of no-good stagecoach robbers, though. Smoke came from the primitive chimneys of several of the structures.

"Well, we found 'em," Salty said. "Now what do we do?"

Matt pointed to a brush corral near the stream and said, "If we stampede their horses, they can't go anywhere. Then from up here we can keep them pinned in the huts until those deputies from Lordsburg get here."

"You're assumin' any deputies'll even come lookin' for us. And to do what you said, we'll have to split up. One fella goes after the horses while the other stays up here and takes potshots at anybody who pokes a head outta them shacks."

"That's right." Matt held out the Winchester toward Salty. "You're a good shot, right? You said you could shoot the whiskers off a gnat at fifty yards."

"Well . . . well . . . yeah, but tarnation, boy, whoever sneaks down yonder is gonna be in a lot more danger than whoever sits up here on this ridge!"

"I don't know about that. They'll likely be shooting back at you. I plan to stampede those horses and then light a shuck out of there. I'll circle back around up here and give you a hand keeping them pinned down."

Salty sighed and took the rifle.

"All right, if you're bound and determined to do it that way. I'll keep my head down until you start the ball down there."

Matt clapped a hand on the old-timer's shoulder.

"Don't waste your shots," he advised. "I brought along extra shells, but we've only got so many."

He took the other cartridges out of his pockets and handed them to Salty as well. With that done, he slid down the ridge a short distance and began making his way along it so that he could circle around to the outlaws' camp.

It was an even bet whether or not they had posted any guards. They had been pulling off those stagecoach robberies for a couple of months, Salty had said, and no one had even tried to track them down yet. They had to be pretty confident that they were safe here in these desolate, isolated hills. Even if there were sentries, they might not be very alert.

Long minutes stretched past as Matt worked his way into position. He crawled over a little hill and slid down it to the creek about a hundred yards downstream from the huts. The scrub brush that grew along the banks provided some cover for him as he crept toward the corral.

He splashed across the creek in a couple of steps and paused next to the corral. A dozen horses milled around inside it, already disturbed slightly by the scent of a strange human being approaching them. Matt reached out to grab some of the branches that had been woven together to form an enclosure. In a matter of minutes, the barrier would be down and he could fire off a shot, yell at the top of his lungs, and send the horses bolting out of the corral.

Before he could do any of those things, the sound of a gun being cocked came from behind him, and a voice warned, "I wouldn't do that if I was you, mister."

Matt froze. He didn't know what was more shocking: that someone had sneaked up on him without him knowing it . . .

Or that judging by the voice, the person who had the drop on him was a little girl.

Chapter 18

"Move away from that corral right now," the voice went on. "I'll shoot you if I have to."

"Now, take it easy with that gun, miss—" Matt began.

"Don't call me miss! I'm not afraid of you."

"Didn't say you were. I just don't want you doing anything that both of us will regret later."

That brought a chuckle from the unseen girl.

"Mister, I promise you, if I have to shoot you I won't regret it later . . . and you won't be around to regret it."

She sounded mighty sure of herself, Matt thought, and he supposed that since she had a gun on him, she could afford to be. With a sigh, he raised his hands into plain sight and stepped back from the brush barrier.

"You're making a mistake here," he said.

"No, you made it." She lifted her voice suddenly and called, "Davey! Pete! Josie!"

Light came from a couple of the *jacals* as their doors were thrown open. Several figures came out hurriedly, one with a rifle, the other two carrying pistols. As they strode quickly toward the corral, the doors of the other huts opened as well. More figures began to appear.

Matt hoped Salty would hold his fire since the horses hadn't been stampeded yet. That should have been enough to warn the old-timer that things weren't going according to plan. Salty could probably hear the voices, too, even if he couldn't make out all the words.

If Salty opened fire, there was a good chance that somebody down here would be killed. Matt didn't want that, at least until he found out exactly what was going on here. And if he was right about what he thought, he still didn't want any killing if it could be avoided.

"SueAnn, what the hell's goin' on out here? What are you yellin' about?"

The question came from one of the newcomers, a young man this time, judging by his voice. Not too young, though. He was almost as tall as Matt. Starlight reflected from the barrel of the gun he held in his hand.

"I caught this varmint sneakin' around the corral, Davey," the girl called SueAnn replied. "I don't know who he is, but he's bound to be up to no good."

"Somebody strike a light," Davey ordered. "Let's have a look at him."

A lucifer flared up. The boy who held it thrust the match toward Matt's face so that the garish light revealed his features.

The light made him squint as its glare half-blinded him, but his eyes adjusted quickly. His captors hadn't stopped to think that while the light allowed them to see who he was, it provided him with a look at them, too, although some of them hung back instead of clustering around him, so he couldn't see them as well.

As he'd suspected, they were young. In some cases, no more than fourteen or fifteen, he guessed. When SueAnn moved around in front of him, still holding the revolver, he saw that she was even younger, maybe twelve. The gun seemed almost as big as she was, but it was plenty steady in her grip.

Davey and a couple of the other boys were older, maybe eighteen. The others were all in their middle teens. Matt counted eight boys and four girls. They had shed the dusters and Stetsons but still wore range clothes, including the bandannas they had used as masks while they were holding up the stagecoach.

When he'd realized that the robbers weren't speaking, the obvious conclusion was that they were silent because they were afraid their voices would reveal something about them. Their age seemed a likely possibility.

The fact that none of the shots struck him and Salty, despite the fact that they didn't have very good cover, also supported that idea. Thinking back on it, the bullets really hadn't even come that close. Salty had told him the same thing had happened during the other holdups.

That indicated to Matt that the outlaws didn't want to kill anybody.

One of the older boys said, "I recognize this fella. He was the shotgun guard on the coach we stopped today."

"Yeah, I knew I'd seen him before," Davey said. "How'd you follow us, mister?"

The other boy who had spoken said, "I'll tell you how he followed us. He cut one of the horses loose from the team. I've been warnin' you somebody would think of that, Davey."

"They never did before," Davey replied sullenly. "But I guess I should have listened to you, Pete."

"Too late now," the boy called Pete snapped. "He's here, he's seen our faces, and he's heard some of our names. If we let him go, he's likely to find out who we are. Worse yet, he knows where this place is. He can bring the law right back down on our heads." Pete squared his shoulders and lifted the gun in his hand. "No, we got to kill him."

Davey reached over, clamped a hand around the cylinder of Pete's gun, and forced the weapon back down.

"No! We said there wouldn't be any killin' unless we had to, to save one of us."

"Well, now we have to," Pete said tightly, "to save all of us."

For a moment, tension hung thickly in the air. Then a pretty, dark-haired girl stepped up to Pete and put a hand on his other arm.

"Why don't we wait and talk to Roman?" she suggested. "He always knows the best thing to do."

"That's a good idea," Davey said. "Roman's supposed to be here in a little while. We'll put this fella in one of the huts and stand guard over him until then. He's not going anywhere."

Pete still looked like he wanted to put a bullet in Matt, but after a moment he shrugged and said, "All right, we'll leave it up to Roman. But you know what he's gonna say. He'll agree with me that this man's got to die."

"We'll deal with that when the time comes," Davey said.

Pete said, "You better take his gun and knife before he tries something, though."

Davey looked like he wished he had thought of that. He pointed his gun at Matt and said, "All right, a couple of you get those weapons. Don't get between us and him, though."

Briefly, Matt considered the possibility of grabbing one of the kids when they came close enough to disarm him and using the youngster as a hostage. He discarded the idea almost immediately. He didn't want to put any of them in harm's way.

They were doing a good enough job of that themselves by deciding to be outlaws.

Anyway, the two boys who took his Colt and knife were careful, as Davey had warned them to be. Matt wouldn't have had a chance to grab either of them. If he had tried, he was sure Pete would have put a bullet in him.

He didn't know who Roman was, but it looked like he was going to have to bide his time and wait for a better moment to make his move.

He had a grizzled ace in the hole in Salty that none of these kids knew about.

They marched him toward one of the huts and prodded him inside at gunpoint. The place was sparsely furnished with a couple of sleeping pallets, a rickety-looking table with a candle burning on it, and a couple of rough-hewn chairs. Two saddles were piled in a corner. A pair of younger boys picked them up and carried them out. Matt figured they were the ones he was displacing from their usual quarters.

"I'll stand watch over him," Pete volunteered.

Davey's eyes narrowed as if he thought that might not be a good idea. Matt thought the same thing. As eager as Pete had been to kill him a few minutes earlier, the youngster might decide to go ahead and put a bullet in him, then claim that he'd tried to escape.

"No, Josie and I will guard him," Davey said. "The rest of you go back to your cabins. Tom, you and Hank can bunk with me for the time being. I won't be there anyway."

The two boys who had carried out the saddles nodded.

"All right, clear out," Davey went on. "Get some rest if you can. It may be a while before Roman gets here. You'll know it when he does."

The other youngsters filed out of the *jacal.* Pete went reluctantly. SueAnn was the last one through the door, and she warned Davey and Josie, "I captured him. He's my prisoner. Don't you let him get away."

"We won't," Josie promised her. When SueAnn was gone, she closed the door.

Davey gestured toward one of the chairs with his gun and told Matt, "Sit down."

Matt took off his hat and dropped it on the table. He sat and cocked his right ankle on his left knee. The pose was more casual than he really felt. His captors might be little more than children, most of them, but he knew he was in danger anyway.

He looked at Davey and Josie and realized that he saw a family resemblance between them. They were brother and sister, he decided. He didn't know if that information would help any, but it didn't hurt to know it.

"Why don't the two of you tell me what's going on here?" he suggested. "How do a bunch of kids wind up robbing stagecoaches?"

"We're not kids," Davey snapped. "Well, not all

of us, anyway. I'm a grown man. A fella grows up fast on the frontier."

Matt had to admit that there was some truth to that. He thought back to the days when he had been Matt Cavanaugh, the only survivor of a massacre in which outlaws had murdered the rest of his family. He'd had to do whatever was necessary to survive during that grim period of his life, before he'd met Smoke and Preacher. Life on the frontier was indeed a hard teacher.

"Maybe so, but most of those others are just youngsters," he said. "They ought to be in school somewhere instead of wearing masks and shooting off guns."

Josie said, "They would be, if they still had families."

"Ah," Matt said as understanding dawned. "You're all orphans."

"That's right," Davey said. "We all grew up together in an orphanage, until Pete and I got old enough that they kicked us out. And then it wasn't long after that the place closed down and everybody who hadn't been adopted was tossed out without a place to live. By then Pete and I had met Roman, and he offered to help us. He knew about this place, and he told us how the stage line runs not too far south of here."

"Davey, you're talkin' too much," his sister warned him.

Davey ignored her. Once the words started

flowing from him, clearly he wanted to talk. He must have been keeping things bottled up inside him ever since leaving the orphanage.

"Roman said if we'd work for him for a while, he'd stake us to supplies and clothes and everything we needed."

"Everything you needed to become outlaws," Matt said quietly.

Davey shrugged.

"The world never cared about the likes of us, mister," he said. "Why should we care about the law?"

"You think you're the only kids who ever had it tough? I was on my own when I was twelve years old. My folks had been gunned down right in front of me."

"That's terrible," Josie said. "What did you do?"

"I met a couple of hombres who helped me out."

"See?" Davey said. "Your story's not that much different from ours, is it?"

"I never turned desperado," Matt said.

"You made your choices, we made ours." Davey frowned. "What's your name, anyway, mister?"

"It's Matt." He started to add his last name, then decided against it. These kids probably wouldn't recognize the name Matt Jensen, but Roman might, when he showed up.

The situation was pretty clear now. This fella Roman was an outlaw himself, Matt thought, and he had taken advantage of the trouble that had befallen Davey, Josie, and the others to recruit them into doing his dirty work for him. Matt had no doubt that when Roman showed up—probably to collect the Wells Fargo express pouch stolen from the stagecoach—he would agree with Pete and decree that Matt had to die.

That meant Matt had to find some allies of his own before that happened.

"When Roman set this deal up, did he promise you that you wouldn't have to kill anybody?"

"That's right," Josie said. "And we haven't."

"You reckon that's going to be true by the time this night is over?"

Davey said, "We all promised each other we'd do whatever we had to in order to survive and stay together. We're all the family any of us has."

"It won't always be that way. You two are old enough to go out and make lives for yourselves now. So's Pete. And the younger ones will be soon. They can grow up, get married, have families, and be decent citizens. They can be happy." Matt paused. "But they can't if they're running from the law with a murder charge hanging over their heads."

"They won't be wanted for murder." Davey took a deep breath. "If there's killin' to be done, I can do it."

"Davey, no!" Josie cried. "I won't let you—"

"You don't have any say in it, sis."

Davey's voice was hard and flat. Matt didn't doubt that the young man would do what he thought he needed to do.

Unfortunately, he didn't have any more time to win them over, because Pete stuck his head in the door and said, "Roman's comin'. Now we'll settle this."

Chapter 19

Davey jerked his gun in a sharp gesture and ordered Matt, "All right, mister, on your feet. Let's get out there."

"Davey, I don't like this," Josie said. "If we kill this man, things will never be the same."

"If we let him live, they won't be the same, either. But we'll let Roman decide." Davey shrugged. "He may want to take Matt here with him when he leaves and handle things himself."

"Handle killing me, you mean," Matt said. "You'll still bear some responsibility for that, Davey. All of you will. Even little SueAnn."

Pete laughed and said, "Hell, mister, SueAnn would pull the trigger on you herself if she needed to. She's one tough little gal."

Again, Davey ordered, "Let's go."

With three guns on him, Matt had no choice but

to cooperate. He stood up and walked out of the hut while they covered him.

The others had all gathered to await Roman's arrival. One of the boys held a lantern that lit up the area along the creek.

Matt heard hoofbeats, and a moment later a buggy rolled into view, followed by a couple of men on horseback. He was a little surprised to see a buggy out here in these badlands. Obviously, there was a trail leading into the hideout that he and Salty hadn't discovered.

The man holding the reins in the buggy drove it up to the group of youngsters and their prisoner. In the light from the lantern, his smooth-shaven face was surprised and angry at the sight of Matt. He was something of a dandy, wearing a dapper brown suit and brown hat and sporting a neatly trimmed mustache. Dark hair curled out from under his hat. As he brought the vehicle to a stop, he asked in a southern accent, "Well, what have we here?"

"This fella was snooping around, Roman," Davey said. "He was the shotgun guard on the coach we held up this afternoon. He followed us."

"I'd say that's rather self-evident, my young friend," Roman drawled. "The question now is, why is he still alive?"

"That's what I told them, Roman," Pete said. Matt got the impression that Pete wouldn't be unhappy if Roman decided to replace Davey as the head of the gang with him. "I said we had to get rid of him."

"Indeed," Roman muttered.

He wasn't exactly what Matt had expected. He had figured Roman would be an outlaw, but he looked and sounded more like a lawyer. Of course, there wasn't usually that much difference between the two.

The two men on horseback who had accompanied Roman here were more of the sort that Matt had expected: hardcases who would be good with the guns on their hips and willing to do just about anything if the payoff was good enough.

So the odds were pretty steep, and things didn't look good, Matt thought. But he wasn't going to give up hope. Smoke and Preacher had taught him better than that.

Besides, Salty was still out there in the dark somewhere.

Josie said, "We'll just turn him over to you, Roman. We figured you'd know what to do."

"Of course, I do, my dear," Roman said. "I always know what to do. My advice has paid off handsomely for you so far, hasn't it?"

"I don't know about that," Davey said. "We're still stuck out here, and you take all the money."

Roman frowned and said, "Your work isn't over yet. And as for the money, you know our arrangement. I put some of it away for you, and the rest goes to pay me back for my legal services."

Yep, a lawyer, Matt thought. In this case, just another word for crook. He had no doubt that these youngsters would never see a penny of the loot they had turned over to Roman. When he decided that he had milked them enough, he would take all the money and disappear.

He might even tip off the law as to where to find the young outlaws.

"Sorry," Davey muttered as Roman glared at him. "I didn't mean anything by it. But Josie's right; it'd be better if you and your men just took Matt away with you." He leaned his head toward the others. "These kids, they don't need to be involved in this."

"On the contrary," Roman said, "this is a very fortuitous circumstance that has arisen. When dealing with children, one must be on the lookout for . . . educational opportunities, shall we say? We can all learn something from this." The smooth voice hardened. "We can learn who actually deserves a place of leadership in our little group."

Matt knew where this was going, and he didn't like it.

"Davey, you've been in charge by virtue of being the oldest," Roman went on. "But perhaps someone else is actually better qualified to be making decisions when I'm not here."

Pete grinned. He understood what was happening, too.

So did Davey. He said, "I don't see where it

matters who gets rid of him, as long as he's not a threat to us anymore."

"But it does matter," Roman insisted. "A person's reaction to trouble is always instructive. One can learn a great deal from how they handle a problem. Peter, what do you think needs to be done here?"

"Somebody needs to shoot this son of a bitch in the head," Pete answered without hesitation.

"I concur. Davey, as the leader it's your responsibility to take care of this."

"No!" Josie exclaimed. "You told us we wouldn't have to kill anybody, Roman."

"Unless it was necessary, dear girl. This is necessary."

"Hell," said Pete, "I'll do it. Davey, step aside."

He raised his gun.

Davey's jaw tightened. His gun came up, too, but it swung toward Pete.

"Nobody's going to die here—"

"That's where you're wrong, my young friend," Roman said. His hand flickered under his coat like a striking snake and came out clutching a pistol.

But the shot that sounded a fraction of a second later came from a rifle cracking from the darkness. Roman rocked back against the buggy seat and his eyes opened wide in surprise and pain as blood welled out into a crimson stain on the snowy front of his white shirt.

At the same instant, Matt dived at Pete and tackled the young man around the waist. As they went down, Matt's hand closed over Pete's gun and wrenched it out of his fingers. Revolvers boomed as Matt rolled to the side. Somebody cried out in pain.

He came to a stop on his belly and angled the gun in his hand toward one of the hardcases on horseback. Both of Roman's men had yanked their guns out and started blazing away. The Colt in Matt's hand roared and bucked, and the slug from it ripped into an outlaw's chest and toppled him from his saddle.

Meanwhile, Davey traded shots with the other hardcase and staggered as he was hit. His bullet tore through the man's throat. The outlaw dropped his gun and clapped both hands to the wound, but he couldn't stop the blood spurting from the severed artery. He pitched to the ground as well, spasmed a couple of times, and then lay still.

Salty rushed up out of the shadows and covered the rest of the youngsters with his rifle.

"Don't none o' you kids move!" he shouted. "Those of you who've got guns, put 'em on the ground *now!*"

Matt came to his feet and pointed the gun he had taken from Pete at Davey and Josie.

"That goes for the two of you as well," he said. "I know you gave us a hand just then, Davey, but

I'll feel better about things when that gun's on the ground."

Josie placed her pistol on the ground at her feet and stepped away from it. She said, "Do what Matt says, Davey. Please."

For a second Matt didn't know what Davey was going to do. He didn't want to shoot the young man, and if he had to, he would try to wound Davey, but there were no guarantees in a gunfight.

Then Davey sighed, leaned forward, and let the revolver slip from his fingers. He stepped back, too, and said, "I reckon it's all over, isn't it?"

"Not quite. Help Pete up, then all of you get over there in a bunch. Salty, keep an eye on them."

"Durned tootin' I will," the old-timer replied. "A bunch o' kid outlaws! I never saw such a thing in all my borned days!"

Pete had hit the ground hard enough to stun him when Matt tackled him, but he was getting his wits back now. He glared at Matt and Salty, but there was nothing else he could do as Davey helped him to his feet and Salty then herded all twelve youngsters into a compact bunch. SueAnn glared and stuck her tongue out at him, giving in to a childish impulse like the child she was.

She looked surprised when Salty stuck his tongue right back out at her.

Matt ignored that exchange and hurried over to

the buggy. Roman was still alive and struggling to lift the gun he had taken from under his coat. Matt reached into the buggy and plucked the weapon from the crooked lawyer's fingers.

"You ought to be damned proud of yourself," Matt snapped. "Getting a bunch of innocent kids to hold up stagecoaches for you."

"You . . . you're wrong," Roman gasped as he fought to hang on to life. "There aren't any . . . innocent people in this . . . in this . . ."

He slumped to the side and his head fell back against the seat. His eyes began to glaze over. He had lost that fight.

Quickly, Matt checked on the two hardcases. They were both dead, as he had thought.

When he returned to Salty's side, the old-timer asked, "What are we gonna do with this bunch? Turn 'em over to the law?"

SueAnn and Salty weren't the only ones who could act on an impulse. Matt said, "No, we're going to turn them loose."

"What! They're outlaws, goldang it! Stagecoach robbers!"

"Yeah, but they never killed anybody," Matt pointed out.

Salty snorted, nodded toward Pete, and said, "That little scalawag would've, if he'd had the chance."

"Maybe. But right now he doesn't have any blood on his hands, and that's the way I'd like to keep it. I'd like to at least give them all a chance for that. Besides, the varmint who was behind the whole business is dead, and I'll bet if we can find out who he is and search his law office, we'll turn up most of the loot that was taken in the robberies."

"I can tell you who he is," Josie said. "His name is Roman Miller, and his office is in Lordsburg."

"There you go," Matt said to Salty. "The real culprit's been brought to justice, we're going to recover the money, and there's no reason to ruin the lives of these kids."

"Well . . . if you let 'em go, it's liable to make Wells Fargo refuse to pay you that reward."

"I can live with that," Matt said with a smile. He was pretty sure he was doing what Smoke would have done in the same situation, and that was good enough for him.

He was still thinking about Smoke a couple of days later in Lordsburg when he checked in at the Western Union office to see if there were any wires for him. Smoke knew the general area of the country where Matt was, and if he needed to get in touch he would send telegraph messages to all the offices in these parts. It wasn't all that often when Smoke needed to get in touch with him, but when he did, it usually meant trouble.

This was no different, Matt thought as he scanned the words printed on the yellow flimsy the telegraph operator handed to him. A grim cast came over his face.

Salty had wandered into the office after him. The old-timer was waiting for another stage-coach run back to Silver City, and Matt intended to go with him to reclaim the horse he had left there.

They had run into a posse on the way to Lordsburg, just as Matt thought they might. They had the bodies of Roman and his two gunnies in the buggy, bound for the undertaker. The deputies had accepted their story about tracking down the gang of stagecoach thieves and rounding up the ringleader and a couple of his lieutenants. The other members of the gang had gotten away, according to Matt and Salty.

Matt had told Davey and Josie to head for Colorado and take the others with them. They needed to go to a town called Big Rock, he said, because there were folks there who would help them start new lives without asking any questions about what had happened in the past. Matt intended to send a telegram to Smoke and ask his older brother to keep an eye out for the kids.

What he hadn't expected was to find a wire from Smoke waiting for him, but here it was, and the message it contained affected Matt enough that Salty said, "You look like somethin's mighty wrong, boy. What's in that telegram? Somebody die?"

"No, but somebody's liable to if I don't get to Colorado as fast as I can," Matt replied. "You'll have to make that run back to Silver City by yourself, I reckon, but at least you shouldn't run into any owlhoots this time."

"What're you gonna do?"

"I've got to go buy a horse," Matt said.

Chapter 20

"Better take your hand away from that gun, mister," Preacher drawled. "If you don't, I'd be happy to take it away from you and stick it in a place where it ain't gonna be comfortable for you at all." The old mountain man paused, then added, "Of course, a dandy such as your own self might just like it."

The gambler on the other side of the poker table was already angry. Now his face flushed even darker, and the hand he had started to slip under his fancy coat moved another inch closer to destiny.

A saloon girl with piled-up blond hair and a low-cut red dress leaned over beside the gambler and said something into his ear in a low voice. Preacher couldn't hear many of the words, but he picked up a few.

". . . old man . . . kill you . . . crazy . . . Preacher . . ."

He narrowed one eye at the gambler and gave him the old skunk-eye. If the fella already thought he was a loco old codger, it wouldn't hurt anything to convince him even more.

The gambler drew in a deep breath and said, "All right. No harm done, I suppose. I can be the bigger man about this."

"What you can do," Preacher said, "is pull your sleeves back so we can all see the rigs you got for holdin' cards you want to switch out when you get a bad hand. Then you can push that pile o' winnin's in front of you back into the center of the table where the rest of us can divvy it up. That's what a lowdown, four-flushin', tinhorn card cheater like you ought to do before he gets hisself kilt."

The gambler's breath hissed between clenched teeth. He said, "If you weren't an old man—"

"If I wasn't an old man, I'd be dead. I ain't, so that ought to tell you I know how to stay alive and make sure the other fella don't. That easy enough for you to understand?"

The other four men sitting at this baize-covered table in the O.K. Saloon in Deadwood, Dakota Territory, had been watching this confrontation with great interest. During the course of the evening, all of them had lost steadily to the gambler, who had given his name as William

Gale. The pots had not been huge, but Gale's "luck" had been such that he'd amassed a pretty big pile of winnings. Clearly, he didn't want to give them up.

One of the men at the table said, "If you're a card mechanic, Gale, you're a pretty good one. I've been in Deadwood since Hickok was here, and I've learned how to spot a cheat. Let's have a look up your sleeves, like the old man says."

It had been less than five years since Wild Bill Hickok was shot by Jack McCall in the Number 10 Saloon, but they had been tumultuous years and anybody who had been there during that time had gained some valuable experience.

A couple of the other players nodded in agreement with the man who had spoken. One of them said, "If you don't have anything to hide, Gale, you won't mind showing us your sleeves."

"An innocent man doesn't like to have his honor impugned!"

Preacher said, "If you was an innocent man, that might carry some weight with me. But since you ain't . . ."

"Oh, all right," Gale said with a look of disgust on his smooth-shaven face. He used his right hand to fiddle with the left sleeve of his coat.

Preacher was ready for a trick. When Gale suddenly thrust out his left arm, Preacher moved even faster. He lunged across the table, caught hold of Gale's wrist, and shoved that arm toward the ceiling. Not straight up, though, because Preacher didn't want a bullet going through the ceiling and into a second-floor room to injure a soiled dove or one of her customers.

Instead, when the derringer in Gale's hand popped, the little slug went harmlessly over the heads of everyone in the saloon and embedded itself in one of the thick beams that held up the ceiling. Preacher's other hand bunched into a fist and smacked into Gale's jaw with enough force to send the gambler's chair over backwards.

Preacher was around the table and kneeling beside Gale before anyone knew what was happening. While he was moving, the old mountain man had drawn his knife. He laid the razor-sharp edge against Gale's throat.

"That little pissant gun o' yours has got a second barrel, I see," Preacher said into the shocked silence that now filled the O.K. Saloon. "If you're thinkin' about shootin' me with it, old son, you got to ask yourself . . . do you really think a skeeter bite like that's gonna kill me 'fore I shove this knife all the way through your neck to your spine? It's sharp enough it'll go through you easier'n a purty little speckled trout a-glidin' through a mountain stream. Are you askin' yourself, Mr. Tinhorn?"

Gale's hand opened. The derringer with its unfired barrel fell a couple of inches to the floor.

A woman's voice asked, "Preacher, are you causing a ruckus again?"

"No such thing," Preacher said without looking around to see who had spoken. He knew the voice. "Just wonderin' why you let cheatin' trash like this in your place, Elizabeth."

A very attractive woman in a stylish dress walked around them. Wings of raven-black hair curled around her face. Her eyes were a beguiling greenish-gray. She had a tiny scar just above the right end of her upper lip, but it didn't detract from her beauty. If anything, it just made her more lovely. Preacher happened to know that she was in her late thirties, but she looked ten years younger than that.

"No one else has complained about Mr. Gale here," she said.

Preacher kept the knife at Gale's throat as he pushed back the man's right coat sleeve to reveal a complicated arrangement of cables and metal clips.

"I was wrong about one thing," the old mountain man said. "I thought he had one o' these contraptions on both arms, but there was a spring holster for that derringer up his other sleeve."

Elizabeth Langston's mouth tightened in anger. That didn't make her any less pretty, either.

"I don't allow card sharps in my establishment, Mr. Gale," she said.

"Get . . . get this madman away from me!" Gale

gasped. He had trouble getting the words out because of the knife at his throat. "He's going to kill me!"

"I'm not sure anyone here would particularly care," Elizabeth said coolly. She waved an elegantly manicured hand toward the pile of money on the table and added, "Gentlemen, help yourselves to Mr. Gale's stake. I'll trust you to divide it in the correct proportions. Please, no squabbling."

"There won't be any, ma'am," one of the cardplayers assured her. "We just want back what Gale took from us by cheating."

While they were doing that, Elizabeth looked down at the gambler again and said, "The only reason I'm asking Preacher not to kill you, Mr. Gale, is because the businesses here in Deadwood are making an attempt to live down, at least somewhat, the town's rather lurid reputation. Not too much, mind you. It wouldn't be good for anyone if Deadwood got too tame. But spilling a gallon of blood on the floor isn't a good thing, either. It's difficult to clean up, as well."

Preacher asked, "Is that your way of sayin' you don't want me to carve this varmint a new grin?"

"I'd appreciate it, yes."

"Well, all right, since I'm in the habit of agreein' when a good-lookin' gal makes a suggestion."

Preacher leaned over and brought his face even closer to Gale's. He said in quiet, dangerous tones, "But you better light a shuck outta this town, mister. If I ever see you again, I ain't gonna be happy, and there probably won't be anybody as generous as Miss Elizabeth here around to ask me not to kill you."

Gale started to swallow, then stopped. He nodded his head, barely moving it, just enough to demonstrate his agreement with what Preacher had said.

Preacher took the knife away from Gale's throat and stood up. A tiny drop of blood showed on the gambler's throat where the blade had nicked it. Gale touched a finger to the drop and smeared it across the tip. Fear and hatred warred in his eyes as he looked at Preacher while he climbed shakily to his feet.

"Leave the derringer on the floor and get out," Elizabeth ordered him.

Gale turned and started toward the saloon's entrance. His gait was none too steady. He didn't even try to pick up the hat that had fallen off his head when Preacher knocked him down, let alone retrieve the derringer.

Preacher picked up the little gun instead, once Gale was gone and things began to get back to normal in the saloon. He broke it open, removed the expended cartridge and the live round from the barrels, and snapped it closed again.

"You want this peashooter?" he asked Elizabeth.

She took it and said, "I'll give it to my friend Andrew. He's a gunsmith. He can probably sell it." She nodded to the money left on the table. "The others have already taken what they had coming to them. You need to get what you lost, too, Preacher."

He grinned and said, "Reckon I'll leave it for the house. Weren't really all that much, and I consider it a fair price for the entertainment value of gettin' to wallop a damn tinhorn."

"He could have killed you, you know. I happened to be watching. He was pretty fast with that hideout gun."

"I was faster."

"By a whisker."

Preacher chuckled and rasped his fingers over the beard stubble on his grizzled jaw.

"I'd say I had the advantage on him there, for sure."

Elizabeth laughed and shook her head. She said, "Come over to my table and have a drink with me."

"Like I said, I always like to oblige pretty women."

Elizabeth signaled to one of her bartenders and led Preacher to a table located in a small alcove in the rear of the barroom. As they sat down, she asked, "How long have you been in Deadwood this time?"

"Just rode in this afternoon," he told her as he thumbed back his battered old hat to reveal thinning salt-and-pepper hair. Mostly salt.

"And you've already been involved in a shooting and a near-knifing. You never change, do you, Preacher?"

"No, ma'am. And I don't intend to, neither."

It was true that change came slowly, if at all, to Preacher. Like Elizabeth Langston, he didn't show his age, but the discrepancy was even greater in his case. He could have passed for fifty, instead of three decades older than that.

Since the days when he had been one of the most famous mountain men of the fur trapping era, Preacher had gotten a little scrawnier. His hair was a little whiter, his permanently tanned skin a little more leathery. He wasn't quite as spry as he had been in his younger days . . . which meant he was still faster, more agile, and more dangerous than nine out of ten men he encountered. He still wore fringed buckskins, but instead of the flintlock pistols he had once carried, he wore holstered Colt revolvers on both hips. He was fast and deadly accurate with them, too, although not at the same level as Smoke and Matt Jensen, the two young men who were the closest thing to family he still had.

The bartender brought a bottle and two glasses to the table. Elizabeth poured the drinks for her and Preacher.

"This is the best stuff in the house, you know," she said.

"I'm sure it's mighty good."

"But it's all who-hit-John to you, isn't it?" she asked, smiling.

Preacher sipped the whiskey and smacked his lips in appreciation.

"Yeah, but it's *good* who-hit-John."

Elizabeth laughed, then grew more serious as she asked, "Did you mean what you said earlier about always trying to oblige a woman?"

"Of course."

"Then I have a favor to ask of you."

"Ask away."

She looked at him over her glass and said, "I need you to kill some men."

Chapter 21

The mining claims around Deadwood were all located in the deep, heavily wooded gulches formed by Deadwood Creek and the other streams in the area. Over the past few years, since the settlement's first boom, many of those claims had been consolidated and taken over by various mining companies and syndicates. It was hard for an individual miner with his pick and shovel, his pan, and his long tom sluice to compete against companies that could afford the latest equipment and the workers to use it.

But some small claims still existed, and one a couple of miles up the gulch from Deadwood was being worked by a man from West Virginia named Frederickson and his four sons. The youngest son, Billy, was only nineteen years old and had recently gotten married to a girl a couple of years younger named Margaret, who was known as Mattie.

"My daughter," Elizabeth Langston said to Preacher as they sat at her private table, after telling him briefly about the Frederickson clan and their mining claim.

Preacher had wondered where she was leading with this tale, and now he had an inkling.

"You're sayin' she didn't want to marry this boy Billy Frederickson?"

Elizabeth shook her head.

"No, not at all. It was Billy's idea, but Mattie went along with it quickly enough, even though I didn't give my permission. She didn't care about that. I think my disapproval made her even more determined to go through with the marriage."

"Yeah, young'uns are like that," Preacher mused. "I never knew you had a daughter, Elizabeth."

She smiled thinly and said, "A woman who's in the saloon business . . . among other things . . . tries to shield her children from the less savory side of her life. In my case, Mattie is my only child, so I was even more protective of her. She'd been in school in Philadelphia, but she ran away and came out here on her own. She wanted to be with me." Elizabeth gave a small shrug. "I couldn't argue with that sentiment, even though I worried a great deal about letting her stay here. As it turns out, I was right to worry."

"She got mixed up with Billy Frederickson and then hitched to him."

"That's right. I tried to explain to her what a primitive, unpleasant business it would be to live on a mining claim, but with the stars in her eyes, she couldn't hear me."

"Well," Preacher said slowly, "I'll allow it's prob'ly a rougher life than what she's used to, but it was her own choice, unless you're claimin' this here Billy Frederickson done kidnapped her. That'd put a different face on things, I reckon."

Elizabeth shook her head again.

"No, like I said, she went out there of her own free will. But what she found waiting for her . . . well, it was worse than just the hardships of living on a mining claim. I started to hear rumors, so I tracked them down. A lot of people in this town owe me favors, Preacher. I heard the same story, independently, from several different sources. It seems the Fredericksons . . . the father and all four sons . . ." She had to draw in a deep breath and visibly brace herself before she could go on. "It seems that they subscribe to a theory of sharing everything equally. All of them regard Mattie as their wife . . . with all that entails."

For a moment, Preacher just stared across the table at her. He didn't trust himself to speak. When he finally did, he said, "That's a mighty rotten thing."

"Yes," she agreed with a faint, humorless smile. "I've been told that Mattie tried to leave, but they wouldn't let her. One of them watches her all the time while the other four work the claim. You can see why I want you to go out there, kill those bastards, and bring my little girl back to me."

Preacher had a hunch that even if he killed the Fredericksons and returned Mattie to her mother, it wouldn't be as simple getting her back as Elizabeth seemed to think . . . or hope. There were other angles to consider, too.

"Most folks'd go to the law with a problem like this," he said. "You've got a sheriff here in Deadwood."

"Yes, and he's a good man, too," Elizabeth agreed, "but Mattie and Billy Frederickson are legally married. You know that the authorities won't step into something like this. In the eyes of the law it's a private matter between husband and wife."

She was probably right about that, he decided. Even though civilization was breaking out all over the frontier these days, in many cases the simplest, most effective thing was for a man to stomp his own snakes.

Or for a woman to do likewise. If he went along with what Elizabeth was asking, he'd be the boot and she'd be the one doing the stomping.

As if sensing his hesitation, she reached across the table and clasped his left hand in both of hers.

"I know it's a terrible thing to ask of you," she said. "To kill those men—"

"I ain't worried about killin' any varmint who's in need of killin'," Preacher interrupted her. "And from the sound of it, them Fredericksons sure fall into that bunch. You're talkin' about five to one odds, though . . . and I ain't as young as I used to be."

"I've known you for fifteen years, Preacher," she said. "I don't think you've aged a day in that time."

"It ain't always the years. It's the miles, and I been a whole heap of 'em."

"You're also the man who used to slip into Blackfoot camps and cut the throats of a dozen warriors while they slept. You're the Ghost Killer."

"Was. Anyway, you've maybe been listenin' to too many stories. You know how some folks like to blow a thing up bigger'n it really is."

"We can talk around and around this, Preacher. What it comes down to is, will you help me and my daughter? I won't insult you by saying that I'll make it worth your while—"

"Good," Preacher said.

"But I can tell you that I'll be in your debt for the rest of my life."

Preacher sat there with a frown on his rugged face. If what she had told him was true, the Fredericksons were skunks and needed to be dealt with as such. And it was true that he and Elizabeth had a history. She hadn't really appealed to that, hadn't asked him to help her for old times' sake, but he couldn't really escape that aspect of the situation, either.

"I'll have to look into it," he finally said. "Make sure that what you've been told is the truth."

"I'm convinced it is, but I can understand why you'd want to be, too," she said, nodding.

"Then, if somethin' needs to be done, I'll do it. Can't promise that all five of 'em will wind up dead, though. If there's only one man guardin' Mattie, it shouldn't be too hard to get her away from him."

"Then they'll come into town, demand that Billy's lawful wife be returned to him, and the sheriff won't have any choice but to go along with what they want."

She was probably right about that. But just because something was legal didn't mean it was right. Preacher had learned that a long time ago.

"We'll see," he said. "Anyway, if they're the sort o' hillbillies and ridge runners who'd do such shameful things to start with, there's a mighty good chance they won't let this be settled peacefully."

"They are," Elizabeth assured him. "You're going to have your hands full, Preacher. And I want you to be careful."

"That probably ain't gonna be possible, neither," the old mountain man said.

Chapter 22

Preacher had been all over this part of the country long before anybody ever thought of finding gold here, and once he had seen a place, tramped over it with his own two feet or ridden it on one of the fine gray stallions he had named Horse, he never forgot it. So when Elizabeth Langston told him where the Frederickson claim was located, he had known right where to find it.

The next day after the encounter with the crooked gambler in the O.K. Saloon, Preacher rode out the gulch west of the settlement and took one of its branches that veered off to the northwest. He had a long, coiled rope hanging from his saddle horn. He wasn't sure how or even if he would use it, but it might come in handy.

He rode to within half a mile of his destination,

then reined in Horse and swung down from the saddle.

"You're gonna have to stay here, fella," he told the gray stallion as he looped the reins around a sapling. "But there's plenty of grass to graze on. I'll try not to be gone too long, but when you're wadin' right into trouble, ain't no tellin' just how long it'll take." He turned toward the slope and added, "Come on, Dog."

There was no telling, either, how many big, wolflike curs called Dog had been his trail companions. Some had been descendants of the original Dog, but eventually that line had died out. Preacher had a knack for finding similar animals, and at times he even wondered if the same spirit animated all of them. That was a fanciful notion, to be sure, but he had seen enough strange things in his life not to rule out too many possibilities, no matter how far-fetched they might be.

The current Dog followed him now as he climbed up the brushy slope on the side of the gulch. In places the slant was so steep that he had to grab hold of tree trunks in order to pull himself higher. When he was about halfway to the top he figured that was far enough and turned to follow the gulch toward the Frederickson claim.

As he approached, he heard men's voices and the metallic sound of a pick digging into rock. Smoke rose up the slope toward Preacher. When he judged that he was right above the diggings, he eased his way down closer. Dog came along behind him, moving as quietly as the old mountain man.

After a few minutes of getting into position, Preacher hunkered on his heels and parted some branches in the brush. That gap allowed him to gaze down on the Frederickson claim. From that vantage point, he couldn't see into the shaft they were digging into the hillside, but the sounds told him two men were working in there. Two more men knelt beside the creek with pans and searched for gold that way, not far from a pole pen where a couple of mules grazed.

That was four of the five West Virginians accounted for. The fifth one was most likely inside the crude cabin they had built, guarding Mattie Langston. Or Mattie Frederickson now, since she was married to the youngest Frederickson brother. It looked like the girl's mother had been right about that part, anyway.

Preacher's eyes narrowed as he studied the layout. He thought there was a chance he might be able to reach the cabin by approaching it from the upstream side. Getting in there could be difficult, though. The back wall didn't have a window in it, and there was a very good chance the side walls didn't, either. Nobody would go to the trouble of putting windows in a primitive log cabin like this when all they did in it was sleep and eat and take advantage of a foolish girl.

The two men he could see working in the stream were both young, not much more than twenty. That meant the patriarch of the Frederickson clan was in either the shaft or the cabin. The best thing to do might be to lure them out, get them all together where he could see them.

Also, he wanted a better look at Mattie before he started killing people over her.

"Come on, Dog," he said quietly to the big cur, who hadn't made a sound.

It didn't take them long to get back to where he had left Horse. He untied the big stallion, swung into the saddle, and started riding along the stream at a deliberate pace, like a man who had all the time in the world and not a care in it, either.

He even started singing an old song in a surprisingly good voice. He wanted the Fredericksons to know he was coming. Men working a mining claim sometimes got a mite jumpy about strangers coming around.

He rounded a bend in the creek and saw the cabin and the diggings in the hillside up ahead. The two men beside the stream set their pans aside and picked up the rifles that were handy. The weapons were fairly new Winchester repeaters, Preacher noted.

One of the men called, "Pa! Wiley!"

As Preacher continued his steady approach, two figures emerged from the shaft. One was thick-bodied and heavy-shouldered, with just a fringe of graying brown hair left around his ears and the back of his head. The other was about thirty, brawny and dark-haired. Both men wore holstered pistols. Their shirts were wet with sweat from the work they'd been doing.

None of the four men Preacher could see looked quite young enough to be Billy Frederickson, who had wooed and wed Mattie Langston. The young couple must be inside the cabin, Preacher decided.

And Billy must have heard his brother call out from the creek, because the door opened and he appeared, a tall, lanky youngster with a shock of sandy hair. He had a rifle in his hands, too.

Preacher saw movement just beyond Billy. A flash of a pale, heart-shaped face surrounded by dark curls. That had to be Mattie. Preacher didn't really get a good look at her, though, before Billy moved a little and blocked his view. Preacher didn't think it was deliberate, but that was the result, anyway.

"Better hold on there, stranger," the elder Frederickson said as he held up a hand with the palm turned toward Preacher. "This is our claim. I'd be askin' what you're doin' here."

Preacher brought Horse to a stop and rested his hand on the saddle horn as he said, "Why, I'm just a-ridin' up this here gulch. What's it look like I'm doin'?"

"If you're just passin' through, where are you bound for?"

"I ain't exactly sure. I thought I'd scout a ways along the crick and see if I could find a likely claim that ain't took yet."

One of the younger men standing at the edge of the stream laughed and said, "You're about five years too late, you old coot. All the good claims are played out, except for the ones the big companies gobbled up. We're breakin' our backs workin' this place, and barely makin' enough to keep beans in the pot."

"You hush, Thurlow," Frederickson said. "What we make or don't make ain't any business of this stranger." He jerked his head toward the north. "If you don't have any reason to be here, just pass on through."

"Well . . ." Preacher rubbed his grizzled jaw. "Speakin' of beans, it's gettin' on toward midday, and I could use somethin' to eat. Seems like I smell somethin' cookin'. Thought I caught a glimpse of a lady in there. Your wife, mister?"

He addressed the question to Frederickson, but it brought a laugh from Billy.

"Shoot, no, she's my wife!" He stepped aside to reveal Mattie standing there in a drab shirt and long skirt with an apron over them. Her face was flushed, probably from cooking, and the look in her eyes reminded Preacher of a rabbit with its foot caught in a trap.

She was a girl who needed help, all right. He had no doubt of that now.

"Get back in that cabin!" Frederickson roared at his youngest son. "Take that trollop with you."

Billy's face darkened with anger. He said, "You got no call to talk about her like that, Pa. I know I said it was all right to—"

"Hush up and do what I told you!"

Glaring, Billy moved back into the cabin. He herded Mattie ahead of him. The door swung closed behind them.

"You'll get nothing to eat here, mister," Frederickson told Preacher.

"I could pay you—" the mountain man began.

"Wouldn't matter. We're on short rations right now, until we take enough gold out of the ground to buy more. Sorry. You'll have to go on your way."

"All right," Preacher said. "Didn't mean to cause no trouble."

He heeled Horse into a walk and started past the men, whistling a tune as he did so. One of the Frederickson boys asked, "Is that a wolf followin' you, mister?"

"Naw, he's a dog. Might have a little wolf blood in him, though. I wouldn't be a bit surprised."

"Keep movin'," Frederickson growled.

Preacher suspected that the old man might have one of the boys follow him, just to make sure he didn't double back. So he rode along the creek for a good two miles before he stopped. He didn't think any of them would have followed him that far.

The Fredericksons were on edge, especially the old man. That was a good indication he knew he was doing something wrong.

Preacher dismounted to study on his best course of action. He knew he had to tread carefully, because there was a chance Frederickson would kill that girl before he'd allow her to be rescued. He wouldn't want her telling anybody about what had been going on here, especially not the authorities. The local lawman might be hesitant to interfere in domestic matters, but he might have to if Mattie's story was bad enough and she told it convincingly enough.

"You might as well graze some more," he told Horse, then added to Dog, "and you might as well go roust up some game if you want to. Best chance of gettin' that girl outta there will be after it's dark, so we're gonna be here for a while."

Chapter 23

By evening, Preacher had figured out what he was going to do. There was something a lot more precious to the Fredericksons than Billy's pretty young wife. That was their claim, and the gold they were taking out of it. Anything that threatened that would make them react in a hurry.

They might take turns standing guard over the mine at night. Knowing that, Preacher moved soundlessly through the dark as he climbed down the slope toward the opening of the shaft. The coiled rope was looped over his shoulder. He had left Dog behind, although the big brute wasn't too far away and could come in a hurry if Preacher called him.

Preacher stopped about ten feet above the opening. He listened and didn't hear anything, but after a moment he smelled tobacco smoke. Somebody had a pipe going.

He was patient, and after a while a man grunted, stirred, and walked out away from the mine. Preacher could tell from the way the figure stretched and rolled his shoulders that he was having trouble staying awake. Preacher couldn't tell which of the Fredericksons it was. Not the father; this man was too tall. It could have been any of the boys, though.

Preacher slipped closer and slid one of his Colts from its holster. He didn't want to fire any shots just yet, but he would if he had to. Soundlessly, he moved out to the end of a jutting slab of rock, timed his leap, and sailed toward the guard just as the man turned back toward the mine.

Whichever of the Frederickson boys he was, he never had a chance. Preacher fell on him out of the dark like a giant bird of prey and knocked him senseless with one swipe of the revolver.

It would have been simple enough to go ahead and cut the unconscious guard's throat, but Preacher decided not to do that. When he had seen Mattie earlier, she had definitely looked scared, like a girl who had gotten into something she desperately wanted out of, but until he talked to her, he couldn't be absolutely sure that the situation was how Mattie's mother had described it to him. Until he knew for certain, he wasn't going to kill any of the Fredericksons in cold blood.

Now, if they decided to up and shoot at him, that would be different, of course. . . .

Preacher dragged the unconscious man away from the mine entrance, cut strips off his shirt to tie and gag him, then straightened from that task and moved toward the dark maw of the mine shaft. He went into it carefully and extended a hand as he searched the stygian gloom.

It didn't take him long to reach the end. The Fredericksons had only penetrated about fifteen feet into the hillside, the shaft sloping downward a bit. Preacher explored the walls by touch and found several support beams fashioned from the trunks of trees.

Working by feel, he took the rope from his shoulder and rigged it around the beams at the end of the shaft. As he played out the strand he looped it around the other beams as well, and when he stepped out of the shaft he had about twenty feet left.

The guard had come to and was moving around a little. Preacher went over and knelt beside him, drew the knife, and put the edge against the man's throat.

"I could'a killed you earlier," Preacher whispered as the man stiffened in fear at the touch of cold steel. "Don't make me sorry that I didn't."

The man lay still. Preacher stood up and sheathed the knife. He went back to what he'd been doing.

A couple of old saddles lay next to the crude corral where the mules were. Preacher opened the gate and took the saddles inside, where he cinched them onto the big, stolid beasts. Then he led the mules to the end of the rope. He had to cut a couple of pieces off of it to come up with an arrangement where he could attach them to the mules and have both the animals pull equally. The mules weren't the least bit skittish while he did this, which was a lucky break for him.

He didn't know if his plan would work. Some dynamite would have been better. But a man had to work with the tools he was given.

"All right, you jugheaded varmints," he told the mules. "You ready to do some haulin'?"

He grasped the halters he had put on them and backed away from the mine. The mules came with him, and behind them the slack in the rope lifted from the ground and became taut. When the mules felt that, they stopped.

"Come on," Preacher gritted. "Don't get balky on me now, you dadblasted critters!"

He cussed and heaved, and after a minute the mules began to heave against the weight. Would the rope hold? Preacher didn't know. Some chain or cable and a bigger team of mules would've been better. So would a donkey engine. But he didn't have any of those things. He had rope, a couple of mules, and some ingenuity.

And the hope that that would be enough.

A scraping sound came from inside the mine. That was one of the support beams coming loose, Preacher thought. Once it gave, that allowed the mules to exert more force on the others, and a moment later the old mountain man heard more scraping.

Then with a clatter, all the beams gave way, and the mules lunged forward and dragged them out of the shaft. Preacher stopped the animals, since their work was done.

Then he held his breath and waited to see what the result would be. There was no guarantee the shaft would collapse just because the support beams had been removed.

The Fredericksons hadn't been tunneling through solid rock. There was a lot of dirt mixed in there, too, Preacher had discovered as he felt his way along the walls. That weakened the shaft. He listened closely and heard a pattering sound. That would be dirt and small rocks falling from the ceiling as the great weight of the hillside shifted a little.

The pattering grew more rapid and got louder. Then it suddenly turned into a rumble, and that rumble changed to a roar as the shaft began to collapse.

Preacher felt like letting out a whoop of triumph, but he didn't want to give away his position. Instead, he left the mules standing where they were and retreated quickly into the trees near the cabin. The place had been dark when he came up, but now the door flew open and light spilled out from a lantern someone inside had lit. Several figures charged out.

Preacher counted them. All four of the remaining Fredericksons appeared. The sons wore long underwear. The elder Frederickson was in an old-fashioned nightshirt.

All of them carried rifles.

"The shaft!" one of the boys yelled in alarm. "The shaft's collapsin'!"

"Where's Arly?" another shouted.

That would be the guard, Preacher thought, the only one of the sons whose name he hadn't heard until now.

Frederickson held the lantern high as they rushed toward the mine opening. He bellowed,

"Arly! By God, boy, where are you? What's happened here? All our work ruined!"

Preacher slipped behind them, putting himself between them and the cabin. He drew both Colts, pointed the left-hand gun into the air, and pulled the trigger. The roar of the mine collapse had come to an end, so the gunshot sounded loud in the following silence.

The shot made the Fredericksons jump and start to turn around, but they froze when Preacher leveled his Colts at them and barked, "Hold it right there, you ridge-runnin' polecats! I got the drop on you, and I'll ventilate the whole lot of you if you give me an excuse."

"You!" Frederickson exclaimed. "I knew we couldn't trust you! What have you done? Why'd you collapse our mine?"

"I reckon if I was you I'd be more worried about that boy o' yours who was standin' guard," Preacher drawled.

"Arly? Damn him, if he let you ruin us!"

"Pa, don't say that," Billy objected. "Mister, what have you done to my brother?"

"He's all right," Preacher said. "Just got a sore head, that's all. But he'll get worse if you fellas don't cooperate with me." His voice hardened. "I've come for Miss Margaret Langston."

"What? You mean Mattie? She ain't Miss Langston! She's my wife!"

"Maybe in the eyes of the law, but if what I've

heard about you varmints is true, I don't reckon it's a real marriage in the eyes o' God."

"See?" Wiley said. He was the oldest of the four sons. "I told you we shouldn't—"

"Shut up!" Frederickson snapped. "What goes on inside a family ain't no business of outsiders!"

That reaction pretty well confirmed the rumors Elizabeth had heard, at least as far as Preacher was concerned. He reined in the impulse to start shooting.

Instead, he said, "Put them rifles on the ground and back away from 'em. I'm takin' the girl back to her mama, where she belongs."

"She belongs with me!" Billy said as the four of them obeyed Preacher's command with obvious reluctance and anger. "She's my wife! We're in love!"

"You may be, but I'll bet she don't feel the same way no more."

"You ask her!" the young man blustered. "You just ask her!"

"I intend to," Preacher said. He raised his voice. "Mattie! Come on out here, gal! I'm a friend your ma sent to help you!"

He didn't take his eyes off the Fredericksons, but a moment later he heard some hesitant, shuffling steps behind him.

"Mattie, is that you?" he asked.

"Yes," came the strained reply. "Who . . . who are you, mister?"

"They call me Preacher. I'm an old friend of your ma's."

Frederickson snorted and said, "Old is right. I'll bet this relic can't even see well enough to hit anything with those guns. We should charge him, boys."

"If you're that eager to get your sons killed, and your own self, too, you just go right ahead, Frederickson," Preacher said.

The four of them didn't move.

"Listen here, Mattie," Preacher went on after a moment. "Your ma asked me to come out here and get you and bring you back to her. I got to hear it from your own mouth, though, that you want to go."

Before she could reply, Billy said, "Mattie, don't! You know I love you, honey. You gotta stay with me!"

Preacher heard Mattie swallow hard. Then she said, "I . . . I can't go, mister. I can't leave here."

Preacher frowned.

"You don't mean that, gal," he said.

Billy let out a whoop and pointed a finger. He said, "You see! She loves me, like I told you! She don't want to leave me!"

"It . . . it's not that," Mattie went on. "I can't go back because of the . . . the shame. After what's been done to me, even a saloon is too respectable a place for . . . for the likes of me. I'm too *dirty.*"

"Now, Mattie, that just ain't right," Preacher

said. “Only reason for somebody to feel shame is because o’ somethin’ they done their own selves. Nobody needs to be ashamed about somethin’ that was done *to* ’em.”

“I’d like to believe that’s true, I really would, but I . . . I couldn’t stand the way people would stare at me and talk behind their hands and snicker.”

“Anybody who did that, your mama would set ’em straight in a hurry. They’d be sorry enough they wouldn’t do it again, neither.”

“I’m sorry, mister. I just can’t go back.”

“I told you,” Billy crowed. “You’ll see, honey, everything’ll be all right.”

Frederickson said, “Except we got to dig out that damned shaft all over again because of what this old bastard did!”

“I’m just a whisker away from shootin’ you just on gen’ral principles, Frederickson,” Preacher warned. “So I’d be careful what I said if I was you.” He turned his head slightly and added, “You got to be sure about this, Mattie. You can make it right if you want to. You just got to be brave enough to do it.”

“I know,” she said. “I already figured that out.”

She stepped beside Preacher. He saw her from the corner of his eye. She wore a long, white nightdress, and her long dark hair was loose around her face and over her shoulders. She had something in her hands, but Preacher couldn't tell what it was at first.

Frederickson saw it, too, and said, "What the hell is that the girl's got? It's not—"

Mattie raised the object with both hands and thrust it in front of her.

Billy cried, "It's your old Dragoon pistol, Pa!"

So it was, Preacher realized, and in that long white gown Mattie looked like some sort of avenging angel as she pointed the long-barreled revolver. The hammer was already pulled back and cocked.

Frederickson said scornfully, "That old thing won't even shoot anymore."

Preacher began, "Girl, don't—"

But Mattie said, "I've got to make things right," and pulled the trigger.

Chapter 24

The Dragoon was a cap-and-ball revolver that fired a heavy .44 caliber round. A tongue of flame lashed from the muzzle as the gun roared.

Billy had started to take a step toward Mattie, but he staggered back as the ball struck his right arm exactly at the elbow. The shot was pure luck; Mattie couldn't have aimed it like that.

But the ball pulverized bone and practically blew Billy's arm off, anyway. He howled in agony as his hand and forearm flopped loosely, held on only by a few strands of muscle and flesh.

"Kill 'em both!" Frederickson bellowed as he lunged for one of the rifles they had dropped on the ground.

Preacher put two slugs from his right-hand Colt into Frederickson's chest before the West Virginian could reach the rifles. He triggered the left-hand gun at Wiley and Thurlow as they went after the Winchesters, too.

At the same time Preacher lunged to his right so that his shoulder hit Mattie. The collision knocked her off her feet and sent her sprawling on the ground, which was exactly what Preacher wanted. At least she was more out of the line of fire down there.

He stood over her and let the twin Colts buck and roar in his hands. The remaining two Frederickson boys got their hands on the rifles and jerked them from the ground. Bullets ripped from the repeaters and whined around Preacher as nearly continuous muzzle flashes tore the night asunder.

The old mountain man had been under fire and faced odds like this countless times in his life. He shifted subtly to throw off the aim of his enemies and drove a slug into Wiley's midsection. That made the oldest son double over and collapse.

A second later, one of Preacher's bullets smashed through Thurlow's right lung and knocked him to the ground. He gasped for air, but the bubbling whistle that came from him testified that he was about to drown in his own blood.

Preacher was worried about Mattie, but he had to check on the Fredericksons first. The old man was dead. Preacher had drilled him twice through the heart. Wiley and Thurlow were both still alive, but not for long. As he was seeing how badly they were hurt, Preacher heard the death rattle in each man's throat.

That left Billy, who writhed and whimpered on the ground nearby. A dark pool of blood surrounded him as it pumped from his mangled arm. But he was strong enough to say piteously, "Mattie . . . Mattie . . ."

Preacher thumbed fresh cartridges into his Colts, holstered them, and went to the girl's side. He knelt and took hold of her shoulders.

"Mattie, are you all right?" he asked as he lifted her into a sitting position. He didn't see any blood on her nightdress, but it was hard to tell in this light.

She seemed too stunned to talk. She clutched at his arms and trembled. He pulled her against him and awkwardly patted her back. Despite his long life, comforting an upset female was something he had never really learned how to do effectively.

"Mattie . . ." Billy wailed.

That made her shudder even more. Preacher tightened his arms around her.

After a few moments, she was able to take a deep breath and say, "I . . . I'm all right, Mr. Preacher."

"Just Preacher," he said. "Forget about the mister."

"Are they all dead?"

"Except for Billy and Arly. He's tied up."

"Is . . . is Billy dying?"

Preacher wasn't going to lie to her. He said, "I reckon so. He's lost too much blood to live."

"I want to talk to him."

That seemed reasonable enough. Preacher picked up the Dragoon Colt she had dropped when he knocked her down and tucked it behind his gun belt. He helped her to her feet. She was none too steady, but with his help she made it over to where Billy lay dying.

"Mattie . . ."

"I'm here," she told him as she leaned on Preacher.

"I . . . I'm sorry," he gasped. "I know what we done . . . was wrong. . . . I tried to stop it. . . . I just never could . . . stand up to my pa and . . . my brothers."

"This was one time you should have, Billy," she said. "You really should have."

"I know. . . . I know. . . ." He grimaced and

spasmed as a fresh wave of pain must have gone through him. "I . . . I'd die easier . . . if you'd forgive me . . . if I knew that . . . you didn't hate me. . . ."

"Billy," she said softly.

"Mattie . . . ?"

"Go to hell. Your family's waiting for you."

Billy gasped. His back arched slightly. When his body sank back to the ground, he was gone, with his wife's condemnation the last thing he heard on this earth.

"Gal, you had it all wrong," Preacher told her. "You're plenty strong enough to make it back in Deadwood, no matter what the folks there do."

"I . . . I don't know. I'll think about it."

Before Preacher could say anything else, he heard a rush of footsteps behind him. He twisted, keeping his left hand on Mattie's arm to steady her, and palmed out the right-hand Colt. He saw the shape charging him and knew that Arly had worked his way free. The last of the Fredericksons had found an ax somewhere, and he had it raised over his head to deliver a killing blow as he shouted in rage.

Preacher blew a .45 slug through his brain.

Momentum kept Arly going for a couple of steps, although he dropped the ax and it fell behind him. Then he pitched forward and lay still on the ground, nearly at Preacher's feet.

"Dadgum it," Preacher said. "I thought I tied

him up better'n that. Maybe I really am gettin' too old for this sort o' rowdy-dow."

Mattie didn't want to stay anywhere near the corpse-littered mining camp and Preacher certainly couldn't blame her for feeling that way. So once she had gone back into the cabin, gotten dressed, and gathered up everything she wanted to take with her, he dragged the bodies back into the crude structure.

"It would be all right with me if you set fire to the place," she said.

"I gave the idea some thought myself," Preacher said. "I surely did. But the fire might spread, and they's other claims up and down this crick. Wouldn't want to cause trouble for any of those folks." He paused. "I'm a mite surprised none of 'em have showed up to see what all the shootin' was about."

"I'm not," Mattie said. "They had to have heard rumors about what was going on here, and they never came to do anything about *that.*"

"I reckon you've got a point there, girl."

He whistled for Dog, who came bounding out of the woods. Mattie flinched a little from the big cur, but Preacher said, "He won't hurt you," and called Dog over. At his urging, Mattie petted the animal and wound up hugging Dog around the neck while he eagerly licked her face.

"Dog's got mighty good judgment. He don't

never have anything to do with anybody except good folks, so that ought to tell you somethin' right there," Preacher said.

She smiled up at him and said, "You've made your point, Preacher. I'll go back to Deadwood with you . . . but it won't be easy."

"Most things worth doin' ain't."

They rode the mules back to where he had left Horse. He switched over to the gray stallion and led the way back into Deadwood. It was almost midnight when they arrived, but the saloons were still open and doing a brisk business, including the O.K.

"There's a back door," Mattie said. "Can we go around that way so I don't have to walk through the barroom?"

"Sure. Whatever you want, gal."

They went along an alley next to the saloon and dismounted at the back of the building. The rear door was locked, but Mattie knocked on it, explaining, "My mother is nearly always in her office at this time of night, toting up the day's receipts. She can hear the knocking from there."

Mattie was right. A moment later a key rattled in the lock and the door swung open a few inches. Elizabeth Langston said, "Who—"

"Mama," Mattie interrupted her in a choked voice.

Elizabeth threw the door the rest of the way open, caught hold of Mattie, and pulled her into a tight embrace. She said, "Oh!", and the simple exclamation showed just how overcome by emotion she really was.

Preacher stood there holding the reins of Horse and the two mules while mother and daughter enjoyed their reunion. After a long moment, Elizabeth looked over Mattie's shoulder without letting her go and said to Preacher, "You brought her home to me.

"And . . . and those men?"

"They won't never trouble you or the gal again."

She mouthed the words *Thank you* at him, and he could tell how heartfelt they were.

Mattie had started to cry. Between sniffles, she said, "I . . . I was such a fool, Mama—"

"Hush," Elizabeth told her. "There's no need to talk about it anymore. What's done is done, and we're going to put it behind us and never talk about it or even think about it again."

Preacher thought that would be a pretty tall order. He had a hunch these two still had some tough times ahead of them. But as he had told Mattie, they were strong enough to deal with whatever came.

He was just glad he wouldn't have to handle that part of it. He was better at things that required tracking and shooting and knife-fighting. The wilderness of the human heart was still largely unknown country to him, despite his age, and he figured it always would be.

Elizabeth finally let go of Mattie and told her, "Go on upstairs to our rooms. I'll be there in a minute. I just have to talk to Preacher first."

Mattie smiled and nodded.

"All right, Mama. I'll be there."

"I know you will. And that makes me happier than I've been in a long time."

When Mattie was gone, the older woman faced Preacher, who held up a hand, palm toward her.

"If you're fixin' to start talkin' about payin' me wages or givin' me some sort o' ree-ward, you might as well get it outta your head. I done what I did 'cause you and me are old friends, and 'cause if anybody needed killin', it was them there Fredericksons."

Elizabeth shook her head and said, "I won't insult you by offering that, Preacher. But I'd be pleased to . . . give you some good memories to wash away all the violence."

Preacher chuckled.

"I won't say I ain't tempted, even at my advanced age, but I reckon I'd better say no thank you to that, too. I'd sort of like to keep things the way they are betwixt us."

"I can understand that," she said with a nod. "But you need to come into the office for a minute, anyway. I have something for you."

"I done told you—"

"It's a telegram," she said. "From your friend Smoke. He sent it in care of me because he knew you were headed in this direction. He asked that I make sure you got it if I saw you."

"Dadgum it," Preacher said. Telegrams from Smoke always meant trouble. "Must be that blasted Indian Ring actin' up again."

Several times in recent years, he, Smoke, and Matt had had to join forces in order to combat the schemes of the Indian Ring, a group of corrupt politicians, industrialists, and financiers out to loot the tribes of as much as they could.

"I wouldn't know about that," Elizabeth said. "I didn't read the telegram that he sent to you."

"I better have a look," Preacher said.

A minute later they were in Elizabeth's office. Preacher tore open the envelope she gave him and read the message printed on the folded flimsy inside. His eyes took on a dangerous squint.

"I've seen that look before," Elizabeth said. "You're going to have to kill somebody, aren't you?"

"A lot of somebodies, more'n likely," Preacher said.

Book Three

Chapter 25

Territorial Capitol, Prescott, Arizona

The governor of Arizona Territory frowned and said, “What you’re asking us to do, Mr. Jensen, is irregular. Highly irregular.”

“I know that, sir,” Smoke said, “but my brother’s life is at stake. I wouldn’t have brought this proposal to you unless it was very important to me.”

The district attorney of Apache County, who had prosecuted Mordecai Kroll and won a conviction in the case, *harummphed*.

“Important to you because this bounty hunter is your brother,” he said. “But the life of one man doesn’t count for much when weighed against the needs of justice.”

The governor frowned and said, “Let’s not be harsh, Claude. I can understand how Mr. Jensen feels.”

“Thank you, sir,” Smoke said.

“But just because I can sympathize with your problem doesn’t mean that I can grant your request. The Arizona Territory simply isn’t in the habit of allowing convicted murderers and outlaws to escape from custody.”

"Especially not when he's been sentenced to hang like Kroll has," the lawyer added sharply.

Smoke regarded the elderly man sitting across the desk from him. At first glance, John Charles Frémont seemed an odd choice for a territorial governor. Famous from one end of the nation to the other as "the Pathfinder," Frémont had been a soldier, a politician, and most notably an explorer, mapping for the first time much of the country west of the Mississippi. He should have been enjoying a well-deserved retirement.

Smoke had heard the Frémont family had suffered financial reverses, though, and had survived mainly on the income derived from the books and magazine articles written by Frémont's wife, Jessie, about his exploits, some of which she had shared with him. Smoke figured the governor's salary came in handy, as well as giving the family a place to live.

Frémont's background also gave Smoke a hole card that he hadn't played yet and wouldn't unless he needed to. Instead, he said, "Kroll won't be escaping, not really, because he'll have somebody going with him. Me. I'm going to bust him out of Yuma."

"That's insane!" the district attorney exclaimed. "A few men have escaped from Yuma and been brought back. No one has ever staged a successful rescue."

"Well . . ." Smoke smiled. "I reckon I'll have some help."

Frémont leaned forward in his chair. A look of interest appeared on his face.

"You want us to help you make the breakout look genuine," he said.

"That's right. Mordecai Kroll can't suspect that it's not real. He has to believe in it before he'll take me to the hideout."

"How do you know he won't just kill you as soon as you're clear of the prison?"

"I won't give him the chance," Smoke replied. "That's why I said he's not really escaping. Once he's out of Yuma, he'll be my prisoner, just like he was Arizona's prisoner. He'll believe that I've agreed to his brother Rudolph's terms, and that I'm taking him to the hideout to exchange him for my brother Luke."

Earlier, Smoke had shown the two officials the letter he had received from Rudolph Kroll. Arranging this meeting with Frémont and the Apache County district attorney hadn't been easy, and he knew this was probably the only chance he would get to convince them to go along with his plan.

The lawyer said, "I still think it's a big risk just to save the life of one man."

"There's more riding on it than that, sir." Smoke was ready to lay down another card, while still holding his trump in reserve. "Over the past few years, the Kroll gang has pulled off dozens of robberies and collected a small fortune in loot. The law hasn't been able to recover any of that money because nobody has any idea where the gang's stronghold is. But they're bound to have one, and chances are a lot of that money is still there. Mordecai's going to lead me right to it."

"And when he does," Frémont said, "you'll have lost your advantage and the Kroll brothers and their followers will kill you and your brother. That seems painfully obvious to me, Mr. Jensen."

"I'm sure that's their plan," Smoke agreed with a nod. "But I plan to have a couple of surprises for them. I have another brother, and an old friend who's like an uncle to me. They're going to trail us, and when I've freed Luke, they'll join forces with us to deal with the gang and recover that loot."

"Four men?" exploded the district attorney. "You really expect four men to take on dozens of vicious outlaws and not get yourselves killed?"

"Well," Smoke said mildly, "we'll try to work it so we don't have to fight all of them at once."

Frémont leaned back again and laughed.

"I can admire your outrageous attitude, if nothing else, Mr. Jensen," he said. "That's the same sort of spit-in-the-Devil's-eye daring that helped get me through my expeditions."

"I know, sir," Smoke said. "By the way, Preacher

told me to remind you of the time you and he and Kit Carson rode into a Cheyenne village by yourselves to reclaim the horses they had stolen from you."

Frémont's eyes grew wide with surprise at the mention of the old mountain man's name.

"Preacher!" he exclaimed. "You know Preacher?"

"He's that old friend I mentioned, the one who's like an uncle to me," Smoke said.

"You mean he's still alive?" The governor sounded like he couldn't believe it.

"Alive and kicking," Smoke said with a smile.

"Good Lord," Frémont muttered. "You say he's going to follow you and help you defeat the Kroll gang?"

"That's the plan," Smoke said.

The district attorney said impatiently, "You're talking about one man. What possible difference could one man make?"

"When he's the right man, all the difference in the world," Frémont snapped. "Anyway, I believe you said you have another brother, Mr. Jensen. . . ."

"His name's Matt," Smoke said. "A while back he got a special commendation from the governor of Colorado for rescuing a young woman and corralling some outlaws."

Frémont nodded slowly and mused, "I think I heard something about that. You make a compelling argument, Mr. Jensen, but the odds would still be so high against you—"

"Like they were against you and Preacher and Kit Carson that day?"

"That was a different era," the district attorney said.

"Boldness never goes out of fashion," Frémont said. "I'm leaning toward granting your request, Mr. Jensen—"

The door of the governor's office opened abruptly and a man strode in. From behind him, Frémont's secretary said, "I'm sorry, governor, I told the marshal that you were in a meeting and couldn't be disturbed—"

"Meeting be damned," the newcomer said. "What's this I hear about you letting Mordecai Kroll go?"

The district attorney was on his feet. He said, "Marshal Ford, this is inappropriate—"

"No, what's inappropriate is turning loose a blasted murderer who should've been stretching a rope by now!"

"I don't disagree with that sentiment, but all the legal angles of the case have to be given a chance to play themselves out."

Frémont narrowed his eyes at his secretary and said, "I'd be very interested in knowing how you heard about this discussion, Marshal, since I assumed only the three people in this room were privy to the details."

The secretary swallowed hard and started to edge back out of the doorway. He froze when

Frémont added, "Don't go anywhere, Horace."

"It doesn't matter how I heard about it," Marshal Ford said. "Is it true?"

"We're not going to release Mordecai Kroll," the governor said. "What we're considering is making it appear as if Mr. Jensen here has broken him out of prison."

Ford swung his baleful gaze toward Smoke and said, "Jensen?"

"That's right," Smoke said coolly as he got to his feet. "Smoke Jensen."

"The outlaw?"

"All the charges against me were dropped a long time ago."

"The gunfighter, then."

Smoke shrugged. He couldn't very well argue with that designation.

"Mr. Jensen," Frémont said, "I don't believe you've met US Deputy Marshal Simon Ford."

"Haven't had the pleasure," Smoke murmured.

Ford was an inch or so taller than Smoke but built along leaner lines. His powerfully rugged face was dominated by a hawklike nose, piercing blue eyes, and a thin mustache that adorned his upper lip and hung down past the corners of his mouth. His hair was the color of mahogany. He wore a brown tweed suit and carried a black hat with a flat brim, a slightly rounded crown, and a thin silver band decorated with bits of turquoise. Smoke saw the pearl-handled butt of a holstered revolver under the right flap of the suit coat. A deputy US marshal's badge was pinned to Ford's dark gray vest.

"It's not a pleasure," Ford snapped. "I'm a lawman, and I don't take any pleasure out of meeting gunmen unless I'm arresting them."

"For the past year and a half, it's been Marshal Ford's special charge to track down the Kroll gang and bring them to justice," Frémont explained.

"I've worn out a dozen good horses and half a dozen posses in that time, too," Ford said.

"Then you ought to be happy there's a chance to round up the whole gang and recover some of the loot they stole," Smoke said.

Ford snorted in disgust.

"It was bad enough that a damned bounty hunter brought in Mordecai Kroll instead of a bona fide representative of the law. But now to let him go in some hair-brained scheme hatched by a gunslinger—"

"Perhaps you should listen to the plan, Marshal," Frémont suggested. "If you had asked, Mr. Jensen might have been agreeable to you sitting in on this meeting . . . instead of you having to bribe my secretary and who knows how many other minor government functionaries to spy for you and listen for any mention of the Kroll brothers."

Horace gulped again and looked like he wanted

to bolt. This time Frémont waved him away, and the secretary quickly disappeared.

"Why don't you sit down, Marshal?" Frémont invited. "Mr. Jensen, do you have any objection to filling Marshal Ford in on your plan?"

Smoke had objections, all right: He didn't know Simon Ford and didn't trust the man. But it seemed that if he wanted the authorities to go along with him, he didn't have much choice but to comply with the governor's request.

"All right," Smoke said as he nodded.

Grudgingly, Ford sat down. So did Smoke, and for the next few minutes he sketched in the idea he'd had to save Luke, save his own life, and bring the Krolls to justice.

The marshal listened with an increasingly skeptical look on his face. When Smoke was finished, Ford shook his head and said, "It'll never work . . . but there might be an outside chance, under one condition."

"What's that?" Frémont asked.

"I go along, too."

Smoke didn't hesitate. He said, "That's impossible. Mordecai is bound to know you, Marshal—"

"He does," the district attorney said. "Marshal Ford was in court every day."

"But he won't know me except by reputation," Smoke went on. "He'll know that I'm trying to help him because Luke's life is riding on it. And that's what'll make him trust me."

Frémont said, "I agree with you, Mr. Jensen. And I also agree with Marshal Ford that the odds of this plan working are very slim indeed."

Ford started to look satisfied.

Frémont dashed that reaction by continuing. "But the chance to break up the Kroll gang once and for all and recover however much we can of the money they've stolen over the years is simply too tempting. I'm going to order that the arrangements be made. And I sincerely hope that you have God and good luck on your side, Mr. Jensen, because I have a feeling you're going to need all the help you can get."

Chapter 26

Bitter anger filled Deputy United States Marshal Simon Ford as he stood at the bar in a Prescott saloon and nursed a glass of bourbon from his home state of Kentucky. All the long, hard months he had spent pursuing the Kroll gang, he thought, and he had been cast aside like he was nothing.

Once a spring blizzard had caught him by surprise in Wyoming after they had robbed a bank in Laramie, and he had come perilously close to freezing to death before he found shelter.

Another time he had been following their trail across the Texas Panhandle when a sudden thunderstorm swooped up and a tornado descended from the clouds and nearly snatched him up. He'd had to pull his horse into a little wash and force the animal to lie down. Then he'd flattened himself as much as possible while the twister roared past only yards away like a runaway freight train.

Then there was the time some of the outlaws lingered behind the others and bushwhacked him. When the weather was damp, his side still ached where the bullet had drilled him. He'd been forced to hole up in some rocks and had nearly bled to death before the human buzzards finally left. He was pretty sure Mordecai Kroll had been among the men who ambushed him.

Ford could come up with a dozen more instances like those, occasions when he had almost caught up with the gang or when he had almost lost his own life trying to bring them to justice.

The knowledge that a bounty hunter—one of the lowest forms of life on the face of the earth as far as Simon Ford was concerned—had brought in Mordecai Kroll was like a knife in the gut to him. He could have lived with it, though, since Rudolph and the rest of the gang were still out there somewhere and he could continue devoting his efforts to tracking them down.

But then this Smoke Jensen—brother to the bounty hunter and a gunslinger and former fugitive from justice himself—had to show up and convince Governor Frémont to let Mordecai go. The crazy scheme that Jensen had hatched would never work. Ford was certain of that. All it would accomplish was having Mordecai Kroll free in the world again to rob and rape and kill.

Ford picked up the shot glass in front of him and threw back the rest of the bourbon.

"You drink that like a man who has some serious business to attend to."

Ford frowned and looked over to see who had spoken. A young, attractive, dark-haired woman stood there with a half-smile on her richly curved red lips. She wore a gray traveling outfit that she made look elegant, despite the fact that it wasn't terribly expensive.

"A saloon like this is no place for a respectable woman," Ford told her. He hadn't downed enough bourbon to be drunk, but he felt the liquor a little.

"I'm not a respectable woman," she said. "I'm a reporter."

"Newspaper?"

"Magazine. I write for *Harper's Weekly*."

"Impressive," Ford said. He signaled for the bartender to refill the glass. "You're wrong about me having serious business to attend to, though.

Right now drinking is the only business I have."

The bartender came over with a bottle, but the young woman put her hand over the top of Ford's glass and coolly said, "You're the one who's wrong, Marshal. Your business is talking with me. I'd like to interview you."

That took Ford by surprise.

"Why in the world would you want to do that?" he asked her.

"You're Simon Ford, the famous lawman who's devoted his life to tracking down the Kroll gang. A lot of people know about you, and yet you've never been interviewed for a national magazine. I'm sure there are many facts about your life and work that would interest the readers of *Harper's*."

Ford grunted and said, "You mean I'm the man who's had the job of tracking down the Kroll gang taken away from him."

"I'm afraid I don't know what you're talking about."

Ford waved a hand and shook his head.

"Forget it," he told her. "It's a sad, sordid story, not worth the telling."

"Sometimes those are the best kind," she said as she leaned in closer to him. "Does this have anything to do with your meeting with Governor Frémont and District Attorney Hampton from Apache County? That's the county where Mordecai Kroll was tried, isn't it?"

"How do you know I talked to the governor?" Ford asked, somewhat surprised.

"A good reporter has her sources, and she doesn't reveal them," the young woman murmured. "I know there was another man at that meeting, too, but I haven't been able to determine who he was. Why did the governor order you to stop pursuing the Kroll gang, Marshal?"

"Who told you that?"

"You did, just a minute ago. You said the job was taken away from you, and I know you met with Governor Frémont, so I just assumed . . ."

"You're smart."

"For a woman, you mean?" she said, and this time her voice had a trace of waspishness in it.

"No, I just mean that you're smart. Being a woman doesn't have anything to do with anything. Except the fact that you're good-looking, and you can't deny that."

She laughed and said, "I had no intention of denying it. So, Marshal, will you give me that interview?"

"Here?" He waved a hand to indicate the saloon around them, which was handy to the territorial capital but a far cry from fancy.

"I'm staying at a hotel not far from here. But before you get the wrong idea," she went on quickly, "I was suggesting that we talk in the lobby there."

"Of course," Ford said, although for a brief

moment he had entertained other ideas. "Before we continue this conversation, though, I really think you should tell me your name."

"It's Darcy," she said with a smile. "Darcy Garnett."

Darcy wouldn't have said that it was easy to get Marshal Simon Ford to tell her what she wanted to know . . . but it wasn't all that difficult, either. Despite his reputation as a tireless manhunter, he was still a man, and Darcy knew how to bend them to her will. The right combination of flattery and hints of a possible romantic interest would get any man to talk.

"I grew up in Kentucky," he said as they sat in armchairs in the hotel lobby. "My father was a horse trainer, but I never had the knack for it. I can ride the beasts, but that's about all. When I was old enough I went to work as a deputy sheriff. It didn't take me long to discover that was where my real talents lay. Enforcing the law, tracking down outlaws, seeing that justice is done . . . those are the things I'm good at, if I do say so myself."

"Everyone else says the same thing about you, Marshal," Darcy told him.

"Well, I never set out to make a big reputation for myself. All I was ever interested in is doing my job."

"After bringing in as many outlaws as you

have, it must have been very frustrating to have the Kroll gang elude capture."

He frowned, and Darcy hoped she hadn't gone too far. But no, her instincts had led her correctly, she saw as he said, "It wasn't really frustration I felt. It was determination. I figured I could do the job better than anyone else."

"But then Luke Jensen captured Mordecai Kroll."

"Luke Jensen was lucky," Ford spat out. His face darkened with anger, and Darcy wasn't sure whom he hated more, Mordecai Kroll for being an outlaw or Luke Jensen for catching him. "And, of course, the most important thing is that an evil man like that was no longer free to harm innocent people. That's what I really care about the most."

He was lying, Darcy thought. She had no doubt about that. But she just nodded sympathetically instead of saying anything. After a moment Ford continued, as she expected.

"Rudolph Kroll and the rest of the gang are still on the loose, you know."

"I'm sure you planned to continue your pursuit of them."

"Yes, of course. I'll never rest until the whole terrible lot of them are either dead or behind bars where they belong."

"But Governor Frémont doesn't agree with that."

"Frémont was taken in by a crazy scheme,"

Ford said bitterly. He took a cigar from his vest pocket and stuck it in his mouth, clamping his teeth down on the cylinder of tobacco without lighting it. He asked around it, "Do you know who Smoke Jensen is?"

"There's a notorious gunfighter by that name." Darcy sat up straighter as genuine surprise gripped her. "Wait a minute. Is Smoke Jensen related to Luke Jensen?"

"Evidently they're brothers."

"I should have known," she murmured.

"Why? Jensen isn't that uncommon a name. There's even a third brother, a young gunman named Matt. Although I gather that he's adopted, not a blood relation."

Matt Jensen's name was vaguely familiar to Darcy, too. She said, "What do those two men have to do with Luke Jensen, other than being related to him?"

"Jensen's been captured by the Kroll gang," Ford blurted out.

Thank goodness for liquor and jealousy, Darcy thought . . . the reporter's best friends.

"You mean Luke Jensen?"

"Yeah. And his brother Smoke has hatched this wild plan to rescue him by breaking Mordecai Kroll out of jail and taking him to the gang's hideout to return him to Rudolph."

Darcy's heart was racing now, but she made an effort not to let the marshal see how excited she was. She said, "Smoke Jensen was the other man at that meeting with Governor Frémont and District Attorney Hampton?"

"Yeah." Ford rolled the cheroot from one corner of his mouth to the other. "I thought Frémont was too smart to go along with Jensen's plan, but Jensen talked him into it."

Darcy listened avidly as the details of Smoke's plan poured out of Ford's mouth. When he sobered up in the morning, he might regret spilling all this to a reporter . . . if he even remembered doing it.

Actually, he started to look a little wary now as he asked, "Are you going to write about all this for *Harper's*?"

"Oh, someday, perhaps," she replied easily. "Right now it's just background, so I can get the whole picture, you know."

Ford nodded and said, "Good. I don't normally talk like this . . . especially to reporters."

She smiled warmly at him.

"I'm not just any reporter," she said. "I feel like you and I are already friends, Marshal Ford."

"Yeah."

She could practically see the wheels of his brain turning. He was wondering whether or not to suggest that they have a drink together in her room . . . or his.

She stood up and said, "Thank you so much for talking to me. I'll keep all this confidential for the moment, I assure you."

He had gotten to his feet when she did. He nodded and said, “That would probably be a good idea. If there’s anything else . . .”

“No, I have all I need for now. Thank you again.”

She put a gloved hand on his forearm for a second, smiled again, and turned to leave.

“You didn’t make any notes while we were talking,” he said.

She looked back at him and said, “I didn’t need to.” She tapped the side of her head. “It’s all up here.”

And so was the use to which she was going to put the information he had given her. She hadn’t lied to him; she wasn’t going to write about Smoke Jensen’s plan and Governor Frémont’s decision to remove Ford from the case. Not yet.

Not when the rest of the story was out there just waiting for her.

Chapter 27

Smoke’s messages to Matt and Preacher had asked them to get in touch with Sheriff Monte Carson when they received the telegrams, and since starting out for Prescott, Smoke had sent wires to Monte himself, keeping the lawman up to date on his progress. When Monte heard from Matt and Preacher, he was supposed to instruct them to meet Smoke in Prescott.

As it turned out, Matt was closer and reached Prescott first. He had been riding shotgun for Wells Fargo, he explained to Smoke when they met in the hotel, and had broken up a gang of unusual stagecoach robbers just before getting Smoke's telegram.

"But that story can wait for later," Matt said. "What's this all about, Smoke? The Indian Ring acting up again?"

"Actually, I'd rather wait until Preacher gets here, so I'll only have to tell it once," Smoke said. "The whole thing's a mite complicated."

"When do you expect him?"

"I'm not sure. When Monte heard from him, he was up in Dakota Territory, at Deadwood, so it's going to take a little longer for him to get here."

When Monte had let the old mountain man know that Smoke was going to be meeting with Governor Frémont, even without knowing what it was all about Preacher had suggested that Smoke bring up the time he and Frémont and Kit Carson had stood up to those Cheyenne horse thieves. Monte had passed that along, and Smoke had made good use of it. Now he was anxious for Preacher to arrive so the three of them could put their heads together and work out the details of the plan.

As it turned out, Preacher reached Prescott only a little more than a day after Matt. He had been able to take the train part of the way, which had cut down on the time he needed to get there. That evening the three of them sat down to supper in Smoke's hotel room, the meal having been brought up from the kitchen. Smoke was staying in the best place in Prescott. Despite his utter lack of pretension, the Sugarloaf had made him a wealthy man.

"The first thing I have to do," Smoke began, "is tell you about Luke Jensen."

"Your older brother who was killed in the war," Matt said.

"Well, that's just it," Smoke said slowly. "Turns out Luke wasn't killed after all."

Both of the other men looked surprised. Matt exclaimed, "What?"

"Luke was badly wounded when some men he thought were his friends betrayed him. They shot him and left him for dead."

Preacher squinted at him and said, "You're talkin' about them varmints you killed up yonder in Idaho a while back."

"That's right," Smoke said. "In fact, I believed that you were dead then, too."

"I'm pretty hard to kill."

"Turns out Luke was, too. He survived, and he's been living for the past fifteen years under another name."

"Why would he do that?" Matt asked. "How come he never got in touch with you?"

Smoke shrugged and said, "He had his reasons. They seemed like good ones to him, I reckon. He called himself Luke Smith, and he made his living as a bounty hunter. Still does, although he's calling himself Jensen again now."

"I reckon the two o' you must'a run into each other," Preacher said.

"He gave me a hand with some trouble a while back," Smoke said. "And we've tried to keep in touch, although I have to say he's not very good at it. I guess he's just gotten too used to being a loner after all these years."

Matt said, "Did you ever intend to introduce us to him, Smoke?"

"Of course, I did," Smoke said. He thought Matt sounded a little put out. "The three of us just haven't gotten together for a while, and I wanted to tell you about this face to face, instead of in a letter or telegram."

"Well, I guess that makes sense," Matt said, mollified by the explanation. "But now the reason you asked us to meet you here has something to do with Luke, doesn't it?"

"That's right."

Quickly, Smoke sketched in the history of the situation, beginning with Luke's capture of Mordecai Kroll. When he was finished, Preacher said, "I figured you sent us them wires 'cause of some shenanigans the Indian Ring was pullin', but this ain't got nothin' to do with them, does it?"

"Not this time," Smoke said. "This time it's personal Jensen family business. They can't go after one of us—"

"Without going after all of us," Matt finished.

"But you and Preacher haven't even met Luke," Smoke pointed out. "Are you sure you want to risk your necks by going up against a whole gang of vicious outlaws like the Kroll bunch, just to maybe save his life?"

"He's a Jensen, ain't he?" Preacher said.

"He's family," Matt added. "Simple as that."

Smoke grinned and said, "I pretty well figured you'd feel that way, both of you."

"All right," Matt said. "Now that that's settled, fill us in on what we're going to do."

Simon Ford stopped with the pencil in his hand poised over the telegraph form he had spread out on the counter. He read the words he had just printed on the form. Just ten words, but they were enough to change the world. *His* world, anyway.

> I HEREBY TENDER MY RESIGNATION AS DEPUTY UNITED STATES MARSHAL

Surprisingly, he discovered that he didn't really have to think about what he was doing. His mind was made up, and he was confident that he was taking the right course of action, the same natural confidence that had carried him through a long, successful career as a lawman.

Following the other words, he printed: STOP SIMON FORD.

That brought a grim smile to his lips under the drooping mustache.

Nobody was going to stop Simon Ford from doing what was right. Not Governor John Charles Frémont, not some backwater district attorney, and sure as hell not a gunslinger like Smoke Jensen.

He didn't work for Frémont, of course, but rather for the United States Justice Department. The governor couldn't order him to step away from his pursuit of the Kroll gang.

But Frémont could make a formal request that he do so, and as the governor of the territory his request would be honored by Washington. It would carry even more weight because of who Frémont was, his own illustrious background, and the fact that his late father-in-law was Thomas Hart Benton, the powerful, long-time senator from Missouri. Benton had been dead for more than twenty years, but his reputation still cast a shadow in Washington. All of that insured that the Justice Department would go along with Frémont's wishes.

Ford couldn't abide that. He put down the pencil, picked up the telegraph form, and carried it over to the window where he handed it to the telegrapher.

"That goes to the Chief Marshal for the Western District at the Denver Federal Building," Ford told the Western Union man.

The telegrapher read the message, then glanced up at Ford from under his green eyeshade.

"I'm not really supposed to ask this," he said, "but are you sure you really want to send this, Marshal?"

"I wouldn't have written it and given it to you if I wasn't sure," Ford snapped.

"Of course," the man said. He reached for his key and started tapping out the message.

When Ford left the Western Union office a couple of minutes later after paying for the telegram out of his own pocket, he felt as if a weight had been lifted from his shoulders. With that chore taken care of, he could get on with his work. His *real* work.

As he walked along the street, he thought briefly about the young woman called Darcy Garnett. He remembered her name and that she was a journalist who wrote for *Harper's Weekly*. He recalled meeting her in the saloon and then sitting and talking with her in the lobby of her hotel. She was a beautiful, intelligent young woman, he knew that much.

What he didn't know was exactly how much he had told her about the Kroll case and the plan Smoke Jensen wanted to put into effect soon. Ford supposed he had had a bit more to drink that night than he'd thought at the time, because his memories of the conversation with Miss Garnett were fuzzy.

Since that conversation several nights earlier, he had hoped to see her again so he could sound her out about what he'd said and maybe ask her again to keep everything confidential for the time being. She had checked out of the hotel, however, and although he had looked from one end of Prescott to the other, he found no sign of her. Clearly, she had left town.

He couldn't do anything about that. He would have to trust her judgment. When faced with a problem he couldn't solve, Simon Ford didn't linger on it or brood about it. Instead, he put it behind him and moved on to the next challenge.

That was what he did now. His career as a lawman had given him a great many odd bits of information, and he had filed them all away in his mind because a man never knew what might come in handy. He had asked around Prescott and had been given the name of a man, a name he recognized. The sort of a man he would have arrested under normal circumstances, but as far as Ford knew, he wasn't wanted, despite all the rumors about his previous activities.

And these were far from normal circumstances, too. Sometimes you had to make a deal with a lesser devil in order to catch a greater one.

He went into a saloon and looked around. He'd

been told that the man he wanted to talk to could be found here most of the time. The description he had was a good one. The man sat at a table in the back, drinking and playing cards with two other men. The pot in the center of the table looked small, meaning the stakes were low and the game was a friendly one.

The man was slouched in his chair, but even so, Ford could tell that he was tall and well-built. He was dressed all in dusty black range clothes, from the boots on his feet to the hat pushed back on a tangle of sandy curls. He was a handsome man, Ford supposed; the former marshal was no real judge of such things.

One of the other men at the table gave Ford a twitchy glance as he approached. He said, "Lawdog." He and the third man, whose face seemed as lean and sharp as an ax blade, tensed and sat up straighter.

Their black-clad companion didn't seem bothered, though. He barely spared Ford a glance, then put down his cards and said, "Three jacks, boys. I don't think you'll beat that."

The other two tossed in their cards. The man in black grinned and raked the pot to him. Then he looked up and asked, "Something I can do for you, Marshal Ford?"

"You know who I am," Ford said.

"Sure. Just like you know who I am. We're sort of in the same line of work, just on different sides." The man chuckled. "Although, nobody's been able to prove that yet."

"You haven't heard the latest news. I'm not a marshal anymore."

The man cocked a bushy eyebrow and said, "Oh? As of when?"

"As of about ten minutes ago. I just sent my resignation to the chief marshal in Denver. I'm just a private citizen now, Clinton, and it's as a private citizen I want to discuss a business proposition with you."

If the notorious gunman Jesse Clinton was surprised by that, he didn't show it. Instead, he said to his companions, "Clear out, boys. It looks like Marshal—I mean, Mister—Simon Ford and I are gonna talk turkey."

Chapter 28

Yuma Territorial Prison

Smoke had never liked wearing a necktie or anything else tight around his throat. Maybe that came from being unjustly outlawed at a fairly young age and having to live for a while with the possibility he might wind up with a hanging rope around his neck.

That made it doubly awkward wearing a priest's collar around his neck. The thing was uncomfortable and made him want to tug at it, and at the same time the idea seemed blasphemous to him. Even though he considered himself a good man, with all the blood on his hands he shouldn't be pretending to be a man of God, he thought as he trudged toward the front gate of Yuma Territorial Prison. This was a good way to go to hell.

Of course, since he was walking into Yuma, some would say that was exactly where he was going.

Not that the prison, which had been open for a few years, was any worse than many others. In fact, it was considerably better than some, as Superintendent Samuel Jesperson had explained to Smoke when they met to discuss the plan to break out Mordecai Kroll.

At the request of Governor Frémont, the prison superintendent—basically the same as a warden, just a different job title—had agreed to get together with Smoke, Matt, and Preacher at the hotel in the town of Yuma, not far from the prison. Jesperson had had a note of pride in his voice as he said, "The place isn't the hellhole it's made out to be. Why, what with it being up on a hill overlooking the Colorado River, there's often a cool breeze. And since the buildings where the prisoners are housed are all constructed of rock and adobe, it's really rather temperate as far as the climate is concerned."

Smoke didn't really care about that; he didn't intend to be inside the prison long enough to care how hot it might get during the summer.

Preacher said, "I hear the place is full o' snakes and scorpions, though."

Jesperson frowned. He was a tall, well-built man with wavy gray hair and a brush of a mustache. He said, "Well, we're located in desert terrain, and it's impossible to keep all the natural wildlife out, Mister . . . ?"

"Just Preacher," the old mountain man said.

"It's true there are snakes and scorpions and other venomous creatures, but there are some amenities to help make up for that. For example, we have one of the best libraries of any prison in the world."

"What about the guard tower?" Smoke asked in an attempt to steer this conversation back to where it was supposed to be.

"The main one is outside the prison itself, overlooking the sallyport . . . the front gate. There's another tower toward the back of the prison, on the wall next to the caliche hill," Jesperson said. "Unfortunately the men posted in the guard towers are sharpshooters."

"Can't you tell them what's going on and give them orders to miss?" Matt asked.

Smoke said, "Too big a chance Kroll would find out about it somehow."

Jesperson said sharply, "The men who work for me are trustworthy."

"I'm sure they are, but it's too big a chance to take. Besides, if they all were to miss, that might make Kroll suspicious, too."

"So what are you going to do?" Matt asked. "If the guards shoot you, that might make it more believable, but it won't help rescue Luke."

"We'll have to take our chances," Smoke said. "I'm counting on Superintendent Jesperson here to do his part and make Kroll believe he's really being rescued."

"Governor Frémont expressed his belief that this plan is worth trying," Jesperson said. "I'm willing to run the risk and go along with what the governor wants."

They spent more time going over the details of the plan. Then Jesperson had shaken hands with Smoke, Matt, and Preacher and headed back to the prison. Once the superintendent was gone, Matt had expressed another worry.

"Even if everything works out at the prison, you'll have to spend who knows how long traveling with Mordecai Kroll back to the gang's hideout," he said. "From everything you told me about him, Smoke, he's lower than a snake. He's a cold-blooded killer. You won't be able to trust him for a second."

"I don't intend to trust him," Smoke replied with a grim smile. "He'll be my prisoner the whole way."

"Yeah, but you'll stand a better chance of

surviving if you don't have to go it alone," Matt argued. "Why not just take me and Preacher with you? The three of us can handle Kroll better than just one man."

Preacher said, "I'll tell you why we can't do it that way. 'Cause when we got to the hideout, wherever it is, then Kroll's brother and the rest o' them varmints'd have the drop on all of us. We're gonna have to have surprise on our side if we're gonna have any chance of roundin' up the whole bunch."

"Besides," Smoke said, "Rudolph Kroll's letter made it pretty plain that I'm supposed to bring his brother to him by myself. If he sees anybody else with Mordecai and me, he's liable to go ahead and kill Luke."

"Assumin' that Luke is even still alive," Preacher said.

Smoke's face was grim as he said, "He'd better be. If he's not, it'll be up to us to avenge him." He paused, and then went on. "The letter from Rudolph Kroll didn't sound like he knows you two even exist, so he won't be expecting you."

"Well, I suppose that makes sense," Matt said grudgingly. "But I don't have to like it."

"No, you don't have to like it," Smoke agreed. "All you have to do is make sure you don't lose our trail."

"You got to get Kroll outta that prison first," Preacher said.

"Yep, that's the first job."

And it was the job in which he was engaged now, wearing the collar and cassock of a priest, along with a flat-brimmed black hat with a slightly rounded crown. He had donned a pair of rimless spectacles as well, although the lenses in them were clear glass. The long robe was baggy enough to partially conceal his broad shoulders and muscular arms, along with the gun he had tucked into the waistband of his trousers.

This masquerade made Smoke feel like a total idiot. He wasn't cut out to be an actor, that was for sure. But the ruse was the only thing he'd been able to come up with that Mordecai Kroll might believe.

Smoke had driven up from the settlement in a buggy and left it parked outside the wire fence that surrounded the front part of the prison compound. Inside the wire were the administrative buildings, the superintendent's quarters, the guard barracks, the kitchen, and several storehouses.

Beyond those buildings loomed the wall that enclosed the prison itself. Built of adobe and stone, it was a massive barrier some sixteen feet high, about eight feet thick at the base and five at the top. Even though it tapered like that, the slope was still too steep to be scaled.

The only way in or out of the prison was through the sallyport, an arched tunnel through the wall. A closely woven strap-iron gate barred the opening, which was heavily guarded inside and out by rifle-toting guards. In addition, as Jesperson had explained, the main guard tower rose just east of the sallyport and gave the sharp-shooters posted there a commanding view of the prison's entrance.

The superintendent walked alongside Smoke as they advanced toward the sallyport. Quietly, he asked, "Are you sure you want to go through with this, Mr. Jensen? I can't guarantee your safety. I can't guarantee the safety of either of us, for that matter."

"I know," Smoke replied, "and I'm obliged to you for taking that chance, superintendent. If we come through this alive, I'll sure owe you a debt."

"And I may well call it in to collect one of these days." With a faint smile, Jesperson added, "If we come through this alive."

The uniformed guards at the sallyport didn't actually snap to attention as the two men approached, but they did stand up straighter and look more alert. One of them nodded and said, "We didn't know you were visiting the men today, Mr. Jesperson."

"A matter came up unexpectedly," Jesperson replied. "Father Hannigan here has some family news for one of the prisoners."

"Bad news, I hope," one of the other guards muttered. He looked away when Jesperson glared at him.

The first guard called, "Superintendent comin' in!" through the gate as he unlocked it. The guards who worked inside didn't have a key to the massive lock, so they couldn't be forced to open it in the event of a prison uprising.

One of the guards gave Smoke a dubious look, as if he wondered whether they ought to search a priest before letting him in. Then Smoke could practically see the mental shrug the man gave. The superintendent was bringing in "Father Hannigan," so that ought to be enough to vouch for the visitor.

Once they were inside and the gate was closed and locked behind them again, Jesperson told one of the inside guards, "The padre needs to speak to Mordecai Kroll."

"He's in the dark cell, Mr. Jesperson," the guard said. "He won't stop causin' trouble. I reckon he figures he don't have much to lose, since he's already been sentenced to hang and all."

Jesperson nodded and said, "I know that. Bring him out."

"Yes, sir."

The man hurried off toward the dark cell. Jesperson had told Smoke about that infamous hole tunneled into the side of the rocky hill. It was a terrible place, prone to being invaded by rattlesnakes, so any man locked into it had to worry whether he would go mad from darkness and isolation or die of snakebite first. Few prisoners actually did either of those things, but the possibility worried them, as it was supposed to.

Smoke watched as the guard went to a thick wooden door set into the wall and unlocked it. On the other side was a narrow tunnel that ran through the wall and into the caliche of the hillside. At the end of that tunnel the space widened out into a chamber big enough to contain a cage made of iron bars. The cage wasn't quite large enough for an average-sized man to either stand up straight or stretch out on the rock floor, so it was impossible to ever get comfortable in there.

The dark cell was used for punishing troublesome inmates, so they weren't supposed to be able to get comfortable. Smoke would have hated being locked up in there.

The guard lit a lantern hanging on a peg beside the door and took it with him as he entered the tunnel. A few minutes later, he reappeared, using the club he carried to prod a prisoner along in front of him. The man wore a baggy prison uniform with alternating black and yellow horizontal stripes on it. The trousers and shirt hung loosely on his bony frame. His head had been shaved when he entered the prison, the same as any other inmate, but his fair hair had started to grow back during the time he'd been locked up here.

That was Mordecai Kroll, Smoke thought.

Some men just looked evil.

Kroll was one of them.

He stumbled a little, probably because his eyes had to adjust to the light after being shut up in the dark cell. His muscles were probably stiff from the confinement, too. Those were good things. He would be less likely to cause trouble for Smoke if he wasn't in his best shape.

"Here he is, Mr. Jesperson," the guard said as he brought Kroll across the yard to the two visitors.

Jesperson nodded and said, "Thank you, Simmons." He turned to Smoke and went on in harsher tones, "You claimed to have a humanitarian message for this prisoner, Father Hannigan. Deliver it so we can shut him back up where he belongs."

Mordecai Kroll blinked bleary, confused eyes as he peered at Smoke.

"I don't know this blackbird," he croaked. His voice sounded rusty, unused.

"But I know your family, my son," Smoke said. The words sounded ridiculously false in his ears, but the guard didn't seem to find them unusual at all. He supposed prisoners here got visits from various clergymen all the time.

"I don't have any family but my brother," Mordecai snapped. "And he wouldn't have anything to do with the likes of you."

"That's where you're wrong," Smoke said. He slid a hand through an opening in the cassock, closed his fingers around the butt of the Colt, and pulled it out. His movements were unhurried, but they were so smooth the guard didn't even notice what he was doing at first.

Not until Smoke lifted the gun and put the muzzle against the side of Jesperson's head.

"It's your brother who sent me to get you out of there, Mordecai," Smoke said.

Chapter 29

Superintendent Jesperson reacted just the way he was supposed to, gasping in surprise, stiffening, starting to pull away. He was a better actor, thought Smoke. He closed his free hand on Jesperson's shoulder to hold him still. He put enough pressure in the grip to cause a genuine wince on the superintendent's part.

"Hold on there, Jesperson," Smoke grated. "You're not going anywhere."

The guard had finally realized what was going on. He ripped out a curse and stepped toward Smoke, lifting his club as he did so.

"Don't do it!" Smoke warned. "I'll put a bullet through your boss's skull."

"If you do that, you'll be dead a second later," Jesperson said in a shaky voice. "My sharpshooters are bound to have you in their sights right now."

Smoke smiled faintly and said, "If their eyes are good enough for them to be sharpshooters, they can see that I've got the trigger tied back on this gun. My thumb on the hammer is all that's keeping it from splattering your brains all over this yard, mister. So you better tell them not to get itchy trigger fingers, because they can't kill me without killing you, too."

That part was true, so Jesperson had to hope that his men were willing to follow his orders. Smoke wasn't going to come in here with an unloaded gun, not when he had to deal with an animal like Mordecai Kroll. He had confidence that as long as he was alive, the gun in his hand wouldn't go off unless he wanted it to.

"Hold your fire!" Jesperson shouted. His voice shook with anger and fear. They had passed the point of no return now, so this escape or rescue or whatever anybody wanted to call it was pretty much real.

Mordecai still looked confused, but he had perked up at the sight of Smoke's gun pressed to the superintendent's head.

"Go on and kill him!" he urged Smoke. "Blow the bastard's brains out!"

"If I do, there'll be so many bullets flying around before Jesperson even hits the ground that you and I both won't make it out of here alive, Kroll," Smoke said. His voice was hard as flint. "And I need you alive, you damned fool."

Mordecai's face twisted in anger, but he didn't take it out on Smoke. Instead, he whirled around, moving faster than a man who had just come out of the dark cell should have been able to manage, and grabbed the bludgeon from the startled guard. Before Smoke could say anything, Mordecai slapped it across the guard's head and drove the man to his knees. Blood welled from a gash the blow had opened up.

"Stop it!" Smoke said as Mordecai drew the club back to strike the guard again. The first blow hadn't done much real damage, but another one might prove fatal. "I swear, Kroll, you kill that man and I'll leave you in here."

Mordecai sneered at Smoke.

"You can't do that, *padre*," he said jeeringly. "You already told me you need me alive."

"You can live with a bullet through the knee."

Mordecai thought about it, Smoke could tell that, but then he tossed the club aside and said, "Ah, hell, it ain't worth it. You say Rudolph sent you to rescue me?"

"I'll tell you all about it later," Smoke said curtly. "Get over here next to me and the superintendent."

By now the prison was full of noise. A few prisoners had been in the yard when Smoke made his move, but the other guards had herded them back through metal gates into the alleys that ran among the stone cell blocks. That didn't stop them from yelling to other inmates that a prison break was going on. The shouts that went back and forth raised a real tumult.

So did the clanging of an alarm bell. The racket had to reach the nearby town. Smoke knew some of the local badge-toters might rush to the prison to help and he didn't need that added complication, but he would just have to deal with that if it happened.

Mordecai crowded up next to Smoke and Jesperson. Smoke could smell the man's stench. He said, "Stay close. We're going to walk out of here."

"You'll never get away with it," Jesperson blustered. "You won't make it out of the prison before someone shoots you both."

"You'd better hope that's not true, mister," Smoke told him coldly. "Come on."

They started toward the sallyport at a shuffling walk. The guards on this side didn't have a key to the gate, so the outer guards could still call his bluff and there wasn't a blasted thing he could do about it. If that happened, the whole plan would collapse.

In that case, Smoke would have to try to persuade Mordecai Kroll to reveal where the gang's hide-out was located. That was a real longshot. Smoke wouldn't have any leverage to force Mordecai to talk.

That was why it was so important that Mordecai believe what was happening now was real. As long as he thought the rescue was genuine and that Smoke had done it solely in an attempt to free Luke, Mordecai would be best served by cooperating. Once they got out of here—*if* they got out of here—everything Smoke told Mordecai would be the truth.

He just wouldn't tell the outlaw the *whole* truth, which included Matt and Preacher trailing them to the hideout.

As they drew closer to the sallyport, Smoke pressed harder against Jesperson's temple with the gun barrel.

"Order those boys outside the gate to unlock it," he said.

"They . . . they won't do it," Jesperson said. He was really scared now, Smoke could tell, scared that everything would go wrong and he'd wind up dead.

"You'd better hope they do."

Jesperson swallowed hard and called, "Unlock the gate!"

One of the guards inside the gate said, "Mr. Jesperson, you know how we handle these things. We can't—"

"Unlock the damned gate! Can't you see this madman's going to kill me?"

The guard gave them a long, hard look, then turned his head and nodded to one of the men outside. Smoke heard the key scrape in the lock. It was a very welcome sound.

So was the squeal of hinges as the gate swung back.

Still moving at a shuffling walk, Smoke and his companions moved through the sallyport. Then they were in the outer yard. Smoke's gray eyes flicked toward the main tower. He saw the riflemen up there pointing their weapons at him and the other two men. But they held off on the triggers, and Smoke steered Jesperson and Mordecai Kroll toward the buggy that was waiting for them.

"You'll have to ride out with us, Jesperson," he said. "Get that other gate open."

Guards armed with rifles and pistols stood at a discreet distance, waiting to see what was going to happen. Jesperson told one of them, "Go open the outer gate, Cramer."

"Sir, are you sure—" the guard began.

"Just do it!"

The guard nodded and trotted off to follow the order. After this, Jesperson would have some work to do to repair his reputation as a tough, hard-nosed prison official. But once he revealed that he had been acting under orders from the governor, that would go a long way toward clearing things up.

The outer gate was opened. Smoke said, "Kroll, you'll have to drive. You can handle a buggy team, can't you?"

"Just watch me!" Mordecai said.

"Jesperson, in the backseat with me. Come on, up you go."

They all climbed into the vehicle. It wasn't easy for Smoke to keep the gun to Jesperson's head as they did so, but he managed. Once they were in the buggy, Mordecai grabbed the reins, yelled at the horses, and slashed the trailing ends of the lines across their rumps. The team took off fast enough to push Smoke and Jesperson back against the rear seat.

Mordecai wheeled the buggy around and sent the horses through the gate at a gallop. The buggy bounced and rocked behind them. Unable to see the passengers because of the black canvas cover over the seats, the guards couldn't risk shooting through it. There was too big a chance they would hit the superintendent.

With Mordecai continuing to whip the horses and yell at them, the buggy careened into the trail that ran north along the river into an area of largely arid wilderness broken by occasional small ranges of low mountains. The Gila River was up there, too, but there was a ferry across it and Smoke already had plans for that.

"Shoot that son of a bitch now that we're outta there!" Mordecai called over his shoulder.

"Just keep driving!" Smoke replied over the hoofbeats of the running team. "They'll be sending Apache trackers and a posse after us! We need to put some distance between us and them!"

Actually, they wouldn't be sending out a posse . . . or rather, they would, but it wouldn't get very far. Jesperson would see to that. As far as Mordecai Kroll was concerned, though, he and Smoke would give the slip to any pursuit.

When they had gone about a mile, Smoke whispered in Jesperson's ear, "Are you ready?"

The superintendent gave a small, nervous nod.

"Slow down!" Smoke shouted to Mordecai.

"What? Slow down? Are you loco?"

"Just for a minute. Do it, Kroll!"

Smoke still had the only gun, so Mordecai hauled back on the reins and slowed the team. Smoke lifted the Colt and struck with it, appearing to smash it down on the back of Jesperson's head.

In reality the blow just grazed Jesperson's upper back, but it would look real enough if Mordecai glanced back, which he did. Jesperson went limp, and Smoke shoved him out of the buggy. He crashed to the ground and rolled over a couple of times.

"What the hell did you do that for?" Mordecai yelped. "He was our hostage!"

"We don't need him anymore, and he'd just slow us down in the long run. Keep going! Whip up those horses again!"

Mordecai obeyed the command, although he still looked angry. He had a man with a gun at his back, though, so he had to do what Smoke said.

Jesperson would lie there as if unconscious until the buggy was out of sight, then get up, brush himself off, and wait for the posse to catch up. That was when he would reveal what was really going on and call off the pursuit.

Pretty soon, the only ones following Smoke and Mordecai Kroll would be Matt and Preacher.

And that was just the way Smoke wanted it.

Chapter 30

After a few minutes Smoke looked back and saw a dust cloud hanging in the air behind them, as if the guards from the prison were giving chase. Smoke figured by now they probably had come upon Jesperson and discovered that the superintendent had been a willing participant in the scheme. They could ride around in circles for all Smoke cared, as long as their horses kicked up that dust and made things look realistic.

Mordecai Kroll saw the dust, too, and said over his shoulder, "They're after us! I told you we should'a hung on to Jesperson!"

"We'll be all right," Smoke told him. "We just have to make it to the Gila."

"What good's that gonna do us?"

"You'll see," Smoke said.

"Mister, who in blazes *are* you? I know damned well you ain't really a priest!"

Smoke laughed and said, "You never saw a gun-toting padre before?"

"Maybe there's been a few, but you ain't one of 'em," Mordecai insisted. "You said my brother sent you. Did he pay you to get me outta there? Why didn't he come himself?"

"Just keep driving," Smoke ordered. "All your questions will be answered in due time."

Mordecai obviously didn't like being told what to do, or being kept in the dark, but he slapped the reins against the horses' rumps and called out to them again. The buggy kept rolling fast over the northbound trail.

They passed through some rolling, brushy hills as they approached the Gila River. The trail veered away from the Colorado. By the time they came in sight of the Gila, the confluence of the two rivers was about a mile west of where they were.

Up ahead, a rope-drawn ferry crossed the stream, which was about sixty feet wide at this point, with a fairly strong current. A horse could swim from one side to the other, but the crossing would be risky.

The ferryman had a shack on the southern bank; there was nothing on the northern bank except the landing that stuck out a few feet into the river. The thick rope that was attached to the ferry looped around a capstan on both sides. A mule was harnessed to one of the poles that stuck out from the capstan on the southern bank and provided the power for the ferry, which at the moment was at this end of the rope.

A stocky, gray-haired man came out of the shack as Mordecai drove the buggy up to the landing. As he walked toward them, he said, "Don't get many buggies goin' across the river. Mostly just prospectors with their mules and outfits—"

The garrulous ferryman stopped short at the sight of Mordecai in his prison garb. Being this close to Yuma, he had to be familiar with what the inmates wore. His eyes widened and he started to back off.

"Say, I can't—"

Smoke hopped down from the buggy and leveled the Colt at the man.

"Sure you can," he said easily. "Let down the bar on the ferry. We don't have any time to waste."

The gray-haired man swallowed hard. He moved to the ferry and let down the bar that closed it off.

"Drive on there," Smoke told Mordecai, who eased the buggy onto the big raft with a railing around it.

Smoke stepped onto the ferry, too, and reached into the buggy to withdraw a Winchester he had placed on the floorboard before he ever drove out to the prison. He worked the rifle's lever and pointed it at the ferryman.

"Just in case you get any ideas about stranding us in the middle of the river," Smoke said. "I promise you I can knock you down with this repeater before you could make it back to your shack."

"Padre, I believe you," the ferryman said fervently. "I never knowed a priest to lie yet."

Despite the seriousness of the situation, Smoke had to make an effort not to chuckle.

The ferryman fastened the gate, then went to the mule and grasped its harness. He pulled on it and said, "Come on, you jughead. If you get me shot, I ain't never gonna forgive you."

The mule began plodding in a circle. That turned the capstan and pulled the rope. The ferry lurched out away from the landing and started across the river. As it neared the middle of the stream, Smoke felt the current tugging on it, but the sturdy rope held easily and the crossing continued.

Smoke kept the rifle trained on the ferryman, who didn't know anything about the escape plan and had to assume that Smoke was really helping Mordecai Kroll get away from the prison. Believing his life to be in danger, the man followed orders and kept the capstan turning until the ferry reached the landing on the north side of the river.

There Smoke unlatched the gate and stepped off first so that he could cover Mordecai with the rifle, too. He backed away a few steps while Mordecai drove the buggy across the landing onto the bank.

"Hold it right there," he said. He walked to the buggy and took out an ax he had concealed in the back along with the rifle.

Most men would need both arms to swing an ax like Smoke did then, but he accomplished it one-handed while he held the rifle in his other hand. With a few swift, accurate strokes, he chopped through the rope. When the first stroke landed, the ferryman shouted indignantly, "Hey!" but Smoke ignored him.

Mordecai laughed when he saw what Smoke was doing.

"Whoever you are, mister, you're pretty smart," he said. "That posse won't be able to cross the river after us now. They ain't likely to try swimmin' their mounts across, anyway."

"That's the idea," Smoke said. He grunted and swung the ax one more time. The keen edge bit through the last strands of the rope. It collapsed into the water.

The ferryman howled in anger at the destruction.

The damage could be repaired, Smoke knew, and anyway, he intended to see to it that the man was compensated for his trouble. It was all part of the price of saving Luke's life. This ought to finish the job of convincing Mordecai that the escape was genuine.

Leaving the ferryman yelling curses at them, Smoke swung up into the buggy and said, “Let’s go.” Mordecai got the team moving again.

“You still haven’t told me who you are, mister. You sure as hell ain’t Father Hannigan.”

“Keep driving,” Smoke told him. “Putting the ferry out of commission will stop any pursuit for a while, but a posse could always go upstream and find a ford somewhere else.”

“Not for a good long ways,” Mordecai said. “I know this part of the country. By the time they can get on our trail again, we’ll be so far ahead of them they won’t be able to catch up.” He laughed. “I’m free, damn it! Free!”

Smoke had seen Mordecai eyeing his guns more than once. He knew what was going through the outlaw’s mind now that they were well clear of the prison. If Mordecai could get his hands on a gun, he could kill his rescuer and set off on his own. That would simplify matters.

Besides, Mordecai wouldn’t like owing a debt to anybody. There was too big a chance they would want something in return. Easier just to accept a benefactor’s help . . . then kill him.

Smoke wasn’t going to let that happen.

Mordecai drove for several more miles. The farther they got from the river, the more arid and rugged the landscape became. Smoke finally pointed to a canyon formed by twin buttes that jutted up from the ground and told Mordecai, "Drive up in there."

"What for?"

"I want to rest the horses, and that looks like a spot where nobody will be likely to see us."

Mordecai shrugged as if that made sense to him. He steered the buggy into the canyon, which was about twenty yards wide.

Smoke, Matt, and Preacher had scouted out this spot a day earlier. It was where Matt and Preacher would pick up their trail, rather than having to follow the buggy all the way from the prison. Smoke's plan was to leave marks along the way to make trailing them easier, without Mordecai noticing what he was doing, of course.

A couple of small cottonwood trees grew at the base of one of the mesas, and marked the location of a tiny spring that wasn't much more than a trickle. It was enough to keep some grass growing there, however. That grass provided graze for the four saddle mounts Smoke had picketed here.

Mordecai saw the horses and grinned.

"You planned out this whole thing, didn't you?" he said. "I was afraid we were gonna have to keep using this buggy."

"No, we'll be leaving it here," Smoke said.

He saw the cunning expression that appeared for a second on Mordecai's face. The outlaw was already trying to figure out his next move, which Smoke was sure would involve getting rid of him.

Unfortunately for Mordecai, Smoke was already a couple of steps ahead of him.

"Pull up over there next to the spring," Smoke said as he pointed toward the trees.

Mordecai brought the buggy to a halt and jumped down from it. He stretched and grinned in satisfaction.

"The air sure smells better when a man is free," he said.

"I reckon you're right about that," Smoke said as he stepped down to the ground. "Hold the horses so they don't drink too much. As small as that spring is, they might drink it dry."

"Yeah, wouldn't want that," Mordecai said. "This is dry country around here."

Smoke set the Winchester on the wagon seat and took off the cassock. It was hot and hampered his movements, and he was glad to be rid of it. He threw it behind the seat, took the collar off, and tossed it into the buggy as well. Under the cassock he wore his usual range clothes, denim trousers and a faded butternut work shirt. He traded the priest's hat for his own Stetson, which was also hidden behind the buggy's rear seat along with his gun belt. When he had buckled it on and slipped the Colt into its holster, he felt normal again for the first time since the masquerade began.

"See, I knew you weren't no priest," Mordecai said as Smoke walked up to him, carrying the Winchester again.

"You're right," Smoke said. "A priest wouldn't do this."

He moved so fast that Mordecai had no chance to stop him. He brought the rifle up and smashed the butt against the back of Mordecai's head, dropping the outlaw senseless to the ground at his feet.

Chapter 31

By the time Mordecai Kroll groaned, shifted on the ground, and started to come around, Smoke had him tied hand and foot. He had dragged Mordecai into the shade cast by the mesa, thus sparing him the blazing Arizona sun.

As far as Smoke was concerned, that was more consideration than the outlaw deserved. Mordecai dying of heatstroke wouldn't bring him any closer to freeing Luke, however.

Mordecai pried his eyes open and saw Smoke hunkered next to a small fire, sipping from a cup of coffee. The pot sat at the edge of the flames, staying hot.

Right away, Mordecai started to curse. Venom

and obscenity poured from his mouth. Smoke let the filth spew for a few moments. Then when Mordecai paused to take a breath, he said calmly, "Keep that up, Kroll, and I'll gag you."

"You can't—"

"Try me and see."

Mordecai lay there glaring murderously at him, then said with a whine in his voice, "Why'd you wallop me? I thought you were helpin' me get away."

"I am," Smoke said. "But I can't afford to let you double-cross me. You were already thinking about killing me since you figure I'm not any more use to you now that you're out of prison."

Mordecai didn't bother trying to deny that. Instead, he asked sullenly, "What is it you want from me? You intend to make my brother pay ransom to get me back?"

"In a way, that's exactly what I'm going to do. You said you don't think I'm really a priest. You're right about that, Kroll. My name is Smoke Jensen. That mean anything to you?"

"Same last name as that no-good bounty hunter who got lucky and caught me." Mordecai frowned. "Seems like I've heard of you, too. Smoke Jensen . . . Hell, yeah! You're that Colorado gunfighter."

"I'm also Luke Jensen's brother," Smoke said.

Mordecai sneered at him.

"I'd say I can see the family resemblance, but to

tell the truth, I can't. I don't even remember that well what the damn bounty hunter looks like."

"Maybe you'll recognize him when you see him again."

"You're takin' me to him?" Mordecai asked as a worried look appeared on his face.

"In a manner of speaking," Smoke said. He took another sip of the coffee. "Your brother is holding him prisoner. Rudolph sent me a letter saying that if I didn't bust you out of prison and bring you to him, he was going to kill Luke."

Mordecai just stared at him for several seconds. Then, abruptly, the outlaw threw his head back and brayed with laughter.

"Mister, that's just about the funniest turn of events I ever heard of," he said as the echoes of his ugly laughter bounced between the twin buttes. "Your brother is responsible for me bein' in that hellhole, and you have to get me out to save his life! Mighty fittin', don't you think?"

Smoke didn't think so at all, but he wasn't going to waste time saying as much to Mordecai Kroll. Instead, he told the outlaw, "Rudolph gave me instructions in his letter. He said I was to get you out of Yuma—although he didn't say how, he left that up to me—and told me I was to bring you to the gang's hideout by myself. He said you'd tell me how to find it and that if I didn't come alone, he'd kill Luke. Once I've turned you over safely to him, he'll let Luke and me go."

Mordecai nodded, solemn now, and said, "He'll do it, too, if that's what he told you. My brother's a man of his word. Just because he's an outlaw, that don't make him a liar."

Smoke didn't believe that for a second, but he wasn't going to make an issue of it at this point. Instead, he said, "I hope you're right, because I've risked everything in order save *my* brother."

Mordecai wiggled around in an effort to get more comfortable where he was sitting with his back propped against a rock. He said, "Now that you've told me all this, how come you got me tied up? Seems to me like we're workin' together, not against each other?"

"I need you alive and well to tell me how to find the hideout, but like I said before, you don't really need me anymore. If you got a chance, you'd kill me and take off back to your brother and the rest of the gang on your own. Once you got there, you could kill Luke. I'm sure you'd enjoy that."

"I won't lie to you," Mordecai said. "I surely would enjoy it. But a deal's a deal. You made one with Rudolph, and he'd be upset with me if I didn't honor it. So you can turn me loose now—"

"Forget it," Smoke cut in. "You're staying tied up until we get where we're going. That's my best chance to get my brother out of this mess alive."

Mordecai glared at him again.

"I'm gonna tell Rudolph how you mistreated me," he threatened. "This is gonna backfire on you, Jensen."

"I'll take that chance. In the meantime, after the horses have rested for a few more minutes, I'll get you in a saddle and tie you onto one of the mounts. We're taking all six animals with us, so we'll always have fresh horses for the journey. If you want to, you can go ahead and tell me where the hideout is."

"So *you* can kill *me* and go after your bounty-huntin' brother by yourself?" Mordecai shook his head. "No thanks. Like you said, you need me alive as long as you don't know where the hideout is. I reckon we'll keep it that way." He grinned. "And we'll see who stays alive the longest. . . ."

Once Marshal Simon Ford had told Darcy all about Smoke Jensen's plan, it hadn't taken long for her to find out even more.

She had sent several telegrams and within a couple of days had received replies that told her considerably more not only about Smoke and Matt, but also about an old mountain man known as Preacher who seemed to be a close friend of the Jensen brothers. Close enough to be considered an adopted uncle or even a surrogate father.

Although the details were sketchy, it was rumored that in the past the Jensens and Preacher had banded together to clash with several powerful politicians and businessmen. In certain circles, they were regarded with suspicion and outright hostility.

This case had nothing to do with their political activities, but that background was still enough to make it a more interesting story. Readers loved tales of corruption and chicanery in the halls of power. The slightest connection to that was enough to perk up a story.

The public also enjoyed reading about outlaws and gunmen. Jesse James, although he seemed to be lying low in recent months, was still a major celebrity known from one end of the country to the other. Before Darcy was through, the Kroll brothers would be even more notorious than Jesse and *his* brother Frank.

Blood and thunder, political wheeling and dealing—what else could you call that meeting with Governor Frémont?—lawbreakers, brotherly love on both sides. . . . It was too bad there wasn't a beautiful woman involved somewhere, preferably as the object of romantic rivalry between two men, she thought as she walked toward a livery stable in the town of Yuma, Arizona Territory. Then the story would have everything.

She would just have to do the best with what she had, she told herself.

To further that end, she wore a riding outfit

today, a split brown riding skirt, a white shirt open at the throat, a brown vest, and a flat-crowned brown hat. She knew she looked fetching, which never hurt when she was about to ask a favor of a man. Or in this case, two men.

Persistent inquiries had led her to Smoke Jensen, and once she'd found Smoke, she found his two companions as well. The young, big, handsome blond man was Matt Jensen. The grizzled old-timer in buckskins was Preacher. They were in the stable saddling their horses when Darcy came in. A couple of pack animals, already loaded with supplies, were hitched nearby.

Matt Jensen glanced at her, then looked again. Darcy was used to that reaction from men, but she had to make an effort not to smile anyway. She nodded and said, "Mr. Jensen?"

She spoke to Matt instead of Preacher because she had already noticed that the older man was regarding her warily. A man of his years was more likely to prove immune to her charms, although if she could get him to remember the days of his youth, she could probably change that.

"I'm Matt Jensen," he said politely. "Have we met, ma'am?"

"Not until now. I'm Darcy Garnett."

Now she smiled. Matt smiled back, which she took as an encouraging sign.

"Matt Jensen, Miss Garnett," he said as he reached up to tug on the brim of his hat. "It is *Miss* Garnett?"

"It is," Darcy said.

Matt leaned his head toward his companion and said, "This is Preacher."

Preacher nodded, but the only sound he made was an unfriendly grunt.

"Don't mind him," Matt went on. "He's rough as an old cob. Not used to being around civilized folks. What can we do for you, Miss Garnett?"

"Well, you see, I'm a reporter. I've been writing for *Harper's Weekly*."

It was only one story she had sold to the magazine, but she didn't consider her statement too much of a stretch.

"When I heard that the famous Jensen brothers were in town," she continued, "I knew I had to see if the two of you would grant me an interview."

Now Matt looked almost as wary as Preacher. He shook his head and said, "No offense, miss, but nobody would want to read about Smoke and me."

"Are you having a bit of sport with me, Mr. Jensen? Your brother is one of the most famous gunfighters in the West, and you're making a name for yourself that's going to rank you as his equal very soon. Everyone wants to read about the two of you."

She paused, weighed the situation, and decided she might as well go ahead and play her trump card. She wasn't going to get anywhere with flattery or playing up to Matt. He might enjoy it, but it wouldn't sway his decisions.

"Especially since you've joined forces to rescue your other brother from the clutches of the Kroll gang," she said.

Matt drew in a sharp breath, obviously trying not to reveal his surprise but failing.

"You know about Luke?" he asked.

"I wrote about his capture of Mordecai Kroll, as well as Mordecai's trial and conviction. And I know that he's been captured by Rudolph Kroll, who has threatened his life if your brother Smoke doesn't rescue Mordecai."

"How the hell—Beg your pardon, Miss Garnett."

"It's all right," Darcy said. "I'd be startled, too, if I were you. You thought all of this was a secret, didn't you?"

Preacher asked in a harsh voice, "What do you want, gal?"

"It's really quite simple," Darcy said. "I know the two of you are going to trail Smoke and Mordecai back to the Kroll stronghold." She smiled again. "I want you to take me with you."

Chapter 32

Simon Ford and Jesse Clinton were in the saloon when a man rode up outside on a lathered horse, swung down from the saddle, and hurried into the building. He came straight to the table in the back where Ford and Clinton were sitting. He was the man with the face like an ax blade, Clinton's segundo Lew Hooke.

Without sitting down, Hooke said, "I followed the buggy all the way to the ferry over the Gila River. They crossed over, and then Jensen took an ax to the ferry rope."

"He was making it look good for Kroll," Ford said. He pushed away the glass of bourbon he'd been nursing. The waiting was over, and he was glad. "He wanted Kroll to think he did that to keep the posse from following them, but the posse had already turned back, hadn't it?"

"As soon as they came up to the spot where Jensen left the prison superintendent," Hooke reported. In the several days Ford had known him, he had never seen Hooke smile even faintly, and that didn't change now.

Clinton, on the other hand, seldom stopped grinning. That's what he was doing as he said,

"Pretty smart fella, that Smoke Jensen. His mistake was letting you find out about his plan, Simon."

Ford managed not to grimace when Clinton used his first name. The gunman seemed to think they were friends of some sort now, just because he and his men were working for Ford. That wasn't the way Ford saw it at all. He could never be friends with a man who was probably an outlaw himself.

But he needed Clinton and the others, so he had to tolerate the man's familiarity. He had promised that Clinton and his men could have all the rewards for the Kroll brothers and their gang, which would add up to a small fortune. Ford didn't want any of the bounty money for himself.

He just wanted to see justice done.

"Are you sure Jensen didn't spot you trailing them?" Clinton asked Hooke.

"I was careful," Hooke said. "Stayed 'way off to the east and watched them through field glasses. It wasn't too hard. They were in a buggy. Jensen got into the prison by pretending to be a priest."

"A priest?" Clinton repeated. He guffawed and slapped his thigh. "I like this man Jensen. He's got audacity."

"He's a stubborn fool," Ford snapped.

"Maybe . . . but he got Mordecai Kroll out of Yuma Prison, didn't he?"

That plan had been risky enough that Ford wouldn't have been surprised if it failed. Clearly, though, Jensen had pulled it off, and now he was on the way to the Kroll gang's hideout.

Soon, Ford would be, too, with his newly acquired allies.

"What do we do now?" Lew Hooke asked.

"Matt Jensen and the old man will follow Jensen and Kroll," Ford said, somewhat irritated that he had to go over this again. Hooke was a good tracker and a dependable man, according to Clinton, but he wasn't too bright. "We'll follow them, and sooner or later they'll lead us to the hideout."

"I've got a man watching the livery stable," Clinton added. "He'll let us know when Matt and Preacher ride out. That'll probably be pretty soon, so you'd better round up the other men and tell them to be ready to ride at a moment's notice, Lew."

Hooke nodded but didn't turn to leave just yet.

Ford pushed himself to his feet, leaving the bourbon undrunk on the table.

"I'll go see to my horse," he said. "All my gear is packed already."

He walked out of the saloon, glad for the opportunity to spend a final few minutes alone, away from the unpleasant company of the hired guns. Soon enough, he would be spending all his days and nights with them.

But the goal at the end would be worth it, he told himself: Rudolph and Mordecai Kroll and all their men, either dead or on their way to prison and ultimately the gallows.

Yes, very much worth it, indeed.

Hooke jerked his head toward the bat wings where Ford had just stalked outside and said, "He's crazy, isn't he?"

"Loco as he can be," Clinton agreed. "He's been chasing the Kroll brothers for so long that they've crawled into his ear and burrowed into his brain like devil worms. But he's going to help us get rich."

Hooke said, "I don't see why we even have to take him along. We can follow the other Jensen and the old man without Ford's help. We can just leave him here." He paused, and then added, "Better yet, kill him and leave him in the desert somewhere."

"No, I believe in following my hunches, and I've got one that tells me it might come in handy to have him along, sooner or later. He's like a dog that's been trained to attack, Lew. When the time comes, we'll point him at the Krolls and turn him loose."

Even though Clinton was still smiling, his voice held a hard undercurrent that made it clear he was the boss here and gave the orders, not Hooke.

"Then once the Krolls and their bunch are

wiped out, we can kill Ford and the Jensens and the old man, and nobody will ever know they weren't gunned down in the fighting. We collect the bounties, but more importantly, we take all the loot the Krolls have cached, too. Nobody'll know that, either. It'll just be a shame that everybody who knew where the money was hidden got killed before the law could question 'em."

"I've said it before, Jesse, but I'll say it again. You are one smart hombre."

The cocky grin flashed across Clinton's face again as he said, "And handsome, too!"

Matt tried not to stare at Darcy Garnett, but it wasn't easy. Preacher didn't go to that much bother. He just looked at Darcy like she was the strangest thing he had ever seen.

Finally, Matt said, "I don't know what you're talking about, Miss Garnett. Preacher and I are going to do a little prospecting."

"Yeah," Preacher said dryly. "We got the gold fever."

"Please," Darcy said, still smiling. "I think it should be obvious that I know a lot more than you want to give me credit for. Lying about the situation isn't going to get you anywhere."

"I don't much cotton to being called a liar," Matt said.

"Then tell the truth," Darcy shot back at him.

"There's only one reason you'd be here in Yuma on the same day that the alarm bells ring up at the prison. Your brother Smoke broke Mordecai Kroll out of there earlier this afternoon, didn't he? There's been no official explanation of all the commotion up there, but that's bound to be what happened. Now the two of you are going to take up their trail." She paused. "Do you really think that three men can defeat the entire Kroll gang? Or four, if you succeed in rescuing Luke Jensen. You'll be outnumbered ten to one."

"We make a habit of dealing with things as they come to us," Matt replied. "Now let me ask you a question, Miss Garnett?"

"It's all right if you call me Darcy."

Matt ignored that and said, "For the sake of argument, let's say that you're right about all these crazy guesses you've made."

"They're not guesses. It's information I've uncovered thanks to my journalistic efforts."

"Doesn't matter what you call it. Let's say you're right. If you are . . . if Preacher and I are about to ride off to God knows where, hoping to find the hideout of one of the worst outlaw gangs in the whole country, what in the world makes you think we'd be willing to take a woman with us?"

"Not a woman," Darcy snapped. "A reporter."

Matt took a deep breath and controlled his temper.

"All right, then. A reporter. We'd have to be looking out for you rather than taking care of the business that brought us there. *If* there was any truth to that wild yarn you've been spinning."

"I can take care of myself." Darcy gestured at the clothes she wore. "You can see that I'm dressed appropriately for riding."

Preacher snorted and said, "For ridin' in one of them danged Wild West shows, maybe."

Matt shook his head and turned to pull the cinch on his saddle tight. He said, "Sorry, Miss Garnett. You've wasted your time. Preacher and I don't have anything else to say to you."

"You're missing a wonderful opportunity," Darcy persisted. "I can make you famous by writing about you."

That statement was so ludicrous Matt had to look at her again and say, "What in the world makes you think I want to be famous?"

Then he nodded to Preacher, put his foot in the stirrup, and swung up on the horse's back. He took the reins of one of the pack animals. Preacher mounted up as well and led the other packhorse. They rode out of the livery stable, leaving Darcy behind to glare after them.

"If that don't beat all," Preacher muttered as they started along Yuma's main street. "Did you ever hear such a loco idea in all your borned days, Matt?"

"You mean letting that reporter gal come along

with us?" Matt laughed quietly and shook his head. "It's pretty crazy, all right . . . but most folks would say that what we're planning to do shows that we've lost our minds, too."

"They just don't know what we can do once we put our minds to it."

Matt grew more solemn as he went on. "What I can't figure out is how she knew about it in the first place. And she knew *all* about it, too, not just hints or rumors."

"Smoke wouldn't have told her," Preacher said, "and I don't figure Frémont would have, either. If I had to guess, I'd say the most likely fella to have done it would be that deputy US marshal who was so put out about the whole thing."

"Simon Ford," Matt mused. Smoke had told them about the lawman interrupting his meeting with the governor in Prescott. "I suppose Miss Garnett could have wormed the story out of him."

"I don't reckon she'd have had to work very hard at it. She struck me as the sort of gal who knows how to twist a man right around her little finger any time she wants to."

Matt grunted and said, "She didn't twist me around her little finger, did she?"

"Nope. But for a second there, when she looked at you with them big brown eyes, didn't you want to give her whatever she wanted?"

Matt didn't answer for a moment. Then he

laughed and said, "Yeah, I did, Preacher. I hate to admit it, but I sure did."

"That's one advantage to bein' old and decrepit like me. Pretty gals can't get under your skin like they do with a young fella."

"Is that true?"

"Well . . ." Preacher sighed. "Well, no, I guess it ain't, not really."

They rode on, heading north out of Yuma and putting the settlement behind them.

Darcy wanted to stamp her foot as she watched the two men ride away. She wanted to cry. She wasn't going to do either of those things, because that was just what people would expect of her because she was a woman.

Instead, she looked around the livery stable. When she didn't see anyone, she went over to the door between the stable and the office and pounded on it with a fist. When the man who ran the place didn't answer the summons quickly enough, she knocked again, harder this time.

The door jerked open and the proprietor said angrily, "All right, damn it, what's the big—" He stopped short at the sight of Darcy standing there in her riding outfit. After a second, he went on, "Uh, sorry, ma'am. What can I do for you?"

"You're right, I *am* in a big hurry," she said. "I need to buy a good horse."

"Um, you mean you need to rent one?" the liveryman asked with a frown.

"No, I meant exactly what I said. I don't know when or if I'll even get back to Yuma, so I don't want you waiting for me to return your horse. That's why I want to buy a good saddle mount."

Still frowning, the liveryman scratched his jaw and asked, "Goin' a long way, are you, ma'am?"

"I won't know until I get there," Darcy said.

But she knew one thing. If that infuriating Matt Jensen thought she was going to give up that easily, he had a lot to learn about Darcy Garnett!

Chapter 33

After an initial fit of stubbornness—prompted more by a sheer contrary nature more than anything else, Smoke suspected—Mordecai Kroll told him that they needed to head east.

Smoke untied Mordecai's legs long enough to get him into the saddle, then lashed the outlaw's ankles together again under the horse's belly. When that was done, he freed Mordecai's hands and let him bring his arms around in front of him again. Then Smoke tied his wrists together and tied those bonds to the saddle horn with a short piece of rope.

Mordecai complained the entire time, but didn't try to make a move of any sort, probably because Smoke never let his guard down even for an instant. Once Mordecai was ready to ride, Smoke roped the four extra horses together so he could lead them. Two of the animals were loaded with supplies.

"You expect me to wear this prison getup the whole way?" Mordecai asked.

"Why not? We're not going to be visiting any towns, so nobody will see you."

"Because it's humiliatin', that's why! If you want me to cooperate with you, Jensen, you got to treat me like a human bein'. You know, decent-like."

Smoke thought for a second about all the people Mordecai hadn't treated decentlike during his career as an owlhoot. Then he put that aside as unprofitable for the moment and said, "There are some extra duds in one of those packs. Maybe later there'll be a chance for you to change clothes."

"That sun's gonna be mighty hot on my head now. You could at least get me a hat."

"You're right," Smoke said with a nod. He went over to the buggy, which he planned to leave here in the canyon, and reached into the back to get the hat he had tossed in there earlier, the one he had worn in his disguise as a priest. He carried it over to Mordecai and told him, "Lean down some."

"You can't be serious. You're really gonna make me wear that priest hat?"

"I'm not going to make you wear anything," Smoke said. "It's up to you if you want to let your brain fry in the sun."

"Oh, all right," Mordecai grumbled. He leaned down from the saddle, as much as the bonds on his wrists would let him. Smoke reached up and clapped the hat on his head.

As Mordecai straightened, Smoke said, "There you go. That'll give you some protection from the sun, anyway."

"And make me look like a damned fool," Mordecai muttered.

"You didn't need a hat for that," Smoke said.

He swung up onto his horse, got hold of the lead rope attached to the other animals, and used his boot heels to prod his mount into motion. Mordecai did likewise and fell in beside him.

When they camped that night, Smoke tried again to get some idea of where they were headed, but Mordecai continued to play it cagey.

"You just worry about keepin' a posse from catchin' us," the outlaw said. "I'll get us where we're goin'."

Smoke was glad to hear that comment. It meant Mordecai was still convinced Smoke was following Rudolph's orders. He didn't suspect that Matt and Preacher would be trailing them.

To preserve that illusion of pursuit, Smoke found an isolated canyon for their camp and built only a small, almost smokeless fire that he put out before it got dark. He used the flames to boil coffee and fry some bacon. Together with biscuits he had brought from Yuma, it made a serviceable supper.

He had left Mordecai's wrists tied together after freeing them from the saddle horn so the outlaw could feed himself. Mordecai's ankles were bound again to keep him from trying to make a run for it . . . although where he would go out here in these godforsaken badlands was a question Smoke couldn't answer.

When they had finished eating, Mordecai set his tin cup and plate aside and said, "You're gonna have to help me into the bushes, Jensen. Either that, or cut me loose so I can get there myself." He smirked. "If you don't, I'm gonna start stinkin' pretty bad by the time we get where we're goin'."

"You're not exactly a fragrant flower now, Kroll," Smoke said dryly. "I'll untie your ankles so you can get up and walk. Your hands stay tied."

"Whatever you say," Mordecai replied with a shrug.

Smoke drew his Colt and held it ready in his right hand while he knelt at Mordecai's feet and used his left to untie the ropes.

"You act like you think I'm gonna try to kick you or something," Mordecai said.

"Just don't want you to get too tempted," Smoke told him. With the bonds loosened, he straightened and stepped back, still covering Mordecai with the gun.

Mordecai laughed and said, "I swear, you're a touchy sort. Don't trust a fella at all, do you?"

"Some I do. Mostly, no."

Mordecai leaned forward and rested his hands on the ground to brace himself as he worked his feet and legs around so he could stand up. He said, "You ought to trust me. We're on the same side, after all."

"How in blazes do you figure that?"

"Well, we're bound for the same destination, anyway. You reckon I really care what happens to your brother as long as I'm free? If Rudolph wants to stick to the deal he made with you, that's just fine with me. All I care about is not gettin' my neck stretched."

He started to heave himself to his feet. As he did, he snatched the empty plate from the ground and threw it as hard as he could. It spun through the air straight toward Smoke's face.

Smoke flung up a hand to try to block it, but the plate was moving too fast. It smacked into his forehead and caromed off, staggering him. Smoke triggered a shot as Mordecai lunged at him, but the blow to the head threw his aim off and the bullet whipped past the outlaw's shoulder.

A split second later, Mordecai Kroll crashed into him and knocked him off his feet.

Smoke went over backwards. When he landed, a rock dug painfully into him between the shoulder blades. Mordecai clubbed his hands together and swung them. The blow slammed into the side of Smoke's face and drove his head to the side.

Mordecai tried to rip the gun out of Smoke's hand. Smoke was stunned, but instinct made him tighten his grip on the revolver. His brain was working just well enough to tell him that he needed a second or two to recover. He heaved his body up off the ground and threw Mordecai to the side.

Mordecai caught himself on his bound hands and swung one leg toward Smoke in a vicious roundhouse kick. The heel of his prison shoe caught Smoke on the wrist and knocked the gun out of his hand. The Colt flew through the air and landed a good fifteen feet away from either man.

That made it more of a fair fight, one in which Smoke should have prevailed easily because of his superior strength and the fact that his hands weren't tied.

But Mordecai fought with a sheer, crazed determination that made him stronger and faster than he should have been. Smoke had once battled a fierce Yaqui warrior whose natural fighting abilities had been enhanced temporarily by his use of peyote. Smoke had barely survived that encounter, and now desperation was driving Mordecai Kroll to a similar deadly level.

Mordecai lunged at him again, but this time Smoke was ready and got a leg up in time to plant his boot heel in Mordecai's stomach. He levered the outlaw up and over him. Mordecai landed hard and rolled across the rocky ground, but he was up almost instantly. As Smoke reached his feet, Mordecai charged him, swinging his bound, clubbed hands again.

Smoke blocked the blow and hammered a punch of his own into Mordecai's chest. Smoke had plenty of natural fighting prowess of his own. His fist landed with enough power to drive Mordecai back several steps.

Wanting to end this battle quickly, Smoke sent a looping left at Mordecai's head. Mordecai ducked under the punch, lowered his head, and rammed it into Smoke's chest. He tried to lift a knee into Smoke's groin, but Smoke twisted and took the vicious blow on his thigh.

That was enough to knock him off balance. Mordecai bulled into him again. Both men fell as their legs tangled up with each other.

Somehow Mordecai twisted and writhed so that he was behind Smoke. His arms rose and fell, and when they came down he had gotten them around Smoke's neck. The way Mordecai's arms were bound together, they made a natural noose. He tightened them on Smoke's throat as he dug a knee into his opponent's back.

Smoke tried to gulp down some air, but he didn't get much into his lungs before Mordecai's brutal grip cut off his breath. He knew he could hold out for a few moments, but unless he broke Mordecai's hold on him, in all likelihood he would pass out from lack of air.

If he lost consciousness, it would all be over. Smoke's life, the chances of rescuing Luke, everything.

Because Mordecai would kill him—Smoke had no doubt about that. If he had to, he would take a rock and bash Smoke's skull until his brains ran out on the rocky ground. Probably, Mordecai would take great pleasure in doing that.

Mordecai's knee in Smoke's back pinned him to the ground. The outlaw hauled back on Smoke's neck, bending him backwards until it felt like Smoke's spine was about to snap. Smoke sank an elbow in Mordecai's midsection, but he didn't seem to even feel it.

Smoke groped out to the side, found a fist-sized rock, and closed his hand around it. He struck up and back, aiming the blow blindly behind him.

The rock connected with something, most likely Mordecai's head because he grunted in pain and his grip loosened just slightly. Smoke struck again and again, and as Mordecai groaned and cursed, the pressure on Smoke's neck lessened even more. Smoke twisted his shoulders and tucked his chin down and pulled loose from the chokehold.

He got his knees under him, heaved upright, and turned to slam a backhanded blow into Mordecai's jaw. Smoke gasped for breath, but he didn't let that slow him down as he dropped the rock and threw another punch that landed cleanly on Mordecai's left cheekbone. The skin split under Smoke's knuckles. Mordecai landed on his back and lay there with his chest heaving. All the fight had been knocked out of him.

Blood trickled from the cut on his cheek Smoke's fist had just opened up, and also from a scratch on the other side of his forehead where the rock had hit him. He gasped, "No more . . . no more, Jensen . . ."

Smoke climbed to his feet and went over to pick up the Colt. He kept an eye on Mordecai the whole time, just in case the outlaw was shamming and tried something else.

It appeared that Mordecai was genuinely beaten, however. Smoke leveled the gun at him and asked, "Why'd you jump me like that? You knew the odds had to be against you?"

"Yeah, but . . . but I almost beat you anyway . . . didn't I?" Mordecai asked. Even in his battered condition, he was able to summon up a grin.

"But I got you out of prison and I'm taking you

back to your brother," Smoke said. "That's got to be what you want. Why try to kill me?"

"If a rattler strikes at you . . . or a scorpion stings you . . . would you ask it why?"

Lying there on the ground, Mordecai started to laugh. Smoke had to force himself not to pull the trigger and put a bullet through the man's diseased brain. After a long moment, he holstered the gun, reached down and took hold of Mordecai, and hauled him to his feet.

Wherever the gang's hideout was, they couldn't get there too soon to suit Smoke. Traveling with Mordecai Kroll was a little like taking a trip with a rabid coyote.

Chapter 34

Matt and Preacher made it to the canyon between the twin mesas with no trouble and found the buggy that Smoke had abandoned there. The sight of the vehicle sitting there alone was a relief to Matt. Although both men had all the confidence in the world in Smoke's ability to handle whatever sort of trouble came along, until that moment they had had no actual proof that the plan was working.

Now, as they followed the tracks left by the six

horses out of the canyon, they knew they were on the right trail and that Smoke and Mordecai were on their way to the Kroll gang's hideout.

"The whole shebang fooled that owlhoot," Preacher said with an appreciative chuckle. "Bet he don't have the least idea we're doggin' their trail."

"Smoke set it up well," Matt agreed. "I just hope the hideout isn't up in Idaho or Montana or somewhere. That would be a long trip to make with a varmint like Kroll."

"You got anywhere you have to be?"

"Well . . . no," Matt admitted.

"Neither do I. That's the good thing about bein' a drifter. Smoke has to worry about Sally and what's goin' on back at that ranch o' his and all the other things that go with leadin' a settled life. While you and me, we're free and ain't got to give a hoot in Hades about such things."

"That's true," Matt said slowly. "And when we're out on the trail somewhere and it's cold and dark and raining and there's not another human soul within miles, we don't have to worry about bothersome things like being snuggled up in a nice soft bed with a warm, beautiful woman. Now do we?"

"Boy," Preacher said, squinting over at him, "you're a-twistin' my words around."

Matt laughed.

"It's all right, Preacher," he said. "I know

you're not ready to settle down just yet. Maybe one of these days . . . when you're too old and feeble to take care of yourself anymore."

Preacher snatched his hat off and swatted at Matt with it.

"Does it look like that day's comin' any time soon, younker?" he demanded. "Well, does it?"

Still laughing, Matt fended off the mock blows and said, "Come on. We've got a trail to follow."

Earlier that afternoon, Ben Terwilliger had hurried into the saloon and reported excitedly to Clinton, "They's leavin', Jesse. The kid and the old man you had me watchin', they're pullin' out now. Want me to go tell the boys?"

"You do that, Ben," Clinton said. "Lew told them earlier to get ready to ride, so it shouldn't take long to round them up."

Terwilliger grinned and bounced up and down on the balls of his feet. He had so much nervous energy that Clinton had thought more than once the twitchy little bastard was going to up and explode. He said, "I'll tell 'em, boss. I'll sure tell 'em," and rushed out of the saloon.

Clinton laughed quietly, reached for the glass on the table in front of him that still contained a little whiskey, and tossed back the rest of the drink. Without getting in any hurry about it, he stood up.

Unlike Terwilliger, who always acted like he

had fleas hopping all over him, or Lew Hooke, who was so stoic his face might as well have been hacked out of rock, Clinton moved easily with a pantherish grace. He never hurried unless he had to, and even then he didn't seem rushed.

He wasn't worried about being able to pick up the trail left by their quarry. Hooke, whose mother was half Mexican and half Apache, had spent some of his life with the savages and rivaled them as a tracker. He'd have no trouble following Matt Jensen and Preacher.

Clinton left the saloon and strolled along the street to the hotel. A moment later he knocked on Simon Ford's door. The former marshal jerked it open so quickly he might have been standing right on the other side of the panel, waiting.

"They're on the move," Clinton drawled. "We'll ride out after them in twenty or thirty minutes."

"Why wait so long?" Ford demanded.

"Because we don't want to tip them off that they're being followed. These aren't babes in the woods we're dealing with, Simon. Matt Jensen already has a reputation even though he's pretty young, and Preacher . . . well, that old-timer is supposed to be as canny as a lobo wolf."

"I just don't want to take a chance on losing them."

"Don't worry about that," Clinton assured the former marshal. "They can't go anywhere that we can't find them, especially if they don't know they're being followed."

Ford looked like he still didn't care for the delay, but he nodded and said, "All right. I'll be ready. Where do I meet you?"

"In front of the saloon will do."

"I'll be there in a few minutes," Ford promised.

By the time Clinton got back to the saloon, the men were starting to assemble. Ben Terwilliger had brought Clinton's horse from the livery stable, saddled and ready to ride. Lew Hooke walked up leading several packhorses loaded with supplies. They had no idea how long the chase would be, so they had to be prepared. There was a good chance they would be traveling through some mighty dry country, so each man had several canteens hanging from his saddle and there were a couple of small water barrels hanging from the rig on one of the pack animals.

True to his words, Simon Ford showed up in short order, obviously eager to be on the trail. He didn't complain, though, as they waited for the rest of Clinton's men to arrive.

Finally, everyone was there and mounted. Twenty-two men, including Ford. Clinton saw how some of the townspeople were eyeing the group warily and taking care to go well around when passing by on the street. They looked like what they were, Clinton supposed: a bunch of hardcases on the trail of trouble.

At the end of that trail, a big payoff waited for them. Chances were, it would be bought with blood, but the price would be worth it, Clinton thought.

He waved the men into motion. They rode out of Yuma with him, Lew Hooke, and Simon Ford in the lead.

Late that afternoon, Hooke returned to the group from scouting out ahead of the rest of the riders by a mile or so. Clinton spotted him coming and frowned slightly as he realized that Hooke was moving pretty fast. Out here in this rugged country, a man didn't run a horse unless there was a really good reason for doing so.

Clinton wasn't the only one who noticed. Ford, riding beside him, remarked, "That's your man Hooke, isn't it? He looks like he's in a hurry."

"Yeah. Let's ride out and meet him."

Clinton heeled his mount into a trot. He and Ford rode ahead of the others, and a minute or so later Hooke reached them and reined in.

Before Clinton could say anything, Ford asked anxiously, "You didn't lose the trail, did you?"

"What?" Hooke frowned in surprise. "No, I didn't lose the trail. But we ain't the only ones following it."

"What do you mean by that, Lew?" Clinton asked.

"I mean there's somebody else trailing Jensen

and the old man. One rider. I got close enough to take a good look with my field glasses."

"He didn't spot you, did he?"

Most men would have leered as they replied, but not Hooke. His angular face remained expressionless as he said, "Wasn't a he. It's a girl who's trailing them, a mighty good-lookin' girl who knows how to ride. Not how to keep an eye on her back trail, though."

Clinton was so startled he forgot to grin. He said, "A girl? Who in the world—"

"I think I have an idea who she might be," Ford said heavily. "And if I'm right, she's nothing but trouble."

As the sun disappeared behind the horizon and night began to fall with its customary suddenness, Darcy couldn't help but wonder if maybe the decision she had made was a little too rash.

It was awfully lonely out here, with the last sign of civilization left miles behind her.

She didn't want to admit that she was scared, but she had lived all her life in cities. Boston, Philadelphia, St. Louis, all had their areas where it was dangerous to be alone at night, of course, but at least there lights burned in the buildings. You could see where you were.

Out here was utter darkness, and anything could be lurking in it.

Anything.

She reached out and ran her fingers over the smooth wood of the Winchester carbine's stock. The man at the store who had sold the weapon to her had said that the carbine's shorter barrel and stock would make it easier for her to handle, and even though it was a smaller caliber than a regular Winchester, it still had enough stopping power to knock down almost anything. Darcy tried to draw confidence from the fact that she had the carbine with her, but the effort didn't quite work.

Nor was the weight of the pistol on her hip particularly reassuring. It was a Colt New Line .32, a streamlined weapon with smaller grips and no trigger guard. Its cylinder held five rounds, but at the moment only four chambers were loaded since the man at the store had advised her to carry it with the hammer resting on an empty chamber.

"Wouldn't want you to shoot your pretty little foot off, miss," he had said with a smile that held a hint of a leer.

So she was well-armed, Darcy told herself, and therefore had nothing to be scared of.

Of course, it didn't actually work that way. She had handled firearms before, but only shooting at targets with men she wanted to impress. Pointing a gun at a living human being and pulling the trigger . . . well, that was something totally different. Darcy didn't know if she could do that.

She wasn't even sure she could shoot a wild animal if it was attacking her.

With any luck she wouldn't have to find out about either of those things.

It would have been so much easier if that blasted Matt Jensen had been more reasonable.

Buying the horse, the saddle and tack, the guns, and the supplies she carried in a bag tied on behind the saddle had taken just about every penny she had to her name. She was counting on getting a good story and being able to sell it. If she didn't, she wasn't sure what she would do.

She had to get the story—and survive in the process—before she could worry about anything else, she told herself. She spotted a large slab of rock that loomed higher than her head and angled the horse toward it. That was as good a place as any to camp, she supposed.

A couple of bushes and a little grass grew at the base of the rock. Although the ground was dry now, during the infrequent rains water probably collected there, which would explain the vegetation. Darcy dismounted and tied the horse's reins to one of the bushes. She removed the saddle and then took off her hat. She poured a little water from one of her canteens into it and let the horse drink. The only reason she knew to do that was because she had read about it in a dime novel.

Maybe she should have given some thought to

doing that sort of writing, she mused. Coming up with imaginary stories had to be easier than concentrating on the real thing. The journalistic instinct was strong inside her, though. She didn't want to lower herself and become a mere scribbler of fiction.

Once the horse had had its drink and started cropping on the grass, Darcy spread a blanket on the ground and sat down. She dug in her sack of supplies and came up with a piece of jerky and a hunk of bread. The bread was already stale, and the jerky was so tough that she worried it would cause her teeth to fall out. Washed down with sips from the canteen, though, it was better than nothing.

The air was already starting to turn cool. She unrolled her bedding, took off her boots, and crawled into the blankets. Millions upon millions of stars blazed in the ebony sky above her, but their light offered cold comfort to her.

She would not break down and cry from loneliness and fear, she vowed to herself.

She would *not*.

Chapter 35

Smoke imagined a line on a map, running from the canyon north of Yuma where he had left the buggy in an east/northeast direction, roughly paralleling the Gila River which lay to the south. Past the Castle Dome Mountains, past other nameless mountains so desolate nothing lived there except lizards and scorpions. Past the occasional village of stubborn Mexicans or Indians who attempted to eke a living from the blasted soil. When he got back to the Sugarloaf and Sally asked about this adventure, as he knew she would, he would get out a map and trace that line with his fingertip and tell her, "This is the way Mordecai Kroll and I went."

And while that would be true, in another way it would be a lie, a lie of omission, because it said nothing about the heat, or the blinding glare of the sun, or the sheer loneliness and isolation and the strain of having to travel with a mad dog killer who would murder him just as easily as blinking if he got the chance, simply because he could.

"What are you thinkin', Jensen?"

Smoke looked over at the man riding beside him and said, "You don't want to know."

Mordecai threw his head back and laughed. He still wore what he scornfully called "the priest hat," but he had changed into jeans and a faded work shirt and a brown vest. The prison shoes were still on his feet. He had complained about not having any real boots to wear, but Smoke couldn't do anything about that, nor did he really care.

"It's mighty temptin', ain't it?" Mordecai said.

Smoke knew it was probably a mistake to engage in conversation with the outlaw, but what else were they going to do out here in the middle of nowhere?

"What's tempting?" he asked.

"You keep thinkin' about how easy it'd be to slip that Colt out of its holster, point it at my head, pull back the hammer, and squeeze the trigger. Don't you?"

Smoke grunted, but other than that he didn't honor the question with a response.

"Oh, yeah," Mordecai went on. "Wouldn't take much to kill me, would it? My life's in your hand, and it wouldn't take much effort to end it. 'Bout like you was holdin' a little baby bird. One little squeeze, that's all. One little squeeze on that baby bird, one little squeeze on the trigger. Ain't nothin' sweeter in this world than havin' the power of life and death over somethin'." He laughed again, a cackle of sheer delight. "Hell, God must stay drunk on it all the time!"

For a long moment, Smoke didn't say anything. Then . . .

"You're wrong, Kroll."

"I am? You can honestly say you don't want to shoot me?"

"No, I don't." Smoke paused. "I'd rather beat you to death with my bare hands. Every breath you take is that much air wasted somebody else more deserving could use. But I won't do either of those things, because somebody else's life is in my hands, at least partially. My brother Luke's. So tell me . . ." Smoke drew in a deep breath. "We'll be getting pretty close to Phoenix in a few days. Where do we go from there?"

"I'll tell you when the time comes," Mordecai said. "Until then, you just enjoy knowin' that you got to keep a piece of scum like me alive. You hear?"

Smoke didn't say anything. Trying to carry on a conversation like Mordecai was a normal human being was another waste of breath.

Darcy wasn't completely sure, but she thought a week had gone by since she'd left Yuma. A week in hell was longer than a regular week, though. That accounted for her uncertainty.

Every bit of exposed skin had been burned red by the sun. She had stayed covered up as much as possible—even though she had never traveled in the desert before, she had sense enough to do *that*—but she hadn't been able to avoid the blistering rays entirely, and for several days she had been in considerable pain before the redness faded and some of her skin peeled off and now her hands and face were brown instead of crimson.

She had been red in other places, too. Much more indelicate places. Long hours in the saddle every day had done that.

But again, time had toughened her. Sometimes she thought she was turning into rawhide as the heat leeched moisture from her body and baked what was left.

Her body might have grown stronger, but at night she still lay for hours sometimes, just staring into the darkness and trying to control her fear. Finally, in the chilliness that would seem impossible the next day once the sun was up again, she dozed off, sleeping for a few hours before she got up and resumed the trek again.

Thankfully, Matt Jensen and Preacher hadn't proven difficult to follow. They weren't trying to cover their tracks. During the long days, Darcy had spent so much time studying the hoofprints left by the four horses that she realized they were all different. Each print had its own peculiarities, and after a while she was able to recognize them. She knew she was still on the right trail.

She stayed far enough back that she felt it was highly unlikely they would spot her. Frontiersmen like them probably looked back from time to time, and she didn't want them to see her and become curious about who was behind them. Because of that, she hadn't seen another living soul since leaving Yuma. She had never spent so much time alone in her life.

It was driving her mad.

One day she had seen the adobe *jacals* of a farming village in the distance and had been tempted to abandon her quest, turn her horse, and ride to the village as fast as she could, just so she could see human faces and hear human voices again. At that moment, it was more important to her than all the journalistic ambition she'd ever had.

Somehow she kept going, kept her horse plodding along next to the tracks left by Matt's and Preacher's horses.

That evening, as she sat on her blankets and gnawed on jerky and watched the stars come out, she counted up the days in her head and decided it had only been a week, even though it seemed much longer.

Her horse suddenly lifted its head. Darcy noticed the reaction and stiffened. The horse acted like it smelled or heard something unexpected.

There could be any number of explanations for that, Darcy told herself. A wild animal of some sort. Another horse. A band of mustangs running free.

Or saddle horses ridden by men.

She had made camp at the edge of a small arroyo. She knew better than to camp actually *in* the arroyo. As unlikely as a rainstorm was, it wasn't impossible, and a sudden downpour could turn one of those dry washes into a raging torrent with little or no warning.

The sky was completely clear at the moment, however, with no thunder rumbling or lightning flickering even in the far distance, so she knew it was safe to slip over the edge and hide in the arroyo until she either saw what had spooked her horse or whatever it was moved on.

She had placed the carbine on the blanket beside her when she sat down. Now she picked it up and hurried to hide in the little cleft that nature had carved across the landscape.

Darcy listened intently. Her horse whickered softly and moved around some, but she had picketed the animal securely and didn't think it would pull free. She didn't hear anything else. No other horses, no men's voices, nothing except the faint sigh of a night breeze as the land gave up some of the day's heat.

Then a tiny, gritty scrape sounded behind her as she crouched just below the rim of the arroyo's bank. Darcy gasped and turned and saw the man-shaped patch of darkness standing only a few feet from her.

In that instant, time seemed to stop. Something

was wrong with the shape's head, something that made it seem grotesque and inhuman.

Then it took a step toward her and enough starlight penetrated into the arroyo for her to realize that the man wore a steeple-crowned sombrero. He lifted a hand and lurched toward her. She saw his face then, twisted and evil, and jerked the carbine up. She started to fire as fast as she could work the weapon's lever and pull the trigger.

Smoke had made good on his promise to blaze a trail for Matt and Preacher. Matt figured Preacher could have followed their quarry anyway—the old mountain man had no equal when it came to tracking—but it was easier because of the marks Smoke had left behind as he and Mordecai Kroll rode east. A small scratched arrow on a rock, a branch on a scrubby bush broken and twisted in a certain direction, pebbles arranged in an almost unnoticeable pattern . . . To Preacher's keen eyes, they might as well have been signposts, and Matt knew that Smoke was clever enough to leave the telltale marks without Mordecai ever realizing what he was doing.

They made a cold camp as usual at the base of a small mesa, and after they had eaten their meager supper, Matt asked, "How much farther do you think it is to the hideout?"

"Why, I ain't got no more clue about that than I

do about what's on t'other side of the moon, boy. Shoot, it could be anywhere. We knew we might be lettin' ourselves in for a long chase when we lit out after Smoke and that Kroll varmint."

Matt lay back on his bedroll with his hands locked together behind his head and said, "Yeah, I know that. But think about it . . . Mordecai Kroll was by himself when Luke captured him up in Apache County. Doesn't it stand to reason that the hideout had to be within a few days' ride from there? Mordecai wouldn't have gone off somewhere weeks away from the hideout unless he was leaving the gang, and from what Smoke said about him, there's never been any indication that he wanted to do that. He's been content to let his big brother, Rudolph, call the shots."

"Yeah, maybe," Preacher said. "What you're sayin' makes sense, but we ain't got no proof of it. And there's a whole heap o' things in this world, younker, that *don't* make sense."

"Can't argue with that," Matt said. "But still, I'm going to hope that we're not too far from the hideout now—"

He stopped short as the unmistakable *crack-crack-crack!* of rifle shots sounded in the night air, coming from a half-mile or so away.

Chapter 36

As Matt bolted to his feet, the heavier boom of revolvers going off followed the rifle shots.

"Smoke!" he exclaimed.

Preacher was up, too. His hand closed over Matt's arm as he said, "Stop and think about it, boy. Them shots come from *behind* us."

"Somebody on our trail?"

"Could be. Or it could be they don't have nothin' to do with us or your brothers. Ain't no law says we got to be the only ones out here in these badlands."

Matt realized the old-timer was right. Despite that, they couldn't afford to leave the possibility uninvestigated.

"We've got to check it out," he said.

"You're right about that," Preacher said with a nod. "Dog! Hunt!"

The big cur had gotten up at the sound of the shots, too. His ears had pricked forward, and the fur on the back of his neck ruffled. Now, without a sound, he bounded off into the darkness, eager to find the source of the shots.

Matt and Preacher saddled up. They left the other horses picketed at the camp and rode off in the same direction Dog had gone. The shooting had stopped now, and as the last echoes faded to nothing, the silence that cloaked the arid landscape had an ominous quality about it.

Whatever the fight had been about, likely somebody had wound up on the losing side of it.

Despite the sense of urgency both men felt, they took their time. The drumming of rapid hoofbeats could be heard for a long way on a quiet night. They had to proceed at a quieter, more deliberate pace.

They had covered almost half a mile, Matt estimated, when he heard men's voices up ahead, raised in loud talk and raucous laughter. Preacher heard them, too, and reined in, as did Matt.

They swung down from their saddles. Matt stepped closer to the old mountain man and said quietly, "Something's off about what I'm hearing."

"That's 'cause them fellas are speakin' Mexican," Preacher replied. "I savvy the lingo pretty good, but we're too far away for me to pick up much of it. They're pleased with themselves over somethin', though."

"We'd better take a look."

"Yep. Leave the horses here."

They dropped their reins, knowing the well-trained horses would stay pretty close to where they were left. With the night shadows thick around them, Matt and Preacher moved forward, crouching low until they got even closer. Then they dropped to their bellies and crawled toward the voices, using the concealment of sagebrush that was barely more than a foot tall.

Matt spoke some Spanish himself, and as they came closer he began to understand more of what was being said. The men were joking about a *puta*—whore—so there was a woman out here, as unlikely as that seemed. Then one of them said something about a *gringa*. They had found a white woman and either captured or killed her.

Matt had an inkling who the victim might be, and he hoped that she wasn't dead.

Although, if he was correct in his guess, he thought, it would almost serve her right!

No, she didn't deserve to die, he rapidly amended in his head. Being annoying wasn't worthy of a death sentence. But as it was, her actions posed a threat not only to her own life, but to Matt and Preacher as well, because they were going to have to rescue her from whatever trouble she had gotten herself into.

"Please." The woman's voice rang out clearly in the darkness, although a faint quiver in it revealed the strain she was under. "*Por favor.* My father can pay you."

His hunch had been right, Matt thought. That was definitely Darcy Garnett up ahead.

And she was in trouble, all right.

A man asked her in thickly accented English, "And who is your *padre*, señorita?"

"His name is John Wilton Garnett." When silence greeted Darcy's words, indicating that the name meant nothing to her captors, she went on, "He owns one of the biggest newspapers in Boston. One of the biggest newspapers on the whole East Coast."

"This means he has money?"

Darcy sounded a little exasperated as she answered, "Yes. He has a lot of money."

"And he will pay to get his *niña* back alive?"

"Of course, he will." Darcy added under her breath, but still loud enough for Matt to hear, "Unless he considers me more trouble than I'm worth, like he always has."

The men talked among themselves in low, rapid Spanish, too quietly for Matt to understand any of it. He could see them now, but only as vague shapes in the darkness as they stood on the edge of an arroyo. He thought there were five or six of them, but he couldn't be sure.

Finally the man who had spoken before said to Darcy, "We have decided, señorita. We will take you back to Mexico with us and sell you to your father. You will not be harmed."

Even Matt could tell that the man was lying about that last part. They might really intend to ransom Darcy back to her father, but she certainly wouldn't be returned untouched.

"We have been up here in Arizona Territory stealing horses," the man went on, openly admitting that he and his companions were bandits from south of the border. "But I think that you are the true prize we will take back with us."

One of the other men said something in swift Spanish.

"José wants to know if there is anyone out here with you," the spokesman translated.

"Yes!" Darcy said, answering too quickly and with too much eagerness to be believed. "I've been traveling with a dozen men . . . bodyguards . . . and they'll be back any minute now."

The spokesman, who was evidently the only one of the bandits who spoke English, told the others what she'd said. They all laughed.

"We just wanted to see what you would say, señorita. We know you are alone. We watched you for an hour before the sun went down and you made camp here. But it's all right that you lied."

The sudden crack of an open-handed slap sounded, followed instantly by Darcy's pained gasp. Matt fought down the urge to leap to his feet, draw his gun and start blazing away.

"Just don't do it again," the bandit said, his voice hard and flat with menace.

He started talking in Spanish again to his companions. After a minute, Preacher touched

Matt lightly on the shoulder and jerked his head, indicating that they should back off.

They crawled away from the arroyo, and when they had put enough distance between them and the bandits for it to be safe, Preacher whispered, "They left that herd o' stolen horses off a ways with a coupla hombres watchin' it. The fella who was talkin' to the gal seems to be the boss. He told three of the others to go back and get the herd and bring it here. That means there'll only be three of 'em watchin' the gal for a little while."

"Best time for us to make our move," Matt said.

"Yep. We'll whittle down the odds while we got the chance. Once the guns start goin' off, though, the rest of the bunch'll come a-larrupin' just as hard as they can."

"We'll have to try to be ready for them."

" 'Less'n you want to go back to our horses and ride away. We got Smoke and Luke to think about."

"And even though we've never met Luke, I feel sure he wouldn't want us to abandon Miss Garnett. I *know* Smoke wouldn't."

Preacher chuckled.

"That's what I figured you'd say. I'd'a been mighty disappointed if you hadn't. Come on."

As they started working their way back to the arroyo where Darcy had been captured by the bandits, the orange glow of flames appeared against the night sky. As Matt and Preacher came closer, they could see that the men who had stayed behind had kindled a campfire. They had to be pretty confident that they weren't in any danger from anybody else who might be out here.

That overconfidence might cost them their lives.

Matt and Preacher didn't have to stop and discuss their plans. They had been in too many situations like this before. They knew what needed to be done and how to go about doing it. When they reached a certain point in their approach to the camp they split up, Matt going right and Preacher going left.

Several more minutes went by while the young gunfighter and the old mountain man worked their way into position. From where he was, Matt could see Darcy sitting with her back against her saddle. Her captors had lashed her wrists together, but her feet were still free. Her face was pale and drawn in the firelight, and the fear she had to feel was easy to see on her features.

But anger and defiance were there in her face, too. She had no way of knowing that help was close at hand, but despite that, she wasn't going to give up hope. If something terrible was going to happen to her, she would fight it every inch of the way.

Matt couldn't help but admire her a little.

But he could understand why her newspaper tycoon father might feel like she was more trouble than she was worth, too. He had a hunch Darcy Garnett had been a handful growing up.

The three horse thieves had the look of typical border outlaws, unshaven, hard-bitten men in well-worn charro clothes and battered old sombreros. Each man carried a gun and a knife, and they would be good with the weapons, too. Matt and Preacher had the element of surprise on their side, though.

Matt heard an owl hoot and knew that was Preacher signaling that he was ready.

Just in time, too, because one of the bandits, a stocky man who had pushed his sombrero back so it hung by its neck strap behind his head, walked over to Darcy and proved himself to be the spokesman they had heard earlier by saying, "It'll be a while before those other hombres are back with the horses. I think we should do something enjoyable to pass the time." He nudged Darcy's left thigh with a booted foot. "What do you think, señorita?"

"I think you should go to hell," she said through clenched teeth.

The bandit lost his affable air and snarled as he reached down toward her, obviously intending to rip her shirt open.

That was when Matt stood up and said, "I think you should do what the lady told you."

The bandit jerked upright, whirled around, and clawed at the gun on his hip.

He had just cleared leather when Matt said, "Go to hell," and squeezed the trigger of the Colt in his hand.

Chapter 37

Flame spouted from the muzzle of Matt's gun and drove the slug deep in the bandit's chest. He staggered backwards, tripped and fell, and crashed down halfway on top of Darcy, who let out an involuntary shriek.

At the same time, Preacher's guns roared and another of the bandits doubled over as a pair of bullets punched into his midsection.

That left just one of the men on his feet, and Matt took care of that a split second later as he pivoted smoothly and fired again. The third bandit had gotten his gun out and jerked the trigger as Matt's shot ripped through his body and twisted him off his feet. The bullet from the outlaw's gun whined off harmlessly into the night.

"Get *off* of me!" Darcy cried as she pushed the corpse to the side. Matt heard hysteria in her voice.

The fight wasn't over and he knew it. They would stand a better chance against the five remaining bandits if they didn't have to worry about Darcy doing something loco.

So he pouched his iron, reached down and grasped her arms, and hauled her to her feet. She started to struggle and cry out. Putting his face close to hers, he said, "Miss Garnett. Darcy! It's me, Matt Jensen! Settle down!"

She stopped yelling and said hesitantly, "M-Matt?"

"That's right. It's Matt, and Preacher's here, too. You're all right. Those men are dead."

"They sure are," Preacher reported. He had been checking the bodies to make certain. "Problem is, they ain't the only ones out here."

"The . . . the others," Darcy said. "Three or four of them . . . they went back to get some horses . . . and some other men."

Matt nodded and said, "I know. They'll have heard those shots, too, and they won't waste any time getting here."

"We could try to slip away whilst we got the chance," Preacher suggested.

"Then we'd have to worry about them being behind us." Matt shook his head. "We don't need that complication. No, I'd rather go ahead and deal with them here and now."

"Reckon I feel the same way," Preacher said. "Just wanted to make sure you did."

Darcy seemed to have calmed down a little. Matt thought she was rational enough to understand what he was telling her as he said, "You need to take your horse, get down in the arroyo, and follow it away from here. Go at least a mile before you stop. Wait for us there, and if we don't come for you pretty quickly after the shooting stops, you'll know you're on your own again."

"I . . . I'd rather stay here with you."

Matt shook his head.

"If you did, and Preacher and I didn't make it, you'd be just as bad off as you were to start with. We're not going to risk getting ourselves killed for that. Do what I told you."

She tossed her head defiantly and said, "You certainly seem to like giving orders, Mr. Jensen."

"You were calling me Matt a minute ago."

"A minute ago you weren't bossing me around."

Preacher said, "Young lady, we're just tryin' to give you a chance to get outta this mess alive. Now, you best take it, or you're just gonna make things harder for ever'body."

She sighed. The sound was full of frustration.

"All right," she said. "Let me get my saddle on my horse."

"I'll do that," Matt said. "Preacher, keep an eye out."

"Already doin' it," the old mountain man said. "An ear, too."

It took Matt only a couple of minutes to saddle

Darcy's mount. He was going to help her get on the horse, but she pulled away from his hand.

"I can take care of myself," she told him.

"You keep saying that, but you don't seem to be doing a very good job of it."

He didn't have to have much light to know that she was glaring at him as she swung up into the saddle.

The banks of the arroyo had caved in here and there. She rode down into the wash at one of those places and started along it, quickly vanishing from sight. Preacher kicked the fire out, then lifted his head and said, "I hear horses comin' fast."

"That'll be them," Matt said as he finished thumbing fresh cartridges into his Colt to replace the ones he had fired. He slid a cartridge into the cylinder's sixth chamber, which he usually kept empty so the hammer could rest on it.

He might need that sixth round in the next few minutes.

"We'll split up again," he said. "Catch them in a cross fire."

"I hope you ain't plannin' on doin' anything stupid, like givin' 'em a chance to surrender."

Grimly, Matt shook his head and said, "Not this bunch. They wouldn't take it anyway."

"Not hardly," Preacher said.

They moved off in different directions in the brush. Matt dropped to one knee and bent lower to make himself inconspicuous in the shadows.

He heard the swift rataplan of hoofbeats now, too, as the other bandits raced back to see what all the shooting was about.

It wouldn't take them long to find out.

A few embers still glowed in the remains of the campfire. Those tiny orange beacons gave the other bandits something to aim for as they galloped up. Matt counted five men and figured they had left the herd of stolen horses somewhere nearby. A couple of them called out in Spanish, and when they didn't get an answer, all the men reached for the rifles they carried on their saddles.

Matt stood up and opened fire.

He was about thirty feet away from the nearest bandit, who jerked and toppled off his horse as the suddenly skittish animal danced to one side. Matt heard Preacher's guns roaring and saw muzzle flashes lighting up the night on the far side of the riders. He shifted his aim and triggered two more shots. One of the bandits threw his arms in the air and slid from the saddle.

It was bleak work, but necessary. Matt knew any of those men would have taken great pleasure in killing him and Preacher if he'd had the chance. Probably would have taken his time and made their dying long and agonizing. And as for what they all would have done to Darcy Garnett . . .

Only one bandit was still mounted. In desperation, he wheeled his horse and kicked it into a run along the arroyo. Matt fired after the fleeing man and so did Preacher. The horse didn't break stride, and the rider stayed in the saddle like he was nailed to it.

It would be better not to leave any enemies behind them, Matt thought as he lowered his Colt, but it was doubtful that one man could really pose a threat to them.

The sudden crack of a rifle shot split the night, along with the spurt of flame from the weapon's muzzle. The fleeing bandit cried out and pitched headlong from the saddle.

"What the hell!" exclaimed Preacher.

"I think I know," Matt said. "Check this bunch. Make sure they're all dead."

While Preacher was doing that, Matt trotted toward where the fifth bandit had fallen. He called out, "Hold your fire, Miss Garnett! It's Matt Jensen!"

Darcy emerged from the arroyo, carrying her carbine in one hand and leading her horse with the other, while Matt nudged the fallen man over onto his back with a toe. He kept his Colt trained on the bandit the whole time, but there was no need. The way the man's head flopped loosely told Matt that not only had Darcy drilled him, he had broken his neck when he fell, too.

"Is he . . . dead?" she asked.

"Yeah," Matt said. "You didn't even go a hundred yards, did you?"

"I thought you and Preacher might need some help. Clearly, you did."

"If this hombre had gotten away, it wouldn't have made any difference—"

"It might have," Darcy interrupted. "What if they had even more friends nearby? He could have gone to summon help. Or he might have lurked around in the vicinity and tried to shoot us from a distance."

Matt had to admit she was right about both of those things, although he considered them unlikely.

"So you went out of sight along the arroyo and waited to see what was going to happen," he said.

"It worked out all right, didn't it?" she demanded. "I was able to . . . to k—to—"

She dropped the carbine and fainted dead away.

Matt uttered a heartfelt, "Blast it!"

Then he shook his head and bent to help her.

A mile away, Simon Ford stood tensely, peering into the darkness as if his eyes could pierce that veil and let him know what had happened in the distance.

Beside him, Jesse Clinton hooked his thumbs in his gun belt and said, "That was quite a ruckus, from the sound of it. Two of 'em, in fact."

"If Matt Jensen and the old man are dead, our plan is ruined," Ford snapped. "We need to go find out."

"And if they ain't dead and we go blundering in on top of them, our plan is ruined, too," Clinton pointed out. "Either way, it's bad. But if they're alive and we wait, we can pick up their trail again in the morning and nothing has to change. We go right on the way we intended. That's the least risky move, Marshal."

"Don't call me that. I'm not a marshal anymore, you know that."

Clinton shrugged.

"Sorry. Once a fella's toted a badge, it's hard to forget."

"How would you know?" Ford said. "You were never a lawman."

"No . . . but I've crossed trails with a heap of them."

Clinton left it at that, and Ford didn't push the issue. He was more worried about what might have happened on the trail ahead of them.

"Even if Jensen and Preacher are dead, it might not ruin everything," he said after a moment's thought. "We might be able to find the trail left by Smoke Jensen and Mordecai Kroll."

"See?" Clinton said. "We'll handle it, Simon. Whatever comes along, we'll handle it."

Ford liked the gunman calling him by his given name even less than he liked Clinton addressing him as "Marshal," but he supposed none of that mattered now. The only important thing was seeing justice done.

What some hired killer called him was nothing. And so was the soul he risked by throwing in with men such as these.

"Whoo-ee!" Mordecai said as the second flurry of shots echoed in the distance. "I thought the entertainment was over for the evenin', but it sounds like there's a second act!"

Smoke heard the shots, too, and frowned in concern. He knew that Matt and Preacher were back there somewhere, and it wouldn't surprise him a bit if those two had somehow landed smack-dab in the middle of trouble. Preacher, especially, had a positive genius for that.

Although it was true of Matt and him, too, Smoke thought. Somehow, whatever they did and wherever they went, somebody wound up shooting at them. If not for the fact that all three of them had come through those deadly dustups alive, he might have started to think that they were jinxed. . . .

"What do you reckon that was?" Mordecai went on. "Apaches raidin' some ranch, maybe? Or *bandidos*? One thing's for sure . . . blood was spilled tonight. I can almost smell it in the air."

"Quit worrying about what you can smell and get some sleep," Smoke said. "You ought to be tired after all those hours in the saddle."

"Ain't you ever heard the old sayin', Jensen?

'A man can rest when he's dead.' I don't plan on that happenin' for a long time yet!"

"How long do you think it'll be before we get to that hideout of yours?"

Mordecai opened his mouth to say something, but he laughed instead as he leaned back against the big rock beside which they had made camp.

"Almost tricked me into sayin' more than I wanted to, didn't you, Jensen? You ain't just slick on the draw. You're slick all the way around. Not slick enough, though. I got all these trump cards in my hand, and I'm playin' 'em one by one. I'm even savin' one of 'em for the last hand. The big casino. Know what I mean?"

Smoke knew.

And the showdown Mordecai referred to couldn't get here soon enough to suit him.

Darcy woke up to the smell of coffee.

She cracked one eye open but saw nothing but darkness at first. Then she became aware of starlight, mainly because a shape appeared and blocked out some of it.

"I know you're awake," Matt said. "You were moving around just a minute ago."

Darcy didn't really remember that, but she was willing to take his word for it. She got her other eye open and saw him hunkered there in front of her with a cup in his left hand.

"You . . . you built a fire for me?" she said. "I didn't think that was safe at night."

"It ain't," Preacher said from somewhere nearby. "Had to dig a goldang hole for it so nobody could see it."

Darcy reached out and wrapped her hands around the cup Matt extended to her. The night was chilly, as nights on the desert always were, and the heat felt good on her fingers.

It felt even better inside her as she sipped the strong, black brew.

"Don't get used to it," Preacher went on. "I ain't always gonna be in such a considerate mood. And if you're gonna travel with us, you got to do what you're told."

"So no more rebelling against your pa who never had time for you," Matt added, "or whatever the hell it is you think you're doing out here."

"I'm going after a story," Darcy said. "Just like I was trained to do. Do you mean that about me traveling with you?"

"What else are we going to do with you?" Matt asked, not bothering to hide the note of disgust in his voice. "Now that we know you've been following us, we can't just leave you out here to fend for yourself."

"I've done a pretty good job of it so far."

"Until you were kidnapped by a bunch of bandits who intended to rape you and then try to sell you back to your father."

Her breath caught in her throat for a second. She said, "You don't believe in pulling any punches, do you, Matt?"

"Why should I? And I see that it's Matt again."

"Well . . . if we're going to be traveling together, we might as well be friends, hadn't we?"

In the long run, that was the most effective first step. Friends . . . and then eventually he would do everything she wanted.

Although Darcy sensed that tactic might not work with Matt Jensen. She wasn't sure *anything* was guaranteed to work with Matt Jensen.

"Do you have any idea how much farther it is to the Kroll brothers' hideout?" she asked.

"I don't have any idea," Matt said. Then he added fervently, "But I sure hope it's not far."

Book Four

Chapter 38

"There it is," Mordecai said. "I keep tellin' Rudolph it needs some sort of fancy name, like *Casa del Diablo* maybe. But he says that's foolishness, and he ain't inclined to foolishness."

Casa del Diablo, Smoke thought as he gazed along the canyon at the big hacienda. *House of the Devil.*

Considering who lived there, the name fit.

This was truly the Devil's stronghold.

Following Mordecai's directions, they had bypassed Phoenix well to the north, then followed a curving trail into the rugged Superstition Mountains. Even though the town wasn't that far away in terms of miles, the mountains were desolate and isolated. Some people even believed them to be haunted, including the Apaches. There had to be a good reason why the Indians avoided the place.

Smoke could see why Rudolph Kroll had chosen this canyon for his gang's hideout, too. His experience instantly told him that it was very defensible. High cliffs too steep to be scaled bordered it on both sides, curving around to seal off the northern end as well, except for a narrow gap. The course of the creek indicated to Smoke that it probably entered the canyon through that gap. The opening was small enough, though, that it would take only a few guards to protect it.

The same was true of the high pass where he and Mordecai now sat on horseback. They had climbed a zigzagging trail to get here. An army would have a hard time getting up that trail without being picked off from above. And any men who made it to the top would then have to go through this pass, where riflemen were posted behind boulders on both sides, ready to lay down a deadly cross fire on anybody foolish enough to try to invade Rudolph Kroll's domain.

It wasn't going to be easy for Matt and Preacher to get in here, Smoke reflected.

But Matt and Preacher were noted for doing things that seemed to be impossible.

One of the guards in the pass called, "Hey, Mordecai! Good to see you!"

Several more men shouted greetings as well. Mordecai waved a hand, the gesture full of casual arrogance as if he were royalty. He was owlhoot royalty, Smoke supposed, the wastrel prince, brother to the king.

"Let's go," he said.

They nudged their horses into motion and started forward through the pass, which ran between high, boulder-littered stone slopes for about fifty yards before the trail dropped down toward the canyon. Mordecai kept grinning and waving. That irritated Smoke, but he didn't waste his breath saying anything.

The trip from Yuma had left him beard-stubbled and hollow-eyed. He hadn't slept much because he didn't trust Mordecai, no matter how securely the outlaw was tied up. In a way, he was actually glad to be here, glad to be surrounded by his enemies. That was less of a strain than traveling with Mordecai Kroll.

As they started down the trail into the canyon, Smoke spotted a man racing on horseback a quarter of a mile ahead of them. Mordecai saw the rider, too, and said, "He'll be goin' to let Rudolph know we're here. Reckon there'll be a big celebration to welcome me back, like in the Good Book where it talks about the fatted calf."

Smoke grunted and said, "I'm surprised you ever heard of anything in the Bible."

"Shoot, yeah, our mama used to read it to Rudolph and me when we was just sprouts. She was a believer, yes, sir." Mordecai paused. " 'Course, that didn't stop her from dyin', just all wore out from how hard life was, before she was forty years old. Hell, she looked twice as old as she really was. All that Bible-thumpin' didn't help her one damn bit."

"If she thought it did, I reckon it was so," Smoke said quietly.

"Only one thing a Bible's good for. If you carry

it in your shirt pocket, you might get lucky and have it stop a bullet or an arrow one of these days."

Smoke's lips tightened. He wasn't going to argue religion with an outlaw. What he really wanted at the moment was to see his brother and make sure Luke was all right.

If Rudolph Kroll had gone back on his word and killed Luke, Smoke would make sure the boss outlaw died, too. But that wouldn't bring Luke back, and Smoke already regretted all the years they had missed out on knowing each other.

As the canyon leveled out, the trail turned into a regular road bordered with trees. On either side lay garden patches and orchards tended by Mexican peasants. With the fruits and vegetables grown there, the canyon could be self-sufficient for a while if need be. From the pass Smoke had seen a small herd of cattle grazing on one side of the canyon, too. That herd would provide beef. This wouldn't be a bad place to live, he mused . . . if it wasn't full of outlaws.

They passed a number of small huts where the Mexican farmers lived, then started up a slope toward the bench at the far end of the canyon where the big house and most of the outbuildings were located. The house, set behind terraced steps, was high enough for Smoke to see the second-floor balcony over the outer adobe wall. A lone man stood there at the wrought-iron railing, and once more Smoke was reminded of royalty. He knew he was looking at Rudolph Kroll as the man stood there like a monarch surveying his kingdom.

Mordecai must have spotted his brother, too. He snatched the hat off his head and waved it enthusiastically.

Then he said, "You're a dang fool, you know that, don't you? Ain't no way in hell Rudolph is gonna let you or your no-good bounty hunter brother outta this canyon alive."

"We'll see," Smoke said.

He hoped Matt and Preacher weren't too far behind them.

For a while Luke had tried to keep track of the days. He had even scratched marks on the stone wall of this dank basement cell to count them off, using a bit of metal he had found while feeling around in the gloom. He thought it was part of an old buckle. There was no telling how long it had been there or who it had belonged to.

Luke figured the poor varmint was long since dead, though. Anybody who was thrown into this hole probably didn't have much of a life expectancy.

Since he was as good as dead himself, he stopped worrying about how many days he had been here. He wasn't giving up, exactly. Surrender didn't come easy to a Jensen.

Here in this dry mountain desert, you wouldn't think anything could stay damp for very long, but Luke's prison, being underground, had moss growing on its stone walls and he seemed to hear the *drip-drip-drip* of water all the time. Maybe that was just his imagination, but he didn't think so.

As he sat there in his tattered clothes with his back against the wall, he heard something to his right. Tiny feet skittered over the stones. He turned his head in that direction and felt his beard brush against his upper chest. It had been several weeks since he'd shaved, and his beard grew fast.

The sounds told him his visitor was back. He didn't know how the rat got in and out of the cell. He had searched all over the place, feeling for an opening large enough for the furry creature to fit through, but he hadn't found one. The rat managed, though.

He had seen it a time or two in the faint light that filtered through the small, barred window in the thick wooden door. It wasn't a particularly big rat. They didn't grow big in the desert. It had stood up on its hind legs and stared at him with what he took to be an evil intelligence, although that was probably giving too much credit to its tiny brain.

Then it vanished back wherever it came from. So far it hadn't tried to gnaw on him, and he was thankful for that. He tried to insure that stayed the same by pinching off little pieces of bread from what he was given and tossing them on the other side of the cell. Maybe as long as he fed the rat, it wouldn't turn on him.

"Hello, old friend," he said now. "Come to relish the sight of a poor human brought low, have you? Man believes himself to have dominion over the whole world, but in the end we're all such fragile creatures, not even masters of ourselves, let alone of our fellow beings. . . ."

His voice was rusty and strained. He tried not to go too long without talking. Sooner or later, he would face Rudolph Kroll again, and he wanted to be able to speak so he could tell the outlaw leader what he really thought of him.

Not that it would really matter.

Footsteps echoed hollowly in the corridor outside the cell. This was the only chamber down here under the house, and Luke suspected whoever had ordered it built had designed it so that whoever was locked up would hear his jailers coming and have to dread their arrival for a few extra seconds.

Why the cell had been built in the first place was a good question. It couldn't have been easy tunneling through the rock, hollowing out the small space, and then walling it up with blocks of stone. Had it been built to house a specific person? A mad relative of the ranch's owner, maybe? No one would ever build such a place just in case they might need to lock someone up, would they?

The answers to those questions were far back in the past. Luke doubted if they would ever be revealed to him. He would die curious.

But then, death was the ultimate curiosity, wasn't it? The puzzle to which no living man was ever granted the solution.

The heavy footsteps stopped outside the door.

A second later a key scraped in the lock. The door swung back. The huge shape that bulked in the corridor, seeming to fill it from side to side, told Luke that Galt had come for him.

That meant he was going upstairs. When it was just a meal arriving, one of the servants brought that, followed by a guard with a shotgun.

Galt rumbled, "Stand up."

Luke thought about not cooperating, but then decided there wasn't any point to being stubborn. His captors fed him barely enough to keep him alive, so he was too weak to fight. Even if he'd been in good shape, he doubted that he could have done much good against Galt, who was almost as big as a grizzly and just as strong and mean.

Luke pushed himself to his feet. Galt had come down here alone, and for a second, Luke considered the odds of jumping him. The idea was ridiculous, of course. He shoved it aside in his brain.

Rudolph Kroll had ordered that he be kept

alive. Luke couldn't understand the reason for that. Kroll needed the threat of his death to force Smoke into doing his bidding, but on the outside of the canyon, Smoke would have no way of being sure whether Luke was alive or dead. He would just have to hope that his brother was alive and proceed accordingly.

Smoke would have some plan in mind. Luke was sure of that. Smoke Jensen wasn't going to just waltz in here, turn Mordecai over, and then wait to be double-crossed and killed. Even though Luke didn't really know his own brother that well. He had heard and read plenty about Smoke. If there was a way to turn the tables on the Kroll brothers, Smoke would find it.

Luke was thinking about that as he struggled to push himself to his feet. When he was upright, he rasped at Galt, "What do you want?"

"The boss sent me to fetch you. That's all I know."

Luke figured that wasn't true. He had seen the way Galt paid attention to everything that went on around him without seeming to. The man might look like a mindless, lumbering behemoth, but he was far from it. He knew why he was supposed to bring Luke upstairs, all right.

He just didn't want to steal Rudolph's thunder, Luke thought.

He felt his pulse quicken. Maybe something was about to happen at last. Maybe after all this time, all these weeks that seemed like years, his ordeal was about over . . . one way or another.

Right now, Luke didn't really care all that much which way it was.

He took a step, almost went down, and then caught himself. He stiffened his legs, determined to walk to meet his fate, whatever it might be, on his own two feet. Galt backed up and raised the lantern he held in his left hand. Luke plodded out of the cell and started toward the stairs at the far end of the corridor. Galt followed behind him.

Luke stopped at the bottom of the stairs to gather his strength. Galt growled, "Up you go, Jensen."

Luke took a step, then another and another. He tried to ignore the weariness that gripped him. It seemed to take an hour, but finally he reached the top of the stairs.

Then he had to do it again, because Galt said, "Mr. Kroll is waiting for you on the balcony."

An attractive, middle-aged Mexican woman stood at the bottom of the curving staircase that led to the second floor. Luke saw sympathy in her dark eyes as he started toward her. He knew her name was Valencia and that she was the housekeeper here, as well as the cook. He suspected she warmed Rudolph Kroll's bed, too. But that didn't stop her from feeling sorry for the prisoner. Luke almost liked her. In a way, she was almost as powerless as he was.

She didn't speak to him as he went past her and started up the stairs. He had to clutch the banister for support. He felt Valencia watching him as he ascended, but he lacked the strength to turn his head and look back at her. He had to concentrate on the task directly in front of him: lifting one foot, then the other. . . .

He reached the second floor. Galt prodded him into Rudolph's library. The first time Luke had seen the room with its shelves of leather-bound books, he'd been jealous. He could have happily spent a great deal of time in there reading. Instead, he'd been locked up in what passed for a dungeon in Arizona Territory.

The French doors on the far side of the library were open, with late afternoon sunlight coming through them. Luke saw Rudolph Kroll standing on the balcony, at the railing. Rudolph turned and beckoned to him.

"Go," Galt growled quietly.

Luke walked across the library, through the doors, and onto the tiled balcony. Rudolph greeted him by saying, "Your salvation has arrived."

He waved a hand toward the tree-lined lane in front of the house. Luke swayed forward, caught himself with both hands on the railing. He saw the two riders approaching the big house.

One was Mordecai Kroll.

The other was Smoke.

Chapter 39

Smoke drew in a sharp breath when he saw the unsteady figure shamble out onto the balcony and stand next to Rudolph Kroll. He and Mordecai still weren't close enough to make out many details, but the newcomer's general size was right to be Luke, and so were the dark hair and beard.

The man's shaky gait as he came up to the railing made Smoke believe that he was looking at his brother, too. There was no telling what the outlaws had done to Luke, what tortures they might have inflicted on him, but at the very least he had suffered through several weeks of captivity. He wouldn't be in top shape.

"Well, what do you know?" Mordecai said. "Looks like Rudolph ain't killed that bounty-huntin' brother of yours after all. I reckon maybe he's savin' that pleasure for me."

"I thought you said your brother was a man of his word," Smoke snapped. "What happened to your claim that he would honor the deal he proposed to me if I brought you here?"

Mordecai laughed.

"Hell, you believed that? I thought you were too smart to get taken in that way, Jensen."

Mordecai paused suddenly and frowned. "You *are* too smart. You got some sort of trick you're plannin', don't you?"

It had taken Mordecai long enough to realize that, Smoke thought. Too long, because they were here now and Matt and Preacher had to be somewhere in the vicinity, too. Soon they would be getting the lay of the land and sizing up the situation, figuring out the best way for them to make their move and get Smoke and Luke out of this canyon.

But Smoke just shook his head and said, "I don't know what you're talking about. I kept up my end of the bargain. You're here, aren't you? Now all I can do is hope that your brother will hold up his end." Smoke slipped his Colt from its holster and aimed it in Mordecai's general direction. "I'm going to give him a good reason to do that."

"You do know there's probably a dozen rifles trained on you right now, don't you? You're lucky you didn't get drilled when you pulled that hog leg."

"I figured as long as I stay close enough to you, nobody will get too trigger-happy." Smoke nudged his horse ahead. "Let's go."

They continued riding up the lane. Smoke's gun never wavered. If he died, Mordecai would die, too. He didn't think any of the outlaws would risk Rudolph's wrath if his brother was killed while right here on the verge of being returned safely.

A massive, bearlike man in a long, beaded vest and flat-crowned black hat waited for them at the open gate in the thick adobe wall. Several other men stood nearby, holding rifles.

"Galt!" Mordecai greeted the big man as he and Smoke reined to a halt. "It's good to see you again, you big ol' buffalo!"

Judging by the scowl on Galt's face, he wasn't as happy to see Mordecai. But he said, "Your brother told me to bring you and this other fella up to see him as soon as you got here."

"Well, let's go!" Mordecai said impatiently. "No sense in wastin' time."

He started to swing down from the saddle, but Smoke snapped, "Hold on a minute, Kroll."

Mordecai froze in an awkward position and glared over at him in disbelief.

"You really mean to tell me you ain't given up yet?" he asked. "Just look around you, Jensen. You shoot me and two seconds later you'll be so full o' lead they could use you as a sinker on a fishin' line! Not to mention ol' Galt there could bust you in half and tear you apart with his bare hands."

"I don't doubt either of those things," Smoke said, "but you'd still be dead, wouldn't you?"

Galt asked, "What do you want, Jensen?"

"I hang on to my gun."

"Nobody's asked you for it, have they?"

Galt had a point there. Smoke said, "I want my brother brought down here. He's going to take a couple of these saddle mounts and ride out of here. I'm going to watch him until he's gone through the pass. Then, and only then, I let you have Mordecai."

"You've gone loco!" Mordecai exclaimed. "Rudolph will never agree to that. Tell him, Galt."

"I don't speak for the boss," Galt said. "I'll have to go talk to him."

"Then do it," Smoke told him.

"Dadgum it!" Mordecai exploded. "I've waited all this time to see Rudolph again, and now you tell me I got to wait more?"

"It won't be long," Galt said. Smoke could see the scorn in the big man's eyes. He had a hunch the rest of the gang tolerated Mordecai because of his brother, rather than him wielding any real power over them.

Galt told the riflemen, "Keep an eye on them," then turned and lumbered through the gate in the wall. Smoke watched the big man as he made his slow, stately way back to the house and disappeared inside.

"I'm gonna see to it that you pay for this, Jensen," Mordecai said. "You should've just gone ahead and died like you was supposed to. Would have been quicker and easier on you that way. Now I'm gonna make you suffer."

"I've been doing that all the way from Yuma," Smoke said. "I had to listen to you."

He thought he saw grins on the faces of a couple of the guards as they quickly looked away. They probably didn't have much use for Mordecai, either. That wouldn't really be any help to him in the long run, more than likely, but it was good to know he wasn't the only one who felt that way.

The minutes stretched out slowly, and Mordecai's continued profane grumbling didn't help them pass any faster. Finally the door into the big house opened, and Galt emerged again.

He wasn't alone this time.

Luke was with him.

And so was Rudolph Kroll.

Even though this was the first time Smoke had seen the man close up, he had no doubt who he was looking at. Kroll was dressed plainly, in brown trousers and vest and a collarless shirt buttoned at the throat. As far as Smoke could see, he wasn't carrying a gun or any other sort of weapon.

But he carried himself as if he were king of this canyon, and in a very real way, he was. He possessed the power of life and death over everyone here.

Smoke didn't really spare Rudolph Kroll more than a cursory glance. Most of his attention was concentrated on Luke, who walked under his own power but was clearly unsteady on his feet. Anger welled up inside Smoke as he saw how captivity had transformed his vital, powerful brother into a gaunt, hollow-eyed, bearded shadow of himself.

Then they were close enough for Smoke to look into Luke's eyes, and he suddenly felt a little better about things. Defiance and intelligence still burned in Luke's eyes. He hadn't given up. Being a prisoner hadn't knocked the fight out of him.

Smoke hadn't expected that it would—Luke was a Jensen, after all—but it was nice to see confirmation of that hunch.

Kroll came to a stop, and so did Luke. Before Rudolph could say anything, Mordecai exclaimed, "Howdy, big brother! I'm back!"

"I can see that," Rudolph said. That curt reply was the only one he gave Mordecai. He swung his attention to Smoke and said, "You'd be Smoke Jensen."

"I would," Smoke agreed.

"Why are you pointing that gun at my brother? Don't you know you won't stand a chance of getting out of this canyon alive if you shoot him?"

"I know that," Smoke said. "I just want you to understand . . . anything happens to me or *my* brother, Mordecai is going to die. That's a hundred percent guaranteed."

"You can't know that for sure," Rudolph snapped.

"Close enough."

Smoke's simple, confident answer made Rudolph frown. Mordecai said, "You see how he is? Just go ahead and kill him, Rudolph. Shoot the son of a bitch. He ain't near as good as he thinks he is."

"You want to bet your life on that?" Rudolph asked. "Because that's what you'd be doing."

Mordecai sat back in the saddle a little and didn't say anything.

Rudolph turned his attention back to Smoke and asked, "What do you want?"

"Your man Galt didn't tell you?"

"I'll hear it from you."

"Fair enough," Smoke said. "I keep this gun pointed at Mordecai until Luke gets on a horse and rides out of the canyon."

For the first time, Luke spoke. In a rusty croak, he said, "No! You can't do that, Smoke. They'll kill you."

"I'll take my chances. First order of business is to get you out of here to where you're safe."

"Hell, no," Luke rasped. "I'm not leaving without you. If the situation were turned around, would you ride out and leave me behind?"

Smoke had hoped his brother wouldn't ask him that question. The answer was no, of course he wouldn't do that. When he'd seen Luke's condition, though, he had hoped that his brother might have enough sense to agree.

It never paid to underestimate the stubbornness of a Jensen, though.

For the time being, Smoke ignored Luke's refusal to go along with his impromptu plan. He looked at Rudolph and said, "How about it, Kroll? Do we have a deal?"

Rudolph fixed him with a cold stare and said, "I've killed men for trying to dictate terms to me."

"They probably didn't have your brother's life for leverage," Smoke pointed out.

"But we have your brother's life in our hands," Rudolph said. "Galt!"

Smoke tensed, ready to open fire. Despite the fact that his gun was aimed at Mordecai, his first shot would be directed at Galt, since the bear of a man seemed to be the biggest threat to Luke. Then he would drill Rudolph and finally Mordecai.

By then he'd probably have several slugs in him. But as long as he could draw breath and pull the trigger, he would continue to kill outlaws.

He hoped Sally would forgive him someday for not coming back to her.

Galt stepped forward and whipped a knife from under his long vest. Moving with surprising speed, he wrapped an arm around Luke's neck and jerked him back against his broad chest. Galt's forearm pushed up against Luke's neck to expose his throat under the beard. Galt put the blade's edge against Luke's throat but didn't press on it.

Smoke controlled the instinct demanding that he kill the big man. Luke's life hung by a thread . . . but then, so did a number of other lives.

"It appears that we have a classic Mexican standoff," Rudolph said.

"Yeah," Mordecai said, "except none of us are Mexicans!"

That prompted a gale of laughter from him. None of the other men gathered in front of the gate joined in his amusement, and after a moment his cackling trailed away.

"What it comes down to, Kroll, is whether or not you're a man of your word," Smoke said. "Mordecai tried to convince me that you are, but then after we got here, he went back on that and claimed you were going to double-cross me. So what's it going to be? I brought you what you wanted. Do you let my brother and me ride out of here or not?"

"So, Mordecai told you I'm not an honorable man, did he?" Rudolph muttered. "I can't say that I'm fond of the idea of letting you go. You Jensens have been a major annoyance to me." He shrugged. "But a deal's a deal. Galt, let the bounty hunter go."

Mordecai's eyes widened in surprise. He exclaimed, "Rudolph! You can't mean it! You can't let these two skunks ride outta here!"

"I still give the orders," Rudolph grated. "You'd do well to remember that, Mordecai."

"But . . . but they know where the hideout is!" Mordecai sputtered. "What's to stop 'em from goin' and tellin' the law or even the army?"

Rudolph looked like he was thinking, and after a moment he said, "That's a fair point. Believe it or not, I like to think of myself as an honorable man. But I'm even more of a practical man. Galt, hang on to Luke Jensen. Smoke Jensen, drop that gun now . . . or go ahead and pull the trigger."

Smoke came mighty close to doing just that. In an earlier time, he would have.

And both he and Luke would have died in the next thirty seconds. Even though surrender ran counter to everything in his nature, a life of danger had forced him to become a practical man, too.

Plus he had a couple of hole cards that no one else here knew about.

"Smoke, don't do it," Luke croaked, his voice even more strained by Galt's grip on his throat. "I'd rather go out . . . fighting. . . ."

"They're not giving me any choice, Luke," Smoke said. He lowered the Colt so that it wasn't pointing at Mordecai anymore, and then tossed it onto the ground.

As soon as the revolver thudded onto the dirt, Mordecai left his saddle in a diving tackle aimed at Smoke. He wrapped his arms around Smoke and the impact of the collision spilled both of them from the horse's back. They crashed to the ground, and hatred gave Mordecai a slight edge as he scrambled up first.

He yelled, "I'm gonna kill you with my bare hands!" and sent a punch speeding toward Smoke's face.

Chapter 40

Matt lowered the field glasses through which he had been peering as he watched Smoke and Mordecai Kroll ride on through the pass and disappear on the other side.

A few moments earlier, he had been studying them through the glasses when he had seen them pause for some reason. Mordecai had tilted his head back a little as if he were looking at something up on the walls of the pass. Matt had shifted the glasses and caught a split-second reflection up there, even though not much sunlight penetrated into the pass.

Then Smoke and Mordecai had ridden on, with the outlaw waving to someone and confirming Matt's hunch that sentries were posted up on those walls of stone.

"I reckon the hideout must be on the other side

of that pass," he said to Preacher and Darcy as he stowed the field glasses away in one of his saddlebags.

"What makes you think that?" Darcy asked.

"The pass is being guarded. The gang wouldn't go to that much trouble unless there was something on the other side of it to protect."

Preacher said, "That makes pure-dee sense. Which means we got to find some other way around."

Matt studied the sheer cliffs, the rocky ridges, and the rugged peaks on both sides of the pass.

"That's not going to be easy," he said. "Looks like that's the only gap for miles."

"We can just ride around," Darcy suggested. "How long can it take?"

"Dependin' on what we find," Preacher said, "it might take days. And I ain't sure Smoke and Luke'll have that much time to spare."

"Neither am I," Matt said. "It'll be pretty dark in that pass come nightfall, though. Somebody who was really good at sneaking around might be able to get through it without the guards noticing him."

"Meanin' me, o' course," the old mountain man said.

"Actually, I was thinking about me."

"Dadblast it!" Preacher said. "I've done forgot more about sneakin' up on varmints than you ever knowed, boy. Besides, it ain't easy for a big ol' galoot like you to move around without makin' some noise."

"You're not exactly small yourself, Preacher," Matt pointed out. "Scrawny, yes, but not small."

"I'm the smallest of any of us," Darcy pointed out, but Matt and Preacher both shook their heads at the same time.

"You're not going anywhere near that outlaw hideout," Matt said. "We'll tell you all about it later, so you can write your story and try to sell it, but we're going to find some place where you'll be safe and leave you there."

Darcy got a stubborn look on her face that Matt was already familiar with, despite the relatively short time they had traveled together, and he knew she was going to argue.

To forestall that, he raised a hand and held it toward her with the palm outward.

"If you give us trouble, we'll tie you up," he warned her.

"You wouldn't dare!" she said. "If you tie me up and then go off and get yourselves killed, I'd starve to death or die of thirst or get eaten by a mountain lion!"

"Oh, we'd fix it so's you could get loose sooner or later," Preacher said. "You'd just be stuck there long enough for me an' Matt to do what needs to be done."

She glared at them for a long moment, and then said, "You two are incredibly annoying."

Preacher nodded and said, "Thank you kindly. I reckon we been doin' things right, then."

Darcy just blew out a frustrated breath.

Preacher ignored her and turned to Matt. He pointed at the mountains to the right of the pass.

"I been studyin' on them peaks," he said. "I got a hunch there's a way through there. See that leetle bitty notch?"

Matt squinted and frowned as he looked where Preacher was pointing.

"Maybe, but it'd take a mountain goat to get there," he said.

The old mountain man nodded and said, "I been accused of worse. Thought maybe I'd get as close as I can on horseback, then Dog and me will scout around up yonder and see what we can find. Might be a way to circle around and come at the hideout from the north."

"Even if you make it to the notch, you don't know what's on the other side."

"You don't know what's on the other side o' that pass, neither. And there's only one way to find out."

"You're right about that," Matt admitted. "I don't much like splitting up, though."

"Neither do I, but the odds are gonna be mighty heavy against us no matter what we do. Catchin' those varmints betwixt us wouldn't make 'em even, but it'd help."

Matt nodded.

"All right, go ahead. I'll find a good place to leave Darcy and then wait for it to get dark so I can try slipping through the pass."

"I'm right here, you know," Darcy said. "You don't have to talk about me like I'm not."

"Wasn't my intention," Matt told her, but he didn't actually apologize.

Preacher lifted a hand in farewell, and then rode off on Horse with Dog padding along beside them.

"Now," Matt said as he looked at Darcy, "what am I going to do with you?"

"You don't want me to answer that," she said with a half-snarl.

Matt turned away so she wouldn't see him grinning. She was feisty as all get-out, but he suspected she wouldn't appreciate it if he said as much.

"Let's go," he said. "We'll have a look around for a good place."

Darcy looked none too happy about it, but she came with him.

A short time later, they found a little canyon that twisted between two rock spires. It narrowed toward the back, so it would be relatively easy to defend. With her rifle, Darcy could hold off quite a few men if she had to.

Although there was no spring or creek, the presence of some grass told Matt water was seeping in from somewhere. He pointed that out to Darcy and told her, "If you're in here long enough to need more water than what you have in your canteens, you can dig for it. Just be careful and make what you have last."

"What about food?"

"Same goes for that. You have enough provisions to last for several days, though." He paused, and then went on. "If Preacher and I aren't back before your food runs out, chances are we're not coming back. What you should do when you have only a couple of days' rations left is pull out and head for Phoenix. If you get down out of the mountains and head west, you'll hit it before you run out of food."

"What you mean is that you'll be dead. The Kroll brothers will have killed you."

"That's the only thing I can think of that'd stop us from coming back for you," Matt said.

He picked out the best place for her to camp, where the graze was thickest for the horses he would leave with her and also where some boulders would provide cover if she needed it. He wished she were back in Boston, where she had come from, or just about anywhere else other than here in the Superstition Mountains not much more than a stone's throw from the lair of some of the most vicious outlaws on the frontier.

But one of the secrets of life was that you had to deal with things as they were, not how you wanted them to be. Despite his relative youth, he had learned that lesson and learned it well. He nodded to Darcy and told her, "All right, I'm going to leave you here now. You'll be all right. Just wait for me or Preacher to come and get you, and in the meantime keep your eyes open. Don't fire any guns unless you absolutely have to. Shots will just announce where you are. Same thing is true for a campfire. You'll have to make do without one."

"I know all that," she said. "There's nothing I can tell you to change your mind about taking me with you?"

"Nope. Not a thing."

"Then maybe I can *do* something."

Without warning, she stepped forward and wrapped her arms around his neck. She was tall and didn't have to stretch up very much to press her mouth to his in a kiss.

When he thought about it later, Matt realized he *could* have stopped her if he tried. The reflexes that had kept him alive in numerous gunfights certainly were fast and sharp enough to have prevented one woman from kissing him. He tried to tell himself that it was because she took him by surprise, but he knew that wasn't exactly the case.

The truth was he didn't mind her kissing him.

But it wasn't going to change his mind about what he'd decided, either.

He slipped an arm around Darcy's waist and held

her close against him for a moment. He had no doubt that her actions were calculated to help her get what she wanted, but from the way her mouth moved under his and her hips surged against him, he thought she found herself enjoying it more than she'd expected.

That didn't make any difference, either. He broke the kiss and stepped back.

Darcy's lips curved in a smile as she said, "Are you sure—"

"Remember, keep your eyes open," he went on as if nothing had happened. "If you see anybody coming up the canyon who isn't me or Preacher, take cover. And if you have to shoot . . . don't shoot to warn."

The grim import of his words was clear.

Darcy looked angry and exasperated at his failure to rise to the bait she had flung his way. But she nodded and said, "All right, I understand. But you be careful, too, Matt. As you put it, don't shoot to warn."

"I don't make a habit of it," he said dryly.

Chapter 41

Mordecai's fist caught Smoke on the jaw and knocked him backwards, but just as the punch landed, Smoke's left hand shot out and grabbed the front of Mordecai's shirt. As Smoke fell he hauled Mordecai with him and gave the outlaw a heave that sent him rolling across the ground.

Smoke slapped his right hand against the dirt and shoved himself up. From the corner of his eye he saw two members of the Kroll gang start forward, obviously intending to intervene in the fight, but Rudolph stopped them with a curt gesture.

"Mordecai bit it off," Rudolph said sharply. "Let's see if he can chew it."

Smoke took that to mean the boss outlaw was going to let them fight. Right now that was all right with him. If he could bust Mordecai up enough to put him out of action for a few days, that was one less threat he'd have to worry about.

Mordecai caught himself after he'd rolled over a couple of times. He got his hands and knees under him and cursed bitterly as he pushed himself upright. Smoke could have stepped in and given him a vicious kick in the belly while he was getting up, but instead Smoke waited for Mordecai to reach his feet before boring in and throwing a left-right combination.

The jab followed by the cross both landed and made Mordecai stagger backwards. He didn't fall this time. He got his back foot braced and lunged forward as he swung a looping right at Smoke's head.

Smoke swayed to the side so that the punch missed by a bare inch. He hooked a left into Mordecai's belly. Mordecai doubled over, but he turned that to his advantage by driving the top of his head into Smoke's chest with enough force to knock the air out of his lungs. Mordecai threw both arms around Smoke's waist and drove with his feet. The outlaw's lean body possessed a great deal of hard, wiry strength. Smoke's feet left the ground, and Mordecai dumped him on his back.

Smoke was already gasping for breath. The impact as he landed stunned him even more. So did the vicious kick that landed in his ribs on the left side an instant later. Luckily, Mordecai was still wearing the blunt-toed prison shoes instead of boots, or the damage might have been even worse.

As it was, Smoke grunted at the sharp stab of pain from a possibly cracked rib.

With a gleeful laugh, Mordecai lifted his foot again and swung it into position to stamp his heel down in Smoke's face. Smoke got his hands up barely in time to grab Mordecai's foot and stop the crushing blow from landing. He twisted as hard as he could. Mordecai let out a startled shout as he fell.

Smoke kept his grip on Mordecai's foot and continued twisting. Mordecai howled in pain as his right knee started to bend in ways it wasn't meant to. Smoke knew if he kept the pressure up for another few moments, he could cripple Mordecai.

Rudolph Kroll must have known that, too, because he snapped, "Galt, get him off of there!"

Smoke heard the boss outlaw's command over the roaring of blood in his ears. A second later, huge fingers clamped down on his shoulders from behind and lifted him. He tried to hang on to Mordecai's foot, but it was torn from his grasp. Smoke's surroundings whirled dizzily around him as Galt spun him through the air and let him go.

Again Smoke crashed to the ground. Getting flung around like a rag doll was starting to annoy him. He let that anger fuel him as he came up swinging.

He drove a right and then a left into Galt's face. The big man's head moved enough that his flat-crowned black hat fell off.

Other than that, however, it was like punching a block of granite, Smoke realized.

Galt grabbed him, lifted him off the ground,

crushed him against the wall of slabbed muscles that was the big man's chest. Those tree-trunk arms closed in a bear hug. Smoke's ribs groaned under the pressure, and once again he felt pain shoot through him. Beyond a doubt, one of his ribs was cracked.

Like the dropping of a curtain, a red haze descended over his eyes. He was already starved for air, and now the situation was even worse. He knew he was going to pass out at any second, and if Galt continued squeezing, Smoke would never wake up. Galt would compress the life right out of him.

"That's enough," Rudolph called. "Let him go."

Smoke barely heard the command. That red haze was so thick it filled his entire head now, and it had started to turn black around the edges. That black tide continued as Galt released him and let him fall to the ground.

Smoke felt himself hit the dirt, but he didn't know anything after that.

The cell was cramped when only one prisoner was in it. With two people incarcerated here, there was barely room to breathe, let alone move around.

Well, brothers were supposed to be close, Luke thought wryly as he waited for Smoke to wake up.

He wasn't sure how much time had passed

since they had been brought through the house, down the narrow stone staircase, along the corridor, and into the cell. Galt had carried Smoke's unconscious form draped over his shoulder like a sack of potatoes. When they reached the cell he'd had Luke go in first, then unceremoniously dumped Smoke at his feet. Guards with rifles had been ready to step in the whole time if need be, although with Smoke out cold and Luke in the shape he was in, the likelihood of that was pretty small.

Then Galt had stepped back and swung the massive door closed with ease, causing gloom to close in around the prisoners.

By now night had fallen, Luke thought, or if it hadn't, it wouldn't be long now. He had no idea how long the Kroll brothers intended to keep them alive.

Although it was Rudolph alone who made the decision, he mused as he sat on his blanket with his knees drawn up to give Smoke as much room as possible. Mordecai had wanted to go ahead and kill both of them right away, but Rudolph had vetoed that idea.

"They'll die when I'm good and ready for them to die," Rudolph had said, and the flat, menacing tone of his voice had made Mordecai stop arguing. They were brothers, but that didn't stop Mordecai from being a little afraid of his older sibling.

The thing of it was, Luke couldn't think of any

reason for Rudolph to delay killing them unless it was a demonstration of his power. Mordecai had caused considerable trouble for his brother by sneaking away from the hideout on his own and getting himself caught. Keeping the prisoners alive reinforced the idea that Rudolph was the boss around here and served the extra purpose of annoying Mordecai.

Smoke stirred and groaned. He was starting to come around. Luke had known it was only a matter of time. His brother was plenty tough.

It didn't look like that was going to be enough to get them out of here, though. Luke's biggest regret right now was that Smoke had been drawn into this fiasco.

Smoke lifted his head, shook it, and grimaced. He was lying on his stomach. He tried to roll over, but the wall stopped him. Clearly surprised, he muttered, "Where . . . where are . . ."

"We're in a cell under the hacienda," Luke said. "Sorry about the cramped quarters. The place appears to have been built for one occupant."

"Luke . . . ?" Smoke turned his head and looked around in an attempt to penetrate the shadows.

"Yeah, I'm right here."

"Matt . . . Preacher . . ."

Luke frowned in the darkness and said, "What?"

He knew who Matt and Preacher were, of course, but he didn't see how they were connected to this affair.

"They haven't been . . . caught?" Smoke asked. "You brought them with you?"

Even though Luke was surprised, when he considered the situation and the people involved, this development made sense. Smoke was a strong believer in family. When he found out that Luke was in danger, he wouldn't have hesitated to recruit Matt and Preacher to help with the rescue effort.

"They're not . . . in here?"

Luke let out a grim chuckle and said, "If two more people were crammed in here, the place would burst at the seams. No, I haven't seen Matt and Preacher. I didn't know they were anywhere around here."

Smoke heaved a sigh that sounded relieved and let himself relax a little, as much as he could on the stone floor.

"They've been trailing me and Mordecai Kroll," he said. "I'm counting on them to help get us out of here now that I've found you."

"So four men—two of them prisoners—are going to take on the whole Kroll gang and win?"

"That was the idea," Smoke replied, and his voice held some grim humor as well.

"Pretty risky plan, wasn't it?"

"Not really."

"How do you figure that?" Luke wanted to know.

Carefully, Smoke shifted around until he could draw his legs up and maneuver himself into a sitting position with his back against the wall alongside Luke. He grunted in obvious pain.

"Are you hurt bad?"

"I think Mordecai cracked a rib when he kicked me," Smoke said. "And then Galt did even more damage with that bear hug. And I reckon I mean that literally . . . Galt's as big as a grizzly."

"He's smarter than you'd give him credit for just by looking at him, too. In some ways, I'd say he may be the most dangerous one of the whole bunch." Luke paused. "You still haven't told me why you thought coming to rescue me this way was a good idea."

"It was the only way," Smoke insisted. "I needed Mordecai's help to find the hideout, and I wasn't going to get it unless I fooled him into thinking that I was following Rudolph's instructions and working alone."

"Then why didn't you just have the army follow you, or even a big posse of US marshals?"

"Too much of a chance Mordecai would spot a large group trailing us. I knew Preacher and Matt could do the job without Mordecai ever realizing they were behind us."

"Maybe so, but now that you're here, there are only two of them to pull us out of this jackpot."

"You've heard about the two of them," Smoke

said, "but you've never actually met Preacher and Matt. I'll take them over a posse or even the army. I'm sure they're out there right now, figuring out a way to give the Kroll brothers a mighty unpleasant surprise."

Chapter 42

Preacher was lost.

It had been many, many years since that thought had crossed the old mountain man's mind. There had been times when he didn't know exactly where he was, of course. That was inevitable when you made a habit of going new places, and the unquenchable desire to see what was over the next hill had always been a part of him. But he had known where he was going, and usually that was all that counted. It was just a matter of figuring out how to get there.

These Superstition Mountains were an unholy jumble, though. Riven by deep gullies, speared by rock pinnacles, bisected by looming cliffs. . . . A man could get lost in here mighty easy by daylight. Finding his way in darkness was damned near impossible.

If anybody could do it, though, Preacher was the man.

Or so he told himself.

"Dog, I'm glad some o' my old pards can't see me now," he told the big cur as he stopped to rest. "I'd be plumb mortified."

Dog whined quietly. He didn't like clambering around through these badlands in the dark any more than Preacher did.

They had left Horse back on the other side of the ridge where the notch was located. Even though it had taken hours for them to reach this spot, what with all the doubling back they had been forced to do, that probably wasn't more than a mile away as the crow flies.

Preacher and Dog had climbed to the notch, which was unguarded they discovered when they got there. The ascent had been a difficult one, if not quite bad enough to require a mountain goat as Matt had said. Preacher was a little surprised the gang didn't have a sentry posted up there anyway. He supposed Rudolph Kroll thought any group of men large enough to pose an actual threat to them wouldn't attempt such a climb.

One man could make it, though . . . and Preacher had.

One man and a dog, anyway.

The terrain on the north side of the notch was almost as rugged, and to make things more difficult, Preacher didn't really know what he was looking for. He knew he was east of the pass Smoke and Mordecai Kroll had used, so he worked his way in that direction. Then he had to backtrack, climb in and out of ravines, and circle around rock spires, until he wasn't even sure which way he was going anymore.

Fortunately, he had stars to steer by, and the brief moment of confusion soon passed. It was troubling, though. Preacher was as close to a man without fear as could ever be found, but there was one thing he was afraid of.

He was afraid of getting too old to go adventuring anymore.

He shoved that thought away and resumed his search. A three-quarter moon rose, and that helped. The silvery light that spilled over the landscape wasn't as bright as day, but Preacher found his way around easier with it.

Even so, the cliff almost fell out from under him with no warning.

He reached down and dug his fingers into the thick fur on the back of Dog's neck as he stopped on the brink of the sheer drop.

"Hold on there, old feller," he said quietly. "Take a look at that."

A canyon lay before him, a good-sized canyon surrounded on all sides by steep, unscalable cliffs. Preacher knew this had to be the Kroll gang's hideout. Lights burned here and there, including one large cluster of them that was probably the headquarters. Preacher could barely make out the lines of some sort of big house.

More than likely an old ranch house, he thought. The Krolls had moved in and taken it over, either finding it abandoned or killing whoever had lived here.

Smoke and Luke were down there somewhere. Finding the hideout made Preacher feel a little better.

The bad part was that he couldn't see any way of getting down there to help them.

But there had to be a back door, he told himself. As long as the Kroll brothers had been raising hell without the law catching up to them, it seemed unlikely Rudolph Kroll was dumb enough to establish his stronghold in a place where his enemies could close off one end and keep him trapped there until he starved to death.

Preacher's keen eyes searched the canyon below him for any clue where that back door might be. Then his gaze fell on a dark line that twisted toward the canyon's northern end. Those were trees, he realized, and they had to mark the course of a stream. The little creek had to come from somewhere.

Of course, the stream might come from a spring at the head of the canyon. But maybe it flowed in from outside. Preacher knew of only one way to find out. He began following the line of cliffs around the canyon.

More than an hour later he came to a ravine that slashed through the cliffs like a giant knife had carved it out of the stone. The gap was about twenty feet wide and at least a hundred feet deep, so there was no way to get across it. Preacher listened and heard the roar of fast-moving water coming from the bottom.

"This is where that creek comes into the canyon," he told Dog. "Look at the way the ravine runs due north. We got to follow it and see if we can find a way down into it. Maybe we can float right into that dang outlaw hideout and get there in time to help Matt!"

A low, heartfelt curse whispered from Matt's lips as he glanced to the east and saw the glow in the sky. The moon was about to rise, charging into view in its constant chase after the sun. He had hoped to make it through the pass before that happened, during the dark gap between the fall of true night and the rising of the moon. His approach to the pass had taken too long, however. The trail had twisted back and forth too much as it made its way through the rugged landscape. Now he was liable to be caught out in the open as the silvery rays spilled over the pass.

He had come too far to turn back. All he could do was go ahead and hope for the best.

He had left his horse well behind him, knowing that he couldn't take the animal through the pass without the hoofbeats echoing and alerting the guards. His passage through the gap had to be almost soundless in order to be successful. It wouldn't take much of a noise to cause a racket.

In his jeans, dark blue shirt, and black hat, he figured he blended into the shadows fairly well for the time being. He had wrapped one of his blankets around the Winchester he carried so there wouldn't be any reflection off the barrel or the action. Also, if he happened to bump the rifle against a rock or anything like that, the blanket would help muffle the sound. His Colt was blued steel, not nickel-plated, and the grips were walnut. The revolver wasn't going to shine in the darkness, either.

Matt was in the pass now, moving slowly and carefully, setting each foot down gingerly until he was sure he wasn't stepping on a rock or about to do anything else that would make a noise. He eased forward, and as he did he heard the guards stationed in the rocks on the sides of the pass talking to each other as they tried to pass the long hours of their shifts.

He paused as he heard one of the outlaws say "Jensen." The name was all Matt caught at first, but then the man continued. "From what I heard, he plans to kill 'em both at dawn."

"He'll make everybody get up to watch, too, won't he?"

"You know how Rudolph is. Runs the gang almost like an army company."

The second man laughed and said, "That's all

right with me. I can take a few orders if it means bein' a rich man sooner or later. I was in the cavalry, you know."

"Naw, I didn't know that," the other man replied. "When'd you muster out?"

That brought another laugh.

"I never did! Just slipped away from a patrol one day and kept ridin'. That was five years ago and they ain't caught me yet."

"As long as you're ridin' with the Kroll brothers, they probably won't. Say, when do you think we'll have the big divvy-up? I'm gettin' a mite tired of the way Rudolph just doles out a little dinero to us. He's got one hell of a lot of loot stashed by now. I want to get my hands on my fair share."

"Why don't you go and suggest that to him?" the other man said. "I'm sure he wouldn't mind takin' your advice."

The response was another suggestion, but a profane one. The second outlaw went on, "I may grouse a little, but there ain't no way I'm tellin' Rudolph Kroll how he ought to run the gang. I'm still too fond of livin'."

"Yeah, me, too. Those two Jensens probably are, too, but they're just plumb out of luck, come mornin'."

The other man changed the subject by saying, "Where do you reckon Rudolph has all that loot stashed, anyway?"

"I don't know. Up there in the big house

somewhere, I suppose. I'll bet him and maybe Galt are the only ones who know for sure."

The men paused in their conversation for a moment. Then one of them said, "You reckon Rudolph will do anything to Mordecai for causin' so much trouble in the first place?"

"Naw. Rudolph's mad, all right. I reckon he'd like to horsewhip the boy. But he won't. Mordecai always gets away with whatever he does, you know that."

"Yeah. But one of these days bein' so reckless is liable to catch up to him."

Matt hoped that day was today, or rather tonight, he thought as he resumed his stealthy trek through the pass. All the information he had picked up from the talkative sentries was interesting, but only one fact really mattered at the moment.

Smoke and Luke were scheduled to die at dawn.

So Matt had until then to make sure they didn't.

Chapter 43

Despite the pain in his side and the threat of death looming over him and Luke, Smoke dozed off after a while with his back and head propped against the stone wall of the cell.

He woke up to the sound of footsteps echoing in the corridor on the other side of the door. He opened his eyes, which were so gritty they felt like the eyeballs had been popped out, rolled around in a bucket of sand, and then shoved back into his head.

Gloom still cloaked the cell, relieved only by the faint glow that came through the barred window in the door. Night and day had no meaning down here in the eternal twilight of imprisonment, Smoke realized.

He heard Luke stir beside him and said, "You reckon it's morning yet?"

"Doesn't seem like it should be," Luke replied. "But I could be wrong about that. Maybe we'll find out if they bring us breakfast."

"How's the food in this place?" Smoke asked wryly.

"Not as good as the steaks at Delmonico's," Luke said with a chuckle.

Smoke was glad to hear that bit of grim humor. It proved that Luke hadn't given up . . . not that Smoke would have expected him to do such a thing. Jensens had never been in the habit of hollering calf-rope.

Their visitor wasn't bringing them breakfast, however. Instead, the footsteps came to a stop outside the door, and Mordecai Kroll put his face close to the bars in the window and said, "Jensen! Both of you! Are you awake in there?"

Neither Smoke nor Luke responded. Chances were that Mordecai had come down here to taunt them. Smoke couldn't think of any other reason the younger Kroll brother would pay a visit to the dungeon. He didn't want to give Mordecai the pleasure of a response, and obviously neither did Luke.

"Go ahead and ignore me, both of you," Mordecai continued. The faint slur in his voice testified that he had been drinking but probably wasn't actually drunk. "I know you're in there, and I know you can hear me. You can't tell it where you are, but it's about five hours until dawn. You know what that means?"

Mordecai paused to increase the drama of the moment.

"It means you've got five hours left until you die," he said after a moment. "Come sunup, I'm gonna even the score with both of you bastards. It took some doin', but I finally talked Rudolph into lettin' me take a bullwhip to you. Listen up, bounty hunter. You're gonna watch me whip your brother to death, and when I'm done with that, I'm gonna take the whip to you until I've cut you into little, tremblin' pieces." Mordecai laughed. "And I'm gonna enjoy every scream, every drop of blood that falls on the ground. You're both done for. Simple as that."

Smoke still didn't say anything, and neither did Luke. Both men had faced death so many times over the years that it held no particular fear for them. If his string was played out, Smoke would regret never seeing Sally again, never being able to hold her and tell her good-bye, but she was the strongest person he had ever known and he was confident she would be all right.

He would be sorry, too, because if he died, that meant the Kroll brothers won, and that idea greatly offended his sense of justice.

But Mordecai had said that it was five hours until dawn and their date with death, and a lot could happen in five hours, especially with Matt and Preacher on the loose somewhere.

"All right, go ahead and be stubborn," Mordecai said when they didn't answer. "Sull up like a couple of old possums for all I care. You'll be screamin' soon enough when I'm usin' that bullwhip to peel every inch of hide off of you!"

Mordecai had brought his bottle with him. Smoke heard liquid gurgle as the outlaw took a long swallow of whiskey from it. Then his footsteps retreated from the door and eventually Smoke heard them ascending stairs, followed by the thump of another door closing.

"He's gone," Smoke said.

"Better make sure," Luke said. "I don't want the slimy son of a bitch eavesdropping on us."

He climbed awkwardly to his feet in the cramped quarters, shuffled over to the door, and peered through the window for a long moment before he said, "Yeah, Mordecai's gone. But he'll be back. You know the old saying about bad pennies. The Kroll brothers are just about the worst."

"That gives Matt and Preacher until then to make their move."

"You've got a lot of confidence in them. I'm not sure I ever put that much faith in anybody."

"Of course, I have faith in them. They're family."

Luke grunted and said, "More so than me, I reckon, even though we're blood relatives and they're not. I turned my back on my family for fifteen years."

"You thought you had good reason," Smoke said. "Anyway, blood's important. But family is more than blood. Preacher was like an uncle to me almost as soon as I met him, and Matt's the little brother I never had, sure enough. But that doesn't make you and me any less brothers."

Slowly nodding in the gloom, Luke said, "That's good to know. Even if we don't make it out of this, we're together now. Nothing Mordecai does can take that away from us."

"Nope. Just don't give up hope."

"Not as long as there's breath in my body," Luke said.

It took Preacher a maddeningly long time to find a place where he could descend into the canyon where the creek ran before it entered the canyon. When he finally did, the slope was too steep and rugged for Dog to manage it.

"I'm gonna have to leave you here, old fella," Preacher told the big cur.

Dog whined deeply in his throat.

"I know, I don't like it any more than you do. But you can't climb down there, and I got to find a way in so I can help Matt when he makes his move. Right now all we can do is hope that Smoke and Luke are still alive."

Dog ran back and forth along the canyon rim. He let out a quiet bark as Preacher lowered himself over the edge.

"Hush, now," Preacher told him. "Maybe you can find some other way down. If you do, I reckon I'll see you in yonder canyon. Just don't do nothin' foolish."

With that warning, he let his weight down onto a foothold he had spied in the moonlight and began searching for the next one.

The descent was harrowing. More than once, Preacher had to work his way to one side or the other for several yards before finding a route that took him lower again. The closer he came to the creek, the slicker the rocks became from spray rising, which added to the danger.

After nearly falling a couple of times, at last Preacher dropped to the level surface of a ledge that jutted out just a few feet above the water. At this point in the canyon, the creek was about thirty feet wide and flowed swiftly, but not fast enough to describe it as rapids.

Some hardy brush grew along the base of the wall. Preacher had hoped to find a few small trees growing in the canyon as well, so that maybe he could hack them down and fashion a crude raft from them, but it appeared he was out of luck where that was concerned.

But the ledge was a good ten feet wide and led in the direction of the outlaw canyon, so he started along it.

The farther he went, the narrower the ledge became. Preacher was sure-footed, but even he had to lean against the rock wall and cling to it with strong fingers to keep from slipping off.

As the ledge narrowed, so did the canyon, until it was a deep gorge no more than fifteen feet wide, through which the creek now raced at breakneck speed. It was too dark down here in the bottom of this slash in the earth to make out many details, but Preacher heard the water roaring and splashing and figured there were rocks jutting up in the rapids.

Eventually the ledge was barely wide enough for Preacher's boots. If it dwindled down to nothing, as it appeared it might, he would have no choice but to go back and look for some other way into the outlaw stronghold. If he had to do that, he might be too late to help Matt rescue

Smoke and Luke . . . if he could get there at all.

But for now he was going to forge ahead, so he clung to the stone wall and moved his feet along the slippery shelf.

He had no warning when it suddenly crumbled underneath him. One second he was perched on the ledge, and the next he toppled backwards, flailing his arms in the air but finding nothing to grab on to.

He hit the water, which was icy from snow melt, and went under. The current caught him like a giant hand and flung him along the rocky gorge.

The eastern sky was gray with the approach of dawn by the time Matt reached the compound. It had taken him this long to get here because he'd had to go to ground several times to avoid discovery by roving patrols of outlaws. As isolated and difficult to get into as this canyon was, Matt was a little surprised Rudolph Kroll would go to that much trouble to guard the place.

But *he* had gotten in here, he reminded himself. So maybe Rudolph's precautions made sense after all.

He didn't know where Smoke and Luke were being held prisoner, but it made sense they would be in the big house where the Kroll brothers were. He needed to get in there and find them, but to do that he would need a distraction of some sort to draw everybody out.

His eyes narrowed as his gaze fell on the big adobe barn with its attached corral where more than two dozen horses milled. The barn wouldn't burn, but the hay stored inside it would, and the smoke and flames would spook the horses into stampeding. That seemed like his best bet.

The buildings were all quiet and dark. People would be getting up soon to greet the new day, but for now nearly everybody was asleep. Matt catfooted from shadow to shadow as he worked his way toward the barn, and he was just about to dart through the opening where one of the big double doors was pushed back a few feet when a man stepped out through that same gap, stretching and yawning. Caught in the open, Matt had nowhere to go, and as the outlaw caught sight of him, the man clawed for the gun on his hip and opened his mouth to give a yell of alarm.

Chapter 44

Matt's superb reflexes were the only thing that saved him. He sprang forward like a striking snake. His left hand closed around the man's wrist and kept him from drawing the gun. At the same time, Matt's right fist crashed into the outlaw's jaw and rocked his head back sharply.

The man's knees folded up as he dropped to the ground, senseless.

No yell, no shot. Matt was still safe for the time being, and more importantly, his plan hadn't been ruined.

Matt dragged the unconscious outlaw away from the barn and stashed him in the shadows of an empty blacksmith shop nearby. He used the man's own belt to tie his hands behind his back and ripped off a piece of the man's shirt, wadded it up, and shoved it between the man's jaws as a gag. He took the outlaw's gun from its holster and stuck it behind his belt.

In a gunfight, he wouldn't have hesitated to ventilate any of the Kroll gang, but he wasn't going to leave a helpless man to burn to death, even an outlaw.

He made it into the barn without further incident and found that it was empty except for several horses in stalls. He led them out through an inner gate into the corral, then went over to the corral gate and unfastened the latches holding it closed. He left the gate pushed up so the horses would stay in the corral for the time being, but once they spooked and began to bump against it, it would swing open and release them so they could get away from the fire he was going to set.

Back in the barn, he found a lantern hanging on a nail and used some cord from the tack room to rig a fuse leading to the lamp's reservoir of kerosene. He poured some of the kerosene on the wooden support pole in one of the stalls directly under the hayloft, and then set the lamp next to a pile of hay by the pole. When the lamp lit it would set fire to the hay, and the furiously burning pile of dry hay ought to climb the oil soaked pole to reach the hayloft and start it blazing as well. From there, everything flammable inside the barn would burn and the horses would stampede . . . if everything went according to plan.

Matt struck a lucifer and lit the fuse leading to the lamp. As soon as he saw it was burning like it should, he hurried out of the barn. The eastern sky was orange now. Smoke came from the chimney of the big ranch house, and also from the cookshack behind what was probably the bunkhouse for the rest of the gang.

People would be up and around. Matt lowered his head so that his hat partially shielded his face and walked toward the adobe wall around the big house as if he belonged here and wasn't doing anything out of the ordinary. An old man stepped out of the cookshack, tossed a pan of water on the ground, and went back inside after barely glancing at Matt.

He reached the shadows along the wall and vanished into them. The wall had a gate in it in front of the house, but there was probably a smaller gate elsewhere. Matt thought that might be his best way in.

He had just found it, not actually a gate but a narrow wooden door, when he heard a commotion from the front of the compound. From the sound of the voices, a lot of men were gathering, maybe the entire gang except for the sentries.

Matt glanced at the sky again. Sunrise was only minutes away. He remembered what the guards in the pass had said about the Kroll brothers planning to execute Smoke and Luke at dawn and how everyone would have to be on hand to witness it. He was running out of time.

The gate was barred on the inside, he discovered when he tried it. But the top of it was in reach of a tall man who could jump. He tensed his muscles, bent his knees slightly, gathered his strength, and sprang upward with his right hand stretching as high as he could reach.

His hand closed over the top of the door—and pain pierced through it. Matt stifled a yell as he hung there. Somebody had fastened barbed wire along the top of the door, and a couple of the vicious barbs had jabbed deep into his palm. Every instinct told him to let go.

Instead, he forced himself to hang on. He had to, for Smoke's and Luke's sake. He had to get in there if they were going to have a chance to escape their execution. Matt reached up with his left hand and got another grip on top of the door, more carefully this time. He managed to let the barbs stick up between his fingers. He pulled his right hand loose and shifted his grip with it. The hand throbbed with pain and grew slick with blood, but that didn't stop Matt from pulling himself up so he could swing a leg on top of the adobe wall next to the door.

A glance toward the barn showed him only pale blue sky above it, streaked with thin, rosy early morning clouds. He thought he ought to be seeing a black pall of smoke from the barn by now. Its absence meant nothing had happened to draw the gang's attention away from the house. They would be gathering there in overwhelming numbers.

It was too late to do anything else now. Matt swung himself over the wall and dropped to the ground inside the compound, bleeding hand and all.

Down here in this crude dungeon there was no way to tell how much time had passed, but it seemed like days to Smoke as he and Luke waited for their fate. Finally, heavy footsteps approached the door again.

Smoke had halfway expected to hear gunshots or even an explosion. It wouldn't have surprised him a bit if Matt and Preacher had pulled off something like that.

But when nothing happened, he began to wonder if something might have befallen them. He had every confidence in the world in them and knew they would never let him down as long as they were alive, but sometimes luck turned on a man and there was nothing he could do about it. Nothing but fight, and maybe in the end lose.

"That's Galt," Luke said quietly as the footsteps came closer to the door. "Nobody else walks like him. I hear some other men with him. Probably rifle-toting guards."

"They've come to get us," Smoke agreed. "Must be getting close to dawn."

Luke grunted and said, "Looks like Matt and Preacher aren't going to get here in time."

"I don't plan to give up as long as I'm still drawing breath."

"I didn't say anything about giving up," Luke responded. "But I'll be damned if I stand by and let a vicious animal like Mordecai Kroll whip me to death. I'm going to get my hands on a gun and take a few of them with me before I make them shoot me."

"Sounds like a good idea," Smoke agreed. "I'd like to send the Kroll brothers to hell first."

Luke grinned in the gloom and said, "That sounds like a good plan to me."

A key rasped in the lock, and the door swung back. Galt's massive form filled the opening, just as Luke had predicted. Smoke couldn't see past the majordomo, but he heard several men shifting their feet in the corridor.

"It's time," Galt said in his voice like the sound of distant drums. "Come on out."

"Or you'll drag us out?" Luke asked.

"I think you know the answer to that question."

Luke lifted a slightly shaky hand and pointed a finger at Galt. He said, "You're a smart man, Galt. Don't try to deny it. I can see it in your eyes. Why do you work for a couple of monsters like the Kroll brothers?"

"Rudolph Kroll isn't a monster," Galt said. "He's a genius. He'll wind up owning this whole territory someday."

"How can you call a man a genius when he lets himself be burdened by a fool like Mordecai?"

This time Galt didn't respond. For a long moment he stood there glaring in the light of a lantern carried by one of the other men. Then he asked, "Are you coming out or not?"

"I don't reckon we've got much choice," Smoke said as he climbed to his feet.

Galt stepped back to let them emerge from the cell. The guards backed off with the rifles in their hands leveled at the two prisoners. The outlaws seemed a little nervous, as if they thought Smoke and Luke might try to jump them. If guns started going off in these close confines and bullets began to bounce around, there was a good chance somebody else would be hit besides the prisoners.

That possibility was enough to make Smoke give it some thought, but he decided against making a move right now. When he glanced at his brother, he could tell that Luke had come to the same conclusion. It would be better to bide their time.

The problem was that their time was running out.

With Galt looming behind them and the guards backing away ahead of them, Smoke and Luke walked along the corridor toward the stairs and then up to the ranch house's opulently furnished first floor. Galt stepped around them then to lead the way to the front door and out onto the first of the flagstone terraces that dropped away from the house and gave a spectacular view of the outlaw canyon.

Two posts fashioned from thick beams had been set up on the terrace. They were nailed at their bases to other beams that formed crosspieces so the posts stood up straight and imposing. They were placed the right width apart so that a prisoner's arms could be pulled out to his sides and tied to the posts. The setup was designed so that a man could be fastened to it and whipped, Smoke realized.

The man who planned to do the whipping stood by waiting in the garish light of a big red sun that had just peeked over the jagged mountains east of the canyon. Mordecai Kroll grinned as he moved his hand and made the long bullwhip dangling from it writhe on the flagstones like a snake.

His brother, Rudolph, was there, too, standing on the other side of the whipping posts with a solemn expression on his dark, dour face. Several yards behind him was the slim form of Rudolph's mistress/housekeeper, Valencia.

The rest of the gang had gathered on the lower terraces, ordered there to witness the execution of the two prisoners. They were silent and unmoving. Some of them had women with them, an assortment of white, Mexican, and Indian soiled doves and camp followers. A few of the men seemed eager to see what was going to happen, but many of them were rather stolid and emotionless, as if they were here only because their boss had told them to be.

"I told you two bastards that you were gonna die at dawn, and I'm keepin' my word!" Mordecai said exultantly. He used the whip handle to point at the sun. "Look there! That's the last sunrise you're ever gonna see!"

Smoke already knew the sun was up. As he and Luke paused at the edge of the terrace, he was looking at something else.

A giant ball of black smoke suddenly burst from one of the buildings outside the wall and rose into the air to form a column. At the same time, shrill whinnies of fear came from what sounded like dozens of horses, followed by the rumble of hoofbeats and an abrupt crash. Everybody on the terraces heard the commotion and turned to look.

"The barn!" Rudolph shouted. "The barn's on fire! Save those horses!"

The outlaws rushed toward the open gate. Mordecai cried, "Damn it, wait! It's dawn! These Jensens gotta die!"

Everybody ignored him. The men rushed toward the barn.

Smoke glanced over at Luke and moved his head in a tiny nod. He knew a distraction when he saw one. This was the work of Matt and Preacher.

Mordecai's face contorted with hate and frustration. He flung the whip on the flagstones at his feet and yelled, "You'll die anyway, damn it!"

He yanked the revolver from the holster on his hip. The gun flashed up toward Smoke and Luke.

Chapter 45

Before Mordecai could fire, a rifle cracked. The gun flew from Mordecai's fingers and he twisted halfway around from the impact of the slug that drilled through his upper right arm.

Matt stepped out from behind some shrubs at the corner of the terrace and leveled his Winchester at Rudolph, who had started to reach under his coat for a gun.

"Hold it, Kroll!" Matt ordered. "Get your hands up or I'll kill you!"

Luke glanced over at Smoke and said, "That'd be our little brother Matt?"

"That it would," Smoke said with a proud smile.

Rudolph thought about making a try anyway, but then he slowly pulled his hand out from under his coat, empty, and raised both arms into the air. Galt growled and took a step forward, but Rudolph snapped, "Galt, no. He's got the drop on us, whoever he is."

"I'm Matt Jensen, that's who I am," Matt said. "The third Jensen brother. Pleased to meet you at last, Luke. I wish it was under better circumstances."

"So do I, Matt," Luke said. "But I'll take it."

With all the commotion going on from the barn being on fire, none of the other outlaws had paid any attention to the shot. The Kroll brothers, Galt, and three other owlhoots were the only ones here on the terrace with the Jensen brothers. Matt was outgunned, but none of the men staring down the barrel of that deadly Winchester seemed to want to start anything, at least not yet.

Matt motioned the guards back with the rifle. Smoke and Luke hurried over to him. Matt said, "Take my Colt and this gun that's stuck behind my belt. That way we'll all be armed."

"Your hand's bleeding, Matt," Smoke commented

as he slipped the revolver from Matt's holster and passed it to Luke. He took the extra gun for himself.

"Yeah, I know. I stuck it on some barbed wire. But it's nothing to worry about. I can still shoot, and that's all that matters right now." Matt raised his voice and called to the three guards, "Throw those rifles away, and your handguns, too. Do it now."

The outlaws hesitated, but then Rudolph gave them a curt nod and they followed Matt's order.

Rudolph wore an angry but pragmatic expression as he said, "The three of you have no chance to get out of here alive. You know that, don't you?"

Mordecai had been whimpering in pain as he clutched his wounded arm. Now he exclaimed, "Don't talk to them, Rudolph! Just kill 'em!"

"Don't be a bigger damned fool than you already are," Rudolph snapped. "If we try anything now they'll kill us. But they're outnumbered and they know it. They can't get away."

"I wouldn't be so sure about that," Matt said confidently. "I reckon we can if we've got some hostages."

For the first time a look of genuine concern flickered over Rudolph Kroll's face. He said, "You're wrong about that, Jensen. My men don't love me that much. They'll gun me down if it means killing you three and preserving the secret of this hideout."

"What about your brother?"

Rudolph laughed coldly and said, "They'll be even quicker to kill Mordecai."

The younger brother forgot about how bad his arm was hurting and stared at Rudolph in amazement.

"How . . . how can you say that?" Mordecai demanded. "The men all love me!"

Rudolph didn't dignify that absurd claim with a response.

"I think you're wrong, Kroll," Matt said. "I think your men will want to keep you alive because you know where all the loot from the gang's jobs is stashed, and they don't. You're worth a lot of dinero to them."

That was news to Smoke, but it didn't come as a real surprise. Rudolph struck him as the sort of hombre who would want to play all his cards close to the vest. That caution might backfire on him now.

Rudolph's face darkened as he glared at the three Jensens.

"*I* won't let you get away with this," he declared. "I'll order my men to open fire on you no matter what happens to Mordecai and me."

"I guess we'll have to put that to the test," Smoke said. He gestured with the gun he held. "Get moving, all of you." He glanced at Valencia. "Except you, ma'am. You can stay here where it's safe."

"What are you going to do?" the woman asked. "What Señor Kroll says is true. There are too many of them."

Matt said, "I figure they'll catch us some of those horses I stampeded with the fire in the barn, and then five of us will ride out of this canyon: my brothers and I and Rudolph and Mordecai. We'll have our guns on them the whole way. If they want to keep Rudolph alive, they'll let us go."

"You overestimate them," Rudolph said. "They'll gun us all down and then come up here and tear the place apart, brick by brick, to find that loot. We'll all die for nothing!"

"It's a chance we have to take," Smoke said. He was getting mighty tired of all the talking. He gestured again with the revolver. "Move!"

"No," Galt said. "No!"

Eyes wide with rage, the big man charged Smoke, Matt, and Luke.

Their guns swung toward Galt, but they hesitated, reluctant to shoot down an unarmed man, even one as big as a grizzly.

The distraction gave the guards a chance to dive for the rifles they had thrown down. They came up firing, but they hurried their shots and the bullets whined over the heads of the three Jensen brothers.

Matt and Luke instantly returned the fire. Working the Winchester's lever with blinding speed, Matt cut down two of the guards while the Colt in Luke's hand boomed and drove a .45 slug into the third man's chest and spun him off his feet.

While they were doing that, Smoke lunged forward to intercept Galt. He whipped the revolver he held against the side of the big man's head. It landed with stunning force, but Galt shook off the effects of the blow and barreled into Smoke. The impact sent darts of pain from his cracked rib stabbing through Smoke's torso as he stumbled backwards, barely escaping the massive arms that Galt tried to throw around him.

Smoke remembered his previous fight with the bearlike majordomo. He wasn't going to let himself get trapped in Galt's deadly embrace again. He summoned up all the speed and quickness he possessed and darted aside as Galt grabbed at him again. Reversing the pistol, he smashed the butt into the bridge of Galt's nose, right between the man's eyes. Those eyes went glassy for a second, and Galt stumbled.

Smoke knew he had done some damage, so he struck again, slightly lower this time. The blow crunched cartilage, flattened Galt's nose, and made bright crimson blood spurt from it. Galt grunted and swung his right arm in a backhand that caught Smoke on the shoulder and nearly knocked him down. Smoke caught his balance as he started to topple.

That gave Galt time to close in again. A huge fist hammered against Smoke's chest, almost paralyzing him. He wondered for a second if the terrible punch had stopped his heart. His muscles responded, albeit sluggishly, as he ducked under a looping left that would have torn his head off if it had landed.

Smoke was an honorable man, but he was also a practical man. Faced with a desperate situation, he did what he had to.

He kicked Galt in the groin.

Even a man as huge and powerful as the majordomo was vulnerable to such a devastating impact. Galt grunted and wheezed in pain as he doubled over. Smoke whipped the gun butt against Galt's broken nose again. Galt's head jerked to the side. He took one stumbling step forward and then collapsed, crashing to the flagstones like a toppled redwood.

Satisfied that Galt was finally out of the fight, at least for the moment, Smoke wheeled around and saw that Matt and Luke had the Kroll brothers covered. The three guards sprawled on the ground in limp attitudes of death.

All the shooting had drawn the attention of the rest of the gang, however, and now the outlaws were streaming away from the burning barn and back toward the big ranch house. The first of them poured through the open gate and opened fire on the little group on the top terrace.

Mordecai yelped in terror as bullets started screaming around his head. Rudolph shouted, "I told you they wouldn't care if they killed me!"

Smoke realized then that the grip the brothers had had on the gang was a tenuous one, motivated by fear more than loyalty. With the Krolls helpless for the time being, the outlaws were seizing the opportunity to overthrow them.

So much for the idea of using them as hostages, Smoke thought. He ordered, "Get back in the house! We'll fort up and hold them off!"

That might be easier said than done, with three guns against more than two dozen vicious desperados. But they didn't have any other option at the moment.

Matt sprayed rifle slugs at the gang to cover the others' retreat. Smoke and Luke prodded the Kroll brothers ahead of them. Smoke saw that Valencia had already fled into the house and was grateful for that. He hoped she would hunker down and hide somewhere until this was all over, one way or the other.

They left the unconscious Galt and the dead guards lying on the terrace and hurried inside the big house. As soon as the door had slammed behind them, Luke covered Rudolph and Mordecai while Smoke and Matt went to a couple of windows, broke them out with gun barrels, and threw lead at the outlaws. There were plenty of places on the terraces where the attackers could take cover. They did so and continued their barrage directed at the house.

In a matter of seconds, all the windows along the front gallery were shattered. Bullets whined and bounced around the long, narrow room. Smoke glanced over his shoulder and saw that Luke had herded Rudolph and Mordecai into a little alcove where they had a little protection against ricochets, but not much.

Matt paused in his firing, dug cartridges out of his pocket, and fed them through the rifle's loading gate. He looked over at Smoke and said, "There are too many of them, and this house is too big. They'll circle and get inside. We can't hold 'em off!"

"I know," Smoke said grimly, "but we'll fight as long as we can."

A grin flashed across Matt's face as he said, "Yeah, I reckon. That's what Jensens do!"

That was certainly true, Smoke thought.

But this time it looked like the Jensen luck might have run out at last. . . .

Chapter 46

The one thing Smoke and Matt had on their side was their deadly accuracy. With a limited amount of ammunition, they had to make every shot count, so every time one of their guns cracked, an outlaw fell, either dead or badly wounded. That was enough to make the attackers cautious . . . for now. Smoke knew it wouldn't last.

"Señores!"

Smoke looked around to see Valencia hurrying across the gallery with several boxes of ammunition in her hands. He motioned urgently for her to get down as bullets continued to whine around the room.

"Slide the cartridges across the floor to me and Matt!" he told her as she dropped to her knees. He was a little surprised that she wanted to help them, but he supposed she was really trying to protect Rudolph, now that the gang appeared to have turned on the Kroll brothers.

Valencia slid a couple of boxes each across the smooth tile floor to Smoke and Matt, then crawled backwards out of the line of fire. Smoke was relieved when she disappeared unharmed through a doorway.

From the alcove where Luke was holding the Krolls prisoner, Rudolph called, “I told you they wouldn’t care whether or not they killed me, Jensen!”

“Which one of us are you talking to?” Matt asked.

Rudolph laughed harshly and said, “Does it matter? You’re both fools, and pretty soon you’re going to be dead fools! You can’t hold them off. Right now they’re out there talking about how they’ll rush the house, make sure we’re all dead, and tear it apart down to the foundation to find the loot they think they’ve got coming to them.”

In a whining voice, Mordecai said, “I told you you shouldn’t treat the boys that way. You always had to lord it over all of us!”

Rudolph turned and slapped his brother across the face.

“Shut up. Having to listen to you just makes things worse. If you’d followed my orders to start with, none of this would have happened. None of it! But no, you had to go and get us mixed up with these damn Jensens!”

Mordecai whimpered and cringed. He said, “If I wasn’t hurt—”

“You still wouldn’t do a damned thing, and you know it,” Rudolph said coldly.

Matt had finished topping off the magazine in his Winchester. He said, “You two might as well save all your wrangling. Looks like that bunch outside is getting ready to rush us."

Smoke agreed. Some of the outlaws would try to flank the house while others attacked it head-on, and in a matter of minutes they stood a good chance of being inside.

From that point on, the only thing Smoke, Matt, and Luke could do was sell their lives as dearly as possible.

"Matt," Smoke said in the lull, "where's Preacher?"

"I don't know. He was going to try to find some other way into the canyon. Were you thinking he'd show up at the last minute to pull our bacon out of the fire somehow?"

"The thought crossed my mind," Smoke admitted with a smile.

It seemed to be a forlorn hope, however. As the outlaws opened fire again, pouring more lead at the house than ever before, several of them leaped up to try to reach the sides of the building.

Only to be cut down from behind by a withering hail of bullets that shredded their bodies mercilessly.

Smoke frowned in surprise when he saw that happen. His astonishment grew when more outlaws leaped up and turned to try to meet this new threat, and they fell, too. Someone was attacking the gang from behind, and while Smoke's first thoughts were of Preacher, he didn't see how the old mountain man could be doing so much damage to the outlaws by himself. It would take a force of equal or larger size to do that.

Matt was equally astounded by this new development. He exclaimed, "What in blazes is going on out there?"

"I don't know," Smoke said. "We've gotten some reinforcements from somewhere."

From the alcove, Luke called questions, too, but Smoke didn't have any answers for him. All they could do was wait and see what happened.

The battle didn't take long. The newcomers—hard-faced men in a variety of range garb and town clothes—swept over the Kroll gang with devastating results. In a matter of minutes, all the outlaws were either dead or so badly wounded that they were out of the fight.

"You reckon that's a posse of some sort?" Matt asked.

"That's the only explanation that makes sense to me," Smoke said.

A few moments later, as several of the newcomers reached the top terrace where the whipping posts stood, that hunch seemed to be confirmed. Smoke spotted a familiar figure. A tall, lean man with a hawklike face strode forward, flanked by a grinning, handsome man dressed all in black.

"That's Simon Ford," Smoke told Matt. "He's a US marshal. Been on the trail of the Kroll brothers for a long time."

"How did he find the place?"

"He must've trailed you and Preacher."

Matt shook his head and said, "We would've seen anybody on our back trail."

"Not if they hung back far enough," Smoke said. "And they could, because Ford knew about our plan, too. He was there when I discussed it with Governor Frémont."

Matt muttered something Smoke couldn't make out. Smoke knew his younger brother was irritated that somebody had been able to follow him and Preacher without him knowing it. Preacher would really be upset when he found out about it. But they weren't the only competent frontiersmen to be found out here, and it would be foolish to think they were.

Simon Ford raised his voice and called, "Hello, the house! Smoke Jensen! Are you in there?"

"We're here, Marshal!" Smoke replied. He had been taking advantage of the chance to reload the revolver. He snapped the cylinder closed as he added, "We have Rudolph and Mordecai Kroll as our prisoners!"

"Bring them on out!" Ford ordered. "You can turn them over to me and my posse!"

Smoke glanced at Matt and then at Luke.

"What about it?" he asked. "Do we turn them over to the marshal?"

"The whole idea was to rescue Luke and bring

them to justice at the same time," Matt said. "It's starting to look like we've done that."

Smoke nodded and stood up from the crouch he'd been in at the window. He motioned for Luke to bring Rudolph and Mordecai over to the door. Broken glass crunched under their boots as they walked across the gallery. Matt, still holding his Winchester, opened the big front door.

"Hold it!" Luke snapped, bringing the Kroll brothers to a halt before they could step through the doorway. "Smoke, is the marshal that tall, hawk-faced gent?"

"That's right," Smoke said, puzzled by Luke's sudden hesitation.

"You know who the hombre is with him?"

"Never seen him before."

"Well, I do," Luke said. "His name is Jesse Clinton. He's a hired killer. He'd never volunteer for a posse, and no decent lawman would ride with him even if he did. Something's going on here, and I don't like it."

Smoke's eyes narrowed as he studied the men who had come up onto the terrace with Ford and Clinton. He had seen plenty of hardcases in his time, and these men fit the bill. He didn't like the looks of them. He liked the situation even less when scattered shots began to ring out down the slope. From the sound of the gunfire, the newcomers were finishing off any outlaws who hadn't been killed in the battle.

"Ford!" Smoke called. "You come on in here . . . alone!"

Ford nodded and took a step forward. His face was set in grim lines that turned to surprise as Clinton snapped, "Hold it right there, Marshal. No need for us to go in. The Jensens can bring Rudolph and Mordecai out to us."

"I'm going to take them into custody," Ford said. "That was our agreement. I can handle that."

"I'm changin' our agreement." Clinton's grin never wavered, but his voice was cold and dangerous. "We don't need the Jensens. Hell, we don't even need Mordecai. Just Rudolph. He's the one who knows where the loot from all the gang's robberies is stashed."

"I don't understand," Ford argued. "I agreed to let you and your men collect all the bounties—"

"That ain't enough," Clinton broke in. "We want Rudolph's cache, too."

"How do you know he's even got such a thing?"

"One of my boys used to ride with the Krolls," Clinton explained while the men inside the house listened tensely. "He was wounded during a holdup, and they left him for dead. That was before Rudolph found this place, so he couldn't lead us here, but he told us all about how Rudolph always kept the loot and doled out just enough to his men to keep them on the string. Personally, I think he was just playin' 'em along and would've double-crossed them one of these days, so he could keep all the loot for himself." Clinton laughed. "Hell, that's what I would've done in his place."

"This is insane," Ford muttered. "I came here to arrest the Kroll brothers, and that's what I'm going to do."

He turned on his heel and stalked toward the door.

Clinton shot him in the back.

Smoke realized what the gunman was about to do, but Clinton struck like a snake and there wasn't time to stop him. The bullet punched into Ford's body and knocked him forward onto the flagstones.

"They're going to kill us all," Luke snapped. He fired past Rudolph at Jesse Clinton. The shot missed, but it came close enough to make the gunman jump for cover.

Smoke and Matt knew that Luke was right. Clinton and his men represented just as much of a danger as the Kroll gang had. The house's defenders had just traded one bunch of bloodthirsty attackers for another.

That realization took only a split second to translate into action. Smoke and Matt opened fire as well, and Clinton's men scattered and began returning the shots.

Movement caught Smoke's eye. Despite being wounded, Simon Ford had started crawling toward the open door. He had to drag himself along by pushing with his elbows as slugs tore through the air above him, but he kept at it stubbornly until he was only a few feet away from the threshold.

As the gun in Smoke's hand roared and bucked to give him a little cover, he leaped into the doorway and bent over to stretch out his other hand to Ford. Ford reached up and clasped wrists with him. Smoke hauled backwards on the marshal's weight and pulled Ford through the doorway as more bullets smashed into the panel and sent splinters flying from it. The effort made Smoke's cracked rib twinge again, but he ignored the pain and dragged Ford into the house, then kicked the door closed behind them.

"You should have . . . left me out there . . . to get shot to pieces," Ford gasped. He tried to stand up but clearly didn't have the strength.

"Just stay down, Marshal," Smoke told him.

"Don't . . . call me that. I turned in . . . my badge. Don't deserve . . . the title. I let my hate for . . . the Krolls . . . make me sell my soul . . . to another bunch of outlaws."

That sort of made sense, Smoke supposed. He could get the whole story from Ford later, if they lived through this ruckus, which seemed increasingly unlikely. A few minutes earlier, they had been about to make their last stand, and despite the brief reprieve, it looked like that would soon be happening again.

"Who the hell is that?" Rudolph Kroll asked.

Smoke turned his head and asked, "You don't know him?"

"Never saw the bastard before in my life."

Simon Ford had devoted *his* life to bringing the Krolls to justice, and his feeling of duty was so strong it had overwhelmed his common sense and led him to make a deal with the Devil, in the form of Jesse Clinton. And despite that, he was still a complete non-entity to the men he had pursued. That didn't seem fair at all to Smoke, but there was nothing he could do about it now.

"Hate to tell you this," Matt said from one of the windows, "but it looks like this bunch is about to charge us, too."

"Give us guns," Rudolph urged. "Let us at least defend ourselves."

"Forget it," Luke snapped. "I wouldn't trust either one of you with a gun if Sitting Bull and all the Indians from the Little Big Horn were out there!"

"We're all going to die anyway," Rudolph argued.

The quiet voice that spoke next took them all by surprise. They turned to look as Valencia said, "No, señores. There is a way out . . . if you trust me."

Chapter 47

Smoke didn't see that they had much choice except to trust Valencia. Their odds of surviving an all-out attack on the house by Clinton's men were pretty blasted small. He said to the housekeeper, "Go on."

"There is a secret way out. My *madre*, she worked here for the Valdez family many years ago when it was the *Rancho Valdez*. In those days, the Apaches were a great danger, so Señor Hernan Valdez had his peons dig a tunnel away from the house, so he and his family could escape if ever they were trapped here."

Mordecai said, "That's the craziest story I ever heard. Rudolph, maybe you could make a deal with that fella Clinton. I got to have a doctor for this arm, or I'm liable to bleed to death!"

"Shut up," Rudolph said. "If you were going to bleed to death, you would have done it by now."

That was true, thought Smoke. Mordecai's wound did need medical attention, but he was in no immediate danger of dying from it.

"Go on, señora," Smoke told the woman.

"I can show you where the tunnel begins," Valencia said. "My mother told me how to find it.

But I do not know what lies at the other end. All I know is that she said it was the way to safety."

Luke said, "I vote we give it a try. We can't be any worse off than we are now."

Smoke wasn't so sure about that—things could *always* get worse—but he agreed they should run the risk. When he looked at Matt, his younger brother nodded.

"All right," he told Valencia. "Show us."

She turned to lead the way out of the room, but Simon Ford said harshly, "Hold it."

"Don't worry, Ford," Smoke began. "We'll take you—"

"No, you won't," Ford cut in. "Give me a couple of pistols and leave me right here. I'll put up enough of a fight to make Clinton, Hooke, and the others think that you're still in here."

"They'll bust in sooner or later and kill you," Matt objected.

Ford laughed.

"Not very likely," he said. "I'll probably be dead by then. I'm shot through the lungs. I can feel them filling up with blood. I ought to be dead already."

Smoke had heard air whistling through the hole in the former lawman's back and knew Ford was right. It would take quick attention from a skilled doctor, preferably in a modern hospital, to save Ford's life, and even that might not be enough.

"Ford's right," he said. He held out his revolver,

which he had just loaded with six fresh rounds. "Here you go, Marshal."

Ford grasped the weapon and rasped, "I told you not to call me that."

"Badge or no badge, you're still a lawman as far as I'm concerned," Smoke said. "Señora, are there any more guns around here?"

"Several extra revolvers," Valencia said. "And more ammunition."

"Get them quickly," Smoke told her. "We don't have much time." He knew Clinton's men could launch a full-fledged attack on the house at any moment.

Valencia hurried to bring the guns into the gallery. Ford sat down with his back against the wall next to one of the windows and arranged the extra revolvers around him. He chuckled grimly and said, "They'll think I've got a Gatling gun in here."

"Wish we did," Smoke said with a bleak smile of his own. "Good luck, marshal."

Ford didn't argue over the title this time. He just nodded and said, "Thanks."

"Come," Valencia told the others. She led the way to the stairs that descended into the crude dungeon underneath the house.

"What the hell?" Luke said. "I'm not fond of the idea of going back down there."

"You will see, Señor Jensen," Valencia said. "I give you my word."

"All right," Luke said grudgingly. "But you'd better not be double-crossing us."

Smoke and Valencia went first, followed by the Kroll brothers with Luke right behind them, holding a gun on them. Matt brought up the rear. Above them, in the main house, shots began to boom as Simon Ford opened fire on Clinton's men.

When the group reached the bottom of the stairs, Valencia hurried toward the cell, where the door still stood open. Light from the bracket lamp on the wall cast a long shadow in front of her.

"You're going in the cell?" Smoke asked.

"You will see," she said again.

Smoke hoped so. If not, they were really going to be trapped, even more than they had been to start with.

Valencia went into the cell and started running her hands over the rear wall. Her movements became more frantic as she didn't seem able to find what she was searching for.

But then Smoke heard a faint click, and when Valencia pushed hard against the wall, it swung back, all in one piece, and revealed the black mouth of a tunnel.

"Son of a *bitch!*" Luke said from the corridor. "You mean that door was right there the whole time I was locked up in here?"

Rudolph Kroll said, "I'm just as surprised as you are, Jensen. Do you think I would have put you in there if I'd known about it?"

"I reckon not," Luke admitted.

Smoke said, "It's a good place to hide an escape tunnel. Matt, go back and get that lamp at the end of the corridor."

When Matt returned with the lamp he handed it to Smoke, who took the lead now as the group started into the tunnel. The floor and walls had been hewn from the stone and left rough, never smoothed. The passage ran straight and level for what seemed like hundreds of yards. Utter blackness loomed in front of them and closed in behind them, and the small circle of light cast by the lamp was the only sign of life in what might have been a vast, stygian universe.

It was enough to give a man the fantods, that was for damned sure, Smoke thought.

They could no longer hear any gunshots coming from the house. Smoke didn't know if that was because of the millions of tons of dirt and stone surrounding them, or because Clinton's men had stormed the house and finished off Simon Ford. If the killers were in the house, it was only a matter of time before they found the escape tunnel. Smoke wanted to be out of there, along with his companions, before that happened.

Rudolph Kroll said, "If I had known this tunnel existed, I would have stashed all that loot down here. That would have been a lot handier."

"Where is it?" Luke asked.

"Don't tell him, Rudolph," Mordecai urged.

"Why not?" Rudolph said. "It's not like he'll ever have a chance to find it. There's an old abandoned mine higher in the mountains, a couple of miles from here. Mordecai and I are the only ones who know how to get there. From the outside it looks like it's all boarded up, but it's really not. There's close to a quarter of a million in gold and greenbacks in there."

Matt let out a low whistle.

"That's a lot of money," he said.

Luke said, "There are old abandoned mines all over the Superstitions. Lost mines, too. I wouldn't be surprised if that's part of the reason these hills got their name."

"Maybe so," Rudolph said, "but that one's not lost. Mordecai knows where it is, and so do I. Nobody else will ever find it, though."

"Sounds like that might be a challenge worth taking."

"You do that, Jensen," Rudolph said dryly. "If you get out of here alive."

That was still a mighty big *if,* Smoke thought. It was starting to look like this tunnel was never going to end.

But then, mere moments later, the floor started to slope upward slightly. That slope quickly grew steeper. Smoke didn't see any light ahead of them, however. If the other end of the tunnel was closed off, then all their efforts had been for nothing. They could sit down here in the dark and die of thirst, or they could go back and be gunned down by Jesse Clinton and his men.

Suddenly, Smoke's eyes were drawn to the lamp. He watched as the flame bent slightly to one side, then straightened, then bent again.

"Air's moving," he said. "There's an opening somewhere ahead. Matt, you still have matches?"

"Yeah," Matt replied. "Why?"

By way of answer, Smoke blew out the lamp.

Instantly, utter, crushing darkness closed in around them. Valencia gasped. Mordecai Kroll muttered a curse that had a whiny, frightened sound to it.

The darkness wasn't absolute, though, Smoke realized after a moment. He made out a faint gray glow ahead of them. As his eyes adjusted, the glow seemed to grow brighter.

"Come on," he told the others. "We need to keep moving."

"How?" Rudolph said. "We can't see where we're going."

But as their vision continued to compensate, they could. As they shuffled along the tunnel, Smoke began to be able to make out the walls on either side of him. He moved faster, and so did the others.

The tunnel took a sharp turn, and the shaft of light waiting on the other side was blinding after so much time spent in the darkness. Smoke looked up and saw boards fastened to the wall to form a crude ladder leading out of the tunnel. Some of them were rotten, but he thought enough of them looked all right that they would serve their original purpose.

At the top of the opening, about a dozen feet over his head, thick brush grew, concealing the opening.

Smoke handed the lamp to Valencia and said, "I'll go up and have a look around."

"Be careful," Luke cautioned. "You don't know what's waiting for you out there."

"Got to be better than where we came from," Smoke said with a quick grin.

He reached up and took hold of a board, got his foot on a lower one, and hoisted himself. The climb would have been easier if all the boards were still intact, but it wasn't too bad. In a matter of moments, he pushed some branches aside and pulled himself out into the morning sunlight.

He heard a roaring sound and looked around. Less than fifty feet away, the creek that ran through the canyon emerged from a cleft in the high stone walls enclosing the stronghold. The water shot through the gap and threw up a white spray as it dropped several feet. It was a waterfall, but a small one.

Smoke's mouth tightened into a grim line as he realized the implications of what he saw. This end of the tunnel was still inside the canyon. He had hoped that it led outside somehow. But as far as he could see, the only way out still lay through the pass at the other end of the canyon, and Jesse Clinton and his men controlled that.

Coming through the tunnel, though, had given them a breather, and maybe they could use this chance to figure out something else. He leaned over the opening in the brush and called, "Come on up!"

Valencia came first. Down in the tunnel, Luke prodded Rudolph in the back with a gun barrel and said, "Up you go, Kroll."

Rudolph complied. Smoke covered him when he emerged from the shaft. Mordecai followed, awkwardly and complaining bitterly about being forced to climb with a wounded arm. Luke and Matt scrambled out behind the outlaw brothers.

"Any chance we can swim up that creek?" Matt asked.

Smoke shook his head.

"The current's too fast. We couldn't make any headway against it. It'd just take us back down by the house."

He looked in that direction as he spoke, and a frown creased his forehead as he saw the sudden fleeting gleam of sunlight reflecting off of something. A gun barrel, maybe . . . or the lens of a telescope or pair of field glasses. . . .

A bullet *spanged* off a nearby rock and whined into the distance, followed a split second later by the boom of the shot that had fired it.

"They've spotted us!" Smoke yelled.

More shots followed immediately, and Smoke saw men on horseback racing toward them, still a good distance away but closing in quickly. Here at the upper end of the canyon, it narrowed down so there really wasn't any place for them to retreat.

But there were some slabs of rock near the creek, lying where they had landed when they sheered off the cliff in ages past, and Smoke waved his companions toward them.

"We'll fort up in those rocks and give 'em a fight!" he called.

But it would be a fight to the finish, he thought, because there was nowhere left for them to run.

Chapter 48

Luke herded the Kroll brothers behind the rocks while Matt opened fire on the riders charging toward them. Clinton's men were still too far away to be in effective handgun range, and Matt had the only rifle.

One of the gunmen toppled out of the saddle as Matt drilled him through the chest. Another slewed to the side and clutched a bullet-shattered shoulder but managed to stay mounted. He circled away from the charge, though, out of the fight for now.

Suddenly another rifle cracked from somewhere nearby, and one of Clinton's men went backwards off his horse as if a giant hand had brushed him loose from the animal. Smoke had knelt behind one of the boulders with Valencia, and he looked around in surprise at the rifle's report.

A familiar, buckskin-clad figure stood beside the creek where it emerged from the gorge. Preacher was hatless, but he had a carbine at his shoulder. The repeater cracked again, and as usual the old mountain man's aim was deadly accurate. One of Clinton's men crumpled and rolled out of the saddle.

Coupled with Matt's shots, Preacher's assault was too much for the charging gunmen. They veered aside and peeled off, abandoning their attack for the moment.

"Come on!" Preacher shouted as he lowered the carbine. "We better get outta here whilst we got the chance!"

"Get out how?" Smoke asked as he took Valencia's hand and led her toward the gorge. "Where in blazes did you come from, Preacher?"

"There's a way along the creek," Preacher replied as he jerked his grizzled chin toward the gorge. "You got to be sure-footed, though. I slipped off once and might've got busted to pieces in the rapids if that gal hadn't helped me."

"What gal?" Matt asked. He and Luke, along with the Krolls, had come up. "You don't mean . . ."

"He means it's a good thing I didn't pay any attention to you," Darcy Garnett said from the mouth of the gorge. "I found Preacher clinging to a rock, about to be washed away. But I was able to tear some strips off my petticoat, knot them together to make a rope of sorts, and haul him in with it."

"She's mighty resourceful, as well as stubborn as a mule," Preacher added.

"You followed Preacher instead of staying where we left you," Matt said.

"And brought her rifle along, too." Preacher gestured with the carbine. "Now come on, we ain't got any time to waste."

He showed them the narrow ledge that ran just above the fast-flowing stream. It was difficult to see unless the person looking for it was standing right in the mouth of the gorge.

"That's the back door that goes along with that tunnel," Smoke said.

Mordecai objected, "It ain't wide enough. We'll fall off."

"You can stay here and take your chances with Clinton if you want," Luke said, "but chances are he'll try to torture the location of that cache of loot out of you."

Preacher asked, "What loot? Who's Clinton?"

"It's a long story," Smoke told the old-timer. "Right now let's see if we can just get out of here."

Smoke didn't know who Darcy Garnett was, either, but Matt and Preacher seemed to trust her, so he didn't protest as she took the lead. Valencia went next, then Smoke. Rudolph and Mordecai Kroll followed them, with Luke close behind them. Matt and Preacher brought up the rear.

The eight figures strung out along the ledge. Smoke knew it was only a matter of time before Clinton and the others came after them. The killers wouldn't wait very long before charging the boulders at the head of the canyon again, and when they did, they would discover that their quarry was gone. Since the gorge was the only possible way out, chances were they would find the ledge pretty quickly.

Smoke saw what Preacher meant about needing to be sure-footed. In places the ledge was less than a foot wide. Spray from the racing creek made it slippery, too. He could see that Darcy and Valencia were terrified, but the women kept moving. They didn't hurry, because rushing could be fatal, but they didn't waste any time, either.

Yard by yard, the fugitives made their way along the perilous escape route. There was no sound except the water's roar, but then a shot blasted somewhere behind them. The sharp report bounced back and forth between the stone walls, setting up deafening echoes.

Matt returned the fire, carefully bracing himself so the Winchester's recoil wouldn't knock him off the ledge.

"We got company coming up behind us!" he called to the others. "Better keep moving!"

"Nobody's stopping!" Smoke said. "Preacher, how far does this ledge run?"

" 'Bout three hundred more yards, I reckon," the old mountain man replied, lifting his voice to be heard over the racket. "And part of the way it widens out! That'll bring us to a spot where we can climb up outta the canyon!"

But they couldn't climb out with Clinton's men coming up to take potshots at them, Smoke thought. They would be easy targets. It looked like once more they would have to stop and make a stand. But now they had an advantage because only one man could attack at a time along the ledge.

That advantage would disappear as soon as Clinton realized he could send men up onto the rims to fire down at them.

It seemed like they kept slipping out of one trap only to find themselves in another, Smoke thought. But as long as they still had an opportunity to fight, that was all he really asked for.

As Preacher had said, the ledge got wider, which allowed them to move a little faster.

Eventually it was ten feet wide, with some brush growing along the base of the wall beside it.

The sound of Dog's barking floated down from above them. Preacher grinned and said, "This is where I climbed down. I had to leave the old fella up there."

"It's a good thing you did," Darcy said. "When I found him, I knew I was on the right track."

Smoke said, "You two ladies see if you can climb out. The rest of us will stay here and keep Clinton and his men back." He thought there might be time for Darcy and Valencia to get away before the fighting got too hot and heavy.

"I'm staying," Darcy said. "I've proven that I can use a gun."

"She can," Matt said.

A shot blasted and a slug whined off the rock wall above their heads.

"Well, miss, it looks like you're about to get your chance," Smoke said. "Preacher, give her back her carbine. Everybody take cover!"

Unfortunately, there wasn't an abundance of cover to be found down here in the gorge. They spread out among the rocks and brush and fired along the ledge at Clinton's men, who hugged the wall and stepped out just long enough to trigger shots at the fugitives. Gun-thunder from both sides filled the ravine with such an overpowering roar it seemed like the whole world was shaking.

A couple of Clinton's men were hit and toppled off the ledge into the creek, where the current caught their bodies and propelled them downstream toward the canyon. Clinton had plenty of men, though, and from what Smoke could see they were gathering along the ledge to rush the fugitives. Smoke knew that he and his companions wouldn't be able to bring down all the attackers. They were minutes away from having their position overrun, and that would mean the end for all of them.

Then a chunk of rock about two feet in diameter sailed down from somewhere above and crashed into the killers clustered along the ledge. The terrible impact killed two men instantly, crushing their skulls, and knocked several more off into the creek, where the current slammed them into rocks and knocked them out to drown. Another missile, just as deadly as the first, followed a few seconds later while the startled hardcases were still shouting curses and questions at each other.

Smoke looked up as the bombardment continued to wreak havoc among Clinton's men. A huge figure stood on the rim, throwing the rocks down into the gorge. It was impossible to mistake the man. That was Galt up there.

Smoke had figured Clinton or one of the others had finished off the majordomo. Galt must have played possum, Smoke thought, and gotten up there somehow to heave the rocks at Clinton's men. If there was a way to reach the rim quickly, Galt would probably know it.

In a matter of moments, Galt had dealt some major damage to Clinton's force. The ones still on the ledge realized where the rocks were coming from, though, and tilted their guns up to open fire on Galt. Smoke saw the big man jerk as slugs pounded into him, but he didn't fall, and he didn't stop the bombardment, either. He hefted a particularly large rock over his head and heaved it, and when it landed on the ledge, it not only crushed one of the killers to bloody pulp, it knocked a big chunk out of the ledge itself. That trapped several men, including Jesse Clinton, ahead of where the ledge collapsed and cut them off from the rest of the gang.

That was enough for the men behind the newly formed gap. They turned to abandon the attack and started back toward the canyon.

"Come back here, damn you!" Clinton yelled at them. His cocksure grin was gone now that the odds were suddenly against him. Screaming incoherently in rage, he thrust his arm up and fired again at Galt.

The big man staggered, swayed, and then plunged off the brink as Valencia screamed. Galt plummeted down and landed in the creek with a huge splash. When he surfaced, he was floating facedown, and the current quickly carried him out of sight that way.

Smoke called, "Clinton! You and the men with you throw down your guns and surrender! Nobody else has to die here today!"

Clinton had seen a fortune snatched out of his hands, and that must have affected his mind. He roared, "You go to hell, Jensen!" and charged the brush with a gun in each hand spouting flame and lead. The two men he had left were right behind him with their own guns blazing.

Smoke slammed two bullets into Clinton's body and knocked the man off his feet. Matt cut down one of the other gunmen, and Preacher ventilated the other. Both men tumbled to the rocky ground. One rolled off into the creek and was washed away. The other lay motionless.

Clinton's hate and greed somehow allowed him the strength to keep moving. He pushed himself onto his knees and raised his gun for another shot at Smoke. Luke fired first and punched a slug into the center of Clinton's forehead. The killer's head snapped back from the impact, and this time when he fell he didn't move again.

Luke had taken his gun off the Krolls to fire that shot, and Mordecai, despite being wounded, struck with the speed and strength of crazed desperation. He tackled Luke, who, weakened by the long ordeal he had suffered, was unable to stop Mordecai from wrenching the revolver out of his hand. Mordecai surged up and started to swing the gun barrel in line with Luke's head.

Smoke, Matt, and Preacher all fired at once, but even as their bullets whipped toward Mordecai, Rudolph lunged in front of his younger brother, crying, "Mord, look ou—"

The slugs slammed into him and knocked him back into Mordecai, causing the gun in the younger man's hand to jerk to the side just as he pulled the trigger. The bullet struck the ground a foot to the left of Luke's head instead of blowing his brains out.

Mordecai staggered under the impact but didn't fall. He caught his balance, saw his brother's bloody body lying crumpled on the ground at his feet, and howled in rage. Screaming curses, he snapped a wild shot at Smoke, Matt, and Preacher, and this time when they returned his fire there was no one to get in the way. The bullets smashed into Mordecai and lifted him on his toes in a grotesque, jittering dance for a second before he dropped the gun and folded up like a rag doll.

The echoes of the shots slowly faded, and the clouds of powder smoke in the air drifted over the creek. Peace settled down over this place of desolation and death, and the silence was marred only by the sobbing of Valencia, who had crawled over to Rudolph's body and pulled his head into her lap as she bent over him and mourned.

Chapter 49

The canyon was empty of life when they reached it again later that day. The survivors who had ridden with Clinton had lit a shuck out of there, no doubt figuring that their gamble for a small fortune had not paid off and it made more sense to leave. Clinton was dead, but that sort of drifting hardcase never felt much loyalty, anyway, except to themselves and their next payday, wherever it might be.

The women who had come to the canyon with the outlaws were gone, too. There was a good chance they had left with Clinton's remaining hired guns, Smoke thought.

They found Simon Ford's body in the gallery at the front of the ranch house, shot so full of holes that it was impossible to count the wounds. An empty six-gun lay next to each of Ford's hands and dead men were piled in front of him, offering mute but eloquent proof that he had died fighting.

Galt's body was among the many that washed downstream into the canyon. Corpses littered the terraces and a number of them were sprawled in the house, as well.

"We'll be diggin' graves for a week," Preacher

muttered when he saw the extent of the carnage. "Danged if it don't look like somebody fought a war here."

Matt canted his Winchester back over his right shoulder and said, "We figured on rescuing Luke and maybe nabbing the Kroll brothers if we were lucky. Instead, the whole gang is wiped out, and most of Clinton's bunch on top of it. Hell sure has a habit of breaking loose when the three of us get together."

"The four of us now," Smoke said as he placed a hand on Luke's shoulder.

"Yeah, well, I hope you gents won't be offended if I don't attend too many of these little family reunions," Luke said dryly. "They get a little too rambunctious for my taste."

That drew laughs from Smoke and Matt. Preacher just shook his head and looked disgusted.

They took Valencia and Darcy Garnett to Phoenix. Valencia had relatives there, and after they said their good-byes, none of them ever saw her again.

Darcy holed up in a hotel room and wrote furiously for ten days straight while Luke rested up and Smoke sent wires to Governor Frémont in Prescott and the Chief Marshal for the Western District in Denver, explaining everything that had happened and asking that Simon Ford be posthumously reinstated as a deputy United States marshal. As far as Smoke was concerned, Ford had died doing his duty as a lawman, and that was how the record ought to read. Frémont promised to use whatever influence he had to make that come about.

The only time Darcy emerged from her writing marathon was to have dinner in the hotel dining room with Matt. The two of them seemed to enjoy each other's company quite a bit, and beyond that, Smoke didn't speculate or ask questions. Eventually, he and Luke returned to the Sugarloaf in Colorado, where Luke was able to recuperate and regain his strength. His iron constitution allowed him to recover fairly quickly, and it wasn't long before he said his farewells and returned to his life as a bounty hunter.

Before he left, though, he told Smoke, "I'll stay in touch so you'll have an idea where to find me. And if you ever run into more trouble than you can handle alone . . ."

"I'll give you a holler," Smoke said with a grin. "Just like with Matt and Preacher."

Luke nodded solemnly. The brothers clasped hands, pounded each other on the back, and then Luke swung into the saddle and rode away.

The Battle at Casa del Diablo; or, The Destruction of the Nefarious Kroll Brothers Gang was published as a yellowback dime novel by

Beadle & Adams under the byline D. J. Garnett and sold well enough that it proved more lucrative than writing an article for *Harper's Weekly*. The final passage of it read:

> As for the alleged abandoned mine where the desperados Rudolph and Mordecai Kroll hid the ill-gotten gains from their many crimes, it has never been located, if indeed it ever existed at all.
>
> It remains just one more mystery hidden among the fear-shrouded peaks of the Superstition Mountains.

J. A. Johnstone on William W. Johnstone
"When the Truth Becomes Legend"

William W. Johnstone was born in southern Missouri, the youngest of four children. He was raised with strong moral and family values by his minister father, and tutored by his schoolteacher mother. Despite this, he quit school at age fifteen.

"I have the highest respect for education," he says, "but such is the folly of youth, and wanting to see the world beyond the four walls and the blackboard."

True to this vow, Bill attempted to enlist in the French Foreign Legion ("I saw Gary Cooper in *Beau Geste* when I was a kid and I thought the French Foreign Legion would be fun") but was rejected, thankfully, for being underage. Instead, he joined a traveling carnival and did all kinds of odd jobs. It was listening to the veteran carny folk, some of whom had been on the circuit since the late 1800s, telling amazing tales about their experiences, that planted the storytelling seed in Bill's imagination.

"They were mostly honest people, despite the bad reputation traveling carny shows had back then," Bill remembers. "Of course, there were exceptions. There was one guy named Picky, who got that name because he was a master pickpocket.

He could steal a man's socks right off his feet without him knowing. Believe me, Picky got us chased out of more than a few towns."

After a few months of this grueling existence, Bill returned home and finished high school. Next came stints as a deputy sheriff in the Tallulah, Louisiana, Sheriff's Department, followed by a hitch in the U.S. Army. Then he began a career in radio broadcasting at KTLD in Tallulah, which would last sixteen years. It was there that he fine-tuned his storytelling skills. He turned to writing in 1970, but it wouldn't be until 1979 that his first novel, *The Devil's Kiss*, was published. Thus began the full-time writing career of William W. Johnstone. He wrote horror (*The Uninvited*), thrillers (*The Last of the Dog Team*), even a romance novel or two. Then, in February 1983, *Out of the Ashes* was published. Searching for his missing family in a postapocalyptic America, rebel mercenary and patriot Ben Raines is united with the civilians of the Resistance forces and moves to the forefront of a revolution for the nation's future.

Out of the Ashes was a smash. The series would continue for the next twenty years, winning Bill three generations of fans all over the world. The series was often imitated but never duplicated. "We all tried to copy the Ashes series," said one publishing executive, "but Bill's uncanny ability, both then and now, to predict in which direction the political winds were blowing brought a certain immediacy to the table no one else could capture." The Ashes series would end its run with more than thirty-four books and twenty million copies in print, making it one of the most successful men's action series in American book publishing. (The Ashes series also, Bill notes with a touch of pride, got him on the FBI's Watch List for its less than flattering portrayal of spineless politicians and the growing power of big government over our lives, among other things. In that respect, I often find myself saying, "Bill was years ahead of his time.")

Always steps ahead of the political curve, Bill's recent thrillers, written with myself, include *Vengeance Is Mine*, *Invasion USA*, *Border War*, *Jackknife*, *Remember the Alamo*, *Home Invasion*, *Phoenix Rising*, *The Blood of Patriots*, *The Bleeding Edge*, and the upcoming *Suicide Mission.*

It is with the western, though, that Bill found his greatest success. His westerns propelled him onto both the *USA Today* and the *New York Times* bestseller lists.

Bill's western series include *The Mountain Man*, *Matt Jensen, the Last Mountain Man*, *Preacher*, *The Family Jensen*, *Luke Jensen*, *Bounty Hunter*, *Eagles*, *MacCallister* (an Eagles spin-off), *Sidewinders*, *The Brothers O'Brien*, *Sixkiller*, *Blood Bond*, *The Last Gunfighter*, and the upcoming new series *Flintlock* and *The Trail West*. May 2013 saw the hardcover western *Butch Cassidy, The Lost Years*.

"The Western," Bill says, "is one of the few true art forms that is one hundred percent American. I liken the Western as America's version of England's Arthurian legends, like the Knights of the Round Table, or Robin Hood and his Merry Men. Starting with the 1902 publication of *The Virginian* by Owen Wister, and followed by the greats like Zane Grey, Max Brand, Ernest Haycox, and of course Louis L'Amour, the Western has helped to shape the cultural landscape of America.

"I'm no goggle-eyed college academic, so when my fans ask me why the Western is as popular now as it was a century ago, I don't offer a 200-page thesis. Instead, I can only offer this: The Western is honest. In this great country, which is suffering under the yoke of political correctness, the Western harks back to an era when justice was sure and swift. Steal a man's horse, rustle his cattle, rob a bank, a stagecoach, or a train, you were hunted down and fitted with a hangman's noose. One size fit all.

"Sure, we westerners are prone to a little embellishment and exaggeration and, I admit it, occasionally play a little fast and loose with the facts. But we do so for a very good reason—to enhance the enjoyment of readers.

"It was Owen Wister, in *The Virginian* who first

coined the phrase *'When you call me that, smile.'* Legend has it that Wister actually heard those words spoken by a deputy sheriff in Medicine Bow, Wyoming, when another poker player called him a son of a bitch.

"Did it really happen, or is it one of those myths that have passed down from one generation to the next? I honestly don't know. But there's a line in one of my favorite Westerns of all time, *The Man Who Shot Liberty Valance*, where the newspaper editor tells the young reporter, 'When the truth becomes legend, print the legend.'

"These are the words I live by."

Center Point Large Print
600 Brooks Road / PO Box 1
Thorndike ME 04986-0001 USA

(207) 568-3717

US & Canada:
1 800 929-9108
www.centerpointlargeprint.com